Desire in the Sun

Also by Karen Robards in Large Print:

Walking After Midnight
Heartbreaker
Nobody's Angel

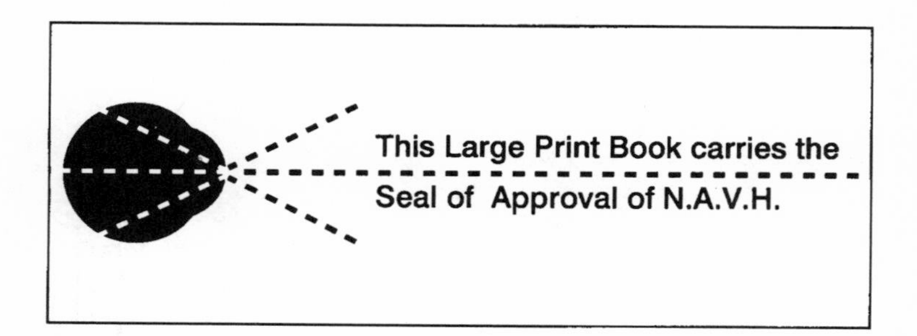
This Large Print Book carries the
Seal of Approval of N.A.V.H.

Desire in the Sun

Karen Robards

Thorndike Press • Thorndike, Maine

Published in 1997 by arrangement with Avon Books,
a division of The Hearst Corporation.

This work is a novel. Any similarity to actual persons or events is purely coincidental.

Thorndike Large Print ® Romance Series.

The tree indicium is a trademark of Thorndike Press.

The text of this Large Print edition is unabridged.
Other aspects of the book may vary from the original edition.

Set in 16 pt. Plantin by Juanita Macdonald.

Printed in the United States on permanent paper.

Library of Congress Cataloging in Publication Data

Robards, Karen.
Desire in the sun / Karen Robards.
p. cm.
ISBN 0-7862-1138-5 (lg. print : hc : alk. paper)
1. Large type books. I. Title.
[PS3568.O196D47 1997]
813′.54—dc21 97-17723

To my brother Tod
and his wife Mary Ann,
in honor of their
second wedding anniversary,
November 30, 1988.
And, as always,
with much love to Doug and Peter.

One

"Miss Remy — Delilah — you are in my thoughts night and day! Like that Delilah of old, you are an enchantress, and you have enchanted my heart! I . . ."

"Pray say no more, Mr. Calvert," Lilah murmured, trying to repossess herself of her hand. The infatuated Mr. Calvert, impervious to her tugging, clung doggedly to her fingers as he sank to one knee before her. She looked down in dismay at the curly brown head bent over her hand.

Michael Calvert was hardly more than a boy, perhaps a year or so younger than her own age of twenty-one. She was no more in love with him than with Hercules, her great-aunt's pampered spaniel, who was curled blissfully beside her in the porch swing at that moment, his short red hairs shedding copiously all over the fragile white silk of her Empire-style gown. But so far it had been as impossible to convince Mr. Calvert of her disinterest as it had been to discourage Hercules. Neither of them seemed the least inclined to take a polite hint. Mr. Calvert had been courting her assiduously for most of the three months she had been visiting her great-aunt, Amanda Barton, at Boxhill. Nothing she had said or done to indicate her complete lack of interest in his suit had served to deter him in the least. Now he was clearly determined to have his say. If he heard her soft-spoken plea, he disregarded it.

Lilah sighed, making no effort to muffle the sound. Trapped in the night-dark corner of the verandah as she was, and unwilling to make a scene, she had little choice but to hear him out.

"I love you! I want you to be my wife!"

Much more had come in between, but she had missed a great deal of it. Now he recaptured her attention by pressing his face to her hand, kissing its back with moist enthusiasm. Lilah tugged at her hand again. He held it in a grip that would not be broken.

"You do me too much honor, Mr. Calvert," she said through gritted teeth.

Under the circumstances, it was difficult to force herself to adhere to the ladylike phrases that had been drummed into her by Katy Allen, her beloved former governess, whose thankless job it had been to supervise her growing-up years. The proprieties had not mattered so much on her home island of Barbados, where, for all the inhabitants' pride in being more British than Britain itself, manners were much freer than they were here in the best houses of colonial Virginia.

At Boxhill manners counted. Though the Colonies had officially freed themselves from British domination more than a decade before, and were by this time, the year 1792, enjoying an ardent love affair with all things French, that love affair did not extend so far as embracing French ideas of what was considered acceptable behavior for unmarried young ladies of good family. In this one area the Colonies remained as Britishly circumspect as ever, with every word and gesture rigidly prescribed.

Following her natural inclination to reward Mr. Calvert's devotion with a shove that would land him on the seat of his breeches was sure to be frowned upon by the old tabbies within, the undisputed leader of whom was her own formidable great-aunt. During the weeks of her visit, Lilah had developed a healthy respect for the vinegar of Amanda Barton's tongue. Unless forced to it by the direst of circumstances, she would just as soon forgo another scolding. It shouldn't be impossible to pass the three weeks remaining of her visit without treading on another of Amanda's sacrosanct tenets on the behavior expected of proper young ladies.

"To do you too much honor would be impossible," Mr. Calvert rhapsodized, pressing his lips daringly close to her wrist. "As my wife, you will be worthy of every honor!"

Lilah stared down at the boy kneeling before her, annoyance puckering her forehead. Really, this was getting absurd! The eligible gentlemen of Mathews County apparently found her particular combination of golden-haired beauty and Barbados sugar plantation riches irresistible, which of course was just as it should be. Never in her life had she lacked for male attention, and she had not expected colonial males to be any different. Four years after her debut, she had nearly two dozen proposals of marriage to her credit, all of which she had unhesitatingly declined. Mr. Calvert's was the third proposal she had received during her stay at Boxhill, and two more gentlemen were paying assiduous court to her, but she had so far managed to keep them from coming to the point.

She sighed again. The truth of it was, she liked none of them any better than the next, and certainly none of them well enough to marry. But she was not getting any younger, she was her father's only child, and as he lost no opportunity to point out to her, it was time she was wed and producing heirs for Heart's Ease. It was beginning to look as though she could do no better than to accept her stepmother's nephew, Kevin Talbott, who had a standing offer for her, made when she was seventeen, that he renewed regularly and she just as regularly refused. Kevin was her father's choice for her, and her father, for all his faults, was the smartest man she knew. At least marrying Kevin would have the advantage of permitting her to live out her life at Heart's Ease, which she loved with an unswerving devotion, while at the same time providing the plantation with a competent manager for years to come. As her husband, Kevin would continue to serve in his present capacity of overseer until her father's death. Then he and she would inherit, and life on the vast sugar plantation would continue as it always had. Her father seemed to find that thought immensely comforting. Lilah found it more than a little distressing.

She had had such hopes for this visit — such dreams that, in this new and (she'd thought!) excitingly different place, she might find a man who'd sweep her right off her practical little feet and make her fall in love. But as her stepmother had warned her before she set sail, such dreams were just that, and harsh reality was this ridiculous boy at her feet. Looking down at him, Lilah had a momentary vision of him climbing into bed with her on their wedding night, and she actually shuddered. Better by far Kevin, who for all his rough-and-ready ways was at least familiar. Her father, as usual, was in the right of it. Love was nothing more than the blather of fools, and if she used the brain she'd been born with she'd marry for sound, sensible reasons.

". . . say you'll be mine!"

Despite her lack of attention, Mr. Calvert was still making declarations of undying love, and kissing her hand with the devotion of a puppy. The tart response that hovered on the tip of her tongue had to be suppressed in favor of the polite phrases fashioned for such situations. She certainly could not tell him that, with his high-pitched voice and curly hair, he reminded her of nothing so much as a large-sized version of Hercules! At least not unless he continued his slavering over her hand past the point where she could bear it.

"Pray release my hand, Mr. Calvert. I cannot marry you." There was the slightest edge to her voice. Her free hand was itching to box his ears. But she would hold off just a little longer, and perhaps Mr. Calvert would see reason before she had to blot her copybook so thoroughly. It would be nice if she could escape from this encounter with Mr. Calvert's image of her as a spun-sugar princess intact. But if his mouth crawled much farther up her arm . . .

Mr. Calvert, carried away by an onslaught of passion and apparently afflicted with deafness besides, began pressing kisses on each of her fingers. Tugging ineffectually at her hand again, Lilah cast despairing eyes around the shadowy verandah to assure herself that the ridiculous scene was unobserved.

An outdoor party had been given by her great-aunt in her honor that afternoon. As night had fallen the company had moved indoors for the dance party that was the traditional finish to such an entertainment. Music and merriment drifted through the open windows onto the verandah and beyond, over the green velvet lawns and carefully cultivated rose gardens. Couples strolled through those gardens, but they were mere murmuring voices in the distance, too far away to cause Lilah any embarrassment. Besides, they were too caught up in their own concerns to spare a thought for what might or might not be happening on the verandah, which except for herself and Mr. Calvert was presently deserted.

Light as well as music spilled out of the long windows, making the corner of the porch where she was trapped seem even darker in contrast. It was July, and the night was warm. The tuneless chirping of cicadas and the scent of the honeysuckle growing around the porch joined with the music and laughter to form a ridiculously romantic backdrop to her predicament. Earlier in the evening she had danced every dance with scarcely a pause in between. At the last break in the music, she had been feeling more than a little dewy (a lady would never sweat!). So she had succumbed to Mr. Calvert's urging that they go outside and sit in the swing to catch their breath. And in the swing she was sitting still, while he knelt before her on the well-swept boards of the wide verandah that wrapped around three sides of the white-columned house, pressing kisses to her hand while she all but gave up on finding a polite way to repulse him. It was becoming increasingly clear that he was not going to release her hand without drastic action on her part.

"Oh, Lilah, if you will but consent to wed me you will make me the happiest of men!" Mr. Calvert, passion inspiring him to an act of uncharacteristic daring, actually went so far as to touch his tongue to her palm. Shocked, Lilah jerked hard at her hand, the slight frown on her face transforming into a full-blown scowl. Beside her, Hercules, disturbed by her sudden movement, raised his head. His disgruntled bug eyes moved from her face to Mr. Calvert's. His glare settled on Mr. Calvert, and he gave vent to a low growl.

"Hush, Hercules!" Lilah snapped, exasperated, then turned her attention back to Mr. Calvert. "No, I will not marry you, so give me back my hand!" she hissed, her patience exhausted at last. Mr. Calvert looked up. His brown eyes that were almost identical to Hercules' glazed with ardor as they met hers.

"This shyness of yours is most becoming. I would not like my wife to be overly bold," were the vexing words that followed. Apparently blind to the expression on her face, he raised her hand to his mouth and pressed his tongue to her palm again. The provocation was too great. Temper flaming, Lilah lifted her dainty slippered foot, placed it squarely in the center of Mr. Calvert's thin chest, and shoved as hard as she could while at the same time pulling on her hand. The effect was not quite what she had intended. True, Mr. Calvert released her hand and fell over backward — but so did she! The force of her push flipped the swing. Before she knew what was happening she was tumbling backwards off the railless verandah, too shocked to manage more than a hoarse cry as she came crashing down on one of the flower-laden honeysuckles that edged the porch. The shock of the impact surprised an unladylike oath from her. Hercules, thrown out of the swing with her, landed on the ground nearby with an indignant yelp.

"Lilah! Oh, dear lord!" Mr. Calvert's horrified gasp was almost as shrill as Hercules' yelp.

For a long moment Lilah lay sprawled across the broken bush, stunned into silence. Sharp little branches poked her skin, but already she felt that more damage had been done to her dignity than to her person. Her temper, already lit, blazed out of control. The horrible certainty of how ridiculous she must appear, lying face-down and spread-eagled across the crushed bush, her skirts twisted anyhow around her legs, baring, she shuddered to think, how much of her person, was less than balm for her sense of outrage.

Hercules' frenzied yapping warned her of Mr. Calvert's approach and unavoidable witness to her dishabille. Lilah wriggled wildly as she sought to escape the bush, but the branches had snagged on her gown and she found herself thoroughly caught. If she tried to rise she would rip her dress, with who knew what disastrous consequences to her modesty. She worked feverishly at disentangling a branch that had attached itself to her bodice.

"Pray allow me to assist you. . . ."

The laughter that he was doing a lamentable job of suppressing distorted his voice. His obvious amusement acted on her anger like alcohol on a fire. Her bottom was up in the air, while her head dangled only a few inches from the ground. She was trapped — trapped! — with her thrashing legs in their garters and white cotton stockings bared to his view. Brown earth littered with a shower of broken twigs and blossoms was all she could see — except for a growing tide of red! She was so angry she could have cheerfully killed the giggling fool! She reached around and tried without success to find the hem of her skirt and jerk it down to the level of decency. To her horror, she felt his hand do what hers could not. His knuckles actually brushed the backs of her thighs!

"Take your hand off me, you blackguard! How dare you touch me! How dare you laugh! This is all your fault, you spineless ninny, and I take leave to tell you that I wouldn't wed you if . . . ! Stop laughing, damn you! Stop laughing, do you hear?"

The uninhibited male chuckles, increasing in volume in response to her tirade (or the ridiculous picture she made flapping around as she tried to extricate herself from the bush!) maddened Lilah past the point of caring about anything except revenge. Thrusting herself up to the accompaniment of a loud ripping sound, Lilah came off that bush like a ball out of a cannon and launched a very unladylike but richly deserved roundhouse punch at the cause of her discomfiture. Just inches before the blow landed, her fist was caught in an iron grip. To Lilah's horror she found that the gentleman who had had the gall to pull down her skirt, whose eyes still twinkled at her even as his hold prevented her from breaking his nose, was not Mr. Calvert at all. Instead he was a complete and total stranger who was laughing at her with the greenest eyes she had ever seen.

Two

"Oh!" she said, completely nonplussed. To put the crowning touch on her discomfiture, a rosy blush swept to her hairline.

The stranger grinned down at her. His teeth were white and faintly uneven, and a piratical mustache slashed the swarthy face above them. His hair, secured in a tail at the nape, was black and thick and softly curling. He was tall, broad-shouldered, and dazzlingly handsome despite the maddening grin. He was dressed for travel in a dun-colored, many-caped riding coat that hung open over a pristine white shirt with an elegantly tied cravat and snug buff breeches. From the riding crop in the hand that was not occupied in holding hers, she surmised that he had just arrived, and had been on his way to the house from the stables when he had witnessed her humiliation.

"You there! Unhand that lady! Unhand her, I say!" Mr. Calvert, having found his own feet and rushed by way of the steps to assist Lilah, was clearly miffed to find himself no longer needed. He came around the corner in an anxious rush, only to stop short, staring, before coming on again, bristling with protective zeal. Hercules, apparently emboldened by Mr. Calvert's advent, let loose with another volley of yaps and made a darting rush at the stranger's dusty boot, only to abandon the attack a good two feet short of its target.

"Oh, be quiet, do!" Lilah snapped, ostensibly to Hercules though her eyes included Mr. Calvert in the admonition. The stranger's grin broadened. The black slashes of his eyebrows lifted slightly as they took in the size and style of the boy advancing on him. But he spared Mr. Calvert no more than a glance before his eyes returned to Lilah.

"I applaud you on your good sense, ma'am. I wouldn't have him either." The confidential note in his voice brought a quivering smile to her lips.

"Why you . . . you . . . !" Mr. Calvert spluttered, his fists clenching at his sides. He stalked over to hover near Lilah's right shoulder, glaring at the stranger all the while. "What business do you have commenting on a private — very private! — matter? Who the devil are you, anyway?"

The stranger inclined his head politely.

"Jocelyn San Pietro, entirely at your service, sir. But my friends call me Joss." His eyes slid back to rest on Lilah's face as he said this last, and she realized that he was blatantly flirting with her. Despite her lingering embarrassment, the very outrageousness of his conduct appealed to her. All the men she had known so far in her life had treated her most deferentially, as if she were a glittering prize to be won. This fellow with his handsome face and bold grin was not at all intimidated by her, and she found that she liked him for it. But he was still holding her hand, and that was beyond the bounds of what was permissible. She tugged discreetly. He looked down with a fleeting expression of regret, but let her go.

"How do you do, Mr. San Pietro? I am Lilah Remy. And this is Michael Calvert." Lilah turned a commanding eye on Mr. Calvert, who sulkily inclined his head.

"I'm very pleased to make your acquaintance, Miss Remy." The formal phrase took on a whole new aspect when accompanied by a meaningful glance from those bold green eyes. He completely ignored Mr. Calvert, who bristled. To her surprise Lilah felt herself growing pleasantly flustered. Ordinarily she was totally in command of herself when talking to gentlemen. After all, she had been much courted and admired for as long as she could remember. But this man was something beyond her ken. At the realization she felt a tingling little sense of excitement spring to life inside her.

"What is your business at Boxhill? You can't have been invited to the party," Mr. Calvert said sharply, his eyes narrowing as they moved between the other man and Lilah. "It was for close friends and neighbors only. And I've never seen you before in my life."

"Are you the new owner of Boxhill?" Mr. San Pietro inquired with a well-feigned expression of surprise. Mr. Calvert, glowering, shook his head. "Ah, then I have not come in vain. My business is with George Barton, and none other."

"Perhaps I could take you to him? He is my uncle — well, really his wife is my great-aunt," Lilah said.

"Indeed?" Mr. San Pietro's smile was charming. "Perhaps you can take me to him — later. For the moment, I am quite happy to let my business wait."

"Lilah, you know nothing about this man! You have no business talking to him! You haven't even been properly introduced! He could be anyone — a bounder! He could even intend Mr. Barton some sort of harm!"

Mr. Calvert's furious whisper caused Lilah to turn angry eyes on him. But Mr. San Pietro, obviously overhearing as he could hardly fail to, forestalled her. The charming grin vanished, and a sudden aura of power seemed to emanate from him as he fixed Mr. Calvert with hard eyes.

"Watch yourself, stripling, or you'll soon be sitting on your backside again." There was cool warning in the eyes that rested on Mr. Calvert's face. Looking from one to the other, Lilah suddenly became aware of the marked contrasts between the men. Jocelyn San Pietro stood a good inch or two over six feet. Broad-shouldered and well-muscled, he was nearly half again the size of the tall but reed-thin Mr. Calvert, and had the look of a man well able to take care of himself in the face of difficulties. Mr. Calvert looked to be exactly what he was, the pampered scion of a prominent family who had never turned his hand to a day's work in his life. Mr. San Pietro had to be nearly thirty. Mr. Calvert could not yet lay claim to twenty. In any sort of physical confrontation between them, Lilah had not the tiniest doubt of who would be the loser. Mr. Calvert, apparently coming to that same conclusion himself, was silent, though he glowered at his rival with fierce resentment.

Hercules yapped again, this time at a couple emerging from the rose garden. The hand-holding pair looked in their direction and immediately dropped hands, putting a circumspect distance between them as they disappeared around the side of the house in the direction of the front entrance. Lilah was reminded of her surroundings, and the party going on within. As reluctant as she was to share Mr. San Pietro with the rest of the company, she really had no choice but to take him inside. Amanda would undoubtedly come looking for her soon if she delayed much longer. And Amanda would scold. . . .

"Hush, Hercules! Perhaps we should go in? When you are ready to talk to my uncle, you have only to tell me, Mr. San Pietro, and I will be glad to fetch him for you. In the meantime, there is a refreshment table, and the musicians are quite good."

"It sounds more than delightful." He was smiling again, his eyes on her face. To her utter amazement Lilah felt her heartbeat quicken. "I must admit to being a trifle sharp-set. I missed dinner to ride out here."

"We can certainly remedy that!" Her answering smile was gay. She felt giddy, like a young, foolish girl, and decided that she quite liked the sensation.

"Shall we go in, then?" He offered her his arm with that blazing smile, his eyes telling her that he found her every bit as interesting as she found him. Which was only to be expected, of course. Lilah was quite aware of the effect of her own beauty, and was not above shamelessly exploiting it to the best advantage. The majority of males from ages ten to ninety who beheld her porcelain-perfect features and fine-boned, gracefully curved body were smitten on the spot. But this was the first time she had felt more than the mildest attraction of her own in return, and she was discovering that it made all the difference in the world.

"Certainly." She placed her hand in the proffered crook of his arm, completely ignoring Mr. Calvert's sharply indrawn breath. As her fingers curled over the canvaslike cloth, she became tinglingly conscious of the hard strength of the muscles beneath. A glow started in the toes of her slippers and radiated all along her nerve endings until it reached the top of her head. She looked up at him, surprise in her eyes, to find that he was looking down at her intently.

"You can't go in there like that, Lilah! Your hair is falling down and it's got twigs in it and you've got a great rip in your dress!" Mr. Calvert's sharp protest brought her back to reality with a thud.

Lilah, who had almost forgotten about her misadventure, stopped and looked down at herself in horror. From what she could see, Mr. Calvert was understating the case. The shimmery silk of her lovely new gown was torn in a dozen places, with a long rip exposing part of her white petticoat down one side. A jagged tear in her bodice just below the low-cut scoop of her neckline allowed glimpses of creamy skin and pin-tucked chemise. Her hands rose in horror to her hair. As Mr. Calvert had said, it had come loose from its moorings. From the feel of the heavy mass, the great knot of pale blonde hair at the back of her head was precariously askew. She had no doubt that the little ringlets that Betsy, her maid, had laboriously coaxed to fall around her face and neck were reduced to unsightly straggles.

With an acute sense of dismay she realized that she must look a perfect fright, which was something she was decidedly unaccustomed to. Lilah Remy was always perfectly turned out, regardless of occasion, weather, or exertion. It was part and parcel of her reputation for matchless beauty. Her eyes flew to Jocelyn San Pietro. His eyes were on her, twinkling. His lips, though firmly pressed together beneath that dashing mustache, gave the impression that they were battling a smile.

"Oh dear," she said, dropping her hands. He leaned over and plucked a twig of honeysuckle from her hair. For a moment only he held it with long, powerful-looking fingers, and then he tucked it carefully into the breast pocket of the black cutaway coat he wore beneath his driving coat so that a single blossom still showed. Lilah was charmed by the gesture. Beside her, she thought she heard Mr. Calvert grind his teeth.

"A slight disarray only serves to point up the perfection of beauty that nature has wrought in you, Miss Remy," Mr. San Pietro said with a slight bow and a soulful look. Lilah could not forbear from chuckling at him, and he grinned in response. Suddenly her ripped dress and untidy hair ceased to matter so much. Perhaps she could be accused of being vain, but she had hated the thought that he was seeing her at less than her best. His too-flowery compliment put her at ease again, as it had doubtless been designed to do.

"I fear you are a flatterer, Mr. San Pietro." She said it severely, but her eyes smiled at him. He shook his head, reaching for her hand again and tucking it back in the crook of his arm.

"Perhaps there is a back entry?" he suggested. Lilah nodded, and with her hand on his arm indicated the way toward the rear of the house. With her free hand she held her skirt clear of the fresh-scythed grass, though she supposed the gesture was useless as the dress was undoubtedly ruined. Or perhaps Betsy could repair it enough to pass it along to one of the kitchen maids . . . ? Mr. Calvert and Hercules brought up the rear of the little procession, and it was not the dog who was growling.

"I must sneak up to my room and do what I can to repair the damage, I suppose." The words were light, though secretly she hated the necessity of leaving him almost as soon as she had found him. Something special had sprung into existence between them, something fragile and delicate and so tangible that it almost shimmered in the warm night air. She was afraid that if she let him out of her sight the magic — or the man himself — might vanish. What was happening to her was almost dreamlike, and certainly too good to be true. . . .

"I hope you will be coming down again? It seems a shame to retire to bed all on account of a tipsy coiffure and a ripped dress."

She looked up at him to find that, though

his eyes were laughing, there was a seriousness behind his words that told her that he did, indeed, very much want her to come back down. She smiled at him, a bewitching smile that promised much. His expression didn't change, but his pupils dilated.

"I'll be back down. The musicians are scheduled to play the boulanger at midnight, and that is my favorite dance in the world. I certainly wouldn't miss it over a ruined hairdo."

"That's the spirit." He grinned at her, and her heart started that absurd doublefast pumping again. What was it about this man . . . ? "I can tell that you're a young lady after my own heart, Miss Remy. I, too, have a marked partiality for the boulanger. Perhaps you would permit me to partner you? As a reward for — uh — having been instrumental in assisting you to leave your bush?"

"I'll have you know, sir, that no gentleman would remind me of such an unfortunate meeting." Coquetry came as naturally as breathing to her, and Lilah pulled out all the stops now with this man who attracted her as no other ever had. She smiled up at him with her chin slightly tilted, knowing from years of practice in front of her dressing table mirror that at that angle her blue eyes would look delightfully exotic and her neck as long and delicate as a swan's. He would be entranced — unless her slipping topknot and scraggly tendrils spoiled the effect. The thought almost made her scowl, but then she saw the appreciation plain in his green eyes, and was reassured. If ever a man looked interested in a woman, he did.

"All Miss Remy's dances are promised," Mr. Calvert said jealously, coming up on Lilah's other side. Lilah spared him an annoyed look. Why didn't he just go away? He was as bad as the mosquitos that were constantly swarming toward the house from nearby Put In Creek. She ached to swat him.

"Indeed, the boulanger was promised, but I believe it was to Mr. Forest and he had to take his mother home earlier in the evening as she was feeling ill." The graceful lie was uttered with another glimmering smile at Mr. San Pietro.

"I am sure I saw him. . . ."

"I'll be delighted to dance the boulanger with you, Mr. San Pietro," Lilah said firmly, giving Mr. Calvert a look that dared him to argue further. She was not about to forgo a dance with Mr. San Pietro in favor of Mr. Forest, who was plump and had perpetually damp hands!

"I will look forward to it," Mr. San Pietro said gravely, but in the darkness she saw his eyes gleam and suspected it was with amusement. Oh dear, she was not usually so obvious — but then, she did not usually have to circumvent a dunce like Mr. Calvert, either!

"You must be longing to return to the party, Mr. Calvert," she said with as much sweetness as she could muster. She lifted her skirt a little higher against the taller grass as they rounded the corner at the back of the house. Surely he would take the hint that he was decidedly de trop.

"I'm not leaving you alone with him," Mr. Calvert muttered. If Mr. San Pietro heard this hissed reply, he gave no indication that he had done so. But from the deepening amusement in his face, she strongly suspected that he had.

Beulah, the rotund black cook who had belonged to the Barton family from her birth, was sitting in a rocker on the stoop in front of the summer kitchen. She fanned herself comfortably with her apron as she watched her three underlings hurry back and forth, carrying heaping platters along the roofed, wall-less passageway connecting the kitchen to the house and bringing empty ones back the same way. On the step below her sat Boot, George Barton's man. The two were engaged in a spirited discussion. Lilah rather suspected that Boot had his eye on Beulah, though they were both old enough to be grandparents several times over. Beulah stopped talking as Lilah, her hand still on Mr. San Pietro's arm, stepped into the passageway, which was lit with flaming torches.

"Lawsy, chile, you done look like you been in a fight!"

Lilah's hand dropped away from Mr. San Pietro's arm as Beulah got to her feet and waddled over to catch her by the chin. She turned Lilah's face to the light to stare suspiciously at what Lilah feared must be a long scratch on her cheek.

"What happened?" Beulah eyed both Lilah's escorts with disfavor. "You got holes all in your pretty dress!"

"I fell off the verandah," Lilah said shortly, pulling her chin from Beulah's hand and casting a fulminating glare at Mr. Calvert. Beulah had no trouble attributing blame from that sizzling look, and fixed her own protuberant eyes on the miscreant as well. Lilah was pleased to see Mr. Calvert visibly wilt under Beulah's stern regard. Reddening, he began to sputter an explanation to which no one paid any attention. Just then Hercules, who had followed them around the house, smelled fried chicken from the platters the maids were carrying, and charged, yapping and jumping furiously. The maid under attack uttered a little shriek and nearly dropped the platter.

"That dog!" Beulah muttered, trying to scare him away with a flapping apron. "Shoo, you, Hercules! Shoo now, you hear?"

Hercules responded with another foray. Lilah had an idea.

"Here, Hercules!" she called, snapping her fingers and patting her skirt. Hercules, expecting a chicken leg, came running. Lilah scooped him up in her arms, ignored an ecstatic lick on her cheek, and thrust him at Mr. Calvert, who accepted the wriggling armful with a horrified scowl.

"I'd be ever so grateful if you'd take him to the stables and lock him in a stall. The poor dear little dog is liable to be hurt if he keeps getting underfoot." She smiled sweetly as she said it, taking a modicum of pleasure in Mr. Calvert's appalled expression. He gaped at her for a moment, but with the dog in his arms and half a dozen pairs of eyes on him there seemed little he could do but go.

As he retreated in defeat, Lilah triumphantly turned back to Mr. San Pietro. "If you like, Boot will take you in to join the company. I must go up and change."

"I'd prefer to wait for you, if I may. As

your young friend pointed out, the party is for close friends and neighbors, and I fear I am neither. I confess to feeling a trifle shy. Perhaps your uncle has a room that's not in use tonight where I can wait without disturbing anyone?"

He was about as shy as a barracuda, Lilah guessed as she led the way along the passage to the house, but she was pleased that he wished to wait for her, however nonsensical his excuse. Beulah and Boot followed them. Lilah stopped at the foot of the steps leading to the house.

"My uncle's office should be empty. But you should really go on in and eat something. You said you missed supper."

"Your uncle's office will do just fine. And I'd much rather miss supper than you."

It was a pretty compliment, prettily given. She smiled at him.

"All right then. Boot, take Mr. San Pietro to Uncle George's office and see that he gets something to eat."

"Yes'm, Miss Lilah."

Lilah climbed the steps as she spoke, pausing on the small back porch. Jocelyn San Pietro came up the steps behind her and stopped at her side. She realized that the light from the open door was spilling over her face and hoped that whatever damage had been done did not render it too unsightly. Apparently not, because his eyes were glinting with approval as they met hers.

"Better let me put somethin' on that scratch, honey, so it won' scar," Beulah said as she tried to herd Lilah into the house.

"Don't worry, it's barely visible now. It won't scar," Jocelyn San Pietro said, running a casual finger over the soft skin of her injured cheek. Lilah felt that touch with every fiber of her being. Eyes widening, she stared up into the lean dark face that was so dizzyingly close. The light that revealed her shortcomings showed his as well. Except to her eyes he had none. He had a broad forehead, high cheekbones, a square jaw. His nose was straight and not overlong. His mustache framed a wide, well-cut mouth. His features were hard and masculine, intelligent and compelling. When combined with the extraordinary emerald eyes and that rakish grin, he was handsome enough to make her go weak at the knees. He must realize the effect he was having on her. . . .

"Chile . . ."

"It's all right, Beulah, I'll get Betsy to take care of it in a few minutes. Boot, you take good care of Mr. San Pietro, you hear?" Then she looked up at him again. "I won't be long," she promised softly. Without waiting for an answer, she picked up her skirts and went into the house.

Three

"Betsy! Betsy!" Lilah called for her maid even as she hurried through her bedroom door. Of course Betsy was not in the room. Why should she be? She would not be expecting her mistress to come to bed for hours yet. Lilah tugged on the bellpull impatiently. She wanted to get back downstairs as quickly as possible. Jocelyn San Pietro was the most attractive man she had ever met, and she didn't mean to keep him waiting any longer than she could help. The refrain "Too good to be true, too good to be true. . . ." kept running through her head.

"What you doin' upstairs so early, Miss — Miss Lilah! What happened?" Betsy came into the room almost at a run, then stopped short just inside the door to stare at her mistress. Betsy was a slender girl with skin the color of coffee mixed liberally with cream. Her aureole of dark hair — which she wore loose at Heart's Ease but which Amanda Barton had decreed must be concealed by a kerchief like those other housemaids wore while at Boxhill — had a reddish tinge. She was very pretty, and was Lilah's friend as well as her personal maid. Betsy was two years older, and had been Lilah's playmate from birth. Lilah's father had officially given the girl to Lilah for her eighth birthday, and Betsy had been her maid and confidante ever since.

"I fell off the verandah," Lilah answered impatiently, as she had to Beulah. The story was too long and involved to go into. "I'm going back downstairs again, so I'll need something else to wear. But first get me out of this dress."

"Yes, Miss Lilah."

Betsy closed the door behind her, then crossed the high-ceilinged room with its elaborate rice-carved bed to unbutton the back of Lilah's dress. Lilah had already untied the sash, and in just a matter of moments Betsy was lifting the dress over her head.

"I don't think it can be mended," Betsy said doubtfully, examining the ruined silk.

"Oh, it doesn't matter." Lilah, clad in petticoat, chemise, and stays, her slippered feet practically soundless on the polished wood floor, crossed to the mahogany wardrobe between the two tall windows and threw open the doors. "Come here, Betsy, and help me pick. Something ravishing!"

Betsy looked at her mistress with a quizzical expression. "You sickening for something? I've never known you to worry about being 'ravishing' before."

Lilah smiled tantalizingly, but said nothing.

"It's a man, isn't it? *The* man? Oh, Lord-a-mercy, it's him at last! You can tell me, Miss Lilah, and you know I won't breathe a word to a soul! Why, I tell you about all my men! And you never tell me a word about yours!"

" 'Cause there's nothing to tell, that's why, and you know it. What about this blue dimity?" She held the dress out and inspected it with a critical eye. "No, blue doesn't show up well at night." She dropped it onto the floor without a second thought and turned back to rummage through the wardrobe again.

"What about the silver faille?" Betsy suggested, reaching around Lilah to find and remove the dress in question. Both girls stared at it with the eyes of connoisseurs.

"It'll do," Lilah decided with a nod, turning away from the wardrobe to cross to the dressing table, where she leaned down to examine her face. "I'll need fresh underclothes, too. Oh, my, I'm a mess!"

As she had feared, her elegant knot was barely anchored over one ear, and the cunning little curls had deteriorated into silvery wisps around her face. A smudge of dirt was on her forehead, and a long scratch marred the creamy skin of one cheek.

"I look dreadful!" she said, appalled.

"No, you don't. You couldn't look dreadful if you tried," Betsy replied placidly, placing the fresh underclothes with the dress on the bed. "You just wash your face, and we'll have you looking good as new in half an hour."

"Half an hour!" Lilah almost wailed, bending over the washstand to splash water on her face. The cold water stung the scratch, but she didn't mind that. She just wanted to hurry downstairs.

"It must be *him,*" Betsy concluded with a chuckle. "I knew Cupid would get you with his arrow one day, Miss Lilah. And from the look of you, you've been hit real bad."

"Don't be silly, Betsy. I told you I fell off the verandah, and I did. Anyway, I've just met the gentleman. I . . . like him, that's all."

"Honey, you like butter on your biscuits. What a girl feels for a certain particular gentleman isn't called like. It's called love."

Betsy began to untie the tapes of Lilah's stays as she spoke. When they were released,

Lilah took a deep breath, the action as automatic as washing her face. She'd been wearing stays for years, and she'd grown accustomed to their strict confinement. Still, it was nice to breathe freely when she could. Next Betsy loosened the ribbons on her petticoat, and lifted the chemise over her head. In minutes Lilah was as naked as a babe, and Betsy was dressing her again from the skin out. The silver faille dress would be left until last, after Betsy had done her hair, so that it wouldn't wrinkle.

"I bet he's handsome," Betsy observed as she pulled the pins from Lilah's hair. Lilah, seated in front of her dressing table, leaned toward the mirror to examine the scratch on her cheek as the silver-blonde strands fell in a shining mass around her face. Her hair reached down past her hips, and although it had to be coaxed to curl with curl papers it was wonderfully thick and shiny.

"I don't want to talk about him, Betsy! Do you think I'll have a scar?"

Betsy shook her head as she brushed out the shining strands. "From that little scratch? I can cover that right up with a little rice powder. No one will hardly know it's there."

Lilah watched in the mirror as Betsy twisted her hair up into an elegant coil at the back of her head. The little curls that had framed her face so charmingly earlier that evening were irredeemably lost for the night. Her hair was as naturally straight as a poker. But the effect of this more severe hairstyle was just as pleasing, she decided, surveying her reflection from first one angle and then another. The cool upsweep of silvery hair enhanced the high-cheekboned beauty of her face, showing off her shell-like ears and the delicate lines of her features. Except for the angles created by her cheekbones and a certain pointiness to her chin, her face was a perfect oval. Her eyes were large with the faintest tilt at the corners, their soft gray-blue enhanced by the thick black sweep of her lashes (which, if the truth were told, Betsy usually darkened with the end of a burned stick). Her nose was straight and finely shaped, and her lips were full and soft yet delicately made. All in all she was quite happy with the face looking back at her — except for the scratch. She hoped Betsy was right about the rice powder.

The silver faille dress was similar in style to the one she had discarded. Lilah stood before the mirror as Betsy pulled the dress over her head, then buttoned up the back. The long satin sash that passed just beneath her breasts to tie in a bow in the back was of a silver just a shade paler than the dress.

The gown was styled in the fashion of the French empire that was so popular, with short puffed sleeves, scooped-out neck and high waist. The skirt was slim and devoid of ornamentation of any kind. It was a simple yet stylish costume that depended for its impact on the beauty of its wearer's figure. On Lilah, with her slender waist and hips and high, full breasts, it was breathtaking. Betsy smiled as she surveyed her mistress in the mirror.

"He's gonna think he died and gone to heaven," she said with satisfaction, reaching for the box of rice powder.

"I told you . . ." Lilah began severely, only to be interrupted by the hare's foot whisking over her face and returning to pass more carefully over her cheek.

"I know what you tole me. I also know what I know."

There was no point in arguing with Betsy, Lilah knew. The maid was exactly as subservient as she wanted to be, and no more. Lilah took one last look at herself in the mirror as Betsy clasped a single strand of pearls around her neck, and then she was ready.

"Oh, Betsy," she said, as butterflies suddenly started to do cartwheels in the pit of her stomach. "I — I think I'm nervous."

"It takes us all like that sometimes, Miss

Lilah. You're just later getting to it than most."

"I am, aren't I? Well, I must go." Taking a deep breath, amazed at the quivering anticipation that made her feel as if she were, in truth, sickening for something — she was normally the most serene person in the world — she went back downstairs.

Four

Lilah still felt absurdly nervous as she walked along the narrow back hall to the out-of-the-way room that her Uncle George used as his office. The door was shut. She hesitated for a moment, then she tapped softly and waited for an answer. When she didn't hear anything, she opened the door and stepped inside. For a moment she feared that he wasn't there. Disappointment struck her like a blow. Her eyes swept the candle-lit room with its cluttered bookcases and leather-topped desk. The remains of a meal were on the desk, but Jocelyn San Pietro was nowhere to be seen. Then she saw him as he got to his feet from a deep wing chair, and she felt a rush of relief.

"I didn't think it would be possible for a woman to look any lovelier than you did earlier. I see I was wrong." He smiled slowly at her. Lilah returned his smile, feeling the magic spark the air between them again. She hadn't imagined it, it wasn't too good to be true. There was an attraction between them so strong that it drew her toward him like a magnetic force.

"You're very good with compliments, Mr. San Pietro. It almost makes me think that you've had a great deal of practice handing them out." She held on to the knob of the open door to resist the urge to walk toward him. His smile broadened. He had shed his driving coat. The black swallowtail coat he wore clung to his broad shoulders and followed the line of his body down to his narrow waist. The knit breeches revealed slim hips, a flat belly, and long, muscular thighs. Lilah caught herself looking at him in a way she had no business doing. A blush stained her cheeks, and she jerked her eyes back up to his face again, hoping that her expression was not as self-conscious as it felt.

"Can it be that you are accusing me of being a flirt, Miss Remy?" The easy banter was all on the surface. The real conversation was silent, and was conducted by their eyes.

"I fear it may be so." Her voice was faintly breathless, despite her best intentions.

He shook his head and came toward her, his walk as lithe as an Indian's. "I never flirt. I'm much too direct for that. If I see something I want, I do my best to get it."

He stopped when he was very close to her, and stood looking down into her face. Lilah felt her pulse quicken at the obvious implication: he had seen her, wanted her, and would try his best to get her. She looked up at him, up at that dark handsome face bent toward hers, and had to fight the urge to sway toward him. He was tall and strong and handsome, and she was shocked at the sudden longing she felt to have him take her in his arms.

"We — should go join the others. My great-aunt will be wondering where I am." That urge to be held by him unnerved her. She had never expected to feel such a thing with a man. Certainly she never had before. Ladies were supposed to be immune to that. Being alone with him was intoxicating, and being intoxicated with him could be dangerous.

"Perhaps we should forgo joining the others."

"Oh, I can't."

"Why not?"

"It — it wouldn't be proper. Besides . . ."

"I have to be on a ship that leaves Washington harbor at dawn the day after tomorrow. I'd like to get to know you better, and if we're surrounded by dozens of people I won't be able to. I know that your relatives won't like the idea of you being alone with a man you barely know, but I can assure you that you've no reason to fear me. Whatever else I may be, I'm a gentleman — or at least I promise to be with you."

"I know that," she answered, surprised because she did. Being afraid of him hadn't even occurred to her. He was wildly attractive, with those predatory eyes and that gleaming smile, but she'd sensed from the first that he'd never hurt her. As he'd said, he was a gentleman — at least with her.

"Well then?"

She hesitated. The idea of spending the rest of the evening with him alone was dazzling. Her aunt would scold for days; the assembled guests would gossip for weeks. But she suddenly found that she didn't care. She gave him a glimmering smile.

"I suppose I could show you the rose garden."

"I've always had an intense interest in horticulture."

"All right then." She smiled at him again, feeling suddenly very carefree. She would show him the rose garden and be hanged to them all if they didn't like it. For once in her life she was going to do what she wanted to do, whether it was the proper thing or not.

"How is it that you are living here at Boxhill with your aunt and uncle? Do your parents live here too?"

"Shhh!" Half laughing, she held a cautioning finger to her lips. They were walking along the back hallway with Lilah in the lead. The sounds of dancing and laughter from the front rooms were faintly muffled, but clear enough so that there was no getting away from the fact that Amanda's party in her honor was still going on. Lilah felt absurdly guilty, like a child sneaking out of a schoolroom. This sensation of illicit freedom was delicious. She felt more alive than she ever had in her life, happier, even daring. Reckless. . . .

She took him out a side door to avoid Beulah and the kitchen maids. When at last they were safe outside, with the darkness all around them sheltering them from prying eyes, she let out a breath of relief. He grinned at her, and she laughed back at him. They were partners in crime.

"So show me the rose garden," he instructed, taking her hand and tucking it in the crook of her arm. Holding up her skirt, Lilah walked closer to him than propriety perhaps allowed, but she didn't care. Already she felt more at ease with him than she did with gentlemen she had known for most of her life. The solid warmth of him beside her felt right, somehow. She looked up at him, at the breadth of shoulder that was just about on her eye level, at the underside of the firm chin that was just faintly darkened as if it had been some hours since he had shaved. Usually she didn't care for gentlemen with mustaches; she preferred them clean shaven, but in his case . . . She caught herself wondering how that mustache would feel if he kissed her, and blushed.

"Tell me about yourself," she said hurriedly as he looked down at her with a gleam in his eyes that made her think he had no trouble at all following the line of her thoughts.

He shook his head. "You first. You never answered my question."

"Oh, about my parents? I don't live here at Boxhill. I'm just visiting my great-aunt, and I'll be going home in a little more than two weeks."

The possibility that she might never see him again after tonight occurred to her with stunning force. Her throat tightened, and her eyes widened on her face. She couldn't bear the thought of never seeing him again. . . .

"And where is home?"

"Barbados. We have a sugar plantation there. It's called Heart's Ease."

"Heart's Ease," he said, as if he were committing it to memory. "My ships sail to Barbados several times a year. I'll make it a point to be on the next one."

"Your ships?" She watched with fascination the different expressions that played over his dark face. He was looking down at her just as intently, his free hand moving to cover the slim, cool fingers that rested in the crook of his arm. Lilah felt the touch of his bare hand on hers with a jolt of her heart. His skin was so warm. . . .

"I operate a shipping company out of Bristol, in England. Sometimes, when I have business somewhere, I captain one of my own ships. As I did to come here tonight. I must warn you, I am liable to be persona non grata when your uncle hears the nature of my business. He may very well order me off his land."

"Uncle George would never do that. He's a very nice man, really. Is it your company that ships his tobacco to England? If so . . ."

He shook his head. "My business with him is personal." His tone was faintly repressive. Lilah wasn't interested enough to probe further. His business with Uncle George had nothing to do with her. She was interested in the man, not what he did.

Another couple strolled toward them. Lilah recognized red-haired Sarah Bennet with a gentleman she thought was Thom McQuarter, and hurriedly tugged Mr. San

Pietro down a bisecting path. She did not want to go through the process of performing introductions, and then have their tête-à-tête turn into a quartet. Knowing how sweet Sarah Bennet was on Mr. McQuarter, she guessed that Sarah would be grateful for her quick action.

"This garden seems a trifle crowded," Mr. San Pietro observed with rueful amusement as minutes later they performed a similar dodging maneuver to avoid another couple.

"Yes. It's a lovely night." She echoed his regret. Then a thought occurred to her that was so daring that she was shocked at herself for even entertaining it. With any other gentleman, she would never have made the suggestion. And if the gentleman had had the bad taste to do so, she would have excused herself from his company and made her way back to the house. Mr. San Pietro might think her bold. . . . But then she remembered that they had only this one night.

"We could walk along the creek to the summerhouse, if you'd like."

He looked down at her with a quick grin. The white gleam of his teeth in the darkness was dazzling.

"I'd like that very much."

The scent of roses faded behind them, to be replaced by the earthier fragrances of grass and woods and water. A mosquito buzzed around her head, and Lilah swatted at it. She would probably pay for her daring in the morning with a rash of insect bites.

Put In Creek sliced through the property at an angle. Uncle George had built an open-walled gazebo of whitewashed birch where the creek formed a vee as it headed toward Chesapeake Bay again. This summerhouse, as everyone at Boxhill called it, had become a favorite retreat of Lilah's, though she had never before been there at night. Now she saw that it stood amidst the grove of rustling willows in which it had been built like a graceful lady ghost. More honeysuckles grew up around the elaborate scrollwork of the railings, their sweet scent lending a heady kind of enchantment to the night. In the creek a pair of ducks swam, their passing silent, marked only by rippling curves of water that gleamed in the moonlight.

Lilah hesitated. She had not realized quite how isolated the summerhouse would be at night.

"Mr. San Pietro . . . ," she began.

"Call me Joss. As I said earlier, my friends all do."

"That's the trouble," she said with a nervous laugh. She made an instinctive move that put a little distance between them. Up to then she had been walking pressed almost against his side. He could not be blamed if she had given him the wrong impression. But though she had been carried away by the man and the moonlight, she was still bound by some proprieties. No matter what he might have been led to believe, beyond a certain point she would not go. "I'm not quite sure how good a friend of yours you expect me to be. I confess I hadn't realized the summerhouse was so . . . so isolated."

He let her hand slide away from the crook of his arm, let her put a few more paces between them until she stood facing him.

"Don't worry, I know a lady when I meet one. You need not concern yourself that you'll have any reason to regret your trust in me. I won't take advantage of it, I promise. But I'd like us to be friends."

She looked up at him a moment, wavering. What she saw in his face reassured her. He was no bounder who would take disgraceful advantage of her lack of discretion in bringing him to this isolated spot. For all his flirting and his roguish smile, he was, as he had assured her earlier, a gentleman.

"Very well then. Friends."

"Joss," he prompted.

"Joss," she echoed, then preceded him up the summerhouse steps.

"I hope you have no objection if I call you Lilah? I like it — it's unusual, and it suits you." He followed her to the opposite side of the octagon-shaped structure, which looked out over the creek. Lilah stopped there, her knees resting against the built-in wooden bench, her hands closing over the polished railing as she stared unseeingly at the creek. Her every nerve ending was focused on the man who stood beside her.

"It's really Delilah," she said inconsequentially.

"That's even more unusual, and suits you even better. Delilah. What a good thing such an enchanting name wasn't wasted on a pudding-faced little miss. Your parents must be people of rare discernment — or else you were an unusually attractive baby."

Lilah smiled up at him fleetingly. "I don't think so. My mother died when I was small, but Katy, my old governess, said that I was the ugliest baby she ever saw. She said I was so ugly my father nearly cried when he saw me."

Joss grinned. "Time has certainly wrought a miracle, then. Because you are the most beautiful young lady I've ever seen."

"There you go, flattering me again."

He shook his head. "Not a bit of it. May God strike me dead on the spot if I'm lying."

"Was that a thunderclap I heard?"

He laughed, picking up her hand from the rail and carrying it toward his lips. He didn't quite kiss her fingers, but looked at her provocatively over the curve of them as he held them near his mouth. Lilah turned a little toward him, her eyes meeting his. She was suddenly nervous, but in a nice kind of way. He had promised not to take advantage of her trust and she believed him, so she wasn't frightened that he might go beyond the line. This giddy anticipation was a new sensation, and her skin tingled with it.

"You know, you've been looking at me all night as if you're trying to figure out what it would feel like if I kissed you." There was a hint of laughter buried under his pensive words.

Her eyes widened, and she felt a blush creep into her cheeks. Was she really that transparent?

"I — I . . ." she stuttered in utter confusion, tugging at her hand. He grinned wickedly, and lifted her fingers to his mouth. His lips just brushed over her knuckles with a pressure so light that the depth of the reaction she felt was shocking in comparison. Her lips parted, and her knees quivered.

"Does it tickle?" he murmured, lowering her hand but still holding on to it. With her senses so disordered from that fleeting kiss, it took Lilah a moment to understand what he had said. When she did, her blush deepened.

"How did you know . . . ?" she gasped, then broke off as she realized what she was admitting.

His grin broadened. "You kept shooting shy little glances in the direction of my chin. At first I thought you were fascinated by my mouth, but then I decided it must be my mustache. I was right, wasn't I? So does it tickle?"

"I didn't notice." Lilah tried to hold on to her slipping composure, lowering her eyes primly and pulling at her hand again. Instead of releasing it, he caught the other one, then slid both his hands up her arms to just above her elbows. The feel of his warm, strong hands against her bare skin caused a jolt that shook her clear to her toes. Her lips parted, and her eyes flew to his.

"So you didn't notice?" He was leaning toward her, deviltry plain in the wicked little half-smile that played around his mouth. Not a handsbreadth separated their bodies. She was so conscious of his nearness that she could barely think. Her eyes locked helplessly with his. For the first time in her life she found herself solely in someone else's power. She couldn't have moved or spoken if her life had depended upon it.

"This time, pay attention," he murmured, and lowered his head toward hers. Lilah froze as his lips touched hers, softly, warmly, just brushing the quivering softness of her mouth. His mustache grazed the tender skin above her upper lip. Then he was lifting his head to look down at her with an intent expression that deepened as he saw how the kiss had affected her. The brief touch of his mouth had left her reeling.

"Lilah . . ."

Whatever else he had been going to say in that dark, soft voice was drowned beneath excited yapping. Lilah, shaken out of the dreamworld she had been caught up in, looked around dazedly to see Hercules darting across the floor toward them. Behind him, not quite at the summerhouse steps, came her Uncle George, his expression boding no good.

Five

"What the devil are you about, girl, flirting like some demmed Jezebel out here in the dark? You ought to be ashamed of yourself! Your aunt's been looking for you this age!"

Her great-uncle's booming voice finished the process of dragging Lilah back to reality. She took a hasty step away from Joss, who obligingly dropped her arms, and turned to face her fuming uncle as he puffed up the shallow steps. Unlike his wife, Uncle George's bark was far worse than his bite. He was not nearly as gruff as he sounded. She was really very fond of him, and gave him a placating smile as he stomped across the floor toward her. He had once been tall, but he was stooped now with age and required a cane to get around. Still, he was an impressive figure with his thick head of bushy white hair and his elegant black evening clothes slimming a frame that inclined toward portliness around the middle.

"I'm sorry if I worried you, Uncle. But the rose garden was crowded, and —"

"And you wanted to find a spot where your young man here could sneak a kiss," Uncle George finished with devastating accuracy. "No use to try to pull the wool over my eyes, girl, I saw what you was about. But don't let on with your aunt. She's a high stickler, she is. Well, now, am I to expect a visit from you in the morning, young man, asking for my great-niece's hand? Or do I crack this cane over your head here and now?"

"Uncle!" Lilah protested, mortified, as she cast a quick look over her shoulder at Joss. He stood tall and silent behind her, his eyes fixed on Uncle George's face. Lilah remembered that he had come to Boxhill on some sort of business that concerned her uncle, and felt a spurt of sympathy toward him. Getting caught kissing one's host's niece was not an ideal way to start a relationship.

"You're not the Burrel boy, are you? Nah, you can't be. His hair's as yeller as Lilah's here. Unless my mind's getting as weak as my knees, I've never seen you before in my life." Uncle George looked at Joss with hard suspicion.

"My name is Jocelyn San Pietro." Joss spoke abruptly, as though he expected the name to have some meaning for the old man. Uncle George glared at Lilah before shifting his eyes back to Joss. Despite her uncle's age and disability, there was suddenly something formidable about him.

"Here in Virginia, we call a man out for less than you've done tonight, sirra. Strangers don't take young ladies out in the dark and kiss them without being called to account for it."

"Uncle . . . !"

"You hush your mouth, missy! Hell, females got no sense, and this proves it! To come out alone with a man we don't know from Adam — you're lucky I came along when I did! He . . ."

"I beg your pardon, sir, but you do know me. Or you should. I believe I'm your grandson."

Astounded silence followed this revelation. Lilah stared at Joss, her mouth open, eyes wide. Uncle George and Aunt Amanda had never had children. . . .

"My grandson? What a load of bull feathers! I don't have a . . ." Uncle George never talked, he bellowed, and he was bellowing now as he reached out to catch Lilah's arm and pull her to him and away from the tall, dark man who stood regarding him inscrutably. The moonlight caught Joss's eyes, making them gleam vividly emerald through the darkness. Uncle George's bluster died. His hand on Lilah's arm tightened painfully as he stared up at Joss. As Lilah watched, her great-uncle's face visibly paled. "Good God! Victoria!"

"Victoria Barton was my grandmother." Joss's voice was expressionless. "Emmelina, her daughter, was my mother. She was also, or so she told me, your daughter. I am sorry to inform you — though I don't believe you ever acknowledged her existence — that she died three months ago. She left some letters for you that I understand were written by her mother, and begged me on her deathbed to deliver them. Once I have executed her commission, I'll take myself off."

"Dear God in heaven." Uncle George sounded as if he were choking. "Victoria! So many years ago! It can't be. . . . You can't be . . ."

Lilah, suddenly embarrassed, realized that she had no business witnessing this emotion-fraught meeting. Her great-uncle had always longed for a son, and she supposed that this newly discovered grandson would be the next best thing. There were difficulties, of course. Obviously Uncle George had, at some time, fathered a daughter with a woman not his wife, and the man confronting him now was the result of that youthful indiscretion. She looked from Joss's hard, set face to Uncle George's suddenly slack one.

The old man looked as if he'd seen a ghost.

"Perhaps you should continue your discussion inside the house?" she suggested, placing her hand on her great-uncle's arm. He shook her off.

"We've nothing to discuss." The old man was more agitated than Lilah had ever seen him. Thinking of her great-aunt Amanda, Lilah understood his concern. If Uncle George's wife should discover the existence of this grandson, what was left of the old man's life was likely to be miserable indeed. Lilah looked at him in sudden sympathy, only to find that his eyes were fixed on his grandson.

"I want you out of here, now. You hear me, boy?"

"I hear you, old man." Joss reached inside his coat for a slim packet that he held out to his grandfather. Uncle George seemed incapable of taking it. Joss didn't move, didn't relent. After a moment, Lilah reached out and accepted it for her uncle. Neither man spared so much as a glance for her. Their eyes were locked on each other in a silent, bitter war.

"Don't come back here," Uncle George rasped. "Ever. Not to Boxhill, not to Virginia. I don't know what you thought to gain, but there's nothing for you here. You go back to wherever your mama brought you up, and you stay there. You hear?"

Joss moved suddenly, striding across the floor. Lilah's heart was in her throat as she watched him go. He stopped short of the steps, and turned back to look at her.

"I'll see you in the spring. Wait for me."

She nodded. Uncle George made a strangled sound deep in his throat.

"You stay away from her! Delilah Remy, he's no good for you, no good for anything! Damn you, boy, stay in your own part of the world and keep away from me and mine!"

"Uncle George . . . !"

"I'll go where I please, and do what I please, old man. It's a free world."

"Not for the likes of you, it's not! You stay on your own side of the Atlantic, and don't come around here again! You . . ."

Uncle George suddenly stopped talking, looked surprised, and clutched at his chest. Then without further warning, he toppled to the floor. Lilah screamed, and tried to catch him as he fell. He was too heavy for her; she couldn't hold him. She dropped to her knees at his side. Joss, his face still taut with rage, was beside her in an instant, his hand going under the old man's coat to feel for his heart.

"Get help. He's in a bad way."

Lilah nodded, and scrambled to her feet,

the packet of letters forgotten on the floor. She ran toward the house like a jackrabbit, screaming for Dr. Patterson, who was a guest. By the time she returned with the medical bag the doctor had sent her to fetch, a crowd had gathered by the summerhouse. Slaves holding flaming torches hovered about, providing light for Dr. Patterson. Joss stood grim-faced as he watched the proceedings. Amanda knelt by the sprawled form of her husband, the packet of papers that Lilah had dropped clutched in her hand. Her face was paper white, but she was dry-eyed. On the other side of the old man's body knelt Boot, his face awash with tears, and Dr. Patterson, who was looking across at Amanda's suddenly skeletal face instead of down at her husband. The little tableau left no doubt in Lilah's mind that her great-uncle was dead.

Six

"He's gone, Howard?" Her great-aunt's voice was remarkably calm. Lilah felt a sudden fierce surge of pity for the old woman whose unbending ways had caused her so much discomfort during her visit. Whatever else she might do or be, Amanda Barton was a lady right through to her core. Any other woman would be screaming and wailing over the loss of her husband. Amanda was meeting the crisis unbowed, according to the tenets of her birth and breeding.

"I'm sorry, Amanda. He was dead by the time I reached him. There was nothing I could do." Dr. Patterson got to his feet as he spoke, and patted Amanda clumsily on the arm. Then, as she started to rise, he helped her do so.

Her movements were very slow and deliberate, as if the shock she had suffered had in some degree affected her muscles. The gathering of guests and slaves was silent, as stunned as Lilah was herself. It seemed impossible that Uncle George was dead. Not ten minutes before he had been yelling at Joss. Her eyes lifted to that gentleman. His handsome face was hard and set. As if he felt her eyes on him, he looked in her direction. Though he had in a way been the cause of Uncle George's death, she felt a great deal of sympathy for him, too. Uncle George had been his grandfather, after all, regardless of how the old man had behaved toward him. Joss must be suffering some measure of shock, just as they all were. He might even be grieving.

She made her way toward him, sliding unobtrusively between the crush of people, only to be stopped in her tracks by her great-aunt's suddenly strident voice.

"Are you the man calling himself Jocelyn San Pietro?"

Amanda's eyes were fixed on Joss with what Lilah could only describe as absolute malevolence. She looked from Joss to the gaunt figure of her aunt and back again, her sympathies divided. Amanda must have discovered who Joss was, and the role he had played in Uncle George's death. She was an unforgiving woman. That Joss was in no way responsible for his own birth and only circumstantially responsible for Uncle George's death would not deter her virulent tongue in the least.

"I am Jocelyn San Pietro, yes," Joss replied evenly, meeting Amanda's eyes over the gapes of the assembled onlookers.

"The grandson of the woman calling herself Victoria Barton?"

"Victoria Barton was my grandmother."

"You admit it?"

"I believe proof of my identity and antecedents are in those letters that you hold in your hand. I see no reason to deny them."

"So you see no reason to deny them, do you?" A ghastly smile split Amanda's wrinkled face. Lilah, watching her, thought that her great-aunt looked almost evil. She felt a momentary shiver of fear for the man being impaled by Amanda's faded blue eyes. How ridiculous! After all, what harm could an old, embittered woman possibly do to such a strong, healthy man?

"That makes you my husband's only grandchild — that I know of. You have no brothers or sisters, have you?"

"I have a stepbrother. He is no kin of your husband's." Joss's expression changed, softened slightly as he took in the extreme frailty of the woman confronting him. "Please accept my condolences on the loss of your husband, Mrs. Barton, and my apologies. Had I any notion that my errand would have resulted in such a tragedy, I —"

Amanda cut short his explanation with a wave of her hand. "You don't know, do you?" she cackled, staring at him. "You don't have the least idea. What a tremendous joke!" She fell to chuckling, horrifying the assembled onlookers. Dr. Patterson frowned at her, looking as taken aback as any of them, then patted her arm again sympathetically.

"You must go back to the house, Amanda, and let me give you something to help you sleep. Boot will take care of the bod— of George, and if you need to you can see him again in the morning. Boot, go up to the house and get a blanket, then come back here and get some of the other boys to help you carry Mr. Barton back to the house. Is Mrs. Barton's maid here? Ah, there you are. . . ."

Boot, tears still streaming down his face, got to his feet and went to obey Dr. Patterson's command. Jenny, Amanda's maid, pushed herself forward from the back of the crowd. She was nearly as old and gaunt as Amanda, with her grizzled hair concealed by a snowy kerchief and her bony frame hidden beneath a voluminous black dress, but she had stood the ravages of time less well than her mistress. She was stooped with age, while her mistress's spine was rigid. Amanda looked at her impatiently, then waved her off.

"Not yet, Jenny, not yet. There's something I must see to. And, no, I've not lost my mind, Howard, so you may stop looking at me in such a way. Where's Thomas? He was about not long ago."

"Thomas" was Judge Thomas Harding. He was politically powerful in Mathews County, and whenever there was any high-level legal business that any of his particular cronies needed taken care of, Judge Harding could usually be counted on to oblige.

"Here I am, Amanda," he said, pushing through the crowd. He looked over at Jocelyn San Pietro as he passed, his expression one of unmasked suspicion. "I understand that you may feel yourself in a somewhat awkward position, now that another heir has presented himself so inopportunely, but —"

"You understand nothing, Thomas," Amanda interrupted brusquely. "Answer me this without any roundaboutation: Have you the authority to secure for me a piece of personal property until Sheriff Nichols can be sent for?"

"What kind of property?" Judge Harding looked both bewildered and a little wary. Like Lilah herself and many of the bystanders, he was clearly beginning to ask himself whether Amanda's mind had been unhinged by the shock of her husband's death.

"A runaway slave," Amanda said clearly, and Lilah knew her aunt's mind had truly snapped. What had a runaway slave to do with Uncle George's death, or anything else that had happened that night?

"Come on up to the house, Amanda. You there, take her other arm. Where's that niece?" Dr. Patterson was trying to urge Amanda from the summerhouse, his eyes searching the crowd for Lilah.

"I'm right here, Dr. Patterson." She attempted to make her way to her great-aunt's side, and the crowd parted for her. Amanda gave the doctor an impatient look.

"Confound it, Howard, I am not going to let you dose me like some old horse until this business gets done! I want your answer, Thomas: Do you or do you not have the authority to order a runaway slave held?" She shook off Jenny's arm and tried to shake off Dr. Patterson's as well, but without success. He motioned to Lilah to take Jenny's place. Lilah tried to slide unobtrusively around her aunt's other side.

"I have the authority, Amanda." Judge Harding's voice was soothing.

"Then I want you to detain Mr. so-called Jocelyn San Pietro here. He's the descendant of one Victoria, a high yeller gal who ran away from Boxhill with her girl-child some forty-five years ago. I owned her, and I owned her daughter, too, and I own this man."

"What?" Joss roared, while Lilah and the rest of the crowd turned as one to gape at him with horrified eyes. "You're insane, old woman! My grandmother was no more a slave than you are!"

Amanda smiled maliciously. "That's where you're wrong, boy. My husband bought your grandmother in New Orleans a couple of years after we were married. He said he bought her to be my maid, but I knew she'd be trouble the minute I set eyes on her. She was real pretty, with skin about the color of honey and red hair, and she had an uppity way about her that I would have cured her of if she hadn't gone off when she did. She could pass for white, and I guess she did, later, because you didn't know, did you, boy, or you wouldn't have come around trying to weasel what you could out of my fool husband. But she was an octoroon, her mother had been a planter's *chère-amie*, and when the planter died the mother and daughter were both sold. Immorality must have been in the blood, because that yeller gal hadn't been here a year before she was with child by my husband. He sent them away — but he never freed them. They were slaves 'til they died, both of them — and that means you are, too. You're as much a darky as Jenny here, for all your white-looking skin. You're a slave, and I own you. Thomas, I want him held."

Seven

Three weeks later, much at Boxhill had changed. George Barton had been laid to rest two days after his passing, and Amanda had already taken the reins of the tobacco plantation into her iron hands. The atmosphere in the house was strained, with most of the slaves grieving for their master while simultaneously suffering under their mistress's demands for unending work. Lilah would not be sorry to sail for Barbados on the *Swift Wind* at the end of the week. Whenever she thought of Heart's Ease, her breast filled with longing and her eyes with tears. So much had happened to her in the Colonies, it seemed as if she'd been away from her home for years.

At the moment she was bowling along the tree-shaded roads of Mathews County in a well-sprung buggy driven by her stepcousin Kevin Talbott, who had been sent by her father to fetch her home. Kevin had arrived without warning three days earlier. One of the maids had brought him into the back parlor where Lilah had been sitting. When she looked up from her book to see the familiar burly form and weather-beaten face, she cried his name and threw herself into his arms. It was so good to see somebody from home! It was quite a sacrifice for her father to do without his overseer for the length of a voyage to the Colonies and back, Lilah knew, but for his only daughter he would put himself out. And the gesture had paid off handsomely, as Leonard Remy had undoubtedly hoped it would: Less than an hour after Kevin's arrival Lilah had accepted his oft-repeated offer of marriage. Her father's fondest dream had come true: His headstrong daughter was finally engaged to the man of his choice, who would take care of both Lilah and the plantation when Leonard Remy was no longer around to do so.

Lilah, picturing her father's jubilation with a rueful grimace, had already written to inform him of the event, though the letter would probably precede her arrival in person by no more than a week. But she wanted to give him the glad tidings as soon as she possibly could. He would be thrilled, she knew. And she also knew that he would not bother to question the motive behind her unexpected decision to do the sensible thing. So long as Leonard Remy got his own way, such details would not concern him. But if truth were told, Lilah had suffered a severe jolting in matters of the heart.

For the first and only time in her life she had trembled on the brink of falling in love, only to have her pretty dream tumble down around her head like a house of cards. The image of Jocelyn San Pietro still troubled her nights, though she forced herself not to think about him during her waking hours. He was gone, removed from her life as completely as if he had died. The man for whom she had felt that violent attraction was a slave, a man of another race. He was as forbidden to her as marriage to a priest. Lilah knew it, accepted it, and tried not to dwell on it. Obviously she could not trust her own feelings when it came to men. Kevin was her father's choice for her, and he would make a kind husband. She would have him — before her untrustworthy heart could betray her again. There would be no more disastrous moonlight dalliances for her.

Through the slave grapevine at Boxhill she had learned that there had been a hasty legal proceeding held the day after Uncle George's death. There Joss was indeed adjudged to be a descendant of the octoroon Victoria, chattel of Boxhill, and George Barton, and thus was legally a chattel himself of Boxhill. He was no longer a free man; no, that was wrong. He had never been a free man, although he had not had the slightest inkling that he had been born a slave. Her great-aunt owned him like a horse or a gown or any of the other slaves at Boxhill, and held his ultimate fate in her hands. From the malevolence of Amanda's actions on that awful night, Lilah guessed that the existence of this illegitimate grandson of her husband's had opened up some old wounds. Uncle George had gotten the slave girl Victoria with child while wed to Amanda, right under the old lady's nose in fact. Amanda was fiercely proud, and had very likely been in love with her husband. The wound would be deep, and her vengeance would be severe. Lilah felt sick whenever she thought of Joss's probable fate. Her aunt would not be kind to him, and even if she were, to go from a free man to slave in the space of an evening must be a fate worse than death.

Sitting there in the buggy beside Kevin, with the breeze blowing tendrils of her hair loose from beneath the brim of her bonnet and the sun shining warmly down all around, Lilah had a sudden mental picture of that lean, handsome face that was so vivid it was almost as if Joss stood before her. She shuddered, and closed her eyes to blot him out. She could not bear thinking of him. His fate was tragic — but it was a mercy that it had happened when it did. If the truth had been revealed a few days later, the tragedy from her point of view would have increased a hundredfold. She would have fallen in love with him, allowed him to take uncounted liberties with her person, maybe even have wed him. And such a thing was unthinkable. If people somehow found out that she'd let him kiss her, she'd be shunned. . . .

"You don't mind if I don't take you straight back to Boxhill, do you?" Kevin was saying. "If I'm going to get to that slave auction, I need to head on over to town. I didn't realize that you'd be visiting so long with Miss Marsh, or I'd have made arrangements to have someone else drive you."

A slave auction fit in so well with her thoughts that Lilah mentally recoiled. "I'd really rather not."

"Come on, Lilah, be a sport. You know I promised your father I'd bring back a new contingent of field hands with us on the *Swift Wind.* Ordinarily I'd take you home first, but the auction's at three o'clock and —"

"Oh, I know. Anything for Heart's Ease. All right, all right, I'll go with you," Lilah capitulated, summoning a smile for her fiance. He was really a nice sort; she'd known him since she was eight years old and he already a man of twenty-two, and he was going to be her husband and the father of her children. She was determined to be agreeable to him if it killed her. Marriages became what one made them, after all, and she meant for hers to be a success. Slaves and slave auctions were something she preferred not to think about at this time, but she would go if Kevin wished her to. Joss San Pietro was an unfortunate chapter in an otherwise serene life, and she was going to put him very firmly from her mind. Doubtless she had imagined the strength of the attraction she had felt for him because she had quite simply been ripe to fall in love. She had willed herself into it, and that was that. The plain truth of the matter was that she had barely known the man.

"If you've any shopping to do in town, I'll be glad to drop you off wherever you wish and pick you up afterwards. Maybe you could get some silk for your wedding dress, or something."

"I'll be wearing Mother's," Lilah answered automatically, her mind not really on the conversation. Her mother had died shortly after Lilah's birth, and Lilah could not remember her at all. Jane, her stepmother and

Kevin's aunt, had come to live at Heart's Ease as her governess when Lilah was five, and had married her father two years later. Jane was kind and good and meek, and suited her blustery father perfectly. But Lilah still sometimes felt a sneaking longing for the mother she had never known.

"Well, what about a new hat? Not that that confection on your head is not charming, of course."

"Thank you." She smiled at him again. He grinned at her in response, his broad, weathered face beneath his thick thatch of tobacco-brown hair turning ruddy with pleasure. Since she had accepted his proposal, Kevin had been the happiest of men. (And why not? one unruly part of her brain kept asking. He was, after all, getting a young and beautiful bride and one of the richest sugar plantations in Barbados in one neat package.) But she . . . she was having to sternly quell second thoughts. This marriage was the sensible thing to do. If Kevin was not precisely the handsome, charming prince of her dreams, well, what of it? Real life was not about dreams, and it was time she accepted that fact. She could make a success of her marriage if she would. And she would!

Mathews Court House was a bustling little town with neat brick-and-frame shops lining cobbled streets. Ladies in their high-waisted, beribboned pastel gowns and deep-brimmed sunbonnets hurried along the streets laden with parcels or shepherding recalcitrant children, some with their more soberly clad menfolk in tow. Here and there she saw acquaintances in the street or in other passing carriages, and she waved to them with a smile. Everywhere her greeting was returned, and she felt a measure of relief.

Lilah had not been sure of her reception socially since that night in the summerhouse. People had been bandying her name about these last three weeks, and she was only glad that the gossip did not seem to have reached Kevin's ears. Exactly what had happened between Lilah and Jocelyn San Pietro was not known, but people were aware that she'd spent a great deal of time alone with him on that fateful night. The memory of her reckless behavior, however, was already fading from the collective consciousness. She had begun to hope that the saga of Jocelyn San Pietro had entered local folklore and been largely forgotten. After all, many of the gentlemen hereabouts had fathered children with their slave mistresses. What made it all so scandalous was that Joss had spent his life as a white man — and that George Barton had died when he'd turned up. Lilah's involvement added just a minor fillip to the story.

More carriages were heading toward the center of town than away, and Lilah supposed that the slave auction was the reason. Slavery was the lifeblood of the great plantations both in the American South and in Barbados. While it wasn't always a pleasant labor system, it was the only way to run the cotton, sugar and tobacco plantations profitably. Slave women were, as a rule, poor breeders, and the only way to replenish the stock of laborers needed to work the fields was to buy them. This had to be done frequently, requiring substantial infusions of cash. The house slaves, of course, were a different breed than the field hands. There was as much difference between a gullah, which was how most of the planters referred to slaves brought fresh from Africa to work the fields, and a gentleman's longtime slave majordomo as there was between a street urchin and a lord in Britain. Many of the house slaves were as much a part of the family as her own Betsy, or Boot, who mourned George Barton more than his own wife did.

The site of the slave auction would be the front and rear lawns of the courthouse, which was an imposing brick building in the center of town. Both lawns were required because there were really two different auctions. The more valuable slaves, house servants, prime field hands and the like, were auctioned off in the front. The rear faced a street known locally as Cheapside, and it was there that the old, injured, recalcitrant or for some other reason less valuable merchandise was sold.

"Shall I drop you off somewhere?"

From the lack of enthusiasm in Kevin's voice, Lilah realized that he was not eager to do so, and guessed that he feared that if he was late he would lose a chance to bid on the best of the field hands. So she shook her head, and got her reward as he smiled at her.

"You're a trump, Lilah! What a team we'll make!"

Lilah smiled in response to that too, which since she had accepted him seemed to be all that was required of her to keep him happy. Kevin maneuvered the buggy into the narrow space some two streets over (all the closer spaces had been taken by earlier arrivals) jumped down, and held up his had to assist Lilah down. His grip on her waist was not unpleasant. When he kept his hands on her for a moment after her feet touched the ground, she managed another smile at him quite easily. He squeezed her waist lightly and released her. Lilah took the arm he offered her, resting her fingers lightly on the fine wool covering the brawny forearm and refused to think of the last masculine arm she had held that way. Talking lightly of desultory things, they made their way to the auction.

The caliber of slaves Kevin was interested in for Heart's Ease would be sold on the upper side, so they headed toward the courthouse's porticoed front. Lilah shortly found herself standing near the front of the crowd gathered before a narrow wooden platform raised perhaps three feet off the ground. On it stood the nattily dressed auctioneer extolling the virtues of a stripped-to-the-waist field hand, age, the auctioneer swore, no more than nineteen. Damon, as the auctioneer named him, was ebony-skinned and heavily muscled, and Lilah was not surprised when Kevin jumped right into the binding. When Damon was knocked down to Kevin for the princely sum of five hundred dollars, the slave grinned from ear to ear, proud of the price he'd brought. He was tagged and at a signal from Kevin led away, to be picked up later that day.

The auction passed swiftly. As it neared the end Lilah lost what little interest she'd had in the proceedings and wandered away. Kevin had bought ten prime field hands for Heart's Ease, as well as a likely-looking mulatto girl who he said could help Maisie, the cook, in the kitchen. His bidding completed unless something that looked exceptionally good should come along, he had fallen into conversation with the gentleman standing next to him, and they were deep in discussion about alternate methods of irrigation. Lilah made her way around the crowd toward the back of the courthouse. No one could accuse Kevin of a lack of interest in his chosen line of work, she thought.

Without any destination in mind, Lilah found herself skirting the edge of the far different crowd attending the auction on Cheapside. The people here were less prosperous farmers and merchants and even white trash who had scraped together enough money to buy an inferior slave or two. Unlike his counterpart on the upper side, this auctioneer was shabbily dressed and raucous, extolling the virtues of a stooped old man with a weary look in his eyes.

"Amos here got a lotta years left in him. And he's stronger than he looks. Why, he can still lift a hoe with the best of 'em, cain't ya, Amos?"

Amos nodded his grizzled head dutifully. But the bidding was unenthusiastic, and in the end he was knocked down for only a hundred dollars to a burly farmer with a mean look in his eyes. Lilah felt a vague pity for Amos as she turned around to head back to the front, where she felt more comfortable. The noise level on this side was giving her a headache, and there was a definite smell of unwashed bodies emanating from the crowd. Besides, Kevin would be wondering where she had gone. . . .

"Now here we have a fine young buck, Joss by name, strong as an ox. Just needs to be broke to bridle a little bit. What am I bid?"

"Why, that's a white man!"

"Nah, he's high yeller. Don' you remember hearin' . . . ?"

"Lookit the chains on 'im! He must be a mean'un! I wouldn't have 'im at any price!"

"I'll give fifty dollars!"

"Fifty dollars! Come on, Mr. Collier! Once he's broke, he'll be worth five hundred sure!" The auctioneer refuted the low bid indignantly.

"Yeah, if he don' kill somebody in the breakin'! Or if ya don' end up havin' to kill him!"

While this exchange was going on between

the auctioneer and a man in the crowd, Lilah glanced up at the auction block and froze. He was dirty, his hair matted and tangled, his mustache gone. Instead what looked like a two-week growth of beard darkened his jaw. He was barefoot, clad only in a pair of tattered breeches that Lilah realized with a shock were the remnants of the buff ones he'd been wearing that fateful night, with something that was more rag than shirt clinging to his shoulders. His chest was mostly bare, revealing corded muscles and glimpses of rib, with a thick wedge of black hair in the center. His mouth was swollen and there was a crust of dried blood at the corner. At the moment it was distorted by a feral snarl. A livid purple bruise extended across his left cheekbone, and there was a half-healed cut on his right temple. Lilah felt her heart stop as she looked at the muscles popping out of the nearly bare arms because his hands were tied so tightly behind his back. A chain linked his ankles, and another chain secured him to a post at the rear of the auction block. Despite his changed appearance, there was no mistaking Joss. Staring helplessly, Lilah felt nausea rise up in her throat, and had to swallow to hold it back. Oh, dear God, that he had been reduced to this . . . The reality of Amanda's revenge was more dreadful than what she had ever imagined.

"Who'll go a hundred? A hundred dollars for a fine young buck!" The auctioneer, keeping a wary distance from the goods he was trying to sell, scanned the crowd. "He's a bargain at the price!"

"I'll go sixty!" a man called.

"Sixty dollars! Why, that's almost crime! You'll get arrested if you take him away for that, Sam Johnson! Come on, folks! I want a hundred!"

"Let's see his back, Neely! I'll wager he's been whipped within an inch of his life! Who needs a troublemaker, huh?"

"Yeah, Neely, let's see his back!"

Reluctantly, the auctioneer yielded to crowd pressure. "Turn around, boy!" he said to Joss.

"Go to hell!" was the growled response. It was clearly audible even to Lilah, who stood in the back row. The auctioneer, scowling, motioned to a couple of burly men who stood on either side of the platform. They climbed up and wrestled the recalcitrant victim around, stripping off the tattered shirt in the process. The exposed back was raw and red, marked with crisscrossing welts. Lilah felt nausea threaten again. She pressed a hand to her mouth, afraid she might actually vomit.

"I withdraw my bid!" yelled the man who had gone sixty dollars.

"Mine stands!" said the fifty-dollar bidder, who added in an aside to the crowd in general: "Hell, you can't buy hog slop that cheap! And if he gives me too much grief, that's just what he'll be — hog slop!"

There was a murmur of sympathetic agreement from the crowd as Joss, released by the burly guards, turned to face them. His face was livid with fury, and with the muscles of his arms and chest tensed and bulging he looked dangerous. In no way did he resemble the dashing, laughing stranger who had flirted with her so boldly and almost stolen her heart. They had made him into a beast, and her heart bled for him.

Her eyes had remained fixed on him from the time she had first recognized him, while his had scornfully challenged the crowd. As they swept the assemblage, daring anyone to bid, they passed over where she stood toward the rear. Then, as if in slow motion, they returned. Those green eyes whose color she remembered more vividly than she did her own fastened on hers.

Eight

Joss was snarling out over the mob like a wild beast at bay when he saw her. She was standing near the edge of the gawking crowd staring up at him, the deep frilled brim of her pale yellow sunbonnet casting a shadow over her face. She was exactly as he remembered her, more beautiful than any young woman had a right to be, looking cool as springwater in the sweltering August heat. The masses of silvery hair that he had seen first in charming disorder were tucked up primly under the sunbonnet, which was trimmed with a narrow ribbon in a soft grayed blue almost exactly the color of her eyes, if his memory served him correctly. She looked as insubstantial as a sunbeam in a pale yellow dress secured under the sweet high curve of her breasts by a ribbon in the same shade of blue that trimmed her bonnet. The long end of the ribbon fluttered down the front of her narrow skirt. The dress itself was made of some gauzy material apparently designed to reveal as much as conceal the delectable curves of her slender body. Below short puffed sleeves her arms were bare, tantalizingly slim and pale in the bright afternoon sunlight. Her expression was hidden from him, but even at that distance he could sense her revulsion, feel her pity for him. Rage flooded through him, covering a tide of humiliation deeper than anything he had ever known.

When he had met her he had been cockily sure of his power over her sex; sure that, if he wished it, he could have nearly any woman he wanted. Females had always found him attractive, and he had managed to take full advantage of that fortunate circumstance more times than he could remember. Then Delilah Remy had gone tumbling into a bush, baring a pair of slender, thrashing, white-stockinged legs to the thigh to pique his interest. When he had done nothing more than the gentlemanly thing by attempting to adjust her skirt for her, she had tried to punch his nose. At first he'd merely been vastly amused. But then, after he'd gotten a good look at her and discovered that the spitfire was a staggering beauty, he'd been enchanted. And had stayed enchanted until this nightmare had caught him in its thrall. There'd been something about her that had appealed to him, something beyond the delicate perfection of her face and form. He had liked her, really liked her. And he had wanted her. Just as she had wanted him, though she was probably too innocent to put what she had felt when he had touched her in those terms. Even that baby's breath of a kiss he'd given her had caused her to catch fire. . . .

But that was in the past. Harsh reality was standing on a platform in the broiling sun, his tongue swollen from thirst and his arms throbbing from being bound so tightly. The rest of his body ached in too many locations to enumerate. He'd been hit and kicked and whipped and beaten so many times that he'd lost count. He'd been stripped of his name and identity and even his race, reduced to the status of a beast to be bought or sold simply because his grandmother had been the great-granddaughter of a gullah, and enslaved.

Impossible to believe — it had taken him some days to become convinced that the whole thing wasn't a hideous mistake — but horribly true. His own ancestry was thirty-one parts white to one part black, a mere teaspoonful of blood, and yet it was enough in this colonial backwater to condemn him to the ranks of the inhuman. His education, his background, even the successful shipping business he had built up, counted for nothing against that soupçon of blood. Never in his life had he imagined being brought so low, or being so powerless to do anything about it. Even his protestations that he had the funds to buy his freedom at that farce of a hearing availed him of nothing. They would not even permit him to send a message to his ship. Slaves had no rights, and could claim ownership of nothing, he had been told as they dragged him away in chains.

He'd been visited in the shed that was his prison by that crazy old woman, Amanda Barton, who had told him — as if she were discussing the weather — that she meant to see him broken. He'd raged at her, spewing profanity that he'd been shocked to find himself using toward any female, even her. She'd cackled with delighted laughter, and left him, chained and ranting, in the dark. Later someone — it had been too dark to make out his assailant's identity — had come in and, without a word, beaten him senseless. He'd been starved and deprived of water, beaten and humiliated and left to wallow in his own filth until he felt himself to be less than human. Ever since the nightmare had started he'd been treated like an animal, no, worse than an animal, with malicious cruelty. And he had, finally, been driven to responding like an animal, earning for his pains more beatings with fists and cudgels, and a bout with a bullwhip.

Eventually he had learned to husband his anger, hoarding it like a miser with his gold, promising himself that if he waited he would have an opportunity to escape. He had not guessed that the old witch planned to sell him like the unwanted property she claimed he was, or that he would be taken from the tumbledown shed where he'd been kept chained and filthy for weeks, only to find himself chained and filthy on an auction block. To be put up for public inspection and bid on like a damned horse — he'd not thought he could sink to any greater depths. Then to find her eyes on him, knowing that she was seeing him dirty and stinking and half-naked and that the shaming marks of the whip were clearly visible to her eyes. . . .

He wanted to kill. The blood-lust that rushed through him was so intense as to sweep every consideration of prudence or even survival before it.

He roared with rage, baring his teeth and throwing every ounce of his strength into the lunge that was intended to break the chain that held him to the post. The post groaned and quivered, and for a moment, just for a moment, he thought he might break free. Though if he did he would likely be shot for his pains. . . .

The more fearful in the crowd cried out while the auctioneer spun around so fast that he tottered and almost fell off the block. Immediately two burly guards were upon Joss, their cudgels falling thick and fast around his head and shoulders. With his arms tied behind him and his ankles chained, there was no way he could protect himself, but he tried, ducking and dodging as best he could to escape the worst of the blows. Inevitably he was beaten to his knees. Then a heavy boot crashed into his ribcage. Pain sharp enough to penetrate the fog of rage that enveloped him stabbed through his chest. He gasped, doubling over so that his forehead touched the dusty wood of the block. Another boot caught him in the lower back. He gasped a second time, and cold sweat break out on his forehead.

"I'll bid a hundred dollars for him!"

Joss had thought his agony couldn't increase, but he'd been wrong. That sweet, softly accented voice from the crowd brought a wave of shame with it so intense that it hurt more than the almost certainly broken ribs. Gritting his teeth, he managed to lift his head to look at her. She had come closer, close enough so that now he could see the delicate perfection of her features beneath the shadowing sunbonnet. She was not looking at him, but up at the auctioneer. Those huge blue eyes were darkened with a combination of what he decided was pity for him and fright at her own daring. For a young lady to buy a male slave was unheard of; females, unless they were confirmed spinsters or widows and lacked the protection of a man, were never even heard to bid at slave auctions at all. In most cases they were prohibited from owning property of any kind; everything was held in the names of their husbands or fathers. And for a young lady such as Lilah to buy a young, virile male slave. . . . It was a courageous act. He recognized that, realized that she would be the talk of the auction, of this little one-horse town and beyond. But he still felt not the smallest spurt of gratitude for what she was doing for him. His blanket hatred and fury at the world stretched in that moment to cover her, too, for being a witness to and a participant in his utter debasement. He was on his knees before her, helpless, bloodied and bowed, his very manhood outraged. How could he not hate her for pitying him?

"Can you beat that? Lookit her, now!"

A scandalized murmur rose from the crowd as necks craned and the bidder was identified as a fashionably dressed young lady. The auctioneer stared down at Lilah as if he were having trouble believing his ears. The guards too turned to look. Lilah, suddenly aware of all the attention she had attracted, turned pink, but her eyes never left the auctioneer. Joss winced for her, and for himself. Her intentions were of the best, he knew, but she was only making things worse. A thousand times worse, and he hadn't thought that was possible.

"Miss, did you really mean to bid?" The auctioneer questioned at last, his tone lowered and marginally respectful. Even the likes of him recognized quality when he saw it, apparently. Joss held his breath without even being aware that he was doing so. She could still back down, and save herself some grief. He hoped she would. Being sold to the meanest, orneriest bastard in the world wouldn't eat at him the way being beholden to her would.

"Yes, I did. I said I'd pay one hundred dollars for him, and that's just what I meant." Her voice was stronger now, the tone and words clear. Her chin was lifted, her lovely eyes bright with defiance. Joss felt intense shame. He growled a wordless protest. The boot of the guard nearest him lifted threateningly, and he shut up. Still she didn't look at him, but he couldn't tear his eyes from her.

"I can't sell a slave like this buck here to a young lady," the auctioneer said, disapproval lacing every word. "What would you want with him, anyway?"

"As you pointed out, properly trained he'll be worth almost five times what I'm paying for him. And I'm not buying him for myself; I'm acting as a proxy for my father. Our overseer bought nearly a dozen slaves at the auction around the front earlier. He'll be taking possession of this one, too."

"Oh." The auctioneer rubbed his chin. "I suppose that makes a difference. If you'll bring your overseer over here . . ."

"He's busy just now with the other slaves we bought." Lilah's chin went a fraction higher, and her voice firmed. "My money is as good as anyone's, I should think. And I don't see anyone else offering you a hundred dollars for him."

The auctioneer frowned down at her for a moment, then looked out over the crowd. "The lady's got a point," he called out. "She says there ain't anyone else offered a hundred dollars. Any of you folks care to top her bid? Do I hear one-twenty? One-ten? No?

Then he's going once, going twice, sold to the young lady here for a hundred dollars!"

"I'll send someone around with the money in a little while," Joss heard her say as the guards unfastened the long chain securing him to the post and hauled him to his feet. A haze of pain made his mind go fuzzy as he was half led, half carried from the block. Newly purchased slaves awaited their masters' convenience in a well-guarded corral at the edge of the lawn. He supposed that was where he was being taken. His injuries would be left to heal on their own, unless his new master — mistress — was compassionate. Bitter laughter shook him, bringing with it another onslaught of pain. The very fact that she had bought him — *bought* him! — testified to her compassion. In his new life as her slave, he could count on being well-treated.

She was waiting at the rear of the block when they dragged him down. The guards stopped, staring at her with speculation and something less than respect in their eyes as she came up to them, to him, oblivious of the milling, murmuring crowd. She did not come too close, but close enough to make him furiously aware of how he must stink, how filthy and debased he was. He was unsteady on his feet, pain making him sweat and grit his teeth, but still he tried to shake off the arms of the guards. It was a mistake. One of them elbowed him sharply in his injured ribs, causing a knife of agony to slice through his insides. Joss groaned, closing his eyes as more cold sweat broke out on his forehead and upper lip.

"You there, don't do that again! I don't want him hurt any more, do you hear?" She came to his defense in a swirl of skirts. Taken by surprise, the guards released their grip and stepped back. To his horror he found that his legs could no longer support him. He crumpled, falling to his knees, then without the use of his hands to catch himself toppled sideways on the soft carpet of dusty grass. Around him the world tilted and twirled sickeningly. For the first time in his life he thought he might faint.

"You've hurt him!" she cried out, dropping to her knees beside him and touching his sweaty, filthy temple with cool fingers. Her touch made his stomach clench. She at least did not regard him as a beast — but he could not allow her to make such a spectacle of herself, knowing the evil that lurked in men's minds. Their obscene imaginations would enjoy this. . . . He gritted his teeth and forced his eyes to open. The world still swam, but by focusing on her face he was able to will himself to stay conscious.

"Get away from me," he growled so that no one else could hear, and was both glad and sorry when her eyes widened and she rocked back on her heels. Glaring up at her, he made an abortive attempt to sit up preparatory to getting back on his feet, but in his weakened condition he found that even sitting was beyond him. Pain swamped him whenever he moved. It was either stay conscious just as he was, or move and risk the indignity of fainting. He chose the former, closing his eyes again as another wave of agony washed over him. When he opened them at last, it was to find her still crouched beside him, the hem of her skirt nearly touching his arm and her face filling his vision. Frowning down at him, she looked sweetly worried, and so cool and lovely that his insides ached from more than his damaged ribs. Her proximity brought a black scowl to his face.

"Damn it, I thought I told you to get away from me!" The fury he felt turned his hissed words into a whiplash. Instead of jumping up and running away, as he half expected her to do, she reached out to touch his ribs as if to check for damage. The feel of her hand sliding so intimately over his side maddened him. He jerked sideways, out from under her touch, and paid for the gesture with another knife-thrust of pain.

"Everything will be all right now, you'll see," she said to him softly, ignoring all his efforts to repulse her. Then a stocky, craggy-faced man loomed up behind her, catching her by both elbows and hauling her bodily to her feet.

"Damn it, Lilah, just what the bloody hell do you think you're doing?" he roared. "Howard LeMasters told me you were over here making a bloody scandal of yourself, but I didn't believe him! Now I see that if anything he understated the case! Suppose you explain yourself, miss!"

The man still had his hands on her arms, looking as if he'd like to shake her. He had turned her around to face him so that Joss could not see her expression. But the man looked furious.

Joss stiffened, and with grim determination tried to force himself to his feet. It was useless. He managed to get to his knees, but could not have risen farther if his life — or hers — had depended on it. If this man became abusive in words or actions, he was in no shape to defend either her honor or her person.

"Oh, Kevin, I was just coming to look for you! I want you to pay the auctioneer a hundred dollars for me, if you please!" She was clearly untroubled by the man's violent reaction to her indiscreet behavior, or by the strength of his grip on her bare arms. At the sight of those beefy hands on her pale skin, a strong dislike for the other man sprang up full-blown in Joss. Then Kevin looked at him over the top of the yellow sunbonnet, and Joss realized that his feelings were well reciprocated.

"Have you lost your bloody senses? I can't believe you would actually bid on a slave — especially this one! He's old George's bastard son, isn't he? The one young Calvert's been telling everyone you were making sheep's eyes at before you found out he was a black buck?"

"Kevin! Lower your voice! He's not deaf, you know, and neither is anyone else!" Her back stiffened in outrage. She turned a little as she said it, glancing down at Joss self-consciously. He noted with the tiny portion of his mind that was not preoccupied with either their conversation or his pain that she had a grass stain on her skirt from where she had knelt beside him.

"Well? That's what he is, isn't he? And now you've actually been fool enough to buy him at public auction! The whole damn country will be talking about you after this!

I can't believe you'd do something so bloody dumb!"

The other man's eyes were a cloudy color somewhere between brown and hazel, Joss discovered as he met them with hatred in his own. He looked Joss over with all the arrogance of a man whose superior position in the world is not in doubt. Joss was naked to the waist, filthy, and covered with welts, bruises and cuts. He was unshaved and unkept and ashamed. But he refused to cringe before Kevin's scathing appraisal. He glared with fierce defiance as the other man's broad nose wrinkled with distaste. At that disdainful gesture, Joss felt killing rage flood his veins. He had not yet accustomed himself to being despised. But before he could say or do anything unwise, Kevin shifted his attention back to the girl.

"Oh, Kevin, don't be cross, please," she coaxed, smiling up at him in a way that made Joss grit his teeth. He'd thought that smile she'd turned on him three weeks ago was special for him. Now he realized that she was an accomplished little flirt who batted her lashes at everything in trousers.

"Don't be cross? You drag your good name through the dirt and tell me don't be cross? You had no business even bidding at a slave auction and well you know it much less for him! I suppose you think I haven't heard the talk? Hah! But I was willing to ignore it, under the circumstances. You couldn't have known what he was, and I know you better than to think that he laid a hand on you. But still you had no business —"

"They were hurting him," she interrupted quietly. "I couldn't bear it."

Kevin stared down at her, shaking his head. "You and your damned soft heart," he said after a moment's silence, and muttered something else under his breath. Joss didn't catch the rest of his words because the knife was twisting in his entrails again. Hot shamed blood rushed into his face. Christ, he hadn't blushed in fifteen years, not since he was a boy of fourteen confronted with his first pair of naked female breasts! But the pity in her voice was more than he could stomach.

"Aren't you going to introduce us, Lilah?" The insolence of his tone was deliberate. She looked at him over her shoulder, her eyes widening. Kevin's face tightened, reddened. He caught Lilah by the waist and moved her bodily out of his path, then walked up to Joss. Joss saw it coming, saw the other man's hand reach toward his waistband, pull out the pistol and lift it high. There was nothing he could do to avoid what was coming but flinch, and pride forbade that. So he took the blow full in the face, his head snapping back as he felt his left cheek split.

"Kevin, no!"

Joss thought she would have rushed to his side if Kevin had not caught her by the arm. But maybe the spreading numbness in his cheek coupled with the awful ache in his side was making him imagine things again.

"Go back to the carriage, Lilah, before you make an even greater scandal of yourself," Kevin said through his teeth. "The slaves are my concern, not yours, and you know it. Go on. I'll join you after I've done what I can to untangle this mess of yours."

"You're not to hit him again, Kevin, do you hear me? Look at him! He's been hurt enough." Anger showed in her voice and her eyes. "I want your word on it!" Someone tittered in the crowd that had slowly gathered to gawk at this new entertainment. Lilah's cheeks pinkened and there was a sudden conscious look on her face as she became aware that she was the cynosure of several dozen eyes.

Kevin, reddening too as he glanced swiftly around, shot her a furious look. "All right, I won't hit him," he said, his voice hard. "Now get out of here, would you? A soft heart is one thing, but you've carried it too far today!

They'll be making jests about you and this — boy — for a month of Sundays! I don't know how you feel about that, but I don't like the notion one bit!"

"I don't care, I've done nothing wrong! I . . ."

"She shore is hot for that dark meat, ain't she?" The man's jocular question was clearly audible over the murmurs of the crowd. Kevin swung around, glaring. Lilah put a cautioning hand on his arm. The man went on, unaware of his danger. "I'd like to give her a taste o' white!"

"Ah, you ain't white, you ole son of a gun. Yer darker than he is!" Another man elbowed the first in the ribs.

"That's jes' dirt! I'd wash it off for the likes o' her — or mebbe not. Mebbe she'd like me better dark!"

"She wouldn't like you any way, you old geezer! You come on away from here, before I snatch you baldheaded!" Before Kevin could explode, a stout woman in the faded clothes of a farmer's wife caught the speaker by the ear and towed him howling out of the crowd. The second man followed, cupping his hand around his mouth to twit the woman to the accompaniment of the crowd's snickers.

"He is bald-headed, Etta!"

This three-sided altercation declined only slightly in volume as the participants crossed the street, but Joss didn't hear any more of it. He was too conscious of the shame in Lilah's face, and the fury in Kevin's. He was furious too, hopelessly, helplessly furious at the entire world, including himself and this incredible, Dantesque situation in which he was trapped. The knowledge that his fury availed him of absolutely nothing made him even angrier.

"Get!" Kevin said to Lilah, his mouth tightening ominously. Lilah glared at him. Hot red color still stained her cheeks, but she lifted her chin with cool defiance.

"Don't you dare talk to me that way, Kevin Talbott! I've taken about enough from you this afternoon, and I'm not about to take any more! I'll go back to the carriage when I'm good and ready and not before! I won't be tyrannized over, and you just better remember that!"

Kevin glared back at her, but Lilah budged not an inch. She was slender and very lovely as she stood there with her face flushed and her arms crossed beneath her breasts, her very attitude daring Kevin to carry the argument further. Kevin apparently knew when he was beaten. He threw up his hands in defeat to more snickers from the crowd.

"You've got the disposition of a mule, and always have had, Delilah Remy! Have it your own way then!" Kevin turned his back on her and the crowd to look at Joss. The two guards, anticipating violence, took a step closer, their cudgels at the ready, unholy appreciation for the unexpected entertainment they were enjoying evident in their faces. At a gesture from Kevin they stepped back again.

"Hear this, boy," Kevin said, his voice low but deadly for all that. "My fiancée Miss Remy has agreed to buy you, and even though I have extremely serious misgivings about it, I will abide by her wishes. But whatever you were or thought you were in the past, you are now nothing more than a slave belonging to Miss Remy's father. I am Mr. Remy's overseer, and I am the boss at Heart's Ease and over all that belongs to it. If I ever hear you address so much as a word to Miss Remy again, much less speak to her familiarly as you just did, I will see to it that you are beaten to within an inch of your miserable life. And you'll discover that I'm not known for making idle threats."

Joss's fists clenched impotently behind him. His injured side was causing him agony, and the split in his cheek burned like fire. His eyes burned even hotter as he glared up at the man standing over him. But he said nothing, did nothing to give the other man an excuse for more violence. He was slowly, painfully, beginning to learn wisdom. He was injured and in pain, unable even to stand. As a slave, he was completely at the mercy of his owners, who could beat him or kill him on nothing more than a whim. For now, he had to play the cards as they were dealt, and not let his own damnable pride and the great blue eyes that were fixed on him so pityingly move him to do something stupid. For now. But every dog had its day. . . .

"Kevin!" Behind him, Lilah clutched at Kevin's arm to pull him back. Kevin tried to shake her off with little success.

"Keep out of this, Lilah. I mean it."

Joss could see Lilah's eyes flare, but she said nothing more. Kevin looked Joss over, contempt and dislike plain in his face.

"You understand me, boy? On Heart's Ease you'll be a slave like all the other slaves. You'll work where you're told, doing what you're told, for as long as you're told. You'll show respect for your betters and keep your insolent tongue between your teeth if you want to keep your hide whole. Do that, and you'll find that your life with us is not so bad. Give me any problems, and you'll wish you'd never been born."

Without waiting for any reply Joss might have made, Kevin nodded curtly at the guards. "Put him with the other slaves for Heart's Ease. Someone will be coming by in a day or so to take them to the harbor and load them on the *Swift Wind.* In the meantime they're to be watered and fed. There are to be no slip-ups. I don't want to lose any of them on the voyage because they haven't been adequately taken care of beforehand."

"Yes, sir."

"Kevin, he's hurt. They kicked him —"

"I'll have a doctor sent over to look at him, all right? Will that make you happy?"

"It will relieve my mind."

She gave him one of those dazzling smiles again. Joss glowered, his bitter anger increasing in direct proportion to the degree of disarming sweetness in her smile. Kevin glanced up from his rapt study of the lovely little face before him to find Joss glaring at the pair of them. He made a gesture to the guards. In response, they grabbed Joss by his arms and hauled him toward the corral. As he was half carried, half dragged away, Joss saw the arrogant bastard turn to Lilah, who had made a sound of protest at the roughness of the treatment accorded him, and, with a conciliatory smile, put his arm around her waist. His insides burned. He told himself it was from his injuries, but he didn't really believe it.

Nine

A week later, Lilah stood on the gently rocking deck of the *Swift Wind*, its white sails billowing against a blue sky overhead, the sound of popping rigging in her ears. Her arms were wrapped around herself in a futile attempt to ward off the stiff sea breeze. She was staring out over the rail toward the far horizon in a desperate attempt not to be aware of the slaves jumping up and down some twenty paces farther along the deck. Kevin was pacing amongst them, shouting, "Jump, you devils, jump!" and prodding malingerers in the leg with the cane he carried in one hand. The chains that were wrapped around the slaves' waists and wrists and bound them to one another clanked noisily as they obeyed. Bare feet thudded arrhythmically on the boards of the deck.

The ship skipped through curling whitecapped waves, the sun dipped toward the horizon in a beautiful display of crimson and pink and orange, and playful spumes of salt spray splattered the fine blue muslin of her skirt every few minutes. Lilah took in none of this. Her whole consciousness was focused on Joss's tall form leaning against the rail perhaps fifteen feet beyond her. His injured ribs had exempted him from the exercising Kevin required of the other slaves, and the chain that ordinarily would link him to the others was undone. She wasn't even looking at him, and yet she was conscious of every shift of his feet. She hated herself for being so aware of him, for even thinking about him now that she had done her Christian duty by rescuing him from the horrible fate he would almost certainly have faced after the auction block. After all, she now knew exactly who and what he was, so there was no excuse she could offer for her weakness in not eradicating him and what had happened between them from her thoughts. But no matter how she wrestled with herself, she was as sensitized to him as a poison ivy sufferer is to the plant. She could not help being aware of him whenever he was anywhere near her vicinity. She refused to give in to it, though; refused even to glance around at him as her instincts urged her to do — *now,* while Kevin had his back turned, his attention fully occupied with the rest of the slaves. No one would ever know, except herself. And maybe Joss. She had the feeling that he was as aware of her presence as she was of his.

Ever the conscientious overseer, Kevin was careful to bring the Heart's Ease slaves up on deck for fresh air and exercise almost daily, depending upon the weather. It was simply good business, he'd responded when, surprised and unnerved to set eyes on Joss surfacing with the other slaves the second day they were on board, Lilah had questioned him. The slaves represented a major investment; he wanted to get them back to Heart's Ease in reasonable health and able to do the work they were bought to do. All but one of the other owners of slaves were content to leave their property to get by as best they might with no fresh air or sunlight for the duration of the voyage, but Kevin was not.

He was right, Lilah knew, yet loss's presence in the rough slave garb that Kevin had issued to all those bound for Heart's Ease made her uneasy. Cleaned up now, his hair restored to glossy coal black waves tied by a bit of string at his nape and the unsightly growth of whiskers gone from his face, he was much as she remembered him from that magical night. The only difference in his appearance was his slave-issue clothes — a loosely woven white shirt and poor-quality black breeches — and the absence of that dashing mustache. Slaves did not sport mustaches. The bruises on his face were nearly healed, and she guessed that the rest of his injuries were mending as fast. If it had not been for the chain around his waist — used to link him to the other slaves when they were on deck — and linking his wrists, she would have had trouble remembering that he was a slave like the rest.

But she had to remember. To allow herself to forget for even a moment would be dangerous to the fragile peace of mind she had achieved since she had accepted Kevin's proposal. And if Kevin were to suspect that she felt the slightest interest in Joss above and beyond the dictates of Christian charity, her forgetfulness would be dangerous for Joss as well. Kevin could be ruthless when it came to protecting his possessions, and as his fiancée she was now considered exactly that. To say nothing of the fact that Kevin and her father and the rest of her acquaintances would be horrified, scandalized and sickened if they guessed that she could not get the gleaming green eyes of a slave out of her mind.

To guard against the possibility of any unwary look revealing her secret, Lilah usually made it a point not to be on deck when the slaves were brought up. But on this particular afternoon she had left the stuffy confines of the cabin she shared with Betsy hoping to regain her usual good spirits with a few swift turns around the deck and the breathing of some brisk sea air, and had lost all track of the time. Then, when Kevin had shepherded the slaves up not twenty feet from where she stood, she had not wanted to rush away for fear of drawing his attention to her discomfort in their — Joss's — presence. She had lived with and around slavery all her life. She took the daily presence of slaves around her as much for granted as she did air to breathe. Never before had she felt the least uneasy around any of them, even the rawest of the gullahs. But it was difficult to consider Joss a slave like those others.

Oh, how she longed to be at home again! It seemed like forever since she had set foot on Barbados's sun-soaked earth. Strangely, now that she was closer to home than she had been for nearly five months, she was homesick. In another three weeks or so, if the weather held, the *Swift Wind* would drop anchor in Bridgetown Bay. And she could put these last dreadful weeks from her mind for good. . . .

"I brought you a shawl, Miss Lilah. You look cold, wrapping yourself up in your arms that way." Betsy came to stand beside her, holding out the lovely Norwich silk shawl that had been a parting gift from Lilah's great-aunt. Grateful for this new distraction, Lilah turned around to smile at her maid. Then she looked down at the shawl Betsy held out to her and shook her head.

"Thank you, Betsy, but I don't want it. In fact, you may have it, if you like."

"This pretty thing? Why, you don't want to give it away! It's new!"

"I guess I can give you a gift if I want to, Betsy. Put it on, you hear?"

Betsy looked at her for a moment, her eyes seeing more than Lilah was comfortable revealing. Then she looked down at the shawl in her hand, and fingered the heavy white silk. "If you say so, Miss Lilah." Betsy wrapped the elegant shawl over the serviceable tan cotton dress she wore and looked down at the six-inch-long fringe as the wind fluttered it against her skirt. "Like my mam would say, gold teeth don' suit hog mouth."

That was a saying common in Barbados meaning that elegant things looked out of place on those who weren't used to them. Lilah shook her head at her maid. "Maida would not say that, and you know it. The shawl looks lovely on you. Ben better look out when you get back. You'll get him this time for sure." Lilah added that last with a teasing half smile.

"What makes you think I want him?" Betsy retorted, tossing her head and grinning. Lilah grinned back at her maid.

"You've been after Ben since you were fifteen years old. You can't fool me."

Betsy suddenly looked grave. "Well, you sure ain't been after Mr. Kevin, Miss Lilah! You can't fool me, either."

Lilah turned back to her contemplation of the sea.

"I don't want to hear any more talk like that," she said sternly.

"Pooh!" Betsy's pretty lips turned up in what was very close to a sneer. "You don't want to hear the truth, is all. You was always like that, even as a little girl. But us who loves you, will tell you: Mr. Kevin's not for you."

"I'm going to marry him," Lilah said determinedly, the lift of her chin signalling that the conversation was closed. Betsy ignored the hint, as Lilah should have known she would. After a lifetime's association, mistress and maid were mere titles. Betsy was family, and family could be as irritating as a burr under a saddle.

"You'll do what you want, just like you always do, but if I were you I'd wait. The right man will come along for you one day. He always do."

"Kevin is the right man for me."

"Mr. Kevin's the right man for your pa and Heart's Ease. He's not the right man for you. And you know it, Miss Lilah, deep down. You're just too stubborn to admit it."

"That's enough, Betsy. I don't want to talk about it anymore!" Lilah glared at her maid. Betsy went on inexorably.

"You don't even like him to kiss you! What you going to do when he gets into bed with you when you're married?"

Lilah's cheeks flushed. "You were spying!" she accused heatedly, knowing that Betsy referred to the scene that had taken place between herself and Kevin the night before.

He had walked her to her cabin after a late turn about the deck. When she opened the door to go in, he had surprised her by stepping inside with her, pushing the door almost closed behind them. Betsy had been asleep — she'd thought! — in the upper berth, but still the cabin was dark and it was late and they were much too private to be completely respectable. She'd looked up at Kevin inquiringly; it wasn't like him to be unconventional. Without a word he'd pulled her hard against his body and covered her mouth with his. The impression she'd formed of his kiss was that he was trying to eat her lips with his mouth. The greedy wetness of his tongue slobbering over her clamped mouth made her feel sick to her stomach. This kiss was nothing like the soft fire of . . . no, she must not remember that. Angry, she'd pushed Kevin away. He apologized immediately, and kissed her hand in gentle remorse before taking himself off, but the whole incident had left her uncomfortable. Was that the kind of thing she could expect from him when they were married? And then it would not be so easy just to push him away. . . .

"I was awake," Betsy corrected, very much on her dignity. "I saw him try to kiss you, and I saw you act like you was going to throw up. That's no way to feel about the man you're meaning to marry, Miss Lilah."

"What do you know about it?" Lilah retorted heatedly, angry because Betsy's words came too close to her own misgivings.

Betsy looked smug. "I know plenty. I kept company with John Henry for a year, and then there was Norman and — well, never you mind. What I'm tellin' you is that I never felt like that when any of them kissed me. And if Ben ever kissed me. . . . Miss Lilah, he'd have to pry me off him with a boat hook! That's how you should feel about the man you're going to marry."

"Ladies don't feel that way about things like that," Lilah said, though with another slight twinge of unease as she once again remembered the excitement of other lips on hers. . . . Resolutely she pushed the forbidden memory away. That single night of madness was not going to be permitted to color her whole life. It had been a night apart from reality, no more substantial than a dream. And she'd better keep that firmly in mind!

Betsy hooted inelegantly. "If you say so, Miss Lilah. But you know and I know you're only fooling yourself. Ladies and maids, we're all alike under the skin — we're women."

The slaves, finally done with their exercising for the day, slogged past, chains clanking as they headed toward the hatchway. Lilah averted her eyes to avoid looking at Joss, now chained securely at the end of the line. Betsy's eyes sharpened.

"You telling me you didn't feel like that with him?" Betsy asked softly, watching Lilah's face with keen knowledge. "You forget, Miss Lilah, I've known you since you was a little girl. And I saw how happy and excited you were, changing into something 'ravishing' for him. You ain't ever been like that before or since! All right, he wasn't the right man for you either, but if you could feel that way about him you could feel that way about another man one day. Don't just settle for Mr. Kevin 'cause you think he's safe! Settling's for old women and old hens, not for a pretty young lady like you!"

"I'm not settling! And I don't want to discuss it anymore!"

"All right, bury your head in the sand if you want to! Me, I've got work to do!"

With a sniff, Betsy took herself off, leaving Lilah to brood. Secretly she feared that there was more than a grain of truth to what Betsy said. Kevin's gentlest kiss did nothing more than rouse in her a desire to wipe her mouth. The one he had tried to give her the previous night had brought with it a tide of revulsion so strong that it had made her feel physically ill. She was not a child; she had a fair idea of what the physical side of marriage entailed. She had just never before taken the time to apply that knowledge to herself and Kevin. Could she let him kiss her like that for the rest of her life, or permit him the kind of intimacies married people shared, the exact details of which were a trifle vague in her mind but she knew involved sharing a bed and begetting children? Could she stand his hands on her naked flesh, not just once or twice but night after night after night for the Lord knew how many years? Lilah actually shivered at the thought. But then her mind ran over all the other men who had begged for her hand over the years, and she realized she couldn't bear the idea of their hands on her either. The only man she'd ever felt the slightest response to was . . .

She shut her eyes at the shameful image. The only man whose touch she thought she might have been able to bear was at that moment chained in the hold with the rest of the slaves Kevin had bought for Heart's Ease.

Her heart lightened fractionally as an idea occurred to her. Once she was safely home again at Heart's Ease, she might speak to her father about freeing Joss. If Kevin was right, he would probably be nothing but trouble, worse than the Africans brought straight from their mother country to work the fields. Leonard Remy refused to have gullahs on the place. Without generations of slavedom behind them to make them docile, gullahs were too unpredictable, he said. They frequently tried to escape, and were capable of stirring up unrest amongst the other slaves with their hankering for freedom.

Her father wouldn't be hard to convince, she thought, as long as he did not get hold of the idea that she wanted the man freed because she was attracted to him. Which was, of course, an entirely ridiculous idea. She wanted him freed because he was a human being like herself. That that might also apply to Betsy and twenty other slaves at Heart's Ease she refused to consider. This man had no business being enslaved, and should be set free. Once he had his freedom, he would depart from Heart's Ease and Barbados and she need never see him again.

The sun had almost disappeared beneath the horizon, and it was getting increasingly colder by the rail. Lilah shivered. Her dress was long-sleeved, but the thin muslin was no protection against the brisk sea wind. Perhaps she should not have been so swift to turn away Amanda's shawl — but she couldn't wear it. Not after what her great-aunt had done to Joss. . . . There he was again, in her thoughts. Did everything have to remind her of him?

Ten

"There you are. I was beginning to worry about you. I thought you would be in your cabin by now, but Betsy said she hadn't seen you since she left you up on deck. I certainly didn't expect to find you still up here in the dark."

Kevin stepped out onto the deck just as Lilah was about to go below. The wind immediately caught his hair and blew it around his face, making him look like a hearty seaman with his broad, weathered face. Despite his stocky build and lack of fashionable accoutrements, he was an attractive man. She smiled warmly at him in the soft glow of the lanternlight that spilled over them both from the passageway behind him. She was fond of Kevin, and she saw absolutely no reason why, after marriage, she should not grow to love him. She knew him well; he would hold no surprises for her, and that was a good thing. Starry-eyed dreams of romance were not going to get in the way of what she knew was the right decision. If Kevin's kisses did not appeal to her — well, it was very likely that she would grow accustomed to them. After all, physical intimacy with a man was very new to her. She could count on the fingers of one hand the number of times a man had kissed her mouth, and Kevin accounted for most of them.

"I was watching the sunset," she said, accepting the arm he offered and allowing him to help her down the stairs. The passenger cabins were just below the main deck. Roughly a dozen of them provided lodging for perhaps twenty-seven or twenty-eight travelers bound for Barbados. Some of them Lilah knew. Irene Guiltinan ran a dress shop in Bridgetown, and John Haverly owned a smallholding near Ragged Point, which was fairly close to Heart's Ease. Like herself, they were returning from visits to the Colonies. Others, whom she didn't know, were bound for Barbados for various reasons that she didn't trouble herself about. After the voyage, she would probably never see them again. The big planters such as her father lived in a kind of splendid isolation, open only to others like themselves and those who served them.

"I'm glad you're not still angry with me." They had almost reached the door to her cabin. Lilah stopped walking and turned to look at Kevin as he spoke. Light from a wall-mounted lantern illuminated each end of the walnut-paneled passage, but the center, where they stood, was in deep shadow. The narrow passageway was deserted, and except for the creaking of the ship, silent. This was the closest they were likely to come to any privacy aboard ship.

"I want to apologize again for my behavior last night. I'm afraid that your beauty quite went to my head. I know I frightened you, and I promise it won't happen again. Well, at least not until you're ready." He added this last with a quick, almost disarming smile.

"You don't have to apologize, Kevin." Lilah took a step closer to him and put her hand on his arm. It was firm and muscular through the fine wool of his coat, and she fought against making the inevitable comparison. This was the man who would be her husband, and this was the man who must fill her thoughts. She was determined it be so. "I was as much at fault as you. I should not have reacted as I did. Being kissed is rather new to me, you see."

He grinned, his hazel eyes twinkling down at her. "Well, I should hope so," he said, and lifted her hand to his lips. "We'll go slow," he promised, and kissed her fingers with a pretty display of gallantry that was totally at odds with his bluff appearance. Lilah, though she tried her best, felt not the smallest tingle. The contact was certainly more pleasant than when Mr. Calvert had slavered over her hand; on the other hand, it did not nearly compare with . . .

"May I kiss you, Lilah? Properly? I won't if you'd rather I didn't."

He sounded so much in earnest, so intent on winning his way back into her good graces, that she had not the heart to deny him.

"It's all right. Go ahead," she said, closing her eyes and lifting her face. Her lips remained primly closed, a silent reminder that he was not to take the privilege too far. She waited.

Kevin bent his head to press his lips to hers. The kiss was soft and not unpleasant. Lilah did not pull away, or repulse him in any way. Eyes tightly shut, she concentrated, willing the feeling to come — but it would not. His kiss meant no more than a kiss she might have received from any relative of whom she was moderately fond. It was just as she had told Betsy — ladies did not have feelings like that. And if she had, once, she must not remember it.

"That wasn't so bad, was it?" Kevin asked

when he lifted his head. A slight smile curved his lips. Lilah could see that he was feeling mighty pleased with himself. He had enjoyed the kiss, and the knowledge cheered her a little. At least he seemed to find nothing lacking in her response. That he could be content with so little augured well for the success of their marriage.

"It was very nice," she told him, patting his arm as one would to humor a nice child. Looking down at her, his smile broadened and his hands, which had been resting lightly on her waist, slid clear around her. To Lilah's dismay he bent his head to repeat the exercise, more lingeringly this time. She closed her eyes and gritted her teeth and endured. At least he wasn't devouring her with his mouth as he had tried to do the night before. . . .

"Oh, Lord Jesus, somebody help me! Millard's took bad!" A woman erupted from her cabin three doors down the passage, her pale face lined with fright and her gray hair untidy. Lilah remembered that her name was Mrs. Gorman, and she was traveling with her husband and grown daughter. At the interruption, Kevin lifted his mouth from hers, his arms dropping from around her waist as he took a quick step backwards. Lilah, secretly relieved to be freed so opportunely, turned toward the woman who was hurrying toward them.

"What's wrong, Mrs. Gorman? Is your husband ill?" Lilah caught the other woman's arm when she would have rushed past them. Only then did Mrs. Gorman seem to become aware of their presence in the passageway. Her eyes, before they focused on Lilah, were wild.

"Aye, he is, and it's Dr. Freeman I'm needin'! Let me go, please, I've got to fetch him!"

"Kevin — Mr. Talbott — will find him for you, if you like. If you want to return to your husband in the meantime, I'll be glad to accompany you."

"You're a sweet gel. I've said it to Millard more than once during this trip."

Taking that distracted compliment for assent to Lilah's plan, Kevin nodded and stepped briskly away. Mrs. Gorman turned back down the passageway, so agitated that she hardly knew what she was doing. Lilah followed, though she was not sure that Mrs. Gorman was even aware that she was behind her.

From the woman's terror, Lilah expected her husband to be in extremus, but she did not expect the terrible stench of uncontrolled diarrhea, or the pools of vomit that had long since overflowed every available container and lay in puddles near the bunk where the skeletal Mr. Gorman lay. Obviously he had been sick for some hours before Mrs. Gorman had summoned help. His daughter — a too-thin spinster whose first name Lilah thought was Doris — was sitting on the edge of his bunk wiping his mouth. Lilah's stomach turned over, but both women looked at her so hopefully that she could not follow her first instinct to flee. Trying to control her revulsion, Lilah stepped carefully toward the bunk, holding her skirt well clear of the floor.

"Oh, Mum, did you get the doctor? Da needs him sore bad."

Miss Gorman's wailing question was punctuated by loud gasps from the man in the bunk. As his daughter leaned over him and Mrs. Gorman ran to his side, Mr. Gorman sat bolt upright in bed, gasping for air. Then he fell back against his pillows like a collapsed balloon.

"Is he dead?"

"No, Mum, look, he's breathing. Oh, we need the doctor!"

"He's coming," Lilah murmured reassuringly, her horrified eyes moving over Mr. Gorman. If he was not yet dead, he was surely near death. He lay unmoving, his face drained of all color, his emaciated body drenched in sweat. Only by looking closely could Lilah detect the faint movement of his chest that proclaimed he still lived.

"What can we do?" Mrs. Gorman asked hopelessly. Lilah was just wondering how she was going to answer that pitiful question when Kevin arrived with Dr. Freeman.

"What's this now?" Dr. Freeman asked as he entered, his black bag in one hand, only to be brought up short by the scene before him. Short, heavyset and plainly dressed, he had a skimpy gray beard and a bald head. Spectacles were perched on the edge of his nose. Lilah stepped back, thankful to leave the whole horrible situation in Dr. Freeman's capable hands. She was very much afraid that Mr. Gorman was going to die. . . .

Dr. Freeman shooed her from the room, and Kevin with her. Kevin was frowning as they walked back down the passageway toward Lilah's cabin.

"What do you think is wrong with him?" she asked, having no idea herself. She had never done much nursing, in fact did not like to be around sick people. Jane did the nursing on Heart's Ease, and she was glad to have it so.

"I don't know," Kevin answered, his voice

deep with worry. Lilah looked up at him sharply. Before she could question him further she heard the sound of a door opening behind them. Looking back, she saw Dr. Freeman step out into the passage, shaking his head. Behind him, framed in the doorway, stood Mrs. Gorman, pale and shaking. He said something to her, shook his head in reply to a question Lilah could not hear, and turned away, coming toward them. Just one look at his face told Lilah that something was very wrong indeed.

"What is it, Doctor?" Kevin asked, his voice tight as though he was almost afraid of the answer.

Dr. Freeman came up to them, and studied Kevin over the top of his spectacles. He looked very tired, far more tired than ten minutes in a sickroom warranted.

"Cholera," the doctor answered briefly, pushing by them. Lilah had no trouble at all recognizing the emotion in his voice. It was stark fear.

Eleven

Three days later, the ship was a floating death trap. The cholera had spread amongst the passengers and crew erratically. Nearly a third of the seventy-odd souls aboard were ill. Four, including Mr. Gorman, were already dead. The able-bodied were divided into two camps: Those who feared the disease but whose conscience or feelings for the stricken drove them to nurse the ill anyway, and those who had forced a quarantine on the sick, and refused to go anywhere near the half of the ship that was given over to them. As the illness advanced each day, striking down its victims seemingly at random no matter what they did to avoid contagion, the quarantine seemed a waste of time. But it was strictly upheld for as long as possible.

Despite her early exposure to Mr. Gorman, Lilah had not so far been stricken. With Betsy at her side she worked tirelessly, soon growing immune to the hideous sights and smells, to the pained whimperings of the ill and the dying and their survivors. The stench of the horrible rice-water diarrhea that was the hallmark of the disease seemed to stretch from one end of the ship to the other. By the seventh day she hardly noticed it anymore.

At least she was able to get up on deck. The slaves, as afflicted by illness as the rest, were confined to the hold. The well among them were recruited to nurse the sick, but conditions in the hold were hideous. Finally, as the disease took its toll, the able-bodied slaves were released from their confinement to do what they could about the ship, which in most cases was not a lot. Most of the slaves had never even been aboard a ship before. Their labors had to be strictly supervised, and with half the crew stricken by the disease and the other half terrified, competent supervision was hard to come by.

Joss was the exception to the general uselessness of the slaves as replacements for the stricken sailors. Having been a sailing man all his adult life and later the captain of his own ships, he was able to take the place of at least three of the crewmen. Lilah saw him everywhere, up in the rigging setting canvas, in the crow's nest wielding a spyglass, on the quarter-deck reading the sextant as he assisted Captain Boone to chart their position and plot the course for the nearest landfall, which was their only hope of salvation. He was unfettered, released from his chains because of Captain Boone's personal request to Kevin, and seemed tireless. He never spoke to Lilah, though they brushed past one another occasionally as each went about their duties. In fact, he did not even seem aware of her, and Lilah was content to have it so. Whatever spark had once flared between them had been extinguished by circumstance, and in truth she was so tired and so frightened that keeping her mind off him was not as difficult as it might have been under better conditions. Though they were less than three weeks out of Barbados, Dr. Patterson had urged Captain Boone to change course for the nearest port. Haiti was to the south, and it was toward Haiti that the *Swift Wind* headed. But then the wind died to a whisper and the ship slowed to a scant two knots. . . . It began to look as though few of them would reach port. Men, women and children were dropping like flies, and dying within days.

Kevin came down with the sickness on the ninth day. Lilah nursed him with a tireless devotion that owed far more to their long acquaintance than to the love she should have borne her fiancé. By the twelfth day she was worn to a shade, thin and so exhausted that she could sleep leaning up against a wall. More than two-thirds of those who were stricken were gone within three days. Kevin passed that milestone, and the vomiting and diarrhea lessened. As the fourteenth day dawned and Kevin was still with them, weak but mending, Lilah and Betsy looked at one another in weary triumph over his sleeping form, too tired to even smile. Then they went on to nurse another victim.

The bodies of the dead were buried at sea. Each evening at sunset the bedraggled contingent of survivors not needed to nurse the sick gathered at the rail in the lee of the main mast. A prayer was said, and the names of the dead were called out as they were heaved over the side. It was a sketchy funeral, and Lilah was not the only one who felt it, but those who still lived were simply too weary to cope with much more.

The good weather held until the evening of the fifteenth day. Then, toward sunset, ominous dark clouds blew in to obscure the horizon. Lilah was too tired to notice, but Betsy, though as worn as her mistress, called her attention to the lowering sky as they struggled across the deck, each weighted down with a pair of buckets brimming with slop to be emptied over the side.

"We're in for some weather," Betsy

grunted as she set her buckets down and arched her spine, glancing at the threatening clouds. The deck moved up and down as the ship plowed through the waves, and a little of the gruesome mess in the bucket splashed out onto the once pristine boards. Once swabbed religiously twice a day, the deck was grimed now with salt and the dirt from many feet, and marked here and there with dried pools of vomit. No one had the energy to think about such unimportant details as the condition of the deck.

"I hope not," Lilah sighed, not even stopping to look. The buckets were heavy, yet they had to be emptied if the ship was not to be overrun with the foul-smelling products of the disease. She who had never even put on her own stockings before was simply doing what had to be done.

"We are — somethin' heavy. I can feel it comin'." Betsy's father was an Obeah man, and her voice was dark with prophesy. Lilah was just too tired to worry about it. After the horrors they had endured, what was a little rain?

A short while later Lilah stood beside Betsy on the deck, head bowed as the captain muttered hasty words over the four corpses that were to be committed to the deep that day. Besides herself, Betsy, and the captain, there was Mrs. Gorman, who had mysteriously escaped the pestilence along with her daughter; Mrs. Holloway, a widow who had lost both her sons to the cholera; Mrs. Freeman, the doctor's wife; and Mrs. Singletary, an elderly lady who looked as if a brisk wind would blow her away but who had as yet escaped the disease. Dr. Freeman was below with Joanna Patterson, who had lost her husband to the disease and now battled mightily to save her young son. Both Irene Guiltinan and John Haverly had already been lost. Two slaves whose job it was to tip the dead into the sea stood a little apart, behind the corpses, which had been sewn into sheets and now lay on planks in a neat row. Joss was present as well, standing with hands clasped in front of him and head bowed as he listened to the prayers. Lilah scarcely noticed him.

"Ashes to ashes, dust to dust, amen," the captain intoned wearily, signalling the end of the prayer. The two slaves, well accustomed to the ritual by now, reached down in tandem to grasp each end of a plank, lifted it to rest on the rail, and tipped the body into the sea. This was repeated four times, as Captain Boone called each victim's name. At the splash that heralded the sea's acceptance of the last corpse, a woman wailed loudly. It was Mrs. Holloway, and Lilah realized that the body must be that of her younger son. A vague pity for the woman's suffering coursed through her, but Lilah remained dry-eyed. She had seen so much death over the past two weeks that she was beyond grief.

With the corpses consigned to the sea, the funeral party went back about its business. Lilah, hurrying to relieve Mrs. Patterson in her tireless nursing of her son, passed by Joss, who seemed to be waiting by the rail. To her surprise, he stopped her with a hand on her arm.

She looked up at him questioningly, so weary that her eyes barely focused.

"Stay below tonight. We're in for a storm."

"A storm?" Conversation was almost beyond her, but from somewhere deep inside her an almost hysterical little giggle bubbled forth. "After all this, what's a storm?"

He looked intently down at her. "You're worn out, aren't you? Well, at least you're alive. And you might stay that way, if you listen to what I'm telling you and stay below deck for as long as it takes the storm to blow itself out, even if it's two or three days. Topside's not safe during a blow like we look to be having."

It occurred to her that he had gone out of his way to warn her, but she had no energy to wonder at it or ponder his reasons. Looking up at him, she saw that, like herself, he was thinner, with lines of fatigue in his face that had not been there before. The place on his cheek where Kevin had hit him with his pistol had healed to a faint red scar. He held himself stiffly, and it struck her that his ribs must still be sore. She realized that he must have been in pain throughout the entire time he was doing the work of three men. Whatever else he was, he was a brave man, and deserving of the gratitude of everyone on board. She smiled at him, the effort feeble because she was so tired.

"Thank you for the warning," she said. He nodded brusquely, and turned on his heel. Lilah looked after him for a long moment before Dr. Freeman, emerging from the causeway, recalled her wandering wits by shaking her arm.

"Mrs. Patterson needs help badly, Miss Remy," he reminded her. Lilah was almost glad to be recalled to the present. She hurried below to do what she could for the desperate mother and her sick child, and gladly banished Joss from her mind once more.

Twelve

Despite what both Joss and Betsy had said, the storm did not break that night. The *Swift Wind* continued on its southerly course, with a skeleton crew at the helm. Around midnight, Dr. Freeman summoned Lilah from a snatched few hours of sleep.

He had more bad news. Three more were down with the cholera, including his wife. He needed Lilah's help. She got to her feet, shaking her head to clear it and feeling her hair tumble lose from its knot to fall over her face. She twisted it back wearily as she first bent over Kevin to check his breathing — he continued deep asleep — then stumbled after the doctor. At least she didn't have to dress. For the last few days she'd been falling asleep in her clothes.

Mrs. Freeman was taken bad. After more than two weeks spent nursing the cholera, Lilah had developed a sixth sense about who would live and who would not. Mrs. Freeman, she very much feared, would not. The doctor knew it too. She could read it in his face as he straightened from his delirious wife's bedside. He was haggard, but still he spent no more time with his wife than with other patients.

"Try to keep her comfortable, and get what liquid into her you can," he told Lilah. As he turned away she saw moisture glimmer in his eyes. For the first time in many days, emotion stirred in her breast. She'd thought she'd become too numb to feel.

"I'll do my best for her, doctor. And if there's any change I'll call you."

He looked down at her, patted her hand where it rested on his sleeve. "Thank you, Miss Remy. I know you will. That's why I wanted you to stay with her instead of one of the other ladies. She was telling me just this morning how much she liked you, and what a goodhearted girl you are." His eyes moistened again. "We've been married thirty-seven years," he added bleakly. Then, before Lilah could do more than look up at him compassionately, he shook his head, cleared his throat, and was gone.

True to her word, Lilah sat with Mrs. Freeman all through the night. The woman never knew she was there. She was burning up with fever, and vomited almost ceaselessly although there was nothing left inside her but yellow bile. The diarrhea scourged her body as well, until the normally plump, motherly doctor's wife was reduced to a waxen, barely breathing shell. Near morning, Lilah knew that the woman had not much time left. She stuck her head out into the passageway and called for help. Mrs. Holloway answered, and Lilah sent her for Dr. Freeman.

When the doctor came, he saw at a glance that his wife was near the end. He knelt by the bed, taking her wasted hand in his and pressing it to his lips. Tears rolled down his lined cheeks. Holding back a sob, Lilah left the two of them alone together and melted into the passageway without a sound. Unconsciously, her feet carried her up the stairs that led to the deck. The hot, sultry wind hit her full in the face, causing her to stagger back almost into the companionway. A hand caught her arm to steady her.

Even through the tears that nearly blinded her she knew who it was. He seemed like a dear friend suddenly, and in her grief she was glad to see him. When his hand lifted from her arm, she missed its warm strength. But she could not give in to the panic and weariness and grief that threatened to overwhelm her. She was needed. She had to be strong a while longer.

"You're crying," he said.

"Mrs. Freeman is dying. They've been married thirty-seven years," she said with just the tiniest quaver, lifting both hands as she spoke to dash the tears from her eyes. She looked up at him to find him regarding her inscrutably. Those emerald eyes gleamed as they caught the light of the blood-red sun that was just peeping over the horizon. The deck was deserted, the few sailors who were not resting below going about their business high in the rigging. She had this sudden feeling of being alone with him and the sky and the sea.

"They were lucky to have thirty-seven years. Most people don't have that."

It was what she needed to hear, sensible, calm and comforting. Lilah nodded, taking a step out onto the deck and swallowing a huge gulp of the sultry air. The wind was drying the tears on her cheeks, and she was beginning to feel that she could go on after all. His hand caught her arm again as the pitching of the deck threatened her balance.

"You shouldn't be on deck. The sea's getting rough."

Only then did she notice that the pitching of the ship seemed more marked than it had before, and that the *Swift Wind* barely seemed to be touching the surface of the water as she skudded over the rising waves.

"I had to have some fresh air. There's so much — so much death below, I couldn't stand it."

He said nothing, just stood there holding her arm and looking down at her. In the orange light of the new dawn, he looked as indescribably weary as she felt. Lilah had a strong urge to lean against him, to rest her tired body against his strength. The urge was so strong that it shocked her back to an awareness of who and what he was, and who and what she was. Stiffening her spine, she took a step away from him. His face tightened.

"I beg your pardon. I shouldn't have touched you, should I? Slaves don't touch their mistresses. They let them fall flat on their faces." There was no mistaking the bitterness that edged his voice.

"It's not that. . . ." she started to protest, but he deserved better than to be lied to. "Yes, it is. You're quite right, you shouldn't have touched me. You mustn't anymore."

"If I do I suppose I can expect the boss man to send his flunkies after me with a bullwhip?"

"Kevin's very ill."

"Is he indeed? Pardon me if I don't say I'm sorry. Tell me something, was he your fiancé when you were letting me kiss you in the gazebo that night?"

Lilah suddenly knew how a deer grazing in a peaceful meadow felt when it discovered a hunter in a blind gunning for it. She had worked so hard to blot that night out of her mind, and she'd hoped that he had put the memory behind him, too. Now he was reminding her of it quite deliberately. She looked up into his eyes, up at the mouth that had kissed her, twisted now in a bitter, mocking smile, and shivered. Even knowing what she did about him, she discovered to her horror that she was not immune to the tantalizing attraction he had held for her from the first.

"No," she managed to get out on a croak.

"Ah, then I owe you an apology for what I have been thinking since learning of your engagement. Apparently you're not such a lightskirt as I'd supposed."

"You mustn't talk to me like that." Lilah could hardly get the words out past the constriction in her throat. She took another step away from him, fighting to get herself under control, her eyes fastened on the handsome face that darkened with anger at her words. "For your own sake, you mustn't, and for mine too."

"Afraid I'll tell about your taste for dark meat?" The barely suppressed anger in his voice lashed at her like a whip. It was all she could do not to cringe. Clearly he had overheard the oaf in the crowd the day she'd bought him, and the man's words rankled with him yet.

"Don't say that!"

"Why not? It's true, isn't it? I can see it in your eyes even now. You'd like nothing better than to have me kiss you again — or do even more. But your conventional little soul is horrified by the very idea. And why? You weren't horrified the night we met. So it stands to reason that what horrifies you now is not the thought of my kisses — we both know you liked that — but of my blood."

"You go too far!" Outraged and embarrassed, she picked up her skirts, meaning to turn and flee along the deck. But he stopped her with a hand on her arm.

"On the contrary, I don't think I've gone far enough," he said through his teeth. Then, before she realized his intent, he jerked her against him and lowered his head to hers. Gasping, she pushed against his chest with both hands as his mouth found hers. But the touch of those soft warm lips jolted her into immobility, stilling her struggles and her mind. Still she fought one last battle against the humiliation of abject surrender, turning her head away from his seeking lips. But when he caught her chin in his hand and turned her mouth back up to his she could fight no more. Her eyes fluttered shut and her body relaxed against his as it longed to do. He gathered her closer, bending her backwards against his arm, his mouth slanting over hers in a ferocious, starving way that did strange things to her heart.

Then, abruptly, he let her go. She stumbled backwards, shocked almost senseless by the violence of what had flared so briefly between them, barely able to keep her balance without the support of his hard arms. Her eyes were huge as they flew to his face. One slim pale hand came up to cover her mouth.

He stared back at her for an instant, his chest heaving as though he had been engaged in some vigorous activity. Then, as he took in the horror slowly dawning on her face, his mouth twisted.

"I think I've made my point," he said. The bitter words scourged her almost as much as the searing kiss. Before she thought, acting solely on instinct, she lifted her hand and slapped him hard across the face.

"Ah," he said, his hand going to his cheek, his eyes fixed on her pale face. For a long moment they stared at one another without speaking. Then the first fat drops of rain splattered on the deck between them. Lilah looked at them without seeing them, her heart pounding as she waited for his revenge. But Joss saw, and realized what they portended. The anger died from his face.

"Boone's carrying too much sail." He made the statement as if their quarrel had never been. His fingers absently smoothing the cheek that she had slapped was the only visible sign he gave of what had happened between them.

"What?" She should run away, she knew, while she had the chance, but he stood between her and the open doorway and she did not want to go along the deck in the rain.

He looked at her impatiently. "He's in a hurry to reach Haiti, and he's carrying too much canvas. If this storm's a bad one, and I think it's going to be, we'll be blown straight to hell."

Lilah bit her lip. The seriousness with which he appeared to regard their situation made her suddenly nervous. "Why don't you tell him?"

He looked angry again, but not at her this time. "Boone won't take my word for it. However experienced a seaman I may be, I'm just a slave, remember? He's bound and determined to captain the *Swift Wind* as he sees fit — and I don't blame him for that.

That's what I'd do myself, but he's making a mistake."

Lilah laughed almost hysterically. "Are you saying that the ship might sink?"

He looked at her without answering. He didn't have to. His face spoke for him. Lilah stood unmoving as the rain darkened the disordered tangle of her silvery hair, bathed her face and splashed over her stained gown. After all that had come before, could God in his mercy truly be going to put them through the additional trial of a deadly storm? Surely not. Surely the *Swift Wind* had been through enough.

"For God's sake, get out of the rain," Joss said impatiently. When she still didn't move but just stared at him he reached out and caught her by her arms, pulling her into the protection of the companionway. The touch of his warm lean hands burned through her thin sleeves like a brand. Vividly it reminded her of the searing heat of his mouth. . . . Her eyes, huge and defenseless, flew to the still-red imprint of her hand on his cheek. Then she looked up to meet those emerald eyes. They were turbulent, glittering, alive as few things were on the *Swift Wind* these days. He stared down at her for a moment, his hands tightening. Then his mouth tightened too, and he released her arms. Beyond the shelter of the companionway the rain came down in silver sheets.

"Stay below," he ordered grimly, then turned on his heel and vanished into the downpour.

Thirteen

The storm was upon them with the fury of a sea monster. Lilah could barely keep on her feet, much less nurse the sick, as the *Swift Wind*, blown hither and yon by the fierce wind, tilted from end to end like a child's teeter board. As day turned to night the wind blew in howling bursts while rain lashed down relentlessly from a sky as black as the sea below. Timbers creaked in ominous warning as the ship fought her way through the turbulence of towering waves. Lightning snaked across the sky, followed by deafening crashes of thunder. Lilah, terrified, wanted to do nothing more than curl up in her bunk with a blanket over her head and pray for deliverance. But the sick continued to need nursing, and the very sick continued to die. She could not give in to the fear that was like a living creature inside her. She had to stay on her feet, had to do what she could to alleviate the horrible suffering that continued unabated regardless of the storm.

Betsy, who had been detailed by Dr. Freeman to nurse the sick slaves in the hold, brought word that water was seeping in below. She was as frightened as Lilah, but there was nothing they could do to help themselves. They, like all those aboard, were at the mercy of God and the sea.

Shivering with fright and cold — because of the danger of fire, all lamps and stoves had been ordered extinguished — Lilah groped her way along the dark, violently pitching passageways as she tended the sick along with the half dozen or so other women left alive and well. With the exception of Dr. Freeman, the few men still on their feet were needed topside to battle the storm.

Mrs. Mingers died that night, as did two slaves. The storm was so fierce the next morning that the bodies had to be consigned to the sea hastily, in the teeth of the howling wind, by two sailors lashed to the deck with ropes. The only prayers were muttered by those who stayed below, listening in vain for the splash that would tell them that more of their number had gone to their final reward at the bottom of the sea. The splash was never heard. It was drowned out by the raging of the wind and the sea.

With the stoves unlit, there was no hot water for nursing the sick, no hot food to sustain the well. The interior of the *Swift*

Wind was cold and dark, damp and terrifying. The ill had to be tied into their bunks to keep them from being thrown to the floor by the pitching of the ship. The few who were recovering — Kevin among them — were fed thin gruel crudely mixed from oats and cold water. The voracious appetite that was a hallmark of those who had had the cholera and survived was not satisfied by this meager diet, and the convalescents were constantly calling for more food. Lilah had nothing else to give them. She was hungry herself, but it was nothing compared with her weariness and fear.

Night came again with a clap of thunder. The wind outside increased in fury until it sounded like thousands of banshees screeching from the bowels of hell. Waves higher than the hills around Heart's Ease crashed over them repeatedly. The *Swift Wind* shuddered at each onslaught and plunged on.

Every couple of hours or so two or three of the men would stagger below for food and rest. Lilah and the other women ministered to their needs according to who was about at the time, wrapping them in blankets as they reeled down the stairs sopping wet, offering them dry clothes and what food was available. Joss came in out of the storm on the same rotating basis as the others. Lilah was present in the common room only twice while he was there, and both times he was already being taken care of. Once it was Betsy who hovered over him, wrapping a blanket around his shoulders as he gulped the thin gruel. The sight of her maid making solicitous noises over the man she, Lilah, had forbidden herself to even think of took her aback. After one look she went on about her business, but the unwelcome picture stayed in her mind for some time to come.

Day was nothing more than a thinning of black to gray. Waves sloshed unceasingly under the closed hatch leading to the deck. Water spilled down the stairs and ran along the passageway to seep under the cabin doors. On Dr. Freeman's orders, the sick were all moved to the common room, which was both the largest and the driest accommodation the ship had to offer. The hard plank floor was soon covered with makeshift pallets laid end to end. Despite the crowding, and the stench, it was much easier to have everyone in one room. Lilah was faintly cheered by the presence of so many others as she saw to the stricken in cold, damp darkness. To comfort themselves, those who were able recited prayers aloud together. Lilah held basins and mopped brows to the muted chant of "Our Father, who art in heaven . . ." and other familiar prayers.

Three days into the storm there was a tremendous cracking sound above them, followed by a huge boom. The ceiling vibrated over their heads as something enormously heavy crashed down upon the deck. The ship shook like a wet dog. Lilah froze in terror, sure the end had come. Screams pierced the gloom as the others faced the same fear. Crying out, Lilah crouched on the floor and threw up her arms to protect her head from the unlit chandelier swinging dizzily above. It seemed sure to fall. . . . Kevin, whom she had been feeding more of the weak gruel, wrapped his arms around her and pulled her beneath him, shielding her with his body as they all awaited the end with baited breath. But the *Swift Wind* fooled them, and went on.

"The mast must have gone," Dr. Freeman announced shakily when at last they all dared to breathe again. Lilah sat up, smoothing her skirt and wiping the tears from her face. The ship had survived again, but she didn't know whether to be glad or sorry. If they were destined to die, surely it would be best to get it over with and end this torturous terror.

"Lilah . . ." Kevin began as she tried to wipe from his blanket some of the gruel she had spilled in her fright. All about the room, the women were wearily going about the tasks they had abandoned. Until they were faced again with approaching death, they saw no alternative but to live and aid the living. "My dear, I want you to know . . ."

He got no further. Just then a wild-eyed, drenched sailor burst through the door.

"Ballast broke lose when the mast hit and knocked a bloody great hole in the prow!" he cried. "Captain's ordered everyone on deck now! We're abandoning ship! Hurry, for your lives, hurry! She'll sink in a bloody whisker!"

"You'll have to help us, man!" Dr. Freeman cried as the sailor turned to leave. "We've the sick to carry, have you forgotten? We need every man Captain Boone can spare us!"

"Captain needs every man he's got on deck to keep the bloody ship afloat until we can get the lifeboats out! Oh, aye, aye, all right then, I'll get you what help I can!"

He vanished, to return moments later with three other men. "Let's go, lets go! She's listing bad to port and could go over at any minute!"

Now that the worst had happened everyone was strangely calm. A lantern was allowed to be lit to assist the evacuation, and it swung from Dr. Freeman's hand as he pointed out those most in need of help. Those too ill to walk were hurriedly laid together on two stretchers made of blankets and hoisted between the shoulders of the sailors. Dr. Freeman lifted little Billy Patterson in his arms while Mrs. Patterson held on to the tail of the doctor's coat with grim-eyed determination not to be separated from her son. Those of the sick who could walk leaned on each other. Betsy had her arm around an elderly lady whose name Lilah couldn't remember, while both Mrs. Gorman and her daughter supported two convalescents each, a man and a woman. Lilah turned to assist Kevin with the frantic exhortations of the sailors to hurry, hurry, ringing in her ears.

"Can you stand?"

"Yes, don't worry." But he was so weak he had to pull himself up by holding on to the wall. Lilah helped him as best she could, but even with the recent weight loss brought on by the disease Kevin was a heavy man. She prayed that they would make it. The common room was emptying, and Lilah noted to her horror that the floor had a definite slant to it. The ship was going under. . . .

"Hurry, Kevin!" she breathed.

"I'm ready," he said, and pushed himself

away from the wall. He was swaying on his feet, his muscles weak and barely able to support him after his illness. He was clad only in his nightshirt, but there was no time now to worry about anything except getting off the ship before it plunged to the depths.

With Lilah's arm around his waist as he leaned heavily against her, they managed to make it into the companionway. It was already crammed with people staggering toward the deck. Lilah and Kevin were halfway up the stairs when the ship tilted a few more degrees to the left. Someone screamed. Most of the women were weeping, and the few men who remained below were grim-faced.

As the ship tilted, Kevin lost his balance and fell to his knees. The people behind them pushed around and over them in a frantic rush for the deck as Lilah struggled to help Kevin to his feet.

"Help him!" she screamed, but her voice was drowned out by the sobbing of the women and the wailing of the storm. Those pushing past were not free to help her in any case; they had their hands full with sick people of their own. At last Kevin managed to rise, and with her arm around him again they made their way up the remaining stairs. They were the last ones out of the passageway.

The scene on deck was like something out

of her worst nightmare. The sails had been torn to ribbons by the wind. The tattered remnants whipped around the two remaining masts like some giant cat-o'-nine-tails. The sky roiled like a boiling pot above; the sea rose and crashed below, showering the deck with salt water that was indistinguishable except by taste from the rain that fell in torrents. Ropes had been strung along the deck, and it was to these that the passengers clung as they made their way to the rail by what was left of the forecastle, which had been stove in by the fall of the main mast. It was from that point that the lifeboats were being launched.

Eight to a lifeboat, and there were four lifeboats. Only thirty-two souls had survived the cholera. Roughly half of those were ill. Most of them likely would not survive. . . . None of them would likely survive. The lifeboats were tiny, they were far from land, and the sea was a monstrous, hungry thing. What chance had their puny boats against such fury?

Kevin made Lilah go ahead of him along the deck. It was all she could do to maintain her grip on the rope while the deck pitched and dropped beneath her and the wind tried to snatch her away with it. Her hair blew free of its knot and whipped around her face, blinding her. Wave after wave crashed over the deck, promising to suck the unwary down into the oceans depths. Thunder boomed, and lightning lit up the churning blackness of the sky. Lilah, numb with fear, lost her footing more than once. The taste of terror was in her mouth, the fear of death strong inside her. She also feared for Kevin, who clung grimly to the rope behind her. How could he find the strength to make it to the lifeboats, weak as he was?

As they fought their way across the deck, the first lifeboat was lowered with a tremendous splash. It was immediately caught up by the waves and lifted high. Lilah caught a brief glimpse of terrified faces and hands clinging to the sides of the boat before it plunged down into a trough, out of sight.

The deck was tilting steeply now, and the fight to get in the lifeboats was more frantic. Through the driving rain Lilah saw Betsy clamber into the second lifeboat, saw too that it was manned by two slaves. As the boat hit the surface of the water the two men bent to their oars. Their effort was wasted against the mighty strength of the waves. She caught only one more glimpse of the boat before it was whirled away.

There were two more boats to be launched. Dr. Freeman clambered into the next one with Mrs. Patterson and Billy, the Gorman ladies, and two others besides the men needed at the oars. Lilah miraculously reached the rail with Kevin behind her as this boat was filled. Clinging for her life as the deck bucked like a wild horse beneath her feet, she realized that she had not seen Joss at all. He was not in the lifeboat, nor in the little group of people waiting, nor had he come below to aid the evacuation. She looked frantically around without ever admitting to herself why she was doing so. It was always possible that he had been in the first boat, or that she had missed him in the second. . . .

But no, there he was, and she was conscious of a great feeling of relief as she spotted him farther along the rail. His black hair was soaked and plastered to his head and his clothes were clinging wetly to him as he worked one of the winches that lowered the lifeboats with another of the slaves. He saw her at about the same time she saw him. She got the impression that his shoulders relaxed a little, as if he was as relieved to discover her whereabouts as she was to discover his. Then he returned his attention to his task. The other boat was swung out over the side and lowered away.

There were six people left to fill the last

boat. She was the only woman remaining. Captain Boone had lashed the tiller, hoping to keep the ship as steady as possible until they were away. The *Swift Wind* was taking on water at an alarming rate. She would not last much longer.

Lilah scrambled into the lifeboat with Kevin behind her, and took a seat near the stem. Wind and rain lashed her face so that she could barely see. Her hair was soaked, the long strands whipping around her shoulders until she caught them and thrust them down the back of her dress. The cold slick wetness against her spine made her shiver. The taste of fear was stronger than the salt on her lips. She licked them, clutching the bench seat for dear life as wave after wave rose to threaten them, suspended as they were high over the sea.

Captain Boone climbed aboard, followed by a compact little man who Lilah thought was named Mr. Downey. Captain Boone motioned to the man to join him in the prow, probably to even out the weight distribution in the boat. The *Swift Wind* was empty now save for Joss and the other man working the winches. Both were slaves, their lives evidently of little value as it became obvious that they were going to be left behind.

"What about them?" Lilah screamed even

as the lifeboat swung out and then hurtled downward, falling toward the sea with sickening speed. No one answered, if they even heard. The howling of the wind and roar of the waves reduced all other sounds to nothingness.

The lifeboat hit the water with a smack, jolting Lilah almost off the seat. The tremendous splash generated by the boat's landing drenched them as the little boat was caught and driven up the side of a wave. Lilah saw that the ropes holding her to the *Swift Wind* were not yet cast away. Looking up at the ship towering above them, Lilah felt sick as she thought of the men who had been left behind. Then her heart rose to her throat as she saw Joss clinging like a monkey to the rope still linking the prow of the lifeboat to the *Swift Wind.* His legs were wrapped securely around it as he lowered himself by his hands with the grace and speed of a circus performer. The other man slid down the rope leading to the stern. Waves washed over them, the mother ship reared and threatened to plunge down on top of them, the wind buffeted them wildly. Lilah thought that they could not possibly make it — but they did! No sooner had their feet touched the decks than the ropes were cast off. The lifeboat was on her own in a dark and vengeful sea.

Fourteen

It could have been hours or days that they huddled in that lifeboat. Lilah didn't know. She knew only that the fury of the storm seemed to increase with every minute that passed, and that she had never been more sure of anything in her life than she was that death would soon claim them. The men, except for Kevin, who was still too weak from the cholera, took turns manning the oars, though it did little good against the raging sea. The boat went where the wind and waves took it, climbing crests as high as mountains before plunging down into deep troughs. Lilah's teeth chattered with the cold. Her clothes clung to her like an icy shroud. Her knees shook with fear. She muttered the prayers of her childhood over and over. Around her she could see the other ships moving, and guessed that they were doing the same.

There was no measure of time. The tiny lifeboat was jerked about at the whim of the sea. Lilah resigned herself to drowning. The question was not if, but when. They were all alone in the terrible black vastness of the storm. She had caught not a glimpse of the other lifeboats since each had been dropped into the sea. They had been borne away like corks in a whirlpool. She doubted that any of them would see land again.

It must have been morning at last, because the blackness that surrounded them lightened just a bit to a fearsome charcoal gray. Lilah lifted her head from where it had been resting wearily on her lap, frowning at a sound that did not seem quite part of the roaring wind and waves. A more rhythmic kind of pounding. . . .

"God's bones!" The expletive came from Joss, and brought Lilah bolt upright with terror. "Breakers! We've got breakers ahead!"

The exact meaning of the warning was lost on Lilah until she saw the white froth of breaking surf through the blackness of sky and sea. At first she was glad to find land so near . . . but then she saw the rocks. Huge gray rocks that rose from the sea like teeth.

It was too late to turn back. The telltale line of surf was just ahead; they had been almost on the breakers when Joss saw them. With the wind blowing them before it like a child would a paper boat, there was no power short of heaven that could have kept them off those rocks.

"Pull! Pull, damn your eyes!" Joss shouted.

They tried. They pulled at the oars like men possessed, muscles bulging against soaked shirts and breeches, oaths and prayers falling from their mouths interchangeably. But the sea came along with a mighty curling hand to scoop the lifeboat up and throw it at the jagged line of rocks with a spear thrower's deadly accuracy. Lilah watched with horror as they hurtled straight toward a huge dark shape towering out of the sea.

"Hang on!" Joss screamed.

Lilah ducked, grasping the edge of the seat so hard that her hands hurt. She closed her eyes — and at that moment they hit.

The lifeboat struck the rocks with a scream like a dying horse, her belly ripping away at first impact. The sea picked the boat up again and hurled her back down against the rock with another shuddering crash. A vast wave of surf poured over them.

Lilah saw the huge wave towering above them and threw her arms up over her face. The wave crashed down into the boat and caught her up with it, carrying her over the side. She had no time, or breath, to scream.

Down into the icy black depths of the ocean she went, fighting and kicking as she tumbled through the churning cold. She had never been a strong swimmer, and she was hampered by her sodden skirt, but she kicked and clawed for the surface, fighting for life-giving air. That she succeeded was no credit to her. The sea, having dragged her down, simply spewed her out again. She popped up on the surface like a bottle.

Waves crashed over her, nearly sinking her. She choked, her head going beneath the surface of the water. At last she managed to gulp a breath of air, and then cried out. The others must be nearby, floundering in the sea just as she was. She thought she heard a faint voice answer, but she couldn't be sure. Then she was caught by another wave and carried under and away.

When she surfaced again she was gasping. Her shoes had come off, and this small loss gave her a slight added buoyancy. An undertow dragged at her, pulling her out to sea. She fought it with all her strength, struggling toward the shore that could not be too far away.

She must have cried out again, because a voice answered. She was sure of it this time, though the sea was crashing all around her and its tremendous roar filled her ears.

"Lilah!"

Gasping, she turned in the water to see a seal-black head swimming up strongly behind her — and a huge dark mountain of a wave towering behind the swimmer. Her eyes widened, and she opened her mouth to cry a warning. The wave broke before she could make a sound. The torrent of water slammed down on her with the force of a collapsing brick building. She was hurtled again into the depths.

She kicked and clawed and fought, but this time the sea seemed inclined to keep her. Just as she thought her lungs would burst from lack of air, the sea spit her out again. She choked as she reached the surface, knowing that she could not hold out much longer. She had reached the end of her strength. It was easier not to fight it, just to sink down beneath the surface of the sea. . . .

Then, out of nowhere, a strong arm hooked itself around her neck, towing her out of the deadly grip of the undertow.

Fifteen

"It's all right, you're safe now," Joss yelled in her ear. Lilah wanted to laugh, wanted to cry, wanted to scream and rage at the fates that had brought them to this, but could do none of those things because another wave broke over them just at that moment, plunging them both under water. For a moment she feared that she would be pulled away from Joss, but he would not let her go, swimming strongly for the surface with her in tow, her feeble paddling little help.

For what could have been hours or days they battled the sea together, Lilah ready to give up more than once but Joss never faltering. If it had not been for his tireless strength she would have drowned countless times. Once the black depths almost claimed her, wrenching her away as she rested tiredly back against his hard body. She was tumbling in the dark quiet world beneath the waves when he found her again, snatching her back up into the horrible reality of the storm with his hand in her hair. After that he stripped off his shirt and tied one sleeve around her wrist and the other around his.

Somewhere during those hours he found a plank, and hoisted her up so that she could cling to it with both arms. He held on to it with one hand, and supported her with the other. They were taken far out and back at the whim of the waves, whirled around and up and down until Lilah lost all track of time or place or even circumstance. The only reality was the brutal fury of the storm.

Then she heard the pounding of the surf again.

"Kick! Damn it to hell, kick!"

She had no idea how long he'd been yelling the order in her ear, but at last the words penetrated. She kicked, and he was kicking beside her, until at last they saw the foaming white spume of waves breaking over a shore. A different shore this time, without the deadly rocks to guard it from all comers. Lilah could make out nothing but a dark mass beyond the breaking waves, but she knew land was there. Land! The knowledge infused her with a last bit of strength, and she kicked frantically as did Joss, but in the end it was no effort of theirs that saved them. A giant wave caught their plank and hurled them toward the shore. Lilah lost her grip on the plank. More waves broke over her, tried to drag her back into the maelstrom again, but the water was shallow here and she was able to wriggle forward on her belly on the sandy bottom until at last she was totally out of the water, free of the deadly pull of the breaking waves. Then she collapsed and lay unmoving. More water washed over her, but it was rain. She barely had time to register the fact that she had not drowned after all before utter exhaustion claimed her.

Sixteen

The heat of the sun on her face woke her. For a long moment Lilah lay still, basking in the blessed warmth, not remembering where she was; not aware of anything other than how very good it felt to lay there soaking up the sun's healing rays. Gradually she sensed the gritty nature of the surface beneath her cheek, and the fact that despite the warmth above and below her she was decidedly damp. Frowning, she opened her eyes.

A long, sparkling expanse of white beach greeted her. Lilah blinked at it, lifted her head to look around. The beach seemed to stretch on for miles, until it curved out of sight as the land did. In front of her, some dozen yards away, palm trees and undergrowth marked the end of the beach. Behind her, less than two feet from her bare toes, lapped the gentle blue waters of a bay. Beyond that lay the sea, as serene as if the recent nightmare had never occurred.

Joss! What had happened to him?

Lilah sat up, her body protesting every

movement, and looked around her. In either direction, as far as she could see, stretched nothing but white sand, pristine, undisturbed. There was no sign of Joss, no sign of life save for a pair of crabs who scuttled toward and then back from the sea, and a single wheeling tern overhead. Her heart contracted. Had he saved her only to drown himself?

The thought brought her to her feet to find that her legs were unsteady beneath her. She stood still for a moment, unexpectedly chilled despite the beaming sun. Shivering, she wrapped her arms around herself and looked down. The front of her once sky-blue dress was covered with sand, and her skirt and petticoat clung clammily to her legs. Her stockings had apparently come off sometime during her battle with the sea. First she brushed off the sand, then she shook out her skirt and petticoat as best she could. The thin muslin of her dress would soon dry on its own, but she knew that if she wanted to get dry she should remove her underclothes. She could not possibly disrobe on a public beach, or walk around in only her dress without the modesty-protecting undergarments beneath. So she would have to stay damp and musty smelling until the sun dried her garments from the outside in, or until she found a safe haven that offered privacy.

Taking stock, Lilah lifted her hands to her hair to find that the silken mass hung in a huge damp tangle down her back. Twisting the thick mass into a knot would be impossible even if she had not lost her hairpins. She could do nothing but leave it hanging untidily. Brushing stray grains of sand from her cheek, pushing back the wayward strands of hair that straggled in front of her eyes, limping, wet, and bedraggled, she started off down the beach.

She could not be the only survivor. The notion horrified her. She had to find Joss; it was impossible to imagine that he might be dead. And what of the others in the lifeboat? What of Kevin? If she had survived, he might have too. Or Captain Boone or Mr. Downey or . . . But she had the feeling that the rocks that had doomed the lifeboat were a long way from where she had washed up. There was little chance that the others had made it to this deserted expanse of beach. Joss had been the only one with her at the end. Joss had saved her life.

Stumbling occasionally as her tender feet made the acquaintance of sharp shells half buried in the sand, Lilah headed in the direction of a small promontory at the far end of the beach where the land turned in on itself again. This outcropping was nothing more than a sand dune covered with scrub grass, she discovered as she climbed it to stand at the top looking around. It afforded an excellent view of the beach in both directions, and a sea so calm in the aftermath of the storm that it seemed to be made of azure glass. A tremor of anger shook her as she stared at that treacherous expanse of blue. How many lives had been lost in those somnolent depths just the night before, to be swallowed up and gone forever? Gritting her teeth, shaken by a terrible surge of anger, Lilah shook her fist at the sea.

The gesture appalled her. By nature she was calm, serene. She should rather be giving thanks for her own survival than cursing the fates for the loss of the *Swift Wind*. But gratitude seemed a little much to ask of herself on this falsely shining morning, when so much had been taken away.

A dark shape on the white sand far down the beach caught her eye. At that distance she could not ascertain what it might be. Whatever it was lay inert. It could very well be nothing more than a piece of flotsam washed up by the storm. But it could also be a man. . . .

Lilah scrambled down the other side of the promontory, picking up her skirts and stumbling along the beach in a near run. Shells cut her feet and she disregarded the pain. Once she fell to her knees, scraping her palms as she caught herself, but still she pushed herself up and ran on. She had to see, had to know. . . .

She was still some yards away when she knew for certain that the shape was a man. He lay unmoving, shirtless and barefoot, one arm flung up past his head and the other cuddled beneath him. She would recognize that coal-black hair and the breadth of those shoulders anywhere.

Joss.

"Joss!" Lilah breathed a prayer that he still lived even as she dropped to her knees beside him. He didn't move. His back with its faint tracery of scars was turned to her. His broad shoulders gleamed a pale bronze in the sun. His breeches were damp but drier than her dress, and his hair was already drying into crisp waves around his head and neck, its confining thong lost in the sea. She could detect no sign that he drew breath.

"Joss!" She put her hand on the satiny skin of his shoulder. It was warm to the touch. Relief flooded through her, until it occurred to her that the warmth of the skin might be due in part to the relentless sun.

Grasping his far shoulder with both hands,

she struggled to turn him onto his back. He was heavy, and the task wasn't easy, but at last she managed it. As his face and chest rolled into view, she gasped. A wicked-looking gash had been sliced into the flesh of his forehead. Although the cut was imbedded now with sand, and any blood that may have flowed from it had been washed away by the sea, Lilah guessed that it had once bled profusely. Was the lack of bleeding now a bad sign, or a good one? Did it mean that he was . . . ? She refused to even think the word.

"Joss!"

Frightened, she shook him. Her hand moved from his shoulder, hesitated, then nestled in the soft wedge of fur on his chest to feel for his heart. There, beneath her fingers, was the faintest of beats.

"Thank God!"

He was alive, then, but at what cost in terms of injuries? He was not merely sleeping, he was unconscious. That great gash might have damaged his skull. The possibility that he had survived the horrors of the night and the sea only to die of an injury on this sundrenched shore unnerved her. Biting her lip, Lilah ran her hands gently around the gash, and then all over his skull down to his neck and behind his ears. The curling tendrils of his hair clung to her fingers like beseeching hands.

His skull seemed to be in one piece. She was no doctor, but she had learned a little about human anatomy from nursing the sick aboard the *Swift Wind*. It was possible that he had some other injury that was not outwardly visible. Moving a little so as to give herself the greatest possible view of his body, she ran her hands over him, probing the broad shoulders, the ribs that seemed to have healed since that day in Mathews Court House, the length of his spine. His skin was warm and smooth and whole, he was lean but firmly muscled, and as far as she could tell the bones in his torso were intact.

Shifting again, she slid her hands down each of his arms. They, too, were warm and sleek, lightly furred and so firmly muscled that they were hard to the touch beneath the satin of his skin. And they, too, seemed to be intact.

That left his hips and legs and feet as possible sites for injury. Unless, of course, he had damage to some internal organ, something she would not find by looking or feeling. If that was the case, she could do nothing about it, so she resolved to put the possibility out of her head.

The thought of running her hands along his narrow hips and hard-muscled legs was unsettling. Lilah glanced at the area of his abdomen covered by his breeches, flushed, and shifted her attention to his legs. For a long moment she stared at them, sprawled out against the white sand as they were, each muscle and sinew clearly delineated by the rough wool breeches that, dampened, clung to him like a second skin. His legs looked straight enough, and the narrow bare brown feet with the toes pointing toward the sky seemed attached just as they were meant to be. That one long look was enough to make up Lilah's mind for her: She would leave well enough alone for the time being. If she were to discover that he had a broken leg, or hip, she would be at a loss to do anything about it anyway.

"Joss!" Her inspection done, she tried once more to rouse him, calling his name and shaking him gently by the shoulder. The stubby black crescents of lashes remained resolutely closed against cheeks that were darkened by several days' growth of beard. He didn't stir, didn't respond in any way. Crouching beside him, Lilah stared down at him in dismay. What ought she do now?

She could just sit on the beach beside him, hoping and praying that he would wake up on his own. But what if he didn't, or what if it took days? They would both have to have water, and she at least would have to eat. And they needed some sort of shelter from the sun. Already she could feel its bright rays burning her tender skin. She could not leave him exposed on the beach to broil like a fish. And she knew from experience with Barbados's blinding sun that her own skin would turn painfully red in a matter of hours if she did not protect it from the sun. There was no one to help her. What needed to be done, she would have to do herself.

Over the course of the next hour, Lilah managed to drag Joss to where the palm trees, with their interlocking tangle of bushes and vegetation, shaded the sand, then erect a crude shelter over him by leaning some driftwood she scavenged from the beach against the trunk of a leafy palm. She found some fresh water in a small rock pool on the promontory. The fresh water, a remnant from the last few days' storm, would evaporate in a day or so. The shelter was so crude that it would keep out nothing more than the gossamer rays of the sun. Her arrangements for survival were strictly temporary, but at least they would keep the two of them alive until Joss woke, or they were rescued, or she figured out what to do next.

Joss stirred and groaned as she tried to clean some of the crusted sand from his wound. Lilah was encouraged by this evidence of life. But he still didn't open his eyes, or respond when she called his name. So she sank back on her heels, disappointed, and continued with what she was doing.

The gash was not particularly deep, but it was long, slicing from just above his right temple all the way across his forehead to end over his left eye. The edges were jagged, and sand clung tenaciously to the scabbing that had already started to form. As Lilah carefully wiped as much of the sand from the cut as she could with the dampened end of her petticoat, it occurred to her that infection was a real danger. Betsy's father was a great believer in salt water as an aid in healing. He used it frequently as he practiced his arts on the other slaves, and Lilah herself had seen the simple remedy work wonders around Heart's Ease. Using a seashell for a cup, she brought some seawater back to the makeshift shelter. Shielding Joss's eyes with her hand, she gently poured the water into the wound.

Joss groaned, and opened his eyes to look right into her face.

"You're awake!" Lilah smiled down at him in delight, and left off pouring the water.

"Water!" he muttered, his eyes closing again, his tongue coming out to touch dry lips.

"Just a minute." She had a little fresh water in another seashell just outside the shelter. Turning, she crawled out, fetched the shell, and, cradling it carefully so that none of its precious liquid spilled, brought it back to him. His eyes opened as she knelt beside him, her hand sliding beneath the back of his head to lift it just enough so that he could drink. He drained the small amount in two gulps, and closed his eyes. Lilah lowered his head carefully back to the sand. Chewing on her lower lip, she looked down at him in concern. He was silent for so long that she had begun to fear that he had lost consciousness again when he spoke without opening his eyes.

"Christ, my head," he mumbled, lifting a hand toward the gash. She caught his hand before he could touch it, and returned it to rest on his chest. "It aches like a sore tooth and burns like hellfire!"

"You've got a bad cut," she said.

"The damned plank hit me. . . ." His voice trailed off as he obviously started to remember the night before. Wincing, he made an abortive movement to sit up. "Where are we?"

"Stay still!" she ordered sharply, her hand flying to the center of his chest to push him back. Her action was unnecessary. He was already falling back with a groan.

"I don't know where we are," she admitted.

"I've got the mother of a headache. But what I can't understand is why the damned thing burns so."

"I put seawater on it to clean it out. That's probably why it burns."

"Seawater!"

"Betsy's father is an Obeah man, and he swears by seawater for preventing infection. He says the salt promotes healing."

"Christ! No wonder it burns!" He frowned as his eyes focused on her face. "Are you all right?"

"I'm fine. In much better shape than you are, believe me. Does anything hurt besides your head? I tried to check for broken bones, but —"

"You did, eh?" His lips sketched a faint smile. "No, nothing hurts. Except my head. It hurts enough for the entire rest of my body."

"I'm sorry."

"I expect I'll survive." He looked up at the rough pieces of driftwood that formed a slanting roof some three feet above his head and torso. "What is this?"

She followed his eyes. "Driftwood. You were unconscious, and I was afraid to leave you lying out in the sun. So I got some driftwood and made a kind of lean-to. And I found some fresh water."

"You built a lean-to over me?" His face was a study in mingled pain and surprise. She smiled down at him.

"Actually, I had to drag you across the beach first, so I could lean the wood against a tree."

He studied her for a long moment, his expression difficult to decipher. "You dragged me across a beach, built me a shelter from the sun, took care of my cut and found fresh water. I'd say that makes you a pretty remarkable lady, Delilah Remy. As resourceful as you are beautiful."

The admiring gleam in his green eyes brought a faint, glimmering smile from her. "And you are an incorrigible flirt," she answered before she thought. Then her eyes widened on his face with dismay. That was exactly the sort of reply she would have made if he were still the Jocelyn San Pietro she had thought him when they had met that never-to-be-forgotten night at Boxhill. But everything had changed since then. He was no longer in a position to tease and flirt with her, and she was no longer free to respond to him. He was a slave, her slave, and to permit any relationship other than mistress to servant to exist between them was both unthinkable and dangerous. Remembering how he had kissed her on the *Swift Wind*, his fierce passion and her fiery response, she flushed. Shipwrecked or no, she could not for a moment forget who and what they both were. The consequences could be disastrous for both of them.

"I'm going to get some more water," she said in a constricted voice. His eyes narrowed on her face. If he could read her thoughts, she didn't care. He had to know just as she did that the attraction that had never died between them was impossible. Forbidden.

Seventeen

When Lilah returned with two seashells full of water, Joss was standing outside the crude shelter. He was half turned away from her, his fists on his hips as he stared out to sea. His black hair fell in disordered curls around the nape of his neck, his shoulders were wide and gleaming in the bright sunlight, his arms corded with muscle. His waist was hard and narrow, and the nether regions of his body discreetly hidden by the sandy black breeches looked just as leanly supple as the rest.

As she stared at him, Lilah's step faltered. When she resumed walking it was at a slower pace. Since nursing the sick aboard the *Swift Wind*, she knew much more about the anatomy of the male body than she had when she'd left Virginia. Bare chests, backs, arms and even legs and other less mentionable parts were no strangers to her anymore. But the brief, necessary glimpses of male flesh that she had been exposed to on the ship had been strictly impersonal. Seeing Joss standing there bare to the waist, muscles sleekly powerful beneath smooth skin, the thick wedge of hair on his chest stretching from one flat brown nipple to the other before narrowing down to disappear beneath the waistband of his breeches — that was personal. He was magnificently, beautifully male, and just looking at him made her mouth go dry.

It was shameful that the mere sight of his unclothed chest should affect her so. Just looking at him aroused the most wanton feelings inside her, and she was not a wanton female. To treat him strictly as a servant would be the hardest thing she had ever done in her life.

Joss heard her approach and turned to look at her, his hands dropping to his sides. His eyes caught hers, held them, then took on a bright emerald gleam that Lilah feared could see clear through to her heart. She returned his stare, determined not to let him know how vulnerable he made her feel. Lilah took a firm grip on her courage and walked right up to him, holding out one of the shells.

"Water?"

Joss accepted the shell without a word, with nothing more than a measuring look, then lifted it to his lips, and drank. Just watching the tilt of his chin and the movement of his throat as the water worked its way down unsettled her. He was far too handsome for his own good — or her peace of mind. When he finished drinking, he dropped the shell to the sand and wiped the back of his hand across his mouth. Lilah felt that simple gesture all the way down to her toes.

She had to get away from him — *soon* — or this thing that existed between them would explode. She wanted his mouth on hers again more than she had ever wanted anything in her life.

"Thank you." His eyes fixed on hers again, as intent as a cat at a mouse hole. Unnerved, Lilah lifted the other shell to her own mouth and drank from it without ever so much as tasting the slight brackishness of the water. When she lowered it, it was to find that his eyes had shifted to her mouth. Her lips tightened in instinctive defense even as her eyes flew to his. Soft blue eyes clashed with hard green ones for a long moment while swirls of an unspeakable tension seared the air between them. Then Lilah deliberately broke eye contact, looking down at the empty shell in her hand. For something to do she bent to nestle the shell in the sand, taking as much time and care as if it had been made of priceless crystal. The physical action gave her time to school her expression, and give a stern lecture to her racing heart.

When she straightened it was to find him heading off down the beach. For a moment she stared after him, nonplussed, and then she picked up her skirts and ran to catch up.

"Where are you going?" she gasped when she reached his side. He barely glanced at her. Certainly he did not stop, or even slow his long strides.

"There's probably a village around here somewhere. I'm going to find it. Far be it from me not to restore your ladyship to civilization as quickly as I can."

There was a hard edge to his voice that revealed his anger. As aware as he always seemed to be of her thoughts, he had undoubtedly divined the reasons behind her flustered withdrawal. Of course he was angry. He had not yet accepted what he was, but it would come in time, just as it would for her. She had only to be strong; just until they were back in the normal structure of society, and she was no longer faced with this unsettling temptation. Danger lay in being alone with him outside the boundaries of her world.

"You really shouldn't be walking with a head injury in this heat." It was all she could do to keep up with him.

"What?" He glanced down in simulated

surprise. "You mean the lady is actually concerned about her slave? Why, Miss Lilah, you surprise me!"

She stopped to glare at him. His mocking falsetto infuriated her. He kept on walking. Fuming, she caught up with him, determined not to speak until he did. Certainly she would never again express so much as a syllable of concern about his well-being! If he wanted to kill himself, that was his business!

The pace he set slowed fractionally as the sun rose until it was almost directly overhead and the heat became stifling. Hot little vapors rose from the sand to quiver in the air ahead of them. Not even the breeze off the ocean was enough to cool the air. Feeling her nose burn, Lilah stopped again. Watching to make certain he did not look around, she reached beneath her skirt to untie the tapes of her petticoat and step out of it. Then she wrapped the folds of white linen around her head to form a crude sunbonnet. With her petticoat on her head instead of around her legs, she felt much cooler, and if her modesty suffered, so be it. She was not fool enough to invite a heatstroke even if he was!

When Lilah caught up with him, Joss took one look at her and laughed rudely.

"How indelicate, Miss Lilah, to flaunt your underwear in public that way! Naughty, naughty!"

Furious, she stopped dead, glaring at him, but he kept walking. "Oh, shut up!" she yelled after him, the rudeness of her remark making her feel a degree better. If he even heard, he gave no indication of it. He just kept walking.

That infuriated her more than anything he could have said or done. If he was determined to be difficult, she would cooperate, she pledged grimly. Catching up with him again, she stuck her nose up in the air and trudged along beside him, waiting for his next broadside with something closely akin to relish. As he ignored her she felt herself growing crosser and crosser. She had never felt closer to committing an act of violence in her life!

They walked for nearly three-quarters of an hour without so much as a word passing between them. So far they'd seen no sign of life except for birds and crabs and lizards. If it hadn't been for Joss, Lilah knew she would have been frightened. But at the moment she was just too furious to have room left for apprehension about their situation.

Climbing over one of the small, grassy dunes that divided the beach into sections,

Lilah stubbed her toe on a rock. Yelping, she hopped about on one foot, clutching its injured mate in her hand. Joss cast her a single glance that correctly assessed the degree of her injury, and kept going. Lilah's temper crackled. She would have plopped down on the sand there and then and refused to take another step if she hadn't been certain he would simply go on without her.

Limping, she followed him, fixing that wide back with a killing glare. Finally she had to skip to catch up. When she did so, she glared at him in earnest.

"You could at least be civil!" she snapped.

He glanced down at her, his expression unpleasant. "I don't feel civil."

"That's patently obvious!"

"A slave is allowed not to talk, isn't he? I don't have to entertain you as well as get you back to your fiancé, do I? Or do I? Please instruct me. I haven't been a slave very long, you know, and I'm not quite up on the etiquette involved."

His sarcasm made her do a slow burn that had nothing to do with the sun beating down on her head.

"You are the most infuriating, arrogant, obnoxious, overbearing . . ."

"Funny, that is exactly what I would have said to you," he said at last, stopping. "If I wasn't a slave, that is."

Those emerald eyes were blisteringly hot with suppressed rage. Lilah sputtered, unable to come up with a sufficiently cutting reply.

Joss was not in a mood to wait. He turned and stalked off again, leaving Lilah nothing to do but glare after him until he walked out of sight as the beach made another curve. Then, picking up her skirts, she trudged in his wake. Her uppermost thought was how much she would like to find a rock with which to bash him over the back of that silky black head!

Eighteen

When she came around the bend, she found him sprawled facedown in the sand.

"Joss!"

Horrified, she ran to him, dropping to her knees by his side. Her first touch on his back assured her that he was not dead. The silky skin was damp with perspiration. He had fainted, and served him right, too! Anyone with a lick of sense would have known better than to go striding off in this heat, and with a head injury, at that.

She was glaring down at him when his eyes opened.

"What a charming sight," he muttered, the words snide, and shut his eyes again. Lilah had to grit her teeth to keep from adding to his injuries with a hard box to his ear.

"I told you it wasn't a good idea to go marching about in this heat," she pointed out virtuously, hoping to annoy him. His eyelashes flickered, and for a moment two slits of green regarded her malevolently.

"Next time I'll let you drown," Joss said

under his breath. Before Lilah could answer, he rolled over onto his back, his hand lifting to shade his eyes.

"Christ, my head aches!"

"I'm not surprised! I told you —"

"If you say that one more time I won't be responsible for what I do."

Silenced temporarily, Lilah rocked back on her heels. Joss lay unmoving, the stubbly growth of black whiskers on his cheeks and jaw and the thick pelt of black fur on his chest making him seem like some wild stranger. Her eyes ran over the breadth of his shoulders and down his arms . . . and suddenly she frowned. The exposed skin of his shoulders and upper arms and chest was an angry shade of deep brick red. Her own skin tingled faintly, but she didn't think she could have much of a burn with the long-sleeved, high-necked dress to cover her body and the deep flounce of the petticoat protecting her face.

"Joss."

The lack of hostility in her tone must have gotten through to him, because he lifted his hand a little to look at her. "Hmm?"

"There's shade up there at the edge of the palm trees. Do you think you can make it that far? It's just a few yards. You can lean on me, if you like. But you really need to get out of the sun."

"What, you mean your ladyship would actually willingly suffer the touch of a lowly slave? Why, I'm overwhelmed!"

Her affability was definitely not contagious, it seemed. "You are the most . . . Never mind! I'm determined not to quarrel with you anymore! Be as obnoxious as you like, I don't care! But you need to get out of the sun! Your shoulders and arms are as red as a lobster!"

"They're about the color of your nose, then," he retorted, but his tone was milder than before. "Actually you look rather fetching, with your nose like a cherry and that petticoat wound around your head. Anyone would be forgiven for thinking that you were human."

Lilah lost her patience and stood up, almost stamping her foot in exasperated annoyance. "You are really the most despicable . . . !" Her voice trailed off as her eyes happened to touch on something down the beach a bit. The outcropping of sand and scrub grass that interrupted her view of the horizon looked amazingly like the promontory she had climbed when she had first awakened and thought herself alone on the beach.

"What's the matter?" Joss followed her

gaze with his eyes, but the promontory meant nothing to him. He'd been well to the west of it when she'd found him.

"I think we're right back where we started." There was a hollow feeling in the pit of her stomach.

"That's not possible! We couldn't have come full circle so fast! Unless . . ." He frowned. "What makes you think we have?"

"That little hill over there — I'm almost sure that's the one where I found the water."

"It can't be."

"Let's get you out of the sun, and I'll go see."

He demurred at first, determined to go with her, but at last Lilah managed to persuade him of the folly of taking a chance on aggravating his injury with sunstroke. As soon as he was upright his head started to swim again. Lilah quickly slid her arm around his waist as he swayed and staggered a pace backwards. Joss leaned heavily against her for a moment, unable to help himself as a wave of dizziness washed over him. Lilah was tinglingly conscious of the intimacy implicit in the way she was holding him, her arm around his naked waist, her hand pressing against the hard flat muscles of his abdomen. If anyone should see — but there was no one to see, no one to know, and if something happened to Joss she would be all alone. Surely it was no more than her Christian duty to do what she could to help him, under the circumstances.

Joss tried to stand on his own two feet without her support, but was hit with another, milder dizzy spell. It was obvious he had little choice: accept her assistance or fall on his face in the sand. With his arm wrapped around her shoulders and her arm around his waist, they hobbled over to where the changing angle of the sun sent shade stretching out across the beach. He was heavy and his skin was damp and warm and gritty with the sand that clung to it. His faintly pungent odor made her wrinkle her nose.

"Smell, do I?" he inquired, seeing her expression.

"Just a little. I imagine I do, too."

He shook his head. "No, you don't," he said. "If that does turn out to be your hill — bring back some water, would you?"

The faintly rasping quality of his voice told her better than words just how exhausted he was.

The promontory was the same one. Lilah climbed to the top of it, found the rock pool, greedily drank until her own thirst was slaked and then filled two shells with water. More than that she could not carry, but the shells were large and would contain sufficient water for Joss for the time being.

When she returned to Joss, he was on his back. The shade had crept down a little more so that it reached a good three feet beyond where he lay. To her surprise, Lilah realized that it must be late afternoon.

Bending to settle the shells carefully in the sand, Lilah knelt beside Joss. She called his name and gently touched his shoulder. His eyes opened, flickered once, then with what appeared to be an effort of will fixed on her face.

"I brought you some water."

With her assistance he managed to lever himself onto one elbow and gulp down the water. Then he lay back in the sand once more, his posture indescribably weary.

"Was it the same hill?"

"Yes." Lilah unwrapped the petticoat from her head, wadded it up, and pushed it under his head for a pillow.

"Mmmm."

She took that as a thank you. After that he was silent for a moment as he lay there with his eyes closed. Finally his eyes opened a slit.

"You realize what that means, don't you?"

"What?" Lilah frowned. She really hadn't

thought much about it, except to be pleased that she had so easily found water again.

"We're on an island — no, not even an island, it's not big enough for that. An atoll in the middle of the Atlantic Ocean. We've walked all the way around it and seen not a solitary sign of life except for ourselves. Unless there's someone in the interior — and I don't think there is, or we would have seen evidence of that — we're all alone."

Lilah's eyes widened. "All alone?" She swallowed as the various ramifications played through her head. "Do you mean we're . . . marooned?" The last word was almost a squeak.

"Exactly," he said, and shut his eyes again.

Nineteen

It was almost dark, and they had shifted position so that they were nestled in a little depression at the very base of the promontory. Joss still felt dizzy every time he stood up, and it had been an effort moving him this far. But he had felt it was better to be closer to their only supply of water, and she had agreed. That the puddle was rapidly diminishing Lilah had not the heart to tell him. There was still enough in it for perhaps another day or two, if they were careful. And tomorrow maybe he would feel better and they would go looking for more.

She was hungry, and she knew he must be too. But making a meal out of a crab or a lizard or a bird was beyond her. First she would have to catch it, then kill it and find some way to cook it — or eat it raw. The very thought made her shudder, hungry as she was. And Joss was in no shape to undertake the task for them both. Surely they could go one night without food. It occurred to her that it had actually been far longer than that since either of them had had a meal of any substance.

Another bodily problem was taken care of on the far side of the promontory at the edge of the trees. When she had finished, she was rewarded by stumbling over a coconut. Another nut was nearby, and she scooped them up with all the triumph of a successful treasure hunter. Looking above her, she saw that the leafy fronds swaying some thirty feet above belonged to coconut palms. The sight was so wonderful that she wanted to jump up and down for joy. At least now they would not have to worry about starving.

Pausing only to break open one of the nuts on a large rock — she hadn't been raised on Barbados for nothing! — she hurried back to Joss. He was sitting up when she returned, his back propped against the grassy dune. It was amazing how safe just the sight of him made her feel.

"Where have you been?" he asked disagreeably, but she was too overjoyed at her find to respond in kind.

"Look," she said, almost skipping as she approached. She carried half of the broken coconut in each hand. The other nut she had left beside the rock, to be reclaimed later.

"What are those?" Joss eyed the hairy brown half-moons with something less than the enthusiasm they deserved.

"It's a coconut." Lilah sank to her knees beside him, holding one out to him. "Here, take it. The milk is good to drink and the meat is good to eat and we can use the shell for a bowl when we're done."

Joss took the shell in his hands and stared down at the milky fluid swimming in its nest of white meat with the same expression he might have worn if she'd suggested he eat a worm.

"It's delicious!" she told him impatiently, and showed him by taking a sip. Watching her, he sniffed warily at his own half. Then he took a small sip, and made a face.

"You don't like it?" Lilah was surprised. On Barbados coconuts were universally beloved. Everybody ate them just as they fell to the ground. They were like fruit in an English garden.

"Not much."

"Drink it anyway."

He did, and then she showed him how to break off the meat into small chunks so that it could be eaten easily. Instead of finishing hers off, she saved a small piece of meat and rubbed it on her burning nose.

"What are you doing?" He was looking at her as if she had suddenly lost her mind. She had to smile.

"There's an oil in the meat that's good for your skin when you've had too much sun. You should rub some over your shoulders and arms. It'll take some of the sting away."

He grunted, looking unconvinced, and continued chewing unenthusiastically on a piece of coconut. Lilah shook her head at him, and moved closer to perform the chore for him. He suffered her to brush the sand away, and then rub the oily meat over his shoulders and back, and down his arms, but his expression was skeptical. For her part, Lilah tried to ignore the pleasure she got from touching him. Despite the fiery heat left by the sun, his skin was as satiny smooth as fine leather. Finally she dabbed a bit on the end of his nose. He ducked, winced, and swatted at her. She laughed at him as she moved away.

"Haven't you ever seen a coconut before?"

He shook his head. "I grew up in England, which, unlike the places where you've apparently lived, is quite civilized. We don't have giant hairy nuts growing on our trees — and we don't have slaves either."

Lilah met that glittering green gaze, and her good mood died. A sudden fierce flare of resentment sent her surging to her feet.

"Look, I'm sick and tired of hearing you whine about being a slave! I can't help what you are any more than you can! It's fate, and I'm not responsible for fate, so you can just stop being so angry at me all the time! You should be grateful to me, if anything! I saved your hide at that auction back there in Virginia, Joss San Pietro. But if I had it to do over again — I'd have let them nail it to the wall!"

Sitting there with his back propped against the grassy dune, he had to tilt his head to look up at her as she stood, arms akimbo, shouting down at him. Instead of getting angry in turn, as Lilah expected, his expression turned pensive.

"Do you know, I think that's the first thing I liked about you: that fiery temper of yours. You cursed when you hit that bush and then when I did the gentlemanly thing and pulled your skirt down for you, you tried to punch my nose. It was charming, especially from such a pretty little thing. I've always liked women who were ready to take on the devil."

He put the coconut down beside him and got slowly to his feet. The move brought him unexpectedly close, and suddenly it was she who had to tilt her head back to look up at him. Dusk was settling over the island, the sun had set, the moon not yet risen, and the only points of light were his eyes. They glittered at her through the gathering darkness.

Lilah took a step backwards in sudden alarm.

"Afraid of me, are you?" He laughed suddenly, the sound grating. She realized with a shock that he was furious. His hand shot out to catch her by the arm and drag her close even as she took another step away. Feeling that steely grip, helpless to free herself as he pulled her so close that no more than a handsbreadth separated their bodies, Lilah was suddenly, frighteningly aware of how strong he was and how helpless she was in the face of that strength. He could overpower her easily. . . .

"You're lucky my mother raised me to be a gentleman, did you know that? Because we're all alone here, there's no one else on this whole damned island, and I'm sick and tired of playing the slave to your lady of the manor. I'm sick and tired of you looking at me like you could eat me up, and putting your soft little hands all over me under one pretext or another, then jumping away as if I have leprosy if I look back, or dare to lay so much as a finger on you. That's a dangerous game you're playing at, Lilah my dear, and if I weren't a gentleman I'd damned well take you up on it. I may anyway if you keep it up, so I suggest you keep your viperish tongue between your teeth and your haughty little nose out of the air and your eyes and hands where they belong. If I find them on me again, I'm going to give you what they're asking for!"

He spoke in a dangerously soft voice that was as smooth as silk. Lilah had never heard quite that tone from him before, and at first she stood frozen as he bit the words out at her. But by the end of this speech her initial surge of nervousness was swamped by a combination of humiliation and sheer rage.

"Why, you conceited beast . . . !" she gasped. "How dare you imply that I . . . that I . . . when we get back to Heart's Ease I'll have you whipped for saying such things to me!"

"Oh, will you now?" he growled, and then he was jerking her all the way against him and his mouth was crushing down on hers. The force of his kiss thrust her head back against his shoulder; the fury of it parted her lips as he staked a harsh claim to her mouth. Shocked and furious, she struggled wildly in his grasp, but he was too strong for her and controlled her struggles with ridiculous ease. She was panting, her breath filling his mouth, while he was as little disturbed by her frantic fists and feet as if she'd been a small child in a tantrum. He wrapped his arms around her, surrounding her with hair-roughened, sweat-dampened bare flesh and the scent of man. One long-fingered hand went up to thread through the thick tangle of her hair, cupping the back of her skull, pulling her head back to allow him easier access to her mouth. Then, shockingly, his tongue was thrusting its way in between her teeth and filling her mouth. . . .

Never in her life had she been kissed in such a way! It couldn't be right, it couldn't be proper, it couldn't be the way decent men kissed ladies they cared for, or respected. . . . A thrill of pleasure shot through her loins as his tongue touched hers, and then Lilah panicked completely.

She bit him. Right on his encroaching tongue. Bit him so hard that he yelped and jumped back, his hand flying to his mouth.

"You — little — bitch!" he ground out, withdrawing his hand from his mouth and looking down at his fingers to find traces of blood on them. His eyes came up to lock with hers. The look on his face was furious enough to give brave men pause, but Lilah was too angry to be afraid.

"Don't you ever dare touch me like that again!" she hissed, and while he still stared at her with that evil look in his eye she whirled, snatched up her petticoat from where it had been serving as a seat on the sand, and marched off into the night.

Twenty

Lilah spent that night and the next huddled under a palm tree away from the promontory. How Joss spent his nights she neither knew nor cared. Savagely she hoped that some giant land crab would crawl up to him while he slept and drag him away. Realistically she knew that that was too much to hope for. He was too blasted big for any such happy occurrence. But oh, with how much relish did she await rescue! He would be singing a different tune when he was her slave again! Though she wouldn't really have him whipped — no slaves had been whipped at Heart's Ease for as long as she could remember. But she would certainly exert her power over him to the fullest! How he would grovel at her feet when she was restored to her proper place!

The third morning on the island dawned bright and hot and clear. Lilah ate another coconut, drank from the pool that was really more like a puddle now, and washed her face with the dampened end of her petticoat, all the while keeping a wary eye out for Joss. He didn't seem to be anywhere on the beach, and she was wondering if perhaps she had gotten her wish and he had been dragged off by a land crab when she spied him standing up to his thighs in the bay, a sharpened stick in his hand. As she watched him in puzzlement, he thrust the stick into the water with a lightning-fast movement. When he pulled it out she saw that he had impaled a squirming fish. Grinning with triumph, Joss headed for shore with his prize.

Lilah climbed down her side of the promontory before she could be seen. God forbid that he should accuse her of eating him with her eyes again! Just remembering his coarse insults and the disgusting way he had kissed her was enough to make her burn with anger, and her anger was enough to steel her against the delicious odor of roasting fish that soon wafted her way. Curiosity, not hunger, she told herself, was what drew her to the top of the promontory, where she dropped to her belly and looked down at him with as much stealth as if she were an enemy scout. He had somehow managed to get a small fire going, and was roasting the cleaned fish on two flat rocks set in the middle of the flames. The thought of a hot meal made her mouth water, but she vowed that she would starve to death before she asked him for so much as a morsel. There were plenty of coconuts on the island. She could make her own way!

The rest of that day they passed as they had the previous one, on their separate sections of beach with the promontory between them as a sort of neutral territory. By late afternoon the freshwater pool was nearly dry, and Lilah knew that on the morrow she would no longer be able to put off going into the interior of the island to search for more. She didn't much like the idea — the thought of invading that thick undergrowth, especially with bare feet, was not inviting — but it would have to be done. The one comfort was that Joss was almost out of water, too. Maybe he'd be the one to step on the poisonous snake instead of herself.

Joss had managed to construct a serviceable-looking hut for himself out of palm fronds and vines, she saw. Looking from her own crude shelter — more chunks of driftwood leaned up against the trunk of a coconut palm — to his sturdy structure set beneath an overhanging jacaranda, Lilah felt her annoyance rise to a new pitch. She had spent the last two nights shivering with cold, even with her petticoat wrapped securely around her shoulders and her knees drawn up to her chest. Amazing that days so blazingly hot that she had been compelled to shed her stays as well as her petticoat, leaving her in the wildly immodest costume of thin dress and even thinner chemise, could turn to nights so cold. The brisk wind that blew nightly off the ocean swept clear through her ramshackle quarters. She had the feeling that he was as snug as could be. . . .

She would not torture herself with such thoughts. Instead she would treat herself to the one luxury of her day: a bath. Heading down off the promontory, she set the water-filled shell inside her shelter and gathered up the rest of her makeshift dishes. Then she headed toward the bay.

"Lilah!"

The sound of Joss's voice yelling her name when they had not spoken for two days brought her head up in disbelief. There was a note of urgency in his shout. She stood up from where she had been rinsing her coconut dishes in the sea — she had already washed her hair, body and clothes by the simple expedient of wading in fully dressed and scrubbing herself from head to toe with sand — and looked in the direction of his end of the beach. Of course she had chosen to bathe where the promontory blocked his view of what she was doing, so in consequence she could not see him either.

"Lilah! Damn it, where are you, girl?"

There was no mistaking the urgency this time. Suddenly he appeared at she top of the promontory, looking wildly around for her. Obviously he was whole of limb, and so she turned her back on him, and continued to clean her dishes in the surf.

Moments later she heard him splashing through the surf behind her. Before she could so much as turn to glare at him he snatched from her head the petticoat she'd bundled around her hair to keep the wet strands off her neck.

"You give that back!" Lilah raged, but Joss was already heading back through the surf with her petticoat in hand. "You come back here with that this minute, you bounder!"

Stamping her foot, she started after him, fury surging through her veins. To steal her petticoat was the outside of enough — if he had need of an extra piece of cloth that was just too bad! Perhaps he was tired of having his chest and back constantly exposed to the sun and meant to fashion a crude shirt for himself. But her petticoat was hers, and she would fight to the last gasp before she gave it up! With her fair skin and blonde hair, she needed protection from the sun more than he did, anyway. What did he think he was about . . . ?

She had not quite reached the shore when he raced to the highest point of the promontory and started waving her petticoat madly over his head. For a moment Lilah stared, wondering if the sun had turned his brain, but then she understood at last.

"A ship!" she screeched, and picking up her skirt raced up the side of the promontory in his wake.

"We're here, we're here!"

She skidded to a halt beside him, jumping up and down and waving her arms in the air and screaming madly just as he was. Though it was a sure bet that the ship whose sails just graced the horizon could not hear so much as a syllable.

"We're here!"

Joss waved her petticoat overhead like a flag. The ship passed majestically down the horizon, silhouetted against the pink and crimson and orange of the dying sun. Impossible to tell if they had been seen or not, but the ship did not seem to be heading their way.

"If only I could get up higher . . . !" Joss looked around distractedly, but he stood on the highest point along the beach. Lilah tugged at his arm. The prospect of rescue had erased all her animosity toward him for at least the moment.

"Lift me up on your shoulders!"

He blinked at her for an instant, then nodded. Lilah had expected that he would kneel down and let her climb onto his shoulders that way. Instead he caught her by the waist, and lifted her up. Her skirt was an obstacle. Without more than the briefest consideration of modesty she hitched it up around her thighs so that he could lift her over his head. Once seated on his shoulders, her bare legs and feet dangling down the front of his chest, she grabbed the petticoat from his hand and waved it frantically. The ship was farther in the distance now, but there was still the off chance that someone might look their way. A sailor in the crow's nest, perhaps. . . .

"They're leaving! They don't see us!"

"No, stop! Come back! We're here!"

Holding on to the top of Joss's head for balance, Lilah managed to get one foot on his shoulder and stand up. He grabbed her ankles, holding her as best he could. If she was to wave her petticoat, she had perforce to let her skirts drop. She did, and they fell down over his head, obscuring it from her view and blinding him. Teetering wildly, she waved the petticoat from that precarious vantage point while he held on to her ankles with a grip like death and tried his best to keep them both upright.

"Come back! We're here!"

Still the ship receded. Lilah raised herself on her tiptoes. . . .

"Christ!"

Joss had taken a step backwards to compensate for her antics on his shoulders. Lilah teetered, and then he was slipping out from under her like an eel. . . .

"Help!"

Lilah shrieked as she tumbled toward the ground, landing with an *oomph* bottom first, right in the middle of his abdomen.

"Arrgh!"

Joss, who fortunately for Lilah had hit the ground first, groaned loudly as she crashed down on top of him. Thankful to have been spared an injury, Lilah shifted around so that she could see his face.

"What happened?"

"I tripped over a damned rock — what were you doing up there anyway?"

He glared at her from his position flat on his back in the sandy scrub grass. She glared back at him from her seat in the middle of his stomach. Then, suddenly, his lips twitched and he grinned. Then chuckled. Then laughed out loud. Lilah, at first affronted, finally had to join in.

"Oh, my," she said finally, shifting off her

perch to kneel beside him. "Did I hurt you?"

He looked at her, his eyes twinkling. "I doubt if I'll ever eat again. My stomach must be permanently bruised."

"I don't weigh that much!"

"You weigh enough, believe me! If I can stand up I'll be surprised."

He grinned at her, and she could not help doing the same. Then he sat up gingerly, one hand pressed to his stomach.

"That's the last time I'll ever put you up on my shoulders."

"That's the last time I'll ever stand on your shoulders! I could have been hurt!"

"I was hurt!"

"Baby!"

That epithet brought another grin from him. Then he looked toward the horizon and sobered.

"I don't think they saw us."

Lilah looked toward the horizon as well. "No."

"If one ship sailed past this island, another will. We'll be rescued before long." He sounded more hopeful than convinced.

"Yes."

They both stared at the now empty horizon for a long moment. Then Lilah looked at Joss. His whiskers had developed into what was very nearly a full beard, and his cut had healed over so that it was no longer so raw and red-looking. His skin was more bronzed than red. He was leaner, she thought, and if possible even more firmly muscled. The only parts of him that she would recognize without a second glance were the brilliant emerald eyes.

"I didn't mean what I said about having you whipped," she said abruptly, her voice low. "When we are rescued, you don't have to worry. Nobody's whipped a slave on Heart's Ease for years."

His eyes sliced to hers. "I'm not worried. Because I don't have the least intention of being a slave on Heart's Ease, ever. When we're rescued, I'm going back to England."

She blinked at him for a moment, dumbfounded. "But you can't!"

"Why can't I? I don't imagine we'll be rescued by anyone who knows us, do you? Unless you tell whoever rescues us about what happened in Virginia, they won't have any reason to suppose that I'm anything but a free man. Which is just what I intend to be."

"But — but . . ."

"Unless you mean to claim me as your property the minute someone finds us," he added, a considering glint in his eyes as they fixed on her.

Lilah stared at him. He was right. When they were rescued, unless it was by someone who knew his history, there would be no reason for anyone to imagine that he was a slave. When he was dressed and shaved he looked every inch the English gentleman — he had been raised as an English gentleman. She had it in her power to set him free. . . .

"Don't get me wrong, I'll see you in safe hands, but I'm not going to carry this farce any further. When I'm home in England again, I'll send you your hundred dollars."

"I don't care about the money. . . ." she began, still at a loss.

"I do." He set his jaw. Looking at him, stubborn and proud and the least likely slave that she had ever met, Lilah made up her mind. He would have his freedom if she could, by her silence, give it to him. It was no more than she had meant to do later, with her father's consent.

"All right then. You can send the money if you want, but my father actually bought you, not me. I just . . . bid."

"So I'll send the money to your father. You agree?"

She looked at him, and slowly nodded. "I agree."

He smiled at her, a sudden charming smile that reminded her heart-stoppingly of the man she had teetered on the brink of falling in love with that first enchanted night.

"Then I apologize for my behavior of two nights ago, and give you my word that it won't happen again. Until we're rescued, you're as safe with me as you would be with your own father."

He got to his feet as he spoke, and held out his hand to help her up. Lilah put her hand in his with mixed emotions. If he went back to England she would never see him again; certainly he would never willingly set foot on Barbados. And for the rest of their enforced stay on the island she would be as safe from his advances as she would be if he were her father. She should be overjoyed on both counts, she knew — but she wasn't.

"Shall we be friends, then?"

He pulled her up beside him as he spoke, and let go of her hand. Lilah nodded, though there was an oddly hollow feeling inside her.

"Friends," she agreed.

"In that case, I'll share my fish with you. If it hasn't burned to a crisp, that is. I was cooking it when I saw that ship."

She smiled at him, but it was an effort. "Lead on, Macduff," she quoted lightly, but her heart was not as light as her words. Maddening as he was, and totally forbidden to her as well, it still hurt to imagine never seeing him again. With a sick feeling in the pit of her stomach Lilah wondered if, once he was gone, her heart would ever be the same.

Twenty-one

The fish was slightly blackened around the edges, but it was still delicious. Lilah ate it off the plantain leaf Joss had cooked it in, licked her fingers, and then rolled up the leaf and ate that too. Joss, sitting across the fire from her, watched her quizzically.

"Is eating one's dishes another of the quaintly barbaric customs you were raised with?"

"On Barbados, baked plantain leaves are considered a delicacy," she informed him with a lift of her chin.

He rolled his up and took a bite, then made a face. "Barbados must be a mighty strange place."

"It's lovely," she said, and proceeded to tell him all about it. From there she progressed to telling about her family, about her mother's death and Kevin's arrival on the scene soon after her father married Kevin's aunt Jane. A shadow must have clouded her face when she mentioned Kevin, because Joss frowned.

"In love with him, are you? Don't worry, if we survived he may well have too. I don't doubt you'll have a touching reunion when you get home to Heart's Ease." There was the slightest trace of sarcasm to his words.

Lilah shook her head. "I hope so. I'm very fond of Kevin. But I don't think I'm in love with him. My father thought he would make me a good husband, and I'm twenty-one, you know. It's time I was married."

"Fond of him?" Joss snorted. "You almost make me sorry for the bastard."

"Don't call Kevin that — he's a very nice man, actually. You just met him under, um, unfortunate circumstances. But why should you feel sorry for him?"

He looked at her without the smallest bit of humor in his face. "I wouldn't want the woman I marry being 'fond' of me. 'Fond' is cold comfort when the two of you are in bed together."

"Joss!"

He smiled crookedly. "Does that shock you? Listen, my girl, I'll give you a piece of advice. Don't marry a man you're just 'fond' of. You'll be miserable inside a year."

"How would you know?" A thought then occurred to her and her eyes widened on his face. "You've never been married, have you?

For goodness' sake, you're not married now?"

"No, I'm not married, and I never have been. And I'll be thirty next month, in case you're wondering."

She smiled, her expression smug. "So you don't know any more about marriage than I do. You just like pretending to be wise to impress me."

He shook his head at her. "Now there's where you're wrong. I do know more than I ever wanted to about the kind of marriage you'll have with your precious Kevin — a loveless marriage of convenience, whether you like to look at it that way or not. My mother was 'fond' of my stepfather when she married him. He had been my real father's best friend, and when my father died — I was eight years old — my mother leaned on him for advice and comfort. She was a very feminine woman, thought she couldn't function without a man, and she was 'fond' of my stepfather. They married a year after my father died. Within another year they were fighting constantly, and within two he had turned into a bitter, mean-tempered man who drowned his unhappiness in drink. He couldn't stand the idea that she didn't love him, you see. Five years after they were married, he fell off a Bristol pier. Drunk again, after he and my mother had had yet another fight. If truth were told, I think by that time she was glad to be rid of him. Certainly I was. He was a mean drunk, and I was afraid that one day when I was no longer living under their roof to protect her he'd hurt her during one of his binges."

"You were close to your mother, weren't you?" Lilah asked softly, remembering that it had been his mother's deathbed behest that had sent him to Boxhill.

He nodded, the single bob of his head curt. "She was soft and gentle and sweet and didn't have a brain in her head. She needed a man to take care of her. My stepfather just wasn't that man."

"You didn't know she was, uh . . ." Lilah's voice trailed off as she couldn't think of a way to phrase the question that wouldn't anger him.

"The daughter of a slave?" he supplied, looking at her keenly. Then he shook his head. "My mother was as pale-skinned as you are. She had red hair and green eyes and was lovely. My black hair and dark skin are from my father, who as far as I am aware was descended from upright British merchants who could trace their ancestry clear back to William the Conqueror. All I got from my mother were her eyes. And she got those from her mother, the notorious Victoria."

"Uncle George seemed to recognize your eyes."

"He did, didn't he? And the shock of finding out that his past sins had come back to haunt him killed him. I'm sorry about that for your sake if you loved him, but the old bastard deserves to roast in hell. My mother never stopped talking about her father, or hoping to see him again. All she knew was that he had sent her and her mother away when she was a little girl and that they were never to return or contact him again. He supported them, though; there was always plenty of money even after I was born. But my mother wanted her father, and could never understand why he was so adamant about not seeing her. Of course she guessed, eventually, that she was illegitimate. But I'm almost certain that she never knew her mother was an octoroon slave. Brainless as she was, she never would have sent me to Virginia if she'd known. My grandmother died when I was young, but I remember her as looking very like my mother. Pale-skinned and lovely."

"I've heard that the octoroons of New Orleans are very beautiful."

He nodded. "She must have been. She

caught old George's eye, didn't she? But then, almost anything must have been an improvement over that witch of a wife of his."

"Amanda is my great-aunt." Her voice was mildly chiding, though she wasn't a whole lot fonder of Amanda than he seemed to be. Still, Amanda was an old woman and her kin, and Lilah had been raised to show both estates respect.

"Then I beg your pardon. But you can't expect me to exactly love her after what she did."

"No." She looked at him, smiled. "I'm glad you're going to be free again. Being a slave doesn't exactly suit you."

His eyes met hers, and he grinned. "It doesn't, does it? I swear to you, Lilah my dear, that ordinarily I'm really the most charming of fellows. You've seen me at my worst."

"You have been rather short-tempered."

"I apologize." He looked at her for a moment and his expression changed. "I promise that my disposition will improve now that we've agreed to be merely fellow castaways."

Lilah laughed. "Castaways? Is that what we are?"

"For the time being." He stood up and flexed his back, then grinned down at her.

"On your feet, fellow castaway, we've work to do."

"What kind of work?" She eyed him suspiciously.

"If we ever want to be rescued, we need to make a few preparations. I doubt that many ships actually drop anchor in our bay here. But as we've seen, they do pass by the island. So I think what we need is a signal fire."

Lilah watched him kick sand over the small fire, then come around its smoking ruin and hold out his hand to her. For a long moment she just looked at it, then she placed her hand in his. His fingers closed warm and hard around her palm as he pulled her up to stand beside him.

Twenty-two

That night, Joss cursed himself for what had to be the hundredth time for being rash enough to ever make her that fool promise.

"You're as safe with me as you would be with your own father," he mimicked in disgust. They'd gathered driftwood and piled it atop the dune together, practiced lighting the tender with the crude flint and steel he'd fashioned out of a rock he'd found on the beach and a buckle from the cuff of his breeches. This way she would know what to do if she should happen to be alone and see a ship. Then they had come down to feast together on a crab he killed with a rock. All the while she'd smiled at him, touched him, enticed him without, he thought savagely, even knowing quite what she was doing. Now it was full night, the moon was high in the sky, and they were going to bed. In his hut. Together. And he'd promised not to touch her. Christ in heaven!

Watching Lilah as she crawled before him into the hut, loss groaned inwardly. He'd given her his word. And however much she might tempt him, with her silky pale skin and rag of a dress that was nearly transparent without the added thickness of her petticoat, he would not go back on his word.

"Damn it to hell and back!"

He hadn't meant to say the words aloud. Lilah heard him, and looked around inquiringly from just inside the hut. She was still on her hands and knees, her tantalizingly round little bottom barely veiled by the thin dress that was pulled tight around it by her position. Her soft eyes that were the exact color of one of Bristol's doves blinked at him over her shoulder as he failed to answer, and he was recalled to himself in a hurry.

"I'll — uh, there's something I need to check. I'll be back in a little while. You go on to sleep."

"I'll come with you." She started to back out of the hut. The soft blue cloth tightened even more around her bottom until Joss, watching with fascination, both hoped and feared it might split.

"No!" His protest was too loud, too vehement, but he couldn't help it. He needed a little time alone, a little time to get a firm grip on his baser instincts. "No, I'll be right back."

That was better, calmer. Christ, he

couldn't let her guess how he felt! He strode away into the moonlit darkness, heading for the bay. A swim was what he needed. It might serve to cool him down.

He swam for what seemed like hours, then, exhausted, emerged from the water confident that he was safe. By now she'd be asleep. And he was tired. . . .

But she wasn't asleep. She was sitting on a rock near where the incoming tide lapped at the white sand. Her hair was pulled over one shoulder, the ends resting in her lap as she wrestled with the tangles that snarled it. The moonlight struck the silken strands and gave them a life of their own, so that they glinted and glittered like molten silver. She looked like a damned mermaid. His breath caught at the sight of her.

"What the devil are you doing out here?" There was more frustration than anger in his voice as he stalked up to her. She smiled at him, her face tilted up so that he could see each lovely feature washed by moonlight. Even the faded blue of her dress took on a silvery sheen in the otherworldly light that poured over the bay.

"Combing my hair. See?" She held up a crudely fashioned comb for his inspection. "I made it by twisting sticks together with vines while I waited for you. You were gone so long I was beginning to be afraid you'd had an accident."

"I was swimming."

"So I see." The dry amusement in her voice warned him. He looked down at himself, turned scarlet, and glared at her furiously before stalking over to where his breeches awaited him in the sand. Soaking wet, he pulled them on, buttoned them, and turned to face her. The brazen wench was still calmly combing her hair, her eyes fixed with serene propriety on the gentle waves rolling in across the bay. But from the small smile that played hide-and-seek across her mouth, he guessed she'd gotten quite an eyeful. His face burned hotter as he planted his fists on his hips and glared at her across the few feet of sand that separated them.

"Damn it, I couldn't swim in my breeches!"

"I realize that."

"I told you to go to bed! How could I know you'd be sitting on a rock like a damned Lorelei when I came out of the water?"

"Nobody's blaming you for anything." Her voice was soothing, her eyes still fixed on the bay. He would have been mollified — if it hadn't been for that damned sneaky smile that kept flickering around her mouth.

"So you got an eyeful!" He sounded belligerent, he knew he did, but he couldn't help it. The notion of her seeing him naked in such circumstances was oddly embarrassing to him. And it infuriated him that that should be so. He'd bedded dozens of females over the course of his life, all of whom had seen him in the altogether. Having a woman's eyes on his body had never bothered him before. Maybe it was because he wanted the minx so badly, and knew he could not have her. Their paths would never cross again once they got off this damned island. And he couldn't just take her body and then cooly abandon her afterwards. She was a virgin, he'd stake his life, and a lady, and a gentleman did not seduce and abandon virgins. Or ladies.

Sometimes it was hell being a gentleman.

"It's all right, Joss," she said gently, sliding around on her rock so that she was looking right at him. With the moonlight pouring over her and the twinkling stars in their midnight velvet background high overhead framing her, she was so beautiful that he felt his blood start to heat. So beautiful that his body reacted independent of his mind. "I wasn't embarrassed."

For a full minute all he could do was stare at her, not quite sure whether or not to believe his ears. She wasn't embarrassed? Was this the haughty lady who would barely tolerate his hand on her arm? Who slapped him and bit him the last two times he'd lost his head and kissed her? Who made no bones about thinking he was so far beneath her that he was hardly fit to dust the ground she walked on? She wasn't embarrassed?!

"Well, I sure as hell was!" he growled, and turning his back, stalked off in the direction of the hut.

If she had laughed, he would have killed her.

But she didn't, or if she did at least he didn't hear her. She followed him meekly to the hut and crawled inside behind him. Joss had built the shelter to accommodate one person — himself. It was scarcely high enough to sit upright in, a little longer than his length if he stretched out flat, and perhaps three feet wide.

Definitely not wide enough for two people. Not when one of them was a man in an acute state of arousal and the other was the woman who had aroused him. Not when he'd given his word not to touch her. Hell and the devil!

He sat with his legs crossed in the far corner, glaring at her as she crawled inside. She sat, curled her legs beneath her, and smiled at him.

"Were you really embarrassed, Joss?"

"I'm going to sleep," he announced, his eyes narrowing to forbidding slits. Suiting the action to the words, he scooted down until he was stretched out full length, and turned his back to her. The palm fronds he had dragged in for bedding stabbed him in the side, but there was no way he was going to turn over and face her.

Not when it was all he could do to keep his hands to himself.

"All right. Good night."

Even the softness of her voice grated on him. He imagined that her skin would feel like she sounded, soft, silky, and exquisitely refined. He gritted his teeth as behind him he heard the sounds of her making ready for bed. Please God she would not take off any of her clothes.

She didn't. She lay down fully dressed, and curled up smack against his back.

He felt the softness of her with every fiber of his skin. The imprint of her shape was seared indelibly into his back.

"This is much nicer than sleeping by myself. I was always afraid something would get me in the middle of the night."

He could feel her warm breath against the back of his neck. Christ, if she got any closer she'd be lying on top of him. Did she want what she was inviting? he wondered savagely. Did she even know what she was inviting?

"I got cold by myself, too. There's quite a breeze that blows in off the bay at night."

Her voice reminded him of the sleepy purr of a kitten. But her shape told him that it was no kitten who was curled against his back.

"Joss?"

"What?" If he sounded irritable, it was because he was. She was driving him insane, either deliberately or out of criminal ignorance. He'd give almost anything he'd ever possessed to turn over and enlighten her in the most basic way possible.

"I'm a little cold now."

She snuggled closer. Joss lay rigid as a board, gritting his teeth as he fought the impulses that threatened to overwhelm him. Finally, no longer able to help himself, he began to tremble.

"Joss! What's wrong?"

"Not a single bloody thing." The words were forced out between his teeth.

"Are you sure?"

"Yes, I'm sure!" He had the trembling under control again, thank God, but for how long he couldn't guess.

"All right, then." She sounded doubtful, but to his relief she quit talking. The softness of her breath stirred the hair at his nape, her breasts burned holes in the skin of his back, and her bare arm rested against his waist.

A gentleman he was. A saint he wasn't.

On that thought he turned over, prepared to sweep her into his arms and give her the education she'd been begging for. Only to find that the maddening female was fast asleep.

"Lord Christ!" He glared at her for a moment, on the verge of waking her, then was defeated by the soft innocence of her face. She looked very young and very defenseless lying there beside him, her head pillowed on her arm, the feathery brown crescents of her lashes spreading out over her cheeks like fans. Her lips were barely parted as her breathing moved them, and her glorious hair tumbled all around her face and body. He lifted a hand toward her, hesitated, and drew it back. It came to him suddenly that she was lying there like that for one reason and one reason only: She trusted him. Grinding his teeth, Joss discovered that the notion of her trust was a greater deterrent to his intentions than his promise ever had been.

She stirred, wriggling, as she tried to find a comfortable position. Cursing himself for a complete fool, he slid his arm beneath her and pulled her against his side so that her head was cradled on his shoulder. She sighed contentedly, snuggling close, but did not waken. Her arm moved to lie across his waist.

The weight and scent and softness of her was unbearable. Joss smiled grimly, set his teeth and closed his eyes. Only once before he fell asleep did he permit himself to stroke her hair.

Twenty-three

When Lilah awoke, she was alone. She sat up, rubbed her eyes, and looked around. Sunlight filtering in through the chinks in the hut turned dustmotes into sparkling gems. The disorder of the palm fronds that served as both floor and bedding were physical reminders that last night she had slept with Joss.

Joss.

A small smile played about her lips. Sometime during the course of the afternoon before, she'd come to a realization. She was so madly in love with him that the mere sight of those broad bronzed shoulders was enough to make her heart quake.

She couldn't marry him. What he was made that quite impossible. She had accepted the reality of that. But she could love him. For a little while. For as long as they were on the island. An enchanted world, for the two of them alone. Something to remember when she was old, when she had been married to Kevin for years and her children were grown and Heart's Ease had enjoyed another fifty years of prosperity.

When they were rescued they would go their separate ways. That was how it had to be. But for now, just for now, just for once in her life, she would indulge herself. She would love him. Just for a little while.

The only difficulty seemed to be letting him know how she felt.

She'd tried the night before, creeping close to him as they settled down to sleep. He had resolutely ignored her, keeping his back turned and fighting his impulses heroically. But he had trembled as if he had had a fever.

Another smile curled her mouth. Whatever he might think, she was not so ignorant as not to know what that meant. He wanted her, but he was determined not to do anything about it no matter how she tempted him.

He was a gentleman. But she had thrown her cap over the windmill and discovered, to her joyous astonishment, that deep inside she was no lady. Not where he was concerned. The knowledge that they had only this little time together had made her bold.

What he'd said about "fond" being cold comfort when two people were in bed together had started her thinking.

Never in her life had she felt about a man the way she felt about Joss. From the very first moment she'd set eyes on him, so dashing and debonair as he had appeared to her then, an instant attraction had quivered to life between them. Even when the truth about him had been revealed, the attraction had never died. It had grown, fed on nothing but glimpses of him. It had flourished, despite her efforts otherwise. And he felt it too. She'd seen it in his eyes every time he'd looked at her: in the gazebo at Boxhill; from the block at the slave auction; on the *Swift Wind* before he had kissed her; and here, on the island, before he had stalked away from her on the beach that first morning, before they'd had that dreadful fight and he'd kissed her so shockingly; and last night when he'd emerged naked and gloriously beautiful from the sea.

Her eyes had riveted on him as he'd walked toward her and she got her first real look at a naked man. He was all hard muscle sheathed in bronze satin and soft fur, and her heart had started to pound as she'd stared.

If she was never again in her life going to feel this way about a man, she'd better do something about it. Or she would go to her grave mourning the wonderful shimmering gift that life had offered her and she had spurned.

What was between them couldn't be forever. Heart's Ease and her father and Kevin were forever.

But Joss could be for now.

Twenty-four

Lilah crawled out of the hut, blinking as the brilliant sunlight hit her eyes. She got to her feet and stood looking around, pushing her hair back from her face. It tumbled free, bleached to an even paler shade by the sun, a thick curtain of silk that reached to her hips. Despite her careful wearing of her petticoat-turned-sunbonnet, she knew her face had to be bloomed with color. The thought of pinkened cheeks was not so bad, but a pinkened nose? Still, Joss did not seem to find any lack in her appearance, and Joss was the one she was concerned about.

Where was he?

"Joss!"

"Over here!"

His voice came from behind the promontory. Lilah made a quick trip into the trees, then picked up her skirt and climbed the hill, stopping at the top to get a drink of water from the puddle and wash her face. There was barely any water left now, and she knew that the day had come when they would have to explore the interior of the island.

Joss was sitting cross-legged in the sand beneath the coconut palms, intent on something he held in his lap.

"What are you doing?"

"Making us both a pair of sandals. See?" He held up an object that had been resting in the sand beside him. Lilah took it, looked at it, and saw that it was really an ingeniously made sole woven of supple vines around a bent twig frame with more vines attached to secure it to the foot.

"I'm all admiration," she said, handing it back.

"Come here. I want to try these on you to see if they work."

Lilah obediently stepped closer, and he picked her foot up by the ankle and guided it into the sandal, carefully adjusting the restraining vines. Then he did the same to her other foot. His hand was warm on her ankle and foot, his touch gentle. Lifting her skirt the few inches necessary for him to work, looking down at his black head bent over her bare foot, Lilah marveled at how natural such intimacy with him seemed. She had known him only a scant two months, but she felt as if she had known him all her life.

"Well? What do you think?"

He looked up as he secured the second

sandal, proud of his handiwork. Lilah smiled down at him with warm amusement. His eyes narrowed, and he abruptly dropped her ankle and stood up.

"They're wonderful," Lilah said, moving her feet up and down experimentally.

"Mmmm." He was already pulling on his own pair and wasn't looking at her. Lilah smiled to herself. Clearly, he was still determined to be a gentleman, in accord with what he thought were her wishes. But just touching her ankle made him uncomfortable.

"We're going exploring today. At least, I am. You don't have to come if you'd rather not." His words were abrupt.

Lilah made a face at him. "You're not leaving me behind!"

He grinned, relaxing, and the familiar flash of white teeth dazzled her. "I didn't think so. Come on, then, let's go."

Making their way through the forest proved harder going than Lilah had expected. The trees grew so closely together that the branches intertwined overhead, shrouding the interior of the island in an eery green glow. Beneath her feet were centuries of debris fallen from the trees, degenerated over time into a spongy mulch. Small twisted trees bursting with huge flowers ranging in shade from milky white to deep crimson sprang up everywhere, their pungent scent spicy as it filled the air. Vines twisted across the bushes like fat snakes. Monkeys, disturbed by their presence, chattered as they fled before the human intruders. Brilliantly colored parrots flew into the air with loud squawks. An orange spider the size of Joss's hand ignored them, busy weaving a huge and intricate web between the branches of two trees. Seeing it, Lilah shuddered and shrank closer to Joss's side. He instinctively took her hand and she clung gratefully to his warm fingers, trying not to imagine what other creatures might be lurking out of her sight. Snakes were her biggest fear, but the only one they saw was a small green one that slithered harmlessly away as they approached.

The island was actually the tip of an undersea mountain thrusting through the surface of the ocean, and for that reason their walk was uphill. The air seemed to get thicker and steamier the farther they went. At last they came across a small stream trickling over a bed of black rock. Joss grinned at Lilah triumphantly.

"Ahah!" he said, and dropped her hand as he moved toward the stream.

Joss bent down to scoop up the water for

a sample taste. As soon as he touched the surface of the creek an odd look came over his face and he drew his hand back, sniffing at his fingers and then cautiously tasting the dampness on them.

"What's wrong?"

From the expression on his face he didn't quite believe what his senses were telling him.

"It's hot! The water's hot!"

"Hot!" Lilah moved forward to stand beside him, then knelt beside the stream to gingerly touch the water. It was indeed hot, about the temperature of a bath she might have had Betsy prepare for her at home. All of a sudden she understood the reason for the odd bubbling noise that had been niggling at her consciousness since they had stopped.

"Come on." Lilah stood up and caught his hand.

"But . . ." He resisted, looking as if he might be inclined to argue, so she gave an insistent tug. He capitulated then and allowed her to lead him along the trail formed by the black rock, following the trickle upstream.

"Where are we going?"

"You'll see."

In a few minutes they found what she'd

been seeking. Lilah saw it first, saw the steam rising from behind a veil of flowering mimosa vines starred with delicate mauve blossoms. Pulling the vines aside, she gestured for him to look.

There, in a crater carved out of the black rock, bubbled a small lake. The water frothed and foamed, obviously fed by a powerful underground spring. From the steamy miasma that hung about it, and the abundance of lush green flora that grew around it, it was clear that the water in the lake was as hot as that in the stream.

"What the devil . . . ?" Joss asked, staring.

Lilah looked over her shoulder at him, smiling at his evident astonishment. "On Barbados we call it a firewater pool. This island must be the tip of a volcano, and the spring is heated by the molten rock deep underground. Most of these islands have them, I would imagine. The water's perfectly good, you know. We can drink it. It's just hot."

She pushed the curtain of vines aside, and stepped out onto the moss-covered rock surrounding the pool. Joss followed her, looking doubtfully at the water.

"If you want to swim, this is the place," she told him. "A firewater pool is like a giant natural bath. Betsy and I used to play around in one near Heart's Ease all the time when we were children. We were strictly forbidden to, of course, but we did all the same."

"One more barbaric custom?" he said with a crooked grin.

Lilah laughed. "If you must put it that way, yes. Would you mind turning your back?"

"What? Why?"

"Because I'm going to have a bath, that's why. This will be the first hot bath I've had in a month, and I wouldn't miss it for the world."

"You're joking." He regarded her, narrow-eyed.

Lilah lifted her eyebrows at him. "No, I'm not. Why should I be?"

"You actually mean to take off your clothes so that you can take a bath in this — cauldron? Here and now?"

"Yes, I do. Now would you please turn around?"

Twenty-five

"All right, you can look now!"

Lilah called to Joss from the center of the pool. It was not very deep, in its deepest spot not over her head, she estimated. At the moment she was covered to her shoulders. The frothing water was impossible to see through, though she had left her chemise on for modesty's sake. Her hair floated on the water around her, and her arms floated at her sides to help her keep her balance against the undertow.

"Are you decent?" he asked, turning cautiously. His eyes found her, and she thought he looked relieved to see just how decent she was.

"Come on in. It feels wonderful!"

Joss looked at her for a long moment, crossed his arms over his chest and shook his head.

"Not right now."

"Why not?"

"Because I don't feel like a bath," he said with an edge to his voice, and sat down on a rock by the side of the pool as if he were prepared to stay there all day.

"Be grumpy, then, see if I care." Lilah then devoted her attention to getting herself thoroughly clean for the first time in weeks. She scrubbed her face and body with sand, then worked sand through her hair. Finally she rinsed by the simple expedient of holding her breath and going beneath the surface, then swimming underwater to the far side of the pool. When she surfaced it was to find loss on his feet at the edge of the pool with his eyes alertly scanning the surface. She skimmed the soaking hair off her face to discover his eyes fixed on her with an ominous glitter.

"You scared the hell out of me!" His furious tone was matched by the fists clenched at his sides.

"I'm sorry. I was rinsing my hair." She smiled at him, and that seemed to make him angrier. He continued to stand by the edge of the pool, glaring at her.

"All right, you've had your bath. Now come out and let's get going."

"But I just got in! I'm not ready to get out yet."

"Suit yourself, but if you stay you'll be here alone. I'm leaving."

"Joss!"

"I mean it. Now are you coming out, or are you staying here alone?"

"That's blackmail," she said, and pouted prettily, one eye on him to see how he reacted. He looked even grimmer than before. In fact, his grimness was so out of proportion to the situation that she began to find it amusing, sure she knew what was annoying him so mightily.

"Oh, all right." As he showed no sign of softening she capitulated with an aggrieved sigh, and started to walk toward where he waited at the pool's edge. She hadn't taken two steps when a small drop-off caught her unawares. Her foot slipped, and then she plunged like a stone beneath the surface of the water.

"Lilah!"

Hearing him shout her name as she went under gave her the idea. Chuckling inwardly, Lilah swam down to the bottom of the pool and held herself there, gently releasing bubbles of air that floated to the surface. As she had expected, far less than a minute passed before she heard an enormous splash. She surfaced, still grinning, to find him swimming with fast economy of motion toward the spot where she had disappeared.

"Joss!"

At the sound of her voice he stopped

swimming and looked around. Lilah grinned at him as his eyes found her. Though she could not see through the water, she guessed from his posture that his fists were planted on his hips. His head was cocked just slightly to one side, and his eyes were glittering ominously as they fixed on her.

"You were faking, weren't you?" The question was calm, especially compared to the look on his face. Her grin widened, but she prudently shook her head.

"Liar!"

He started toward where she waited for him. Lilah waited until he was almost upon her, then dived beneath the surface and came up on his other side, splashing him playfully.

"So you got me in here with a trick and now you want to play, huh? All right, then, I'm willing! Anything to oblige a lady!"

He grabbed at her. Laughing, Lilah half swam and half ran away from him. When he caught her and pulled her around to face him, she was still laughing even as she shook the hair back from her face.

"You'd better take a deep breath, my girl, because you're going un—" he started to say, when she reached out to tickle his ribs. Caught by surprise, he clamped his elbows to his sides and lost his grip on her. Lilah swam around behind him, trailing teasing fingers over his broad back as she did so.

"Come back here, you!" Joss whirled, grabbing for her again. A grin was beginning to lurk around his mouth, banishing the scowl with which he had started after her. Lilah dived beneath the surface, running a tickling finger down the length of his arm. This time he caught her, his hand clamping over hers, and pulled her to the surface.

"Got you!" he said, exulting openly as he pulled her up beside him. She tried to tickle him again, but this time he was ready for her, dodging and catching her hand. He pulled both hands against his chest, grinning down at her in triumph. Lilah laughed back at him, content to be caught.

"Aren't you glad I made you get in?"

"You *were* faking!"

She nodded, her eyes twinkling. His black hair was now as wet as her own and slicked back along his skull to curl around his neck. A full beard had grown to cover his lean jaw. The water hit him two-thirds of the way up his chest, so that his shoulders and the tops of his muscular arms showed above the frothing surface. He held her hands nestled half in and half out of the water, her fingers pressed against the silky wet pelt that covered his chest.

"You're playing with fire, my girl." He still

held on to her hands even as he shook his head at her.

"Oh?" Lilah moved a little closer, smiling bewitchingly. His jaw clenched, and he let go of her hands. Her eyes never leaving his, she slid her palms up his chest to rest on the warm wet skin of his shoulders. Touching him like that was intoxicating. Unable and unwilling to stop, she ran her fingers lightly over the tops of his shoulders.

Joss caught her hands again, pulled them down. His eyes were a deep, fathomless green as they bored into hers.

"Do you have any idea what you're inviting?" His voice was hoarse.

Lilah looked up at him, the smile leaving her lips. Wordlessly she nodded.

His eyes widened, then narrowed. "No, you don't. You don't even know how to kiss properly. You bit me."

She had to smile at that despite the sudden wild drumming of her heart. "You can teach me, can't you? And I bit you because — because you were scaring me, and because I thought that — people don't really kiss like that most of the time, do they?" She ended on a note of interested inquiry.

"I'm afraid so." Her naive question wrung a slight, wry smile from him. "If they're lovers, that is."

Her eyelids flickered down, then up again. "Lovers. I always expected to have a husband, but never a lover."

"Well-brought-up young ladies usually don't think along those lines."

"But . . . once we're off this island you'll go back to England and I'll go home to Barbados and we'll never see one another again." Her voice was scarcely louder than a whisper.

"That's occurred to me."

"I'll miss you, Joss." She was not looking at him now, but rather had her eyes fixed intently on his Adam's apple.

"I'll miss you, too." The words sounded as though his throat was constricted. Lilah looked up at him then, only to be helplessly caught in the emerald depths of his eyes.

"Couldn't we just . . . be lovers, then — just while we're on the island? Just for a little while?"

For a moment it seemed as if he'd stopped breathing. Then his hands clenched on her waist, and he closed his eyes. When he opened them again, his jaw was taut.

"You don't realize what you're asking," he said at last. "Sweetheart, from my point of view there's nothing I'd like better than to be your lover. But you — there can be consequences for a woman."

She frowned. "What kind of consequences?"

"Babies," he said tersely, and took a deep breath.

"Oh." Lilah thought about that. She'd known, of course, that babies resulted when people married and shared a bed. Somehow she hadn't applied that knowledge to what she felt for Joss.

"But there are — things we can do. Things that won't make a baby." The words sounded as if they were being forced out of him against his will.

"Does kissing cause a baby? The — the kind you did with me the other night? When I bit you?"

Again his lips curved in a reluctant half-smile. "No."

"Then you can kiss me like that, and teach me everything else that doesn't cause a baby."

"Christ." He shut his eyes again, swallowed, then opened them to regard her intently. "Lilah, are you sure?"

She nodded. His tongue came out to wet his lips.

"All right." It was scarcely more than a hoarse whisper. Slowly, as if giving her time to change her mind, he dipped his head toward hers, his mouth just grazing her lips.

"Put your arms around my neck," he muttered, and she did. Her heart was pounding and her knees were weak. As her arms slid around his neck she took a step closer to him — and looked down in shock.

A large, protuberant something was poking at her belly. The murky water kept her from seeing what it was, but she already knew. It was that mysterious part of him that she had caught just a glimpse of as he had walked out of the sea the night before.

"I left my breeches on the bank," he said, correctly interpreting her look. Knowing that he was naked made Lilah's throat go dry. Her hand slid from behind his neck down over his chest to dip beneath the water and find that intriguing part of him. She touched it, found it hot and hard and swollen as her fingers stroked lightly along it.

"Whoa!"

His hand caught hers, pulled it away from him, held it. Looking up at him, she saw that there was a wild glitter in his eyes.

"Shouldn't I — touch you there?" Her voice was husky.

He nodded once, curtly. Then he bent his head and kissed her slowly and gently, his tongue just barely meeting the line separating her lips. She pressed against him, quivering.

Joss lifted his head abruptly, taking a deep breath, while she leaned against him, looking up at him with huge, languid eyes.

"I think you had the right idea after all," he muttered, and brought her hand back to him again.

Twenty-six

He guided her fingers as they closed over him, then showed her how to please him. Lilah moved her hand, at first slowly and then faster. His eyes closed, and he gritted his teeth almost as if he were in pain. Lilah felt a strange tightening at the place where her thighs joined, felt her breasts swell against the wet fabric that covered them. Then all at once he groaned, and groaned again, and the thing she was holding quivered and jerked in her hand. She dropped it, shocked, but whatever she had done to him it was too late to undo. Joss shuddered all over. When his eyes opened again she was regarding him in wary surprise.

"Oh, Lilah!" A broken laugh escaped him as he put his arms around her and pulled her close against him. "You are so innocent! If I were a gentleman I'd stop this right now."

"I'm tired of you being a gentleman," she said, her voice muffled against his shoulder. "I've never felt about anybody in my life the way I feel about you, and I want you to do something about it."

He slid a hand up through her wet hair and cupped her skull, gently pulling her head back so that he could look down into her face.

"You do, do you?" A tiny smile flickered on his lips and died. His eyes were both tender and rueful as they met hers. "How about if I teach you to kiss properly?" Lilah nodded, unable to trust her voice. His hand left the back of her head and stroked her cheek, his thumb just brushing her lower lip.

"Promise not to bite me?" It was a husky whisper. She nodded again, feeling her heartbeat quicken, and he bent his head. At first his lips brushed over hers so softly that she lifted her chin to deepen the contact. The bristles covering his cheeks and jaw abraded her soft skin, but she barely noticed. Every ounce of her concentration was focused on the gentle fusing of their mouths.

"Open your mouth." He whispered it against her lips as his tongue probed at her closed teeth. Lilah trembled, her arms going up instinctively to clutch his neck. She opened her mouth. His tongue slid inside, touched hers. She felt a quickening start deep inside her belly, felt her knees weaken. As she quaked in his arms they tightened around her, pulling her full up against him so that she felt the entire length of him. The hairs on his legs were rough against her soft thighs; the hairs on his chest cushioned her breasts that might as well have been as naked as he was, covered as they were only by the thin layer of soaking cloth. The secret part of him was huge again, and hard as it pressed against her belly. Now that she knew what it did, it held no fears for her.

Around them the water bubbled and hissed, but she wasn't even aware of where they were. She was only aware of him, of his body against hers, of his lips and tongue teaching her things that she had never dreamed of.

His tongue was still a gentle invader, still stroking the inside of her mouth. Lilah had never imagined that such a disgusting act could make thrills run over her from head to toe. Acting from some deep primordial instinct, her tongue moved too, to stroke his.

He groaned into her mouth, then lifted his head despite her grip on his hair, pulling his lips from hers.

"What's wrong?" Her eyes flickered open to stare dazedly into his. His eyes were a dark smoldering green, alight with a kind of wildfire.

"This is harder than I thought. I want

you so much I ache."

"Do you?" she whispered. He drew in a breath, standing very still as her lips plied sweetly over his. When he took over the kiss its character changed. No longer so carefully gentle, his mouth slanted over hers and his tongue thrust between her teeth with bold possession. His arms tightened around her as if they would squeeze her very breath from her, but Lilah didn't care. She was in the grip of new and exciting sensations, trembling from head to toe, intoxicated with this new world of the senses that he was teaching her.

She was bent back against his arm, her head pillowed on his shoulder, her arms tight around his neck. Her eyes were closed, her head whirling as she gave herself over to his kiss. Then she felt his palms slide down over her back, his touch warm through the thin wet linen of her chemise. His hands lingered at her waist, testing the smallness of the curve, moved on over her buttocks to stroke the backs of her bare thighs. Then, before she could even breathe again after the intimacy of that gesture, his hands slid up under the hem of her chemise to close on the soft round cheeks of her behind.

Lilah gasped, the sound swallowed by his mouth. Her eyes flickered wildly open only to shut again. His hands on her bottom pulled her close against him, lifting her up on her tiptoes so that the soft mound of her womanhood was pressed tight against the stiff protuberance of his flesh.

"Jo-oss." It wasn't quite a protest, wasn't quite a sound of pleasure. Her head was awhirl, her heart quaking in her chest, and she was both shocked and exhilarated by the way he was holding her, the things he was making her feel.

"Shhh." He gentled her with kisses until she was weak and pliant and quivering in his arms. Then his mouth grew hot and hungry as he rocked her against him. At the rhythmic contact she felt her body tighten as flares of pleasure radiated out from that central spot. She gasped her pleasure into his mouth.

"Oh, Joss!"

His hold on her shifted so that only one hand stayed beneath her chemise. The other came up to cup her breast, squeeze it.

Lilah cried out. Her nails dug into the back of his neck as exquisite pleasure exploded inside her. She shivered and shook and at last went limp in his arms. It was some time later before she even became aware that he still held her.

"Does that . . . always happen?" Her face

was pressed to his neck as he rested his cheek against the top of her hair. His arms were tight around her, his heart drumming urgently against her breasts. That part of him that had given her so much pleasure still pressed swollen and hot against her belly.

"Not always. Not to females. You're lucky. Hell, I'm lucky." He sounded as if he were having trouble getting the words out. Lilah felt pleasantly lethargic and warm and comfortable in his hold, but she bestirred herself to look up at him.

"You're lucky?"

"To have such an apt pupil."

He smiled down at her, a tender ghost of a smile, but his eyes were strained.

"What's wrong?" she asked, frowning faintly. She felt wonderful, and it seemed odd that he should not feel the same.

"Never mind." His grip on her loosened, and his hand came up to stroke the hair back from her face. "You still have lots to learn."

"Mmmm." She stepped back away from him, feeling almost self-conscious now in the aftermath of their lovemaking. His eyes were intent on her face, and it seemed to cost him an effort to let her go. As he looked at her a rueful smile curved his lips.

"You are soaking wet and your nose is red and you are still the most beautiful thing I've ever seen in my life. I think you've been sent by a malevolent fate to be the death of me."

She frowned. "What are you talking about?"

"Nothing. Come on, let's get out of this bloody pool. I don't know about you, but I'm getting waterlogged."

It occurred to her that she would get to see him naked again, that she would get a good look this time at what she had only glimpsed and touched. It also occurred to her that he would get almost as good a look at her as she stepped out of the water in her wet chemise. The garment covered her to the thighs, but it would provide little in the way of concealment. At the thought of Joss looking at her in such dishabille, Lilah felt a little glow of mingled excitement and embarrassment start to grow inside her.

She slid her hand into his.

"I quite like being lovers," she said seriously, then looked at him in surprise when he laughed then groaned.

Twenty-seven

"Avast, there, Magruder, you're goin' too bloody fast for me old bones!"

The shout came from somewhere close at hand. It froze Lilah and Joss in their tracks, still shoulder deep in the pool.

"Aw, step lively, Yates! If my ol' peg leg can set this pace, sure to God your two good ones can keep up!"

Joss and Lilah exchanged astonished looks. The voices were coarse, the accents rough, but they were certainly no ghostly utterances. There were at least two flesh-and-blood men on the island with them. After nearly a week of being alone, and a growing fear that it might be a long time indeed before they were rescued, the voices struck Lilah as manna from heaven. With a delighted grin at Joss, she opened her mouth to call to the strangers.

He quickly silenced her by clapping a hand over her mouth. "Don't. You're the next thing to naked, and there might be more than two of them."

Lilah had forgotten about her state of undress. She nodded, and Joss removed his hand with a cautioning look. The voices grew closer, arguing loudly now about who was carrying the heavier end of the load. Joss edged Lilah over into the lee of a large rock, and they stood silently, their heads just above the water, listening. It occurred to Lilah suddenly that with rescue at hand, her time with Joss might be over before it had truly begun. At the thought, her throat tightened, and she clutched his hand.

The voices of the intruders faded away into the distance. Joss listened intently, then with his hands braced on the sides heaved himself out of the pool. He reached down and pulled Lilah out of the pool to sit on the rocky ledge at his feet.

"Get dressed," he said in a terse whisper. "I want to follow them."

He was already stepping into his breeches. The heady lover of the firewater pool had turned in an instant into a grim-eyed man with his mind on matters far removed from the pleasures they had just shared. He hardly even looked at her as she pulled her dress on over her soaking chemise. His attention was totally focused on the intruders, whose fading voices could still be heard cursing one another in the distance.

"Joss!" It was a whisper. He turned to look at her, his expression impatient.

"Do up my buttons, would you, please?" Though she had managed to get out of the dress on her own, buttoning it up again was beyond her. The buttons were tiny and slippery from where her chemise had already soaked her dress. Even when dry, she found buttoning herself up a slow, arduous process. Dressing herself was one of many things she would not miss a bit once they were rescued from the island.

In fact, the only thing she would miss was Joss.

She turned her back to him and he did up her buttons with quick efficiency, clearly no stranger to assisting a lady's toilette. His thoughts were not on what he was doing, she could tell, or even on her at all. The ramifications posed by the intruders occupied all his attention. But when he finished, he bent to slide the sandals on her feet, taking care to wrap the vines securely around her ankles. At that evidence of his care for her she felt a lump rise to her throat.

She almost wished they would never be rescued.

"Come on," he said, taking her hand and pulling her after him as he set off in the direction the strangers had taken.

Once in the forest, they marched single file with Joss in the lead. The undergrowth was thicker in this direction, which was due south, away from the small bay. Joss tried to shield her from the worst of the vines and branches, but a long scratch quickly decorated her arm, and her dress suffered a triangular tear in the skirt that made it just this side of indecent.

Lilah came up beside Joss and was astonished to see the blue of the ocean glinting beyond the thick curtain of vines that he had moved a scant few inches aside.

"We must be at the opposite end of the island," Lilah whispered. Joss nodded.

"Look there."

They had emerged at the edge of a cliff overlooking a small, half-moon-shaped bay. Joss pointed toward the curve of the beach below them.

Lilah looked, her eyes widening. The scene was incredible. On its side in shallow water lay a ship nearly as large as the *Swift Wind* had been. At first Lilah thought she must be looking at the results of another shipwreck, although there had been no storms since she and Joss had washed up on the island and they had already tramped its circumference on foot and found themselves alone. But then she saw that the ship was held on its side by blocks and tackles tied to trees, and that men in rowboats were busy scraping her hull. The ship had been denuded of everything: topmasts, sails, seabags and chests, weapons and a welter of miscellaneous stores and goods that were scattered along the beach helter-skelter. Some piles were protected with tarpaulins, some were not. Not far from the ship two men hauling logs stomped up to where a fire blazed under a huge kettle. It was too far to hear the exchange that took place between these two and the stocking-capped man stirring the kettle, but Lilah guessed from the peg leg on one of them that these were the men they'd heard.

"What are they doing?" she asked.

"She's being careened."

At Lilah's look of incomprehension he added patiently, "Having her hull scraped, caulked and repaired. She must have taken some damage in the storm. Smell that?"

Lilah sniffed, then nodded, wrinkling her nose.

"Hot tallow. They'll coat the hull with it, make her watertight again."

Lilah watched for a minute or two, then looked at Joss again. "Shouldn't we go down and tell them we're here?"

His eyes ran over her face, down over her

body, whose feminine curves and hollows were clearly delineated by the wet-through dress. He shook his head.

"I think we'd better keep an eye on them for a while first. If the whole crew of them decided to take a fancy to you, there wouldn't be much I could do to stop them."

His eyes ran over her again. Looking down at herself, at the full mounds of her breasts pressing wantonly against the cloth, at her nipples clearly visible as the wet friction of the cloth rendered them hard as buttons, at the transparent nature of the skirt, which had never been intended to be worn without a petticoat around her legs, Lilah blushed. When it was just herself and Joss, she had not worried about her state of undress. But at the thought of so many strangers seeing her like this, her cheeks burned.

"My dress will be dry in an hour or so."

He shook his head. "Wet or dry, you'd be too much of a temptation. They don't strike me as a simple crew of honest sailors."

Her brow wrinkled. "What else could they be?"

"Pirates. An honest ship would not be likely to do their careen on a deserted island in the middle of nowhere. Not when there are livelier ports around."

"But . . ."

At that moment a woman screamed, the sound high and shrill and frantic.

Lilah looked down the beach to see a woman running, her black skirts and equally black hair flying behind her. Chasing her was a man with a red kerchief tied over his head, his chest bare except for a leather strap cutting across it that might have held a sheath for a knife. As Lilah watched, wide-eyed, he caught the woman by the ends of her long hair and jerked, tumbling her to the ground. As she hit the ground she rolled onto her back, her hands going up as if to ward off the man, though the gesture was useless. He fell on top of her, and as she screamed again Lilah saw that he was pulling up her skirt and fumbling with his own breeches. Lilah's eyes widened as the man's thin white rump was revealed to her view. It settled into position between the woman's bare thrashing legs, and began to move.

"You don't need to watch that," Joss said roughly, catching her by the shoulders and pulling her around and into his arms so that her face was pressed against his chest.

"But we have to help her!"

"What do you propose we do, run down there and punch him in the nose? We're unarmed, remember? And you are a far more fetching package than that poor woman down there."

"Oh, dear God!" The thought that she might suffer the same degradation as was being visited on that woman had not even occurred to her.

"Come on, I've seen all I need to."

Joss's expression was grim as he led her away from the cliff. He kept her hand in his, and Lilah followed him meekly, shocked by what she had seen. If she had followed her original impulse and shouted out from the pool when she'd first heard voices, she might very well have shared that unfortunate woman's fate. That Joss would have fought to the death to protect her she had not a single doubt, but he was only one man and unarmed. If not for his caution, he would very likely have lost his own life and she would even now be worse than dead.

They'd been lucky. She'd been lucky. For the time being.

But a serpent had invaded their small paradise. The island was tiny, and the chances of their being found by the intruders were good. They would have to hide until the ship had finished with its careen and left.

The taste of danger was bitter in her mouth.

Twenty-eight

By nightfall they had removed every trace of their presence from the beach. Joss had even swept away their footprints. If anyone came looking, there'd be nothing to indicate that the two of them had ever been on the island.

Their new shelter, a small hut that Joss constructed out of palm fronds and vines, was hidden behind a wide, flowering snow-on-the-mountain tree and the huge, half-rotted trunk of a tamarind. Unless someone stumbled right over it, the low hut was almost impossible to distinguish from the rest of the undergrowth around it.

They had an ample supply of coconuts, and fresh water fetched from the firewater pool and stored in empty shells. There was no reason for them to leave the protection of the rain forest, not even to fish or catch crabs. On the white sandy beaches, they would be all too visible to chance passersby.

With the coming of night could be heard strange rustlings from the forest floor. Lilah and Joss looked at one another, then turned and crawled into the hut as one.

It was not much bigger than the last one he had built, but the bedding he had piled on the ground was thicker and more comfortable. With Lilah's petticoat spread over it, it made a very adequate bed. Once inside, Joss stretched out flat on his back and Lilah curled naturally against him, her head on his shoulder and her arm curved cross his chest. Her fingers idly stroked the silky hairs beneath them, but at the moment she was not really aware of what she was doing.

"I keep thinking about that poor woman," she said into the darkness, and shuddered.

"There's nothing we can do for her, so you may as well try to put her out of your mind." His voice was soft but grim.

"Where — how do you suppose they got hold of her?"

"I don't know. Maybe she was a passenger on a ship they attacked."

Lilah was silent for a while. From outside could be heard the sounds of the wind blowing through the trees and the calls and shrieks and rustlings of the island's nocturnal creatures as they went about their business. The inside of the hut was so dark that she could not even see her hand as it rested against Joss's chest, or the gleam of his eyes.

"Do you think they'll find us?"

"I don't know. I doubt it. Why should they? They're not looking for us; they don't even know we're on the island."

"That's true." The thought was comforting. "How long does a careen usually take?"

"It depends on the crew. Not more than a week. From their progress I'd guess they've already been at it for at least two or three days."

"Maybe that was the ship we saw!" At the notion that they might actually have succeeded in attracting the pirates' attention, Lilah shuddered.

"Maybe."

"Joss?"

"Mmmm?"

"We may not have very long together."

"No."

"The pirates could find us. Even if they don't, another ship could stop here if they did. At any time."

"Yes."

"Whatever happens, there's something I want you to know. I — I love you."

A long silence greeted this gift that she had expected him to return with delight. Lilah lifted her head and tried to read his expression, but the darkness was so thick and so all-enveloping that it was impossible for her to see anything.

"Joss?"

"What?"

"Aren't you going to say anything?" She almost whispered the words.

"What do you want me to say?"

"What do I want you to say?" Lilah sat up, suddenly angry. "What do I want you to say!" she sputtered as she repeated it for the second time.

"You want me to say that I love you, too, I take it. If I do, what good will it do me? You've already made it quite clear that you're in the market for a lover while we're on the island. Once we're rescued, I won't be good enough to kiss the hem of your skirt, much less your mouth. You'll take a husband like your precious Kevin, and he'll sleep in your bed and put his hands on your white skin and give you children. But you know what?"

She didn't say anything, shocked at this sudden bitter outpouring.

"You won't ever again in your life feel with any man what you feel with me. Do you know how rare what we have is? Hell, no, of course you don't! You say you love me, Lilah, but I don't think you even know what that means!"

"I do! And I do love you. But —"

"The bloody hell you do! There are no 'buts' when you love someone!"

With that he jackknifed upright and crawled from the hut.

"Joss!" Lilah was right behind him, hurt and frightened by his sudden fierce anger. He got to his feet outside where it was light enough that she could at least see him. He stood with his back to her, his arms crossed over his chest, his legs braced slightly apart. Lilah looked at that broad muscular back, the set of that black head, and felt her throat tighten.

"I do love you, Joss," she said pitifully, and coming up behind him stroked soft fingers along his shoulder. He stood there, rigid, for just a moment, then as she stroked him again he turned on her with an expression so hard that she was momentarily frightened.

"You don't," he said through his teeth, his hands coming out to catch her by the shoulders. "You just think you do. You think you can play at loving me for a little while, then when we're rescued your life can resume along the nice smooth path you have mapped out for it. Well, that won't work, my dear. We've come too far for that, you and I."

His hands tightened on her shoulders, and he pulled her against him, his eyes glittering down into her face.

"By God, you will love me," he said, then bent his head to take her mouth.

Twenty-nine

His mouth slanted over hers brutally, hurting her, making her gasp out a protest against his bruising lips. He paid no heed to her cry, forcing her back over his arm so that her head was wedged against the unyielding strength of his shoulder. His arms around her were like steel bands, holding her so tightly that she could scarcely breathe. She had to clutch at his shoulder with the hand that was not trapped between them or lose her balance entirely. The heat of that satin-sheathed muscle seared her palm.

The fury of his kiss forced open her mouth. His tongue penetrated deep inside with none of the gentle wooing he had shown her earlier. He took her mouth, forced it to his will, used it ruthlessly. His tongue met the feeble protest of hers and conquered it without mercy. Then he staked his claim to the whole of the warm wet cave with a ferocity that made her tremble. The violence of the sexuality he had so suddenly unleashed frightened her. Clutching him, suffering that savage kiss, Lilah felt the world spin around her and feared she might swoon. Then he shifted his hold on her, loosening his fierce grip by the merest of degrees so that she was again able to get her breath.

His hand closed over her left breast.

Lilah gasped and started, feeling the heat and strength of that hand burn clear through the thin material of her dress and chemise to her skin. Her nipple puckered, hardened against his palm, sending a shaft of pure fire straight to her loins. The sensation was like nothing she had ever experienced. Her eyes flew open. Instinctively she fought to free herself.

His kiss deepened savagely, and his hand remained on her breast, caressing her, searing her skin like a brand. Her eyes fluttered shut and she moaned, no longer struggling to get free. Her nails curled into the flesh of his shoulder, but not in punishment.

His hand moved upward to the satiny arch of her neck. He stroked the bare skin, then, without warning, slid his hand down. His fingers thrust inside her bodice, and the much-put-upon muslin gave with a soft ripping sound. His hand closed over her soft breast, and Lilah cried out as her knees gave way.

He caught her, lowering her with utmost

gentleness to the ground. She lay quivering, helpless to do anything but stare up at him through the shifting darkness as he knelt wordlessly beside her, his hands sliding behind her back to find the buttons to her gown. He undid one, then another, then a third, quickly, efficiently, with a controlled savagery that made her heart shiver in her breast. Even if she had wanted to protest, she could not have. She was incapable of making a sound, incapable of making a move to help or hinder him. Her blood boiled within her, her limbs trembled, and a fierce need built up inside her to match the savage hunger she read in his face.

Whatever he was going to do to her, however he was going to do it, she wanted it. She wanted him. She felt as if she could die from the wanting.

He had her dress unbuttoned and pulled it down to her waist, not bothering to first free her arms from her sleeves. The unfastened bodice bound her elbows to her sides, increasing the sense of helplessness that both frightened and thrilled her.

Beneath the dress she wore only her chemise. The thinness of the primly pin-tucked garment provided scarcely more than a tantalizing veil over the nakedness of her breasts. As her nipples thrust against the white cloth, Joss growled under his breath. Then he reached out with fingers that suddenly were less than steady to yank her chemise down to just beneath her breasts, baring the satiny white globes to his touch and view.

For a long moment he stared without moving, the shifting moonlight behind him casting his head in dark silhouette and making it impossible for Lilah to read the expression on his face. As he looked down at her she felt her breasts swell and tighten, causing an ache inside her that was both pleasure and pain. The sudden quickening in her loins drew a soft, wordless murmur from her. In an instinctive movement as old as woman, her back arched and she offered her breasts to him. He sucked in his breath, the sound ragged and harsh. Then, the movement so swift it startled her, he was coming down on top of her, lying on her, his weight crushing her into the thick dusty carpet of vines and mulch and leaves. There was a rock beneath her spine and she shifted her hips to get away from it.

The movement seemed to inflame him. His arms wrapped around her back, crushing her to him. His mouth closed over hers, and he kissed her with a fierceness that drew a small impassioned cry from her. The wiry mat of hair on his chest was abrasive against her breasts. They burned, and she trembled violently. He must have felt her response because all his muscles hardened. For just a moment he went rigid, then reached down for her skirt with both hands, jerking it up until it was wadded around her waist. She was left naked from the waist down while he moved atop her, still clad in the coarse black breeches. Lilah barely had time to register the feel of him against her before he was wedging a thigh between her legs, fumbling with the buttons on his breeches at the same time. Before she knew what was happening he was shoving himself against her, inside her. She murmured a small protest, moving her head from side to side, writhing as she sought to escape this sudden unexpected discomfort. But with her arms pinioned by her bodice and her legs spread wide by his thighs, escape was impossible. He thrust against her, hurting her. Even as she cried out he was thrusting again, breaking through the barrier, burying himself deep inside.

The pain was startling, knifelike in its intensity. Lilah screamed, the sound swallowed up by his mouth. Then he moved again, convulsively, stretching her, filling her. Through the pain she felt him, huge and hot and moving inside her, and all at once she forgot the pain, forgot everything but the exquisite pleasure that swept away all before it.

He thrust again, so deep this time that she feared being split in two. She gasped, her hips grinding against his in his urgent, instinctive response. The wonderful quickening inside her exploded, splintering into a shimmering whirlwind of shapes and textures and colors. Lilah cried out, quivering. Joss cried out too, thrusting one final time before wrapping his arms tight around her and holding himself deep inside her.

For a few moments afterwards they lay unmoving, entwined together, collecting their thoughts along with their breath. Then without warning Joss stiffened, lifting himself partially off her. His face was deep in shadows, the moon a silvery glow high overhead. Lilah could not decipher his expression, did not even try to. She did not speak either, but looked up at him in a sort of dreamy wonder that was beyond words. Her eyes were shining softly as they moved over his face. One slender hand came up to touch, slide down over his tensed forearm.

At that small touch Joss swore, the words harsh and shockingly profane. He rolled off her and got to his feet. Lilah struggled up on her elbows, calling out to him as he strode off into the darkness of the forest, barely taking time to yank his breeches up around his waist as he disappeared into the night.

Thirty

Joss was swimming, as Lilah had assumed he would be. She felt a small measure of relief as she found his breeches discarded on the beach, then spotted that seal-black head slicing through the glimmering green phosphorescence that sparkled in the moonlight over the bay. He was angry, that much she knew from the abrupt way he'd left her, but whether with her or himself she could not guess. What had happened between them had been violent and primitive, the product of desire ignited by rage. If he had not been blazingly furious with her, he would not have lost that iron control and taken her as he had sworn not to do. How he must despise himself now! He had no way of knowing that she had gloried in his fierce possession.

Well, she would tell him.

A small smile played around her lips as Lilah found the same rock on which she had waited for him before and curled up on it to wait again.

The sliver of moon washed the beach and

the bay in iridescent shades of silver and midnight blue. A warm wind faintly scented with salt blew in off the sea. The muted rush of the waves and the rustling of the wind through the trees some yards behind her were the only sounds beside her own breathing. Nothing stirred along the beach. Even the gulls had settled down to sleep, and the crabs had disappeared into their holes for the night. Lilah hugged her knees to her chin and waited, her hair blowing in shimmering billows around her face.

When at last she saw him walking out of the sea her heartbeat speeded up. As the dark water fell away from his waist, his thighs, his calves, until he was wading ankle deep, she stared at him wide-eyed. He was beautiful, broad-shouldered and lean-flanked, the muscles of his arms and thighs rippled as he moved. His black hair was slicked back from his head to fall in a tangle of wet curls around his neck. His skin was pale in the moonlight, with only the shadows of his black body hair to darken his chest and the soft nest between his thighs. In the darkness, she could barely make out the thing that had invaded her body, first hurting her and then giving her so much pleasure that she felt a quickening just remembering it.

At that distance his features were indistinct, but there was no mistaking the sudden tensing of his body as he saw her. He braced himself as if for blow or battle. He moved stiffly toward her. Finally, when he was perhaps six feet away, he stopped and folded his arms over his chest. Unlike the first time she had surprised him when he was swimming, he appeared oblivious now to his nakedness. He stood bold as a pagan before her, making no attempt to protect either her modesty or his own. Unbidden, Lilah's eyes swept once more over the magnificence of his body. When they returned to meet his eyes, it was to find them narrowed to forbidding slits of emerald green.

Though she felt a wash of color stain her cheeks, Lilah managed to meet his eyes without faltering. After a moment a corner of his mouth quirked downward, and his eyes shifted away from hers to flit restlessly over the beach beyond where she sat.

"Lilah." His voice as it at last broke the silence was gruff. His eyes came back to meet hers, and she saw a faint trace of something in them that made her heartbeat quicken. "I hurt you, and I never meant to. For that, if nothing else, I'm more sorry than I can say."

Lilah gazed at him without speaking, weighing the words and the tone in which they were uttered. The oddly formal apology was at odds with the harshness of his voice. He spoke as if it hurt him to do so. . . .

Still without speaking, Lilah got to her feet. The fine, dry sand was warm and comforting. She curled her toes in it. The wind caught her hair and blew it around her face. Lifting a hand to catch the wayward strands, she fixed her eyes on him. He looked away from her again.

"You didn't hurt me. At least, not very much, and not for very long," she finally said, her voice soft. That brought his eyes back to narrow on her face. Lilah saw that he was taut with tension. He was frowning, and his lips were clamped together.

"I was angry." The explanation, if explanation it was, was abrupt. The guilt was well hidden, but she who knew him well heard it for what it was. He regretted what he had done, regretted it bitterly, while she . . .

Lilah looked at him consideringly. He had closed himself off from her. Words of forgiveness or even love would not reach him. In his mind he had violated his own code of honor, violated her innocence however much she might have wanted it.

Searching for words that would both ease his guilt and let him know just how very un-sorry she was over the loss of her virginity, she could come up with nothing.

Instinct saved her. Suddenly, from somewhere deep inside her, came the intuitive knowledge of the one answer that would get through to him. Instead of speaking with words, Lilah reached behind her back to the buttons she had managed to fasten again only after much effort.

"What the devil are you doing?" His voice was hoarse, his stare disbelieving. Lilah pushed the dress down over her hips and stepped out of it, her eyes never leaving him.

"What does it look like?"

He watched her warily as she stood before him clad only in her chemise. As his eyes moved almost unwillingly over the slender curves of her body, down the length of her bare legs silvered by the moonlight, Lilah looked back at him gravely. When he again met her eyes, she managed a small, nervous smile.

"Lilah —" His voice broke off as she caught her chemise by the hem and pulled it over her head in a single fluid motion. For just an instant she held the garment before her, shielding her nakedness from his view. Then her fingers unclenched and it too dropped to the sand. She was as naked as he, fine-boned and exquisitely lovely against the background of pale sand and dark star-strewn sky. The shimmery ashen strands of her hair reached to her thighs, providing the lightest of teasing veils. Through it her nipples peeked, dark and proud against the creamy whiteness of her breasts. The shifting veil revealed tantalizing glimpses of the supple curves of waist and hips, and the tawny triangle of hair at the apex of her thighs.

Joss stared as if mesmerized. His eyes darkened, glittered. His mouth tightened. He neither spoke nor moved, just stared while Lilah stood motionless before him, waiting, her heart pounding like a kettledrum in her ears.

At last it became obvious that he was not going to do or say anything to make this easy for her. Whatever happened next was up to her.

Lifting her chin, she moved slowly and steadily across the few feet of sand that separated them. She felt no shame. Instinct more powerful than reason whispered that what she was doing was right. He had made her truly a woman, his woman, and no matter what might come to them in the future, that could never be taken from her. She would have the memory of this moon-washed night safe inside her, to pull out and relive if real life became too gray and dull. Though they might part physically she would carry the brand of his touch imprinted on her mind and heart and body forever. He had made her senses come alive, had awakened a wellspring of physical hunger deep inside her, that she had never even guessed existed. He had made her want him before she ever really knew what wanting was. Well, now she knew. And she still wanted him. Her body burned with the wanting.

When she was less than an arm's length away from him, she stopped. Still he made no move to touch her, said no word to encourage her. His face was set and hard, his mouth an unyielding line. Lilah looked into those green eyes, and felt a shiver run clear down through her soul. She felt as if she were being bewitched, by the man and the moonlight and her own hungry body.

"Joss," she said softly, breaking off as her voice deteriorated into a husky rasp. His eyes flickered, and the muscles around his mouth tightened. Lilah put out her tongue to wet her lips, then tried again.

"I want you to — be my lover. Please." Her voice was so low by the time she got out the last word that it was scarcely audible above the murmur of the surf. He stared at her a moment longer, his eyes taking on a glint that was bitter and hungry at the same time. Then he reached for her, his movement violent. His hands caught her by the upper arms, and he pulled her the few steps necessary to bring her close. Still he did not pull her right against him, but held her a little away, so that she could sense more than feel the heat of his body. She looked up at him, her eyes wide and smoky, her lips softly sensual. His eyes blazed down at her. Lilah was suddenly aware that she could see the pulse in his throat pounding through his sun-bronzed skin.

"You are a witch and I'm a damned fool," he muttered, but even as he said the words he was jerking her hard against him, his mouth coming down on hers as if he could deny himself no longer.

His mouth was hard and hot and hungry as she opened hers to it with matching desire. Her hands slid up the hard muscles of his arms, stroked his shoulders, closed behind his neck. She kissed him as if she'd die if she didn't, pressing close against him, glorying in the feel of his hard male body against hers.

When he pulled her up on tiptoe, she twined her arms tighter around his neck, her fingers curving into his hair, her thighs throbbing against his. His hand found her bare breast and her knees gave. This time he sank with her, following her down to the sand, covering her body with his as she melted onto her back. This time there was no violence, only mutual, urgent need. She spread her legs and her back arched as she waited in trembling anticipation for the flaming torch of his entry. But he held himself back, poised just on the brink, and lifted his head so that he could look down at her. Those green eyes blazed clear through to her soul.

"Now tell me," he muttered between gritted teeth.

"What?"

"That you love me."

She smiled at him, a tiny smile made tremulous by passion. His arms tightened around her, but still he held himself back, waiting for the words he wanted.

"I love you."

"Joss," he prompted, the word a growl.

"I love you, Joss," she whispered obediently, and his eyes glittered with a fierce kind of satisfaction. Then he entered her and it was wonderful, glorious, a mating born more of heaven than of earth. Lilah took and took and gave and gave, gasping and panting and finally sobbing with ecstasy as he showed her how the act of love was meant to be between a man and a woman. When it was over, when he rested quietly atop her, she was smiling dreamily as she stroked the silken back of his head, the sweat-damp skin of his shoulders.

After a while he propped himself up on his elbows to look at her, a considering expression on his face.

"There's no taking it back, you know. Whatever happens."

"I don't want to take it back."

"You gave yourself to me. You're mine now, and your bloody precious Keith can go whistle himself up another fiancée." His eyes were brilliantly green in the otherworldly light as they fixed on her face.

"Mmm. I love being yours." That sensuous response, coupled as it was by her hands stroking over his broad shoulders, seemed to satisfy him. She saw no point in pointing out that his name was Kevin, he was likely drowned, and that whether he was or wasn't, the gulfs between herself and Joss were still as enormous as ever. Not tonight. Tonight was special, a magic few hours out of reality. Besides, it was always possible that they would never get off the island, that they would live out the rest of their days here, marooned together. It was amazing just how appealing that idea suddenly seemed.

His face relaxed, and he rolled off her. She curled cozily against his side, her head pillowed on his shoulder. One arm rested on his flat, furred belly. Her fingers busied themselves by walking through the soft wedge of curly black hair that stretched across his chest. They marched down the line of his ribs, across the ridged hardness of his abdomen, found his belly button and dipped teasingly inside. When that provoked no response other than a slight flicker of his eyelids she delicately tickled his belly.

That broke through his pensive inattention at last. He shifted sideways slightly to escape her mischievous ministrations even as he grunted a protest. She followed, tickling his side this time, and he caught her hand. His slow-dawning grin earned him an answering smile and a soft kiss pressed against the stubbly side of his cheek.

"If you don't watch yourself, I'll be making love to you all over again before you even have a chance to catch your breath." His eyes glinted at her threateningly.

"I'd like that." She twinkled back at him.

He laughed then, the sound a trifle rusty but definitely a laugh, and hugged her closer, her hand still safely imprisoned to prevent further assaults on his ribs. "Shameless little thing, aren't you? Whoever would have guessed it?"

Lilah looked up from her interested inspection of his chest to frown at him. His words caught her by surprise, stung. It was a moment before she spoke, and when she did her voice was low.

"Joss, am I truly — shameless? Aren't . . . well, most ladies like me? When it comes to — to . . ." She broke off, her eyes troubled.

"No, my darling, most ladies are definitely not like you. In my experience, most *females* are not like you. From ladies to whores."

"Oh." Her voice was very small, and she felt a sickening wave of humiliation. She had been too bold, too frank in her enjoyment of him. He must think her wanton. . . .

Joss saw the look on her face, and quickly scooped her up and rolled with her so that he was on his back and she sprawled on top of him. His hands cupped her bottom, his fingers lightly stroking the soft, rounded flesh.

"No, most women are not like you," he said again, holding her in place when she would have wriggled off him to find a more dignified posture. "You've been given the gift of passion, and I thank God for it. It's a rare gift in females, precious and beyond price."

"Truly?" she asked, her eyes still faintly troubled.

"Truly," he answered gravely, then he pulled her face down to his.

His mouth was warm and gentle and softly persuasive. He held his passion in check, letting her set the pace of the kiss. She grew bolder, her tongue urging his into playful battle.

When at last she lifted her head his eyes were turbulent with passion. Lilah smiled into them, feeling a drowsy heat spiral through her loins. But when she would have bent her head to kiss him again, he eluded her with a shake of his head, his hands catching her shoulders and pushing her upright. As she obediently sat up his hands slid down the front of her body, moving intimately over her breasts and belly and the soft thatch of hair between her legs. Then he showed her how to straddle him.

With her hands resting on his chest for balance, Lilah frowned down at him, confused. Was this his way of putting a brake on their passion? Perhaps men could only pleasure females once or twice before needing a rest? She realized anew how very little she knew of men.

"If you're tired . . ."

Her words were hesitant, wanting to offer him a way out without damaging his male pride, which she knew from hearsay was very sensitive in this area. He looked up at her then, shifting his eyes from their interested study of her body. The heat in his eyes was only intensified by the slight smile that quirked his lips at her words.

"Not yet," he said, the words husky even as his smile broadened until it was a lopsided grin. "We've hardly gotten started. You've still got lots to learn. If we're going to be lovers, you need to know what I like."

"What you like?" He sounded as if he were a gourmet at a feast, choosily selecting his menu. Surely there was not more than one way to perform the physical act. He must mean something else. . . .

"Mm-hm. For example, sometimes I like to see you — all of you — when we make love. So every once in a while I'll want you to be on top — just like this. So I can see your beautiful breasts. . . ." As he spoke he reached up to cup them. Lilah's lips parted slightly as he seemed to weigh them, then ran his thumbs teasingly across her nipples. Shafts of pure fire shot through her.

"Joss. . . ." His name as she moaned it was half protest, half pleasured cry.

He abandoned her breasts to slide his hands over her ribcage, over her small waist and the delicate curve of her hips, over the slight roundness of her belly. Heat followed in the wake of his touch, melting her bones until all she wanted was to collapse on top of him and have him make the exquisite ache he had caused inside her go away.

Although Lilah had often, guiltily, tried to imagine what it would be like to perform the marriage act with a man, in her wildest imaginings she would never have pictured this: herself naked, slender and pale and washed by moonlight, sitting on her lover's chest as he lay sprawled in the sand as naked as she, the wind blowing her hair in a silvery cloud around them both and the night enclosing them in a cocoon of mystery. It was something out of a dream, though she would never have dreamed of such a thing. Her dreams of love were gentle things, as sheltered and innocent as she had been herself. If she had lived a thousand years her dreams would never have included anything like this pagan lovemaking.

Not before tonight.

She gasped as the warm strength of his hands touched her knees, slid from them up the silk of her inner thighs. She froze as exploring fingers found her soft nest of hair, stroked over it softly, burrowed to discover secret wellsprings of passion that Lilah had not even guessed she possessed. As his fingers pressed against her she cried out, moved, her head falling forward and her eyes closing at the intensity of her desire. Only her hands braced against his chest kept her from collapsing.

"Now I want you to love me."

His husky whisper came as she was on the verge of falling into the vortex that awaited her. Lilah's head lifted and her eyes struggled open as she tried to make sense of what he had said. He must have seen the incomprehension in her eyes, because his fingers pressed against her one last time before his hands moved to her hips, lifting her bodily away from his chest and lowering her carefully onto him. Lilah gasped as she felt the fiery heat probing against her. Then he was inside the first little bit and his hands on her hips were tugging her down, down until he filled her and she was squirming against the hugeness of him.

"Love me," he muttered again, the words thick. His eyes were glazed, his face flushed with passion. The muscles of his arms and chest stood out in corded relief beneath his bronzed skin as he fought to keep himself in control so that she could set the pace. Gasping, Lilah did as he asked, clutching his wrists as with his hands he guided her hips in the motion he sought. When she had learned the motion to his satisfaction he released her hips to find her breasts.

Lilah cried out as his hands closed over them.

As if that small sound had snapped something inside him, he groaned and pulled her down to him so that he could take her breasts in his mouth. He suckled with savage hunger, his hands hard and hot on the silken roundness of her bottom as he held her still above him and ground himself upwards into her. Helpless to do anything but respond, Lilah gave herself over to the fierceness of his passion. Finally with a hoarse cry he clutched her close, trembling in her arms. As he held himself inside her she cried out too, swept away on that firestorm of passion that had claimed her before.

Then at last they lay quietly in each other's arms, quivering with exhaustion and sated passion. The warm breath of the wind caressed them, the moonlit stillness of the beach stretched all around them, the surf rolled in to kiss the shore in a gentle rhythm. But the two entwined together in the sand were aware of nothing beyond themselves.

Caught up in the drugging aftermath of passion, they slept.

Thirty-one

Rough hands grabbing her beneath her armpits and dragging her out of the warm cocoon in which she slept woke Lilah. She had a single shocked instant to register that it was no longer night but dawn. Pink and purple pinwheels spiralled out from the pale yellow sun just peeking over the eastern horizon. The tide lapped far up the beach, dangerously close to where she had been lying, narrowing the strip of sand to a width of less than a dozen yards.

Then in the same instant she realized that she had been sleeping in Joss's arms on the beach, and she was now being dragged away from him, her bare skin scraping over the gritty sand. A grinning, dirty-looking man in a scarlet shirt and black breeches whom she immediately took for one of the pirates stood with his bare foot on Joss's shoulder, aiming a pistol point-blank at his face.

Joss, too, seemed stunned by what was happening. As Lilah looked on in horror, Joss's head rose an inch or two from the sand, swivelled in her direction. The pirate holding the pistol said something, cocked the pistol, and Joss's eyes swung back to the pistol and the man who held it. Joss froze, every muscle in his body seeming to tense. The pirate's grin broadened. His finger seemed to tighten on the trigger. . . .

Lilah then understood that the hands holding her belonged to another pirate, one with a lush red beard and a missing front tooth, who was leering at her nakedness as he dragged her farther along the beach. Lilah had no doubt that in a matter of seconds the pistol in the hand of the first pirate would explode, Joss would be killed, and she would be brutally raped by one and possibly both men.

The reality of what was happening sank in at last and she screamed.

The sound was as loud and shrill as a steam whistle. The man dragging her jumped and cursed, kicking her in the back with his bare foot. Lilah barely felt the blow as she struggled to escape his hold. Her scream had apparently distracted for a vital instant the pirate bent on murdering Joss. Even as she fought to break free of her captor, she was aware of Joss's hand closing over the hand holding the gun, of the pirate who had threatened him twisting through the air. . . . Suddenly there was an explosion, and then she was free. The red-bearded man abandoned the fight and took to his heels as Joss came running toward them. The other pirate lay motionless in the sand. Lilah sank to her knees, shaking. After a single glance at her that seemed to register in a millisecond that she was unharmed, Joss chased the red-bearded man along the beach and into the forest. And it was then that Lilah thought that even if Joss caught and killed the other man, the pirates would certainly miss two of their number. They would come looking for their crew-mates. More pirates might even at that moment be watching her.

Eyes wide, Lilah looked around, fear causing a sour taste in her mouth.

Except for the dead man, the beach was deserted. She was alone. At least, she seemed to be alone.

Her eyes scanned the forest. If they were watching her, they would come out. They had no need to fear a lone woman. On the contrary. . . .

The memory of the fate that had befallen that other woman taken prisoner by the pirates flashed into her mind as vividly as if it was happening before her eyes at that very moment. Lilah shuddered.

She was naked. Her eyes swept the beach for her clothes.

Funny how different everything looked in the brightening light of dawn. Some half-dozen yards away, just beyond the dead man, loomed the rock from which she had watched Joss swim. The tide had almost reached it. Her dress lay in its lee.

Whatever happened, she would face it fully clad.

Barely taking time to brush the sand from her body, she shook the clothes out and pulled them on, doing up the buttons and lacings with a frantic haste slowed only by trembling fingers.

She had no sooner swept her hair out of the back of her dress than Joss emerged from the forest. Heart pounding, she ran up to him.

"He's dead."

The words were in response to the unspoken question in her eyes. Without a pause he walked past her to the other man, stared down at him for an instant, then bent and cautiously turned him over. Lilah, following, shuddered and turned away at the sight of blood oozing from where the left side of the man's face had been. Joss's shot had blown it clean away. When she looked again, it was to find that Joss had emptied the pirate's pockets and was in the process of stripping him of his breeches.

"What are you doing?" Her voice was faint.

"We need his clothes."

"Why?"

Joss looked up from what he was doing only briefly, but she saw that his eyes were dark and hard, his expression grim.

"When they find us — *if* they find us — I want them to think they've found two men. You'll be safer by far if we can keep them from guessing that you're a woman."

Thirty-two

Joss carried the body inland. With a rock, he scraped a shallow grave out of the loose undergrowth and dirt that lay beneath the wildly tangled vegetation. He repeated the exercise with the second body. Joss was quiet, grim, a far different man from the impassioned lover of the night before.

As he carried the second man through the forest Lilah followed silently, carrying the clothes and other possessions Joss had stripped from the body. When both naked corpses were covered with a thin layer of dirt, she helped Joss pile rotting vegetation on top of the graves. Finally he dragged a large, uprooted oleander to lie across the spot.

When he was finished, no one could have told that the jungle had been disturbed in any way, much less that two fresh graves had been dug. Not quite an hour had passed since Lilah had first been so rudely awakened on the beach.

"Come on, we need to hurry," Joss said at last, stopping to scoop up the pirates' belongings and tuck them under his arm before heading back toward the beach. Lilah, still practically speechless with shock, followed close behind. Joss had donned his breeches before hoisting the first body, but his chest and back were bare and streaked with dirt and sweat. The day was already starting to get hot. In the interior of the island the dense vegetation caused a steamy, hothouse atmosphere that was unpleasant. Lilah swallowed air that was as thick as pudding, and fought valiantly not to get sick.

"Do you think the rest of the crew will come looking for their shipmates?"

"Yes."

"Soon?"

"Who knows? Before nightfall, probably. How hard they look depends on who the men were, and how much they need them. If they were just two sailors who weren't much good to anyone, the crew may look for a day or two, chalk their disappearance up to the mysteries of fate, and leave."

"I hope so." Lilah's worlds were heartfelt. She and Joss reached the edge of the beach, and stopped. Joss put the bundle of clothes down, straightened, and looked at her, frowning. For his sake Lilah forced a tremulous smile. He returned her smile with one of his own, a gleam that could almost be described as tender coming to light in his eyes. Then he reached for her. One hand caught her waist, pulling her close, and the other one cupped her chin so that she was looking up at him.

"You're a female in a million, Delilah Remy. Most women would have swooned dead away long since, or treated me to a case of screaming hysterics."

"I've never had hysterics in my life." Lilah was revolted by the very idea. Joss's grin turned teasing. Some of the strain eased from his face, and Lilah felt better than she had all morning. They had faced horror and death together, and survived, thanks to Joss. He had kept her safe. So far.

"You're wonderful," she said. His eyes narrowed on her face. He bent his head to drop a quick, hard kiss on her mouth. Then he let her go, turning away with a familiar little smack on her behind.

"Enough of this. We have to do what we can to clean up the beach. Let's get to it, woman."

Lilah followed him as he stepped briskly onto the sand. Some quarter-hour later all traces of the deadly battle that had taken place on that white strip had disappeared. Joss had turned over the bloodstained sand so nothing looked unusual. Then he and

Lilah eradicated all traces of human presence from the beach by sweeping the sand with palm fronds.

"That should do it," he finally said. Lilah followed him as he headed back toward their hut, trying not to think that even now the pirates might be searching the jungle for their shipmates.

Thirty-three

To Lilah, it seemed as though centuries instead of hours had passed since she had left the small clearing in search of Joss the night before. If the snow-on-the-mountain tree had not caught her eye, Lilah would have walked right by the camp. It was comforting to realize how difficult it would be for someone who didn't have any idea of its existence to find it.

"Now for you," Joss said, dropping the bundle of clothes in front of the hut and turning to survey her with a critical eye.

"M-me?" His sudden grimness scared her all over again. It reminded her anew that they faced mortal danger. From Joss's expression, he anticipated trouble, and soon. Lilah swallowed.

"We have to transform you from the beautiful young lady that you are to a grubby youth not worth a second look. Let's see what we have to work with."

With that Joss started rifling through the pile of clothes. Two pairs of breeches, both black, the scarlet silk shirt that had been worn by the pirate who had tried to murder Joss, now stained with blotches of blood, a once-white shirt and scuffed leather boots that had belonged to red-beard, a leather pouch containing six poured-lead bullets, flint and steel and some chewing tobacco, a pistol and a sheathed knife were the sum total of the booty. Joss loaded the pistol, stuck it in the waistband of his breeches, and stood up, holding the smaller pair of breeches in one hand.

"Take off your clothes," he instructed. "We're going to try to turn you into a boy."

He was frowning at her impatiently as he waited for her to obey. Staring back at him, Lilah felt a sudden surge of shyness. To undress in front of him in broad daylight was something totally different from her bold seduction of him by the light of the moon. She couldn't just . . . strip off her clothes while he watched.

"Turn your back."

He looked at her for a moment as if he couldn't believe his ears.

"You're joking."

"No. Turn your back." Her expression was as stubborn as she felt.

"Lilah . . ."

Whatever argument he had been going to

make he gave up on. Throwing up his hands in a silent gesture of defeat, Joss tossed her the breeches, then turned his back.

Wrinkling her nose, she stepped into the filthy breeches. They were miles too big, and if she hadn't kept a tight grip on the waistband they would have immediately fallen around her ankles.

"What about a shirt?"

"The white one. The red's too fancy, too easily remembered. We don't want anyone connecting these clothes with their original owners."

Lilah silently agreed. She also did not want to wear a garment that was still wet with its previous owner's blood. Picking up the specified shirt, she closed her eyes to its grimy state and tried to close her nose to its smell as she pulled it on over her chemise. Ignoring the smell proved impossible. It was a combination of fish and sweat and other things that were too horrible to contemplate.

"All right. You can turn around now."

Joss turned, looked at her once, grinned at her expression of acute distaste. Then he studied her again, more slowly, and frowned.

"Well?" She cocked her head to one side, regarding him anxiously. The long spill of her white-blonde hair swung around to cascade over one shoulder. Her eyes were huge pools of gray-blue in the delicate oval of her face. The skin of her face and neck was white and satiny smooth as it stretched across her high cheekbones and fragile jawline. Within the open collar of the filthy shirt her collarbone was visible. Despite the hugeness of the oversized shirt, her breasts still thrust provocatively forth. Of her waist and hips nothing was evident. The breeches were so large on her that she was forced to hold them up with one hand.

Joss groaned. "If I ever saw anyone look less like a male, I can't remember it."

"The breeches are too big, but if I tied them up with something and wore a kerchief over my hair, don't you think I could pass?"

"At midnight if you stumbled across a blind man, maybe. Hell, let's try it. You couldn't look any more female than you do right now unless you ran around without your clothes."

He picked up the second pair of breeches and slit them with a knife. Ripping three long strips from the cloth, he knotted them to form a single strip.

"Tuck the shirt in."

She did as he told her, then he wrapped the strip of cloth around her waist and tied it in a knot. Cautiously she let go of the breeches; they now stayed up. Encouraged, she looked up at him hopefully.

"Better?"

He rolled his eyes skyward in an expression of utter defeat.

"What's wrong now?" Her fists rested on her hips as she stared at him narrow-eyed. His pessimism about her chances of passing for a male was beginning to annoy her. The least he could do was be encouraging. She was doing everything she could to please him.

"Sweetheart, you are simply too . . . too —" His hands made a gesture in front of his chest that indicated that her front had too much curve to it. "What are you wearing under that shirt?"

"My chemise."

"Take it off. Maybe that will help. Something bloody well has to!"

Lilah hesitated a moment, then nodded. "All right. But turn around again, please."

"Oh, for God's sake . . . !"

He bit off the rest, and spun around. Lilah could tell from the set of his broad shoulders that her insistence on a modicum of modesty was beginning to irk him.

She slipped out of the shirt, then pulled the chemise over her head and dropped it on the ground. The idea of putting the filthy shirt next to her bare skin was unappealing, but there was no help for it. Buttoning it up, she told Joss she was now decent.

He told one look at her and shook his head.

"No better?"

"Worse, if anything. You're simply too female."

"Well, I beg your pardon." Lilah was beginning to feel more than a little out of sorts. "I can't help it, you know."

"Don't get mad now. God graced you with a luscious figure and I'm thankful for it. But at the moment it presents a problem. We'll come about. It just needs . . . something. . . ."

His voice broke off, and he turned away to cross to the hut. Lilah watched with some suspicion as he disappeared inside. Whatever his idea was, she was quite sure she was not going to like it. Her guess was confirmed when he emerged with her petticoat, which he proceeded to slit and rip into strips as he had the breeches.

"What are you doing?" Over the course of their sojourn on the island, she had come to value the garment highly. It was supremely useful in a variety of ways, it was in one piece, and it was hers. Joss had better have a good reason for inflicting mayhem upon it.

"Binding's what we need, I think," he said, not even looking at her as he blithely continued to tear the garment into strips.

"Binding?" Lilah lowered her hands, frowned, and considered. "Binding?" Her voice rose to a squeak.

"That's what I said. Take off the shirt. And don't give me any more of that 'turn your back' nonsense. It's ridiculous, I won't do it, and in any case you've far more to worry about at the moment than misguided attempts at maintaining a ladylike modesty."

"You —"

"Take off that damned shirt!" he roared.

Lilah jumped. Hearing Joss shout was such a novelty that she was taken by surprise. For just a moment she gaped at him, but at the emerald glare that met her stare she turned her back and meekly started to unbutton her shirt.

Even as she was undoing the last button he was pulling it impatiently from her shoulders. Cheeks flushing hotly, Lilah covered herself with her hands as he turned her around. Despite everything that had passed between them, she could not control the blush that suffused her cheeks as he looked down at her breasts. Her hands spread over them seemed a very inadequate protection for her modesty. If anything, they only seemed to emphasize her nakedness.

"Lilah." The single word, uttered in a soft, compelling voice, brought her eyes up to meet his. Her blush deepened, heated. Her lashes fluttered down to cover her eyes on the ridiculous hope that if she couldn't see him, he couldn't see her.

"Stop being so idiotic, will you please?" At these distinctly unloverlike words, Lilah stiffened and her eyes flew open. Her cheeks were still flushed the same hectic wild rose, but as she met his steady gaze some of her embarrassment faded. When he reached for her wrists she allowed him to pull her hands away and then, when he let go, kept them at her sides. Chin high, she stood before him without flinching, bare to the waist. He smiled faintly at her, then looked at her breasts and frowned in concentration. Only the deepening color of his eyes told her that her nakedness affected him in any way.

"If you'll hold your arms out to your sides, we'll see what can be done."

Lilah did as he instructed. Joss then took the torn strips of petticoat and wrapped them around her chest, trussing her up like a mummy and flattening her generous curves.

"It's too tight! It hurts!" she protested as he jerked the two remaining ends into a hard knot at the back. "Ouch! Can't you make it a little looser? Please?"

"Let's see how it looks," he said, ignoring her plea as he picked the shirt up from the ground and handed it to her.

Shifting uncomfortably as she tried to ease the pressure of the bandage around her breasts — to no avail — Lilah pulled on the shirt and buttoned it with many an uncomplimentary mutter. Joss stood a few feet away, regarding her critically.

"Well?"

After a long moment he nodded grudgingly. "Not good, but . . . better. Now twist your hair up on top of your head."

Lilah held her hair up while he ripped a large triangle from the seat of the breeches and wrapped it around her head bandanna-style. He tied the coarse black material so low over her forehead that it nearly obscured her vision, then tucked it in the back so that it completely hid her hair. When he was done, he stepped back and inspected her. Finally he shook his head with evident disgust.

"Maybe they won't find us, and we won't have to worry about how I look," Lilah offered hopefully, discouraged by this latest evidence of failure in her disguise.

"We can't take that chance," he said, his eyes moving over her with disconcerting slowness. Suddenly intent, he caught her arm, holding her still while he bent to scoop up a handful of dirt. While she gasped a protest, wriggling, he rubbed the dirt over her face and into the skin of her neck.

"Joss! Stop it! What do you think you're doing?"

"A good layer of dirt will help camouflage that female soft skin of yours."

By the time he was done with her she was so filthy that she felt like a walking dung heap. Her skin was caked with grime, and the shirt and breeches were so dirty that if she'd taken them off they could have stood up by themselves.

Standing a little back from her as she shook mud from her fingertips, Joss eyed her again. This time he didn't shake his head.

"Better?" Lilah asked.

"Better," he affirmed. "Walk around for me, would you?"

Scowling, Lilah walked. When she came back to him he was frowning again.

"What now?" she asked with a sigh.

"Could you try not to wiggle your bottom? That seductive sway will give you away in about two steps."

"I do not wiggle my bottom, and I do not have a seductive sway!" The words were a growl.

"Is that so? Walk, will you please?"

Lilah walked while Joss watched critically. Although she concentrated on keeping her body motionless as she moved, he was still dissatisfied.

"Here, put these on," he said, picking up red-beard's boots. Before he handed them to her he dropped a good-sized stone into one. Taking the boots, Lilah frowned at him and automatically started to fish the stone out.

"Leave it," he ordered sharply. "It'll make you limp."

She left it. The boots were huge on her small feet, but the stone seemed to have an uncanny knack for wedging itself under the tenderest part of her sole. This time, when she walked for him, he pronounced himself marginally satisfied.

"You still don't look like a man, but I guess this is the best we're going to be able to do. Just pray the pirates don't find us and we don't have to worry about it."

"Don't worry, I will," she answered fervently. And she did.

Thirty-four

Lilah and Joss spent the next three days dodging the search parties that scoured the island for the missing pirates. From the intensity of the search, Joss concluded that at least one of the men was extremely valuable to the ship. Which one, or why, he could only speculate.

Lilah was chronically miserable. The brackish-smelling mud that Joss insisted must always be smeared over her exposed skin itched and drew tiny biting flies that left her itching even more. Her breasts ached constantly beneath the strips of cloth that smashed them flat. In the layers of clothes she was forced to wear — Joss had ripped up her dress to form a crude jerkin, which, worn over the outsized shirt, further disguised her sex — she was also hellishly hot. Her misery was compounded by the fact that they had to keep constantly on the move.

Only after nightfall did they dare retreat to the relative comfort of the hut and relax their vigilance. The pirates had proven to be a cautious lot, made nervous by the disappearance of two of their number. As night approached, the search parties headed for their ship, not to be seen again until the sun was well up in the sky the next day. Clearly the men did not care to risk the dangers of tramping about an unknown tropical island by torchlight. From what Joss and Lilah saw and overheard, most of them didn't appear too keen on it even in the bright light of day. They searched for their shipmates under strict orders from their captain, but they were unenthusiastic and so avoiding them was not as difficult as it might have been.

During the day Lilah followed Joss's lead as they played hide-and-seek with the pirates. As long as they kept their wits about them and their eyes and ears open, she did not think they would be captured. At least, she hoped not. But the threat of discovery was ever present. Despite the brave face she kept up for Joss — he was lavish in his admiration of her courage — Lilah was frightened a good deal of the time. She knew that if they were discovered, their chances of surviving were not good. And that was if the pirates were convinced that she was a male. If they saw through her disguise, both she and Joss were doomed. He would fight to the death to defend her, she knew, while she

. . . well, the fate the black-haired woman had suffered would be worse than death. To be at the mercy of the pirates was a horror she could not contemplate without shuddering.

At night, in the privacy of the hut, was the only time Joss would allow her to discard her disguise. In truth, he was not overly enthusiastic about it even then, but after more than fourteen hours of relentless discomfort Lilah was not going to listen to his nay-saying. If she did not get some relief from the itching she would go mad! To add to her woes, the tight binding had caused a heat rash to break out along her back and beneath her breasts. Joss soothed it by applying the creamy juice of a plant Lilah knew from Barbados, and had discovered growing wild on this small island. Each night, as the cream did its work, the rash would disappear, only to return the next day to drive her out of her mind anew. So as the sun blazed relentlessly down on their tropical paradise, Lilah scratched, and despaired.

Bliss was discarding the filthy clothes she wore by day and washing with the water Joss fetched for her in coconut shells. With her skin clean, she would pull the concealing kerchief from her hair, wash the encrusted strands as best she could with the small amount of water available, and comb it dry. Then she would climb into her own chemise — the only whole female garment she still possessed — and suddenly she was herself again. Unbound, her chest would ache, but she was so happy to be back in her own skin again that she barely noticed the throbbing discomfort.

Joss, who could not seem to fully comprehend the misery she found in being filthy and evil-smelling, observed these time-consuming ablutions with interest and a quizzical half-smile. He would watch her, his green eyes alight with humor and something that might have been appreciation. He would grin at her, and she would go into his arms, curling beside him, resting her head on his shoulder, her hand on his chest.

In the magical dark hours betwixt dusk and dawn, they learned all there was to know about each other. Joss taught her about her body and his own, and she learned how to please him and how to be pleasured. Afterwards, she would lie in his arms and they would talk, lovers' nonsense mostly, but also about their childhoods and families, their deepest secrets, their fears. The one thing they didn't talk about was the future. It was too uncertain, too painful to look ahead. The truth was that if they were ever able to resume their normal lives they didn't have a future. Not together. With the part of her that was practical Lilah knew that. But her heart — her heart grew more enchanted with every hour that she passed in his company.

During those nights in Joss's arms, Lilah fell ever more deeply in love. He was tender and gentle with her even in the throes of a passion that drove him to wake her again and again from the exhausted sleep to which his lovemaking reduced her. He could make her laugh even while she trembled with need, and once or twice — only once or twice! — she caught herself thinking how wonderful things would be if they could only get off this island, if she could only take Joss by the hand to her father and announce that this was the man with whom she had chosen to spend her life.

The fantasy was impossible, of course, on every count. Number one, it was seeming ever more likely that they would never get off the island, alive or otherwise. Number two, even if they did, her father would never in a million years accept Joss. His ancestry forever precluded that. Lilah knew that, and tried to put the fantasy from her mind. It hurt too much when compared with cold, cruel reality.

But when she lay in Joss's arms, her head

on his shoulder, his fingers lightly stroking the bare skin of her arm as they talked about everything and nothing, the only reality was the two of them together. She loved him, and she thought he loved her though he never said the words, and she didn't push for them. She was afraid that if she did, those words would precipitate the discussion of their future that she dreaded. She had come to realize that Joss for all his strength was a hopeless romantic. He couldn't seem to comprehend just how huge was the obstacle between them.

Since there was no happy solution, Lilah resolved to put the whole horrible mess out of her mind for as long as she could. "Sufficient unto the day is the evil thereof," as Katy Allen would have told her, and Lilah decided to live by that. Until something happened that made it impossible, she was going to love Joss with all her heart.

Lilah's modesty with Joss faded too, gradually but inexorably. By the morning of the fourth day she was largely unself-conscious in her nakedness with him. Before dawn broke each day she had to don her hated disguise. On that fourth morning, while he watched, propped on his elbow with a fugitive half-smile lurking around the corners of his mouth, Lilah braided her hair and twisted it up, then pulled the chemise over her head. A proprietary gleam came into his eyes, and he caught her hand as she picked up the cloth to bind her chest. Sitting up, he stilled her with a hand on her arm, and dropped a light kiss on each soon-to-be-flattened nipple.

"Let me," he said, taking the cloth from her hand.

"Sadist!"

He chuckled, and kissed her mouth this time before turning his attention to the business at hand. Grimacing, Lilah lifted her arms. Joss wrapped the strips tightly around her chest, transforming her in the space of a few moments from seductively curvaceous female to flat-chested youth. While she donned the rest of her disguise, he pulled on his breeches and went outside. When Lilah emerged from the hut, he was standing at the edge of the clearing, frowning toward the interior of the island.

"What is it?" she asked, coming to his side and staring out at the lush panorama of entwining trees and vines that met her eyes as far as she could see. Thin fingers of sunlight were just beginning to poke through the canopy overhead, but the world before them remained deep green and shadowed, with steam from the forest floor rising like lazy fingers of mist. Besides the few threads of sunlight, only the screeching birds gave evidence of the coming of day.

"Hear the birds? The pirates are up early this morning, and it sounds like they're headed this way. We need to get moving."

The birds were far louder than usual, Lilah realized with a shock. Alone, she never would have noticed. The familiar surge of fear tasted like metal in her mouth as Joss closed his hand around hers and pulled her after him through the undergrowth, away from the warning cries of the birds.

The tedious, familiar game of playing hide-and-seek with the pirates was begun anew.

Later that day, Lilah and Joss were on the same cliff from which they had watched the rape of the black-haired woman. Lying on their stomachs in the tall grasses that covered the top of the cliff, with the woven canopy of vine-covered treetops shielding them from the brilliance of the afternoon sun, they watched the activity on the beach below them.

The pirates' careen had been completed two days before. The ship, which Joss identified as a brigantine because of its square masts, was afloat again, anchored in the sapphire waters of the bay. Small rowboats moved occasionally between ship and shore, ferrying men and materials both ways. There was no sign today of the unfortunate woman, or the majority of the crew. The *Magdalene*, the name painted in crude black letters along the ship's prow, appeared largely deserted. Most of the crew had apparently come ashore early that morning in an all-out search for the missing crew members, which Joss reluctantly admitted worried him. As he told Lilah, no pirate crew likes to prolong their stay in such a small-mouthed bay. A ship at anchor in such a berth was, to all intents and purposes, helpless. Another ship approaching from the sea would have her trapped before she could even get her sails unfurled. The *Magdalene* could be captured without so much as a shot being fired.

For her captain to put his ship in such a position, delaying her departure by days, the missing men must be very sorely needed indeed.

On this day the search seemed to be concentrated on the far side of the island where Joss and Lilah had been living, thus they both felt reasonably secure in their perches, secure enough for Lilah to nearly give in to the heat and nap.

"We done looked up there oncet!"

The surly words brought Lilah fully alert.

Joss was staring behind them, toward where a crude path wound up the overgrown cliff-side from the beach.

"Hell, like Cap'n said, you can see the whole beach from up there. Mebbe they fell off a cliff and was washed out to sea. Their bodies might turn up anytime, rolling in on a wave just as neat as you please. And we'd be the ones to find 'em."

The voices were nearby, perhaps some twenty feet below. Lilah couldn't believe that the pirates had gotten so close without either herself or Joss hearing their approach. Disaster loomed. At the realization Lilah's heart began pounding so loudly that it drowned out the next part of the pirates' conversation. Panicked, she darted a look at Joss.

He shushed her with a gesture, then turned and slithered to where the nearly flat clifftop overlooked the path. On his stomach, he inched to the edge and peered over. Cautiously, crawling on her hands and knees, Lilah followed him. They both must have been nearly asleep for the pirates to get so close without being heard. They had made love until nearly dawn the night before. They were both tired, and being tired had made them careless. And being careless could cost them their lives. They were lucky, very lucky, that the pirates were taking no pains to be silent. If the pirates had climbed the cliff without speaking, Joss and Lilah would have been easy prey.

"Cap'n Logan is dead set on finding McAfee. Otherwise we'd a set sail yester-morn."

The speaker was a small man, grizzled, wearing bright yellow pantaloons and an orange-striped shirt. His hair was shoulder-length and scraggly, and he had a patch over one eye. Lilah thought he looked as little like a bloodthirsty pirate as any man she'd ever seen. He was resting his hands on his knees as he stood bent over, trying to catch his breath. The climb from the beach was steep, and his words were punctuated by gasps.

"That log we took off the *Sister Sue* ain't no good without someone to read it, is it? And McAfee's the only one who knows how to read it."

The second pirate was younger and bigger, less short of breath but no less raggedy. Lilah frowned as she looked down at them. When she thought of pirates she thought of rich plunder and chests of jewels and gold, shared alike by all the crew. But from the looks of the men she had seen, if they possessed any chests of jewels and gold they'd converted none of it to clothing or personal possessions. To a man, the *Magdalene*'s crew seemed something less than prosperous. Or perhaps they just had an aversion to being well-dressed, or even clean.

"So? Who needs to read it? We got along just fine before we took it. Cap'n can steer by the stars. What's he need a blamed book for?"

The younger of the two started to say something, hesitated, then looked about carefully. Satisfied that he and his companion were alone on the cliff, he continued in a lowered voice. "If I tell you somepin, Silas, you got to promise me it won't go no further. Cap'n'd have my hide, did he know I listened to him talkin' to McAfee."

"What about?"

"Well . . ." The man again hesitated, clearly of two minds whether or not to reveal his secret.

"C'mon, Speare, you know you can trust me. Silas Hanks tells no tales, and never has."

"Aye. Well, seems Cap'n's heard tell of a treasure. It's supposed to be hidden in a cave on an island marked in that log. That's where we was headed when we finished the careen. Only now McAfee's gone, and nobody else can make heads nor tails out of the scurvy book. That's why Cap'n's looking so bloody hard for McAfee."

"Treasure, eh? Cap'n's a mighty covetous man. I shoulda known it was somepin like that. I did know we sure weren't lookin' for Sugar-lips. That red-headed son-of-a-gun ain't no loss to nobody. If he ever did an honest day's work in his life, I never saw 'im at it."

"Nah. All he was good for was diddlin' the wimmin, and braggin' about it afterwards."

The two men looked at each other, and chortled. Then the older one, Silas, suddenly sobered.

"What you reckon happened to those boys, anyhow? We been over every blasted inch of this island twice. It's like they just disappeared with nary a trace."

"I don't know. I don't know as I want to know."

"No."

Both men glanced around uneasily.

"You don't suppose as there's headhunters on this island, do you? Or cannibals?"

"Damn it all, Silas, you think I know? All I know is I ain't seen none. Yet."

"Mebbe they hide during the day. Mebbe they're watching us right now. Mebbe they ate McAfee and ole Sugar-lips, bones and all, and that's why we ain't found so much as a hair."

Both men shifted closer together. Despite the danger of her position, Lilah could not repress a smile at their hypothesis and the nervousness that resulted from it. Joss was grinning, too, clearly enjoying the flights of fancy that were going on below. If the situation were not so deadly serious, it would have been funny to let out a war whoop and watch how fast those pirates hightailed it back to their ship. Cannibals, indeed!

"Cmon, let's go up there and get it over with. Cap'n tole us to search the point again," Silas said.

Joss slithered back away from the edge, and Lilah followed suit. Or at least she tried. As she pushed against the scrub grass at the edge of the cliff, a large hunk of earth became dislodged. She watched with horror as it fell down, squarely at the pirates' feet. For just an instant Lilah's hand showed over the edge, and then she snatched it back.

"What the hell . . . ?"

"Somebody's up there! And it sure as hell ain't McAfee or Sugar-lips!"

The two pirates came charging up the path, drawing their pistols. Lilah and Joss had only an instant to stare at each other in horror. There was no time to run, no place to run to. If they fled along the path that led to the forest they would be heard, seen, and chased. Once the pirates knew that there were others on the island besides themselves they would be pursued relentlessly, and caught in a matter of days. . . .

Joss grabbed Lilah, swung her around, shoved her to her knees and then her belly in the leafy thicket behind him.

"I don't care what the hell you see or hear, or what happens to me, you stay put and be quiet, do you hear me?" It was a quick, fierce whisper. Then Joss was stepping out into the middle of the clearing, drawing the pirate's pistol that he'd worn in his waistband. Lilah had time to do no more than blink up at him in terror before the pirates exploded into the clearing, pistols drawn. At the sight of Joss, tall and bronzed and stripped to the waist, formidable enough without the pistol he leveled at them, standing with feet apart and cool challenge in his eyes, they came to a sudden, bumbling stop. Silas, who'd been slightly to the rear, almost bumped into the other man. Both pistols wavered, were snapped up to point at Joss threateningly. He met their wide-eyed stares, his own pistol trained on Speare's heart.

"Well-met, gentlemen," he said calmly. Despite her fear, Lilah felt a small, warming spurt of pride in him. He looked and sounded as calm as if he had run into a neighbor while on a Sunday stroll. He had to be afraid, he would not be human if he wasn't, but even she who knew him so well could not detect the slightest sign of it. This was a man to spend a lifetime with. . . . As quickly as it came, she banished the thought.

"Who the bloody hell are you, and where the bloody hell did you come from?" Speare spluttered. Behind him, Silas suddenly took three steps to the side. For a moment Lilah couldn't imagine why. Then she guessed. With such a space between the two pirates, Joss couldn't hope to kill them both. At least not without offering at least one of them an excellent chance at killing him first.

"I might ask the same." Joss still sounded unruffled, but a hard note had entered his voice that seemed to make the pirates uneasy. Silas sidled another step to the left. Lilah, watching, was not certain that Joss even noticed. She longed to cry out a warning — but he had told her to stay still. If she did reveal herself, and her disguise proved inadequate after all, she could be signing both their death warrants. Biting her lip, she remained silent, her eyes huge as, with a sense of helpless horror, she watched events unfold.

"Blimy, Silas, did you hear that? The cheek of 'im!" Speare's pistol steadied, its muzzle pointed squarely at Joss's chest. "I'll ask ya once again, mate. Who be ye?"

Joss was silent for a moment. Lilah held her breath. The answer he finally gave caught her by surprise.

"The name is San Pietro, Captain Joss San Pietro, late of the *Sea Belle*. My ship went down in a storm off these shores a week or so ago. I'd be much obliged if you'd take me to your captain so I can claim the hospitality of the sea."

The two pirates were evidently as startled by the calm audacity of Joss's words as Lilah was. They looked sideways at each other, then back at Joss with suspicion plain in their faces.

"What should we do, Speare?" Silas asked.

"Blimy, Silas, how should I know?" He looked Joss over. "We're missing two shipmates. You seen aught of them?"

"I've seen many of your shipmates over the past few days. Hell, they've been all over the island, and I've been watching them. But as to two in particular, no, not so as I noticed. Now, as I mentioned, I'd like to talk to your captain."

Silas and Speare glanced at each other again. Then Silas shrugged. "Hell, let Cap'n Logan sort it out."

Speare nodded. "Come on, then, you. But

I warn you, try any kind of trick and you're a dead man."

"You've no need to fear me, gentlemen," Joss said placidly, lowering his pistol and then, to Lilah's horrified astonishment, tucking it carelessly in his waistband. The two pirates seemed to relax slightly, though they still regarded Joss with extreme wariness. Their pistols never left him.

"You go on ahead." Speare motioned to Joss to precede them down the trail. Joss complied, with Speare right behind him. It occurred to Lilah that in a matter of seconds she would be left totally alone! Before she could decide what, if anything, she should do, Silas fell in behind Speare and they were marching Joss away down the trail.

Thirty-five

When the men were gone, Lilah remained motionless for a few minutes, not knowing what to do. What would they do to Joss? It was inconceivable to her that they would at any point just let him go. Maybe he meant to overpower Silas and Speare farther down the trail, before they got in sight of the *Magdalene*? But he had put his pistol in his waistband, while both of the pirates had theirs trained on his back. It did not seem likely that even Joss could get the better of two armed men in the space of time it took to descend to the beach.

The question was, what could she do to aid him? Showing herself would achieve nothing. There was nothing she could do, and that was the hard truth.

When the voices had receded sufficiently, Lilah squirmed out from beneath the sheltering undergrowth and made her way cautiously to the edge of the cliff. The men were already out of the range of her vision. She moved to the opposite side of the promontory overlooking the beach. And she was still crouched there when Joss emerged from the cliff path, followed by the two pirates, who still kept him carefully covered with their pistols.

If Joss was going to try anything, he had at best only a few more minutes to make the attempt.

The trio headed toward the bay. The distance was too great to permit her to hear anything of what was said, but the pirates motioned Joss toward another man, who sat under a palm at the edge of the beach. At the trio's approach, the man rose, fumbling for his pistol. When Joss and his captors stopped walking, the four men appeared to exchange only a brief bit of conversation. Then the fourth man picked up a scarlet flag from where it had been lying beside him in the sand, and by waving it overhead seemed to be sending a signal to the brigantine. A short while later a small punt with two men at the oars headed from the ship to the beach. As it approached, Joss was herded into the surf and pulled aboard the punt. Silas and Speare followed. The oarsmen reversed directions, pulling for the *Magdalene*. Joss sat in the stern as though he hadn't a care in the world while Speare's pistol kept him under guard. Not by the slightest gesture did Joss reveal any nervousness, though he must have feared for his life.

As the punt reached the ship, Lilah watched with her heart in her throat. Joss, a tiny figure in the distance only identifiable because of his black hair, climbed a dangling ladder to the deck, where he was grabbed by two pair of hands and pulled from her sight before he had done more than sling a leg over the rail. When he was gone, she stared blindly at the other men ascending the *Magdalene*'s ladder. A huge knot formed in her stomach. She was so frightened for Joss her insides churned.

As the afternoon progressed, nothing happened. Though she watched the ship with eagle eyes, there was no sign of Joss. Lilah's fear was relentless, both for him and for herself, too. With Joss gone, she was alone and very vulnerable. If he should be killed, or if the Magdalene sailed away with him on board, she might be alone for days, weeks . . . forever even! The thought was terrifying. Being marooned with Joss was almost fun, a kind of exotic, romantic adventure. Being marooned alone, with no idea of Joss's fate, would be a nightmare of the worst sort.

Afternoon turned to evening, and still Lilah crouched, watching, on the promontory. She was hungry and thirsty, but she dared not move in case Joss somehow managed to get word to her. As the shadows lengthened, search parties straggled onto the beach, where the waiting pirate signalled for a punt with his scarlet flag. By nightfall, she thought most of the men were off the island.

She was alone in the dark.

The *Magdalene* bobbed gracefully on the midnight blue waters of the bay, lights shining from her portholes. Lilah toyed with the thought of swimming out to the ship under the cover of darkness. She knew this was ridiculous and extremely dangerous, but she felt as if she would go crazy if she did not do something! Perhaps she could at least determine if Joss was dead or alive. . . .

Then a punt was launched from the *Magdalene* with two men in the prow and two at the oars. It headed toward the beach. As the punt drew closer to shore she thought that one of the men in the prow looked like Joss. Her heartbeat stopped, speeded up. Torchlight illuminated broad bare shoulders and black hair, a heavily muscled chest above a narrow waist and tattered black breeches. And there was something about the way he moved his head. . . .

But Joss, if Joss he was, did not appear to be under any kind of restraint. As far as Lilah could tell, no pistol was trained on him, and he was talking easily to the man who sat just behind him. Crazily, hope began to bubble inside her.

As the punt reached the beach, the men jumped out and splashed through the shallow surf to shore. The two who had been manning the oars dragged the punt behind them. When they were all on the beach, the man who might or might not be Joss pointed up toward where Lilah crouched, and said something to his companions. All four men looked in her direction. Appalled Lilah scooted back.

When she looked again, the black-haired man and one other were heading up the path from the beach. The others stayed behind.

Panic churned in Lilah's stomach, her breath was labored. What in the name of heaven was she to do? Run? Hide? Had Joss been tortured into revealing her presence? Was that man even Joss?

If it was, he would not reveal her existence without a good reason. If he was leading the pirates up to her hiding place, then perhaps it was because they had misjudged everything. Perhaps the pirates were harmless. Perhaps they were honest sailing men, and not pirates at all.

And perhaps pigs could fly.

Lilah remembered the black-haired

woman, and shuddered.

She could hear the men coming up the path. Listening to the low rumble of their voices, she no longer had any doubt: The taller one was Joss. She would recognize that voice anywhere in the world, under any conditions.

They stopped on the path just below. Crouching, Lilah scooted to the spot where she and Joss had spied on Speare and Silas — had it only been a matter of hours ago? It seemed like centuries!

Only one man stood there. The moon had gone behind a cloud, and it was too dark to tell which one he was. But there was only one, of that Lilah was sure.

She quickly scooted for cover even as a tall dark shape strode into the clearing.

For a moment she stared, dry-mouthed, as the shadowy figure looked around. She was almost certain it was . . .

"Lilah!" came the hoarse whisper.

"Joss!"

Lilah scrambled from her hiding place and flew across the intervening space to throw herself against him in a paroxysm of relief. He caught her in his arms, and hugged her to him for just an instant.

"The captain — Logan — insists that I join the crew," Joss explained in a whisper.

"The only thing that kept them from stringing me up or putting me to an even more unsavory end is the fact that I can use a sextant. That makes me valuable, at least until they get where they're going. I told them that I was captain of a ship that went down off these shores during the storm that wrecked us, and that I and a lone shipmate were the sole survivors. You are the shipmate, a cabin boy named Remy. You're my young nephew, and I promised your mother I'd look out for you. You're slow-witted by nature, and the wreck left you positively addled. You haven't spoken a word since. The ship was the *Sea Belle*, out of Bristol. Can you remember all that?"

Before Lilah could reply, a voice floated up from below.

"You still up there, San Pietro?" The question was heavy with suspicion.

"I sure as hell haven't taken wing over the ocean," Joss shot back. "I'm explaining things to my nephew, so he won't be frightened out of what few wits he has left. We'll be right down."

"See that you are! I ain't standin' here all night!"

Joss turned back to Lilah, urgency in his gestures and lowered voice.

"They don't trust me, but they need me,

and it's either go with them or be killed. You'll have to come too, never forgetting your role for a minute. Not one minute, you understand? You're my addled nephew Remy, and you stick to me like a shadow. Got it?"

Lilah nodded, her throat tightening with fear. She was actually going to join the pirate crew — as an addled boy? Could she play the part for days on end without slipping up? It seemed absurd, impossible. She had never really thought to have to put her boy's guise to the test. But as Joss said, what was the alternative? If she gave herself away, it would almost certainly mean death for them both. Lilah thought about that for an instant, then lifted her chin with determination. She could play the part, because she had to. There was no choice, for either of them.

"I won't slip up."

Joss nodded. Looking around once, moving quickly, he pulled the kerchief from her head, and caught the thick braid of her hair in his fist as it tumbled down.

"What are you doing?" she whispered, wincing and catching his arm as he yanked at her tender scalp.

"I hate like hell to do it, but all this hair is just too damned much of a risk. If they find out you're a female . . ." His voice trailed off. She knew the risk as well as he. With a twisted expression that told more than words how much the action pained him, Joss pulled a knife from his breeches and began sawing through the thick braid. The painful tugging on her scalp brought tears to Lilah's eyes, but she made not so much as a sound of protest. Joss was the one who looked sick scant moments later as he stood there staring at the severed rope of silvered hair that lay across his palm.

"It'll grow back, silly." She felt a ridiculous urge to comfort him even as her fingers moved in increasingly appalled exploration over the ragged bob he'd left her with.

"I know." With a breath like a sigh he too ran his hand over her shorn head.

He stepped past her and with a pair of long strides carried the shimmering braid to the edge of the cliff overlooking the ocean. For just an instant he held it tight in his closed fist, as if savoring the feel of the silken strands one last time. Then he drew his arm back and threw the glimmering rope as far out to sea as he could. As the braid fell from sight he turned back to look at Lilah.

"San Pietro? You still up there?"

"We're coming now."

Even before he finished speaking, he bent down to scrape off some of the slimy fungus that grew along the base of the rocks by the edge of the cliff. Straightening, he crossed to Lilah and caught her chin. As she looked up at him wordlessly he smeared the oily fungus into her scalp, spreading his fingers to work it through the choppy cap that was left of her hair. Then he grabbed a handful of dirt, and rubbed that into her hair too. That done, he wiped his dirty fingers over her face with quick, rough movements.

"Ow!"

"Sorry." He retied her kerchief and studied her a moment.

"God help us," he said under his breath, "but that's the best I can do. Remember, don't speak, and keep your eyes down. You're addled and frightened. And for God's sake, don't act shocked at anything you may hear, or see. A blush could ruin us. Stay close to me at all times, like you're afraid of everyone else. Understand?"

Lilah nodded. Staying close to him and pretending to be afraid would require little in the way of acting. She was terrified, and she had no intention of letting Joss out of her sight if she could help it. She needed him now, as she had never needed another human being in her life.

He looked down at her for an instant longer, his expression grim. Then he caught her chin in his hand, and kissed her. Before she could respond, he headed down the path, and she followed.

They rounded the turn in the path. The pirate who had escorted Joss stood there, smoking. Lilah hung her head and allowed one shoulder to droop, giving her what she hoped was a scrawny, concave appearance. The stone in her boot wedged under her insole, making her limp real. Joss moved as if he hadn't a worry in the world, while her heart pounded so loudly that she was afraid the pirate might hear it.

"Took you long enough," the pirate grumbled as Joss came up to him and Lilah hung a little back. Even though she kept her eyes downcast, she was tinglingly aware of the hard look he ran over her. She devoutly hoped that the confining strips of cloth and the loose shirt and jerkin were enough to conceal her shape. As the man's eyes swept her body, it was all she could do not to cringe.

"Get over here, Remy, and try not to be such a bloody little coward," Joss said with evident disgust, reaching out to catch her by the shoulder and yank her across the few feet of path that separated them. Stumbling, she ended up standing beside him, his hand on her shoulder, her head hanging. Darkness shrouded the three of them, providing her some protection. Lilah was concentrating so hard on acting addled that when a nightbird screeched close by she didn't even jump.

"This gentleman's name is Burl," Joss said to Lilah, overemphasizing the words as if she were hard of hearing. Lilah stared at the ground, managing to work up enough saliva for a creditable drool. As it dribbled from the corner of her slack mouth and dropped to the ground, Joss made a disgusted sound even as his hand on her shoulder gave her a secret, applauding squeeze. The pirate looked away with revulsion.

Then, to Burl, Joss said, "This is my nephew Remy. His ma thought a sea voyage would make a man of him, but you can see what's come of that. I'm not looking forward to taking him back to her. He's in worse shape than when he left, and she's sure as hellfire going to blame me."

Lilah, knowing that she couldn't stare at the ground forever, grunted and rolled her eyes, trying to shrug out from under Joss's hand. He let her go, frowning as she squatted at his feet, tracing aimless patterns with her finger in the dirt path.

"Half-witted, ain't he?" Burl said, and shook his head. "Well, let's get on back to the ship. Cap'n'll be glad to see that he won't have no worries about your shipmate causin' trouble."

"Get on your feet, Remy." Joss's tone of controlled exasperation was well done, Lilah thought. She pretended not to hear him, concentrating on tracing more circles in the dirt. There was just the right amount of roughness in the jerk with which Joss finally hauled her to her feet. As soon as he had her up, Lilah squatted again, and went back to her task. Burl guffawed. Joss cursed, and yanked her up for the second time. This time he kept a hand twisted in her collar.

Burl, grinning at Joss's struggle to keep his idiot nephew on his feet, stood back so that Lilah and Joss could precede him down the path. Lilah limped and stumbled, drooled and sagged. Joss let go of her collar to grab her upper arm and keep her going that way. Burl followed, seeming to accept her for what she pretended to be without a qualm. As she let Joss drag her along, Lilah found to her surprise that some of the edge had left her terror. She had played her part, and played it well. Burl seemed to be convinced that she was Remy, an idiot boy. Of course, the real test was yet to come. She had yet to spend any time with any of the pirates, or appear in the harsh light of day.

Fooling the entire bloodthirsty crew of the *Magdalene* would be difficult. But she didn't think it would be impossible. Not anymore.

Thirty-six

Joss's mouth was dry as he watched Lilah climb the ladder onto the pirate ship. She made a great show of fumbling at the ropes, keeping her supposedly bad leg stiff as she hauled herself upward. Positioned behind her, he had an eagle's-eye view of her backside, as did the other men in the boat. He breathed a silent sigh of relief. In the baggy breeches, there was nothing to reveal that she was a female. Her waist was small, but then so were the waists of many a scrawny lad. With the oversized shirt hanging outside the breeches, and her dress ripped into that ragged jerkin on top of that, her shape was almost impossible to determine. He only prayed to God that the cloth binding her breasts would hold. If it did, if she remembered to keep her eyes down, limp whenever she moved and remain constantly mute, they had a small chance of pulling this off. He hoped.

"Step lively, Remy," he shouted.

Lilah continued her slow pace up the ladder as if she had not heard. Joss shook his head for the benefit of the onlookers.

When Joss reached the deck, Lilah was at the center of a crowd of pirates, being looked up and down by none other than Captain Logan himself. They formed a loose circle in front of the forecastle, and four flaming torches lit the small area so that it was almost as bright as day.

"Um — what's your name?"

Joss opened his mouth to reply when Lilah, appearing to take no notice of the question or the staring men around her, squatted and began drawing aimless patterns on the deck with her finger.

"By damn, is he deaf?" Logan sounded more puzzled than angry, staring down at Lilah with a growing frown on his face.

"Addled, like I told you," Joss said, joining the group. "He's always been a little slow-witted, but the wreck really did him in. He hardly seems to understand what even I say to him, and I'm his bloody uncle."

"Don't know as I care to have any dead-wood on my ship." This was said in a thoughtful tone, as if Logan was pondering the point. "On the *Magdalene*, we all pull our own weight."

"I'll pull his oar and mine too, if necessary," Joss said sharply. "What I won't do is leave him. He's my dead brother's boy, and I'm responsible for him. You want me to read your sextant for you, you take him as well as me."

"Hmmph." Logan pondered this too, his eyes studying Lilah. Joss felt his heart stop as that hooded gaze ran over the slender figure crouched at his feet. To her everlasting credit, Lilah appeared unaware that their very lives hung in the balance while Logan considered whether the liability of taking on a useless mouth to feed outweighed the plus of Joss's ability with a sextant. To Joss's eyes, even with the black kerchief pulled low over her head, hiding her forehead and what was left of her hair, her breasts flattened and the rest of her shape concealed by the baggy men's clothes, and covered with dirt, she still looked unmistakably like a woman, like the one he loved. But she was playing her part well. She even managed to drool at this point.

If she hadn't been a lady, the girl should have been an actress. Joss's heart swelled with pride as Logan turned his eyes away from her in distaste.

"Can he write? Enough to sign his name? He'll have to sign the articles of agreement, same as the rest."

"He can make his mark. Can't you,

Remy?" Thus addressed by Joss, Lilah drooled again, never ceasing in her endless pattern-drawing. Joss almost applauded. He had to bite back a grin.

"Get out the articles of agreement."

To Joss's relief, Logan turned away from Lilah to give the order to a man at his left. Now that he had decided to allow the two of them on board, he seemed to have no further interest in his addled crew member. Attention shifted from Lilah to the pirate Logan had addressed, who disappeared briefly below, then returned with a tattered roll of white foolscap. A hogshead barrel was dragged forward, a quill and ink pot were produced. Joss was motioned over; he smoothed out the paper and glanced over it carelessly. It was nothing more than the standard rules of shipboard life and the formula for division of the spoils, calculated to give the most to the captain with a decreasing percentage according to the importance of the crew member. He and Lilah would, he deduced, receive one twenty-fifth of what was left after the captain and other officers took their share. Which was fine with Joss. He didn't intend for either of them to hang around long enough to collect. At the first chance offered, hopefully at a well-populated port, they were going to jump ship.

Their lives hung by a thread, and that thread would be cut as soon as Logan got where he wanted to go, or decided that Joss and his addled nephew were more liability than asset. Before that happened, they had to win free. In the meantime, they would have to be very, very careful if they were to survive.

The names of the crew members were signed round-robin fashion. Joss picked up the quill and, with a flourish, signed his name at the far edge of the circle. Then he bent, caught Lilah by the arm, and hauled her up to stand beside him.

"Make your mark. Here, on this paper," he ordered, thrusting the quill into her hand. She promptly dropped it, dribbling ink over the barrel and the boards of the deck as the quill rolled toward the rail. With a pained look, Joss retrieved the quill, only to find Lilah squatting again when he got back to her side. The watching pirates howled with mirth, slapping each other on the back in their merriment at his expense. Even dour Logan had to smile. Starved for entertainment, the pirates were finding their new shipmate an unexpected treat.

Cursing loudly, Joss hauled Lilah to her feet again, thrust the quill into her hand, closed her fingers around it and held them while he tried to convey to her what he wanted. The girl was fantastic. She frowned and drooled, tried to squat and had to be held upright, let her head roll limply on her neck. If he hadn't known better, he would have thought she really was addled. Finally he was forced to trace a scraggly X for her by holding his hand around hers and guiding the quill in the direction he wanted. When it was done and he let her go, she immediately squatted again, while he was left to write beside that lopsided X: "Will Remy's mark."

With the articles signed and put away, Lilah was left to trace her endless patterns on the deck while Logan called for a tot of rum all around. As Joss drained his mug, he thought with relief that they had passed the test. Until and unless something happened to show them otherwise, the pirates had accepted Lilah as what she pretended to be: a half-wit boy.

If she could keep up the act, they would be safe. As he had told her once, she was a female in a million.

Which was why he loved her, although he had never told her that. Maybe he would, one day soon.

Or maybe, just maybe, she was the last person that he would ever tell. He had a feeling that admitting to Lilah that he loved her would give her a hold on his heart that neither time nor circumstance would ever be able to break.

Somebody thrust another tot of rum in his hand. Joss drained it as rapidly as he had the first. For the time being, he and his addled nephew were members of a pirate band.

Thirty-seven

A week later, the *Magdalene* was at sea. Lilah's disguise had held. Captain Logan and the others noticed her only when she got in their way. She had a feeling that even then they weren't really seeing her. Her supposed half-wittedness made her blend into the woodwork.

The daylight hours she spent lurching after Joss, or squatting on the quarterdeck while he and the captain plotted their course by means of complicated calculations. As Speare had said, Logan had obtained from a captured ship a sextant with markings that supposedly led to an island where treasure was buried. Joss's job was to lead the pirates there by deciphering these markings. Until that was done, she and Joss were relatively safe. After that, when they were no longer needed . . . she hated to think what their fate might be.

The *Magdalene*'s cabins had been cut out of her, the bulwarks raised to afford the pirates better concealment when chasing a prize. The crew from Captain Logan down to the lowliest cabin boy slept rolled up in pallets on the deck. At night, when Lilah lay huddled in her blanket, curled alongside Joss in his, a guard was posted not far from where they slept. Every gesture, every whispered word had to be strictly guarded lest it be overheard and their secret exposed.

Logan did not suspect her sex, but he was wary of Joss and not the kind of man to take chances. Though what he thought one man and his scrawny nephew could do against an entire crew of pirates she had no idea.

There were twenty-three of them, not counting Lilah and Joss. Armand Logan was tall and lanky, perhaps in his early forties, dark-haired, with a pockmarked face rendered even more unsightly by a livid scar slicing down from his right temple to his chin. The angry-looking scar was the likely result of a saber cut, Joss said in reply to Lilah's question, whispered while they were settling down for sleep their first night on board. Alone amongst the pirates, Logan dressed well, in suits of fine materials and shirts frothing with lace. The elegant attire went oddly with his marred face. But for all his ugliness he seemed a man much the same as any other, and Lilah had difficulty picturing him in the role of bloodthirsty pirate captain. He treated Joss with as much courtesy as he did anyone, and ignored her completely, which suited Lilah just fine.

The black-haired woman whom Lilah had pitied was one of three captured from the same ship which had yielded the sextant. During the day they were kept locked below, and after dark they were passed around to whichever pirate had a fancy for a bedmate. Each woman would be raped four or five times a night, the repeated horror apparently having dulled their senses so much that they did not even bother to scream any longer. No doubt they had learned that screaming earned them the additional pain of a blow or a kick. Certainly it did not save them from being violated.

It was all Lilah could do to ignore the pathetic things, but Joss warned her fiercely that to attempt any kind of alleviation of their plight would almost certainly bring about their own downfall. She was to close her eyes and ears to what she saw and heard, and concentrate on saving herself.

It was one of the most difficult things she had ever done, but Lilah obeyed. By going to bed with the sun and pulling her blanket over her head she was able to block out much of the drunken debauchery that went on at night. Only once did the sounds of forced fornication reach her ears.

The woman was not screaming, not crying, only whimpering, the helpless, hurt keening of an animal. The grunts of the man who used her nearly covered her soft sounds. But Lilah heard, and was sick. By the time it was over, the woman gone and the man left to sleep off the effects of rum and sated lust, Lilah was shivering violently. For hours she lay awake, unable to banish the horror from her mind. Then when she slept she had a nightmare that she was the victim. It was a miracle that she did not awaken the ship with her screams. As it was, she disturbed only Joss, who was on her in an instant, his hand clamped over her mouth while he denounced her loudly for waking him.

There were two other women who were not prisoners, who sailed on the *Magdalene* willingly. One had hair of an improbable shade of brassy red, and a bosom to make strong men go pale. Her name was Nell, and she had been McAfee's paramour. Now that McAfee was gone, she appeared resigned to choosing a new protector from amongst the remaining crew. If she'd ever been unwilling, Lilah saw no signs of it. She seemed only too eager to bed anything in trousers.

The other woman was Nell's sister,

Nancy. Nancy was Captain Logan's woman, and had a tendency to queen it over her sister. The two women appeared to dislike one another cordially.

By the morning of the eighth day at sea, Lilah's fear of discovery was receding. It was replaced by a new worry: Nell had her eye on Joss, and was making every effort to put more than her eye on him. She had chosen a replacement for McAfee, it seemed, and Joss, willing or no, was it.

Intellectually, Lilah couldn't blame her. Joss, clean shaven except for the dashing mustache that he'd saved when he scraped off his beard the first day at sea, was easily the handsomest man aboard the *Magdalene*. He'd inherited McAfee's wardrobe as well as his task of deciphering the sextant, and in the flamboyant silk shirts that the man had favored he was breathtaking. Lilah's temper sizzled when the floozy came flouncing past wherever Joss was working (which happened easily a dozen times a day!), twitching her skirts and fluttering her eyelashes. The hussy even had the nerve to touch him, once running her finger teasingly down the open vee of his shirt; once grabbing at his shoulder as she pretended to stumble; once even going so far as to press her enormous breasts full against his chest as she pretended to have a cinder in her eye and asked him to get it out.

In her guise as Joss's nephew, there was little Lilah could do to thwart the woman's designs. Even so much as a hot glare at Joss could raise questions in the minds of any who might see it. So she had to play deaf and dumb and blind, and save her fury for when she could get Joss alone.

"I can't help it!" he protested when she hissed at him late one night. Lilah thought she heard amusement in his voice, though it was too dark to properly see his expression. The idea that he found the situation even remotely laughable made her even angrier.

"You can keep your blasted shirt buttoned!" she spat in response, and this time there was no mistaking his laughter. Lilah stiffened and shot him a look that by rights should have slain him on the spot.

Lilah's greatest worry was that Nell would come crawling into Joss's pallet one night. Lilah didn't know how she would react to that. Even if Joss turned the woman away — which there was no certainty that he would do — she would be furious. If Joss did not turn the woman away, she would not be answerable for the consequences. This she tried to convey to him after several days of maintaining a discreet but increasingly furious silence, which seemed to amuse more than chasten him.

"How can you let her flirt so with you? Not that flirt is the word for what she does!" This was delivered under cover of slapping waves and rushing wind as Joss came to his pallet for what remained of the night. He'd stood first watch, so it must have been long past midnight. Lilah had been deemed useless as far as standing watch and most other shipboard duties were concerned so she was free to retire when she wished. But she had not been able to sleep, wondering what Joss was getting up to without her supervision. Not an hour earlier, she had peeped from her blanket to find Nell sashaying along the deck to where he stood near the prow, the steaming cup in her hand her excuse for approaching him. It had been all she could do to remain quietly lying in her pallet. By the time Joss rolled up in his blanket beside her she was spitting mad.

"So you saw that, did you? You must have eyes like a cat," he replied to her accusation with a long-suffering sigh. The notion that he considered himself hardly used made her temper heat even more.

"What I didn't see was you sending her on her way!"

"You couldn't expect me to do that, now

could you? Nell is quite an armful for any man."

He was teasing her, baiting her for his own amusement, Lilah realized after a moment's shock. She passed from steaming to full boil. Laugh at her, would he!

"If you like her so well, then be my guest." Lilah flounced over on her side so that her back was to him. "Just don't expect to come mooning around me, you horny goat!"

Joss laughed, and reached out with a questing finger to stroke the vulnerable nape of her neck. Captain Logan had apparently grown more trusting the longer the pair of them had been on board, so there was no longer a guard stationed feet from where they slept. Still, shipmates slept all around, and Joss's action entailed some risk.

Lilah slewed around to glare at him. The clouds shifted away from the frosted moon long enough to allow her to see his face as he lay on his side not two feet behind her, his head resting on his arm.

"You are despicable!"

"And you are adorable. I'm only teasing you about Nell, you know. Though you can't expect me to repulse her out of hand. To do so would be too suspicious. After all, if you *were* my addled nephew I would probably be glad of the comforts she's offering."

"If you bed her . . ." It was a slit-eyed threat.

He grinned. She could see his white teeth through the shifting darkness.

"I won't. The only female I feel like bedding has a bosom that's squashed flat as a board, is crusted with dirt and lying right next to me at this moment hollering at me for something that is not my fault. She's a shrew and a witch, and she's ruined me for any other woman. Any attention I pay Nell is just show. Satisfied?"

"No!"

He chuckled, the sound low. "It figures. Now be quiet, shrew, and go to sleep. And for God's sake, don't start shooting Nell any filthy looks. You'll give away the game."

"Then you'll just have to watch yourself, won't you?"

"I'll try to discourage her, all right?" His tone told her that he was trying to be conciliatory.

Lilah was in no mood to be appeased. "You'd better! Or you'll think shrew, indeed!"

But to mitigate the severity of her words, she turned over, scooted a little closer, and under cover of the blankets stretched out her hand. Her fingers found his, stroked them. His hand closed around hers, wrapped it warmly, carried it to his lips. And he kissed her fingers, one by one, lingeringly, right there on the deck of the pirate ship.

Thirty-eight

The second week out dawned clear and hot. The *Magdalene* was on a southeasterly course, fighting a brisk head wind. On this particular morning some twelve days after they had joined the pirate crew, Lilah awoke when Joss pushed her roughly. She grumbled, yawned, and sat up, blinking at the brightness of the early morning sunlight.

"Get a move on there, Remy!"

Obediently she staggered to her feet and rolled up her blanket, as did Joss. Then, limping and vacant-eyed, she followed him to a deserted section of the port bow where he attended to nature's needs with flagrant disregard for any considerations of modesty, letting fly over the side as did the other men when weather and circumstance allowed. Lilah had of necessity to be more discreet. Retiring behind a hogshead, she made hasty use of a chamber pot, which Joss had on the first day out thoughtfully discovered and concealed for her there. Finished, she quickly emptied the contents over the side and returned the pot to its hiding place with no one the wiser.

When Lilah emerged from behind the barrel, it was to find Nell simpering up at Joss. The woman's mass of coarse red hair hung in deep waves around her face and halfway down her back. Her skin was swarthy, and her face was round with slightly overlarge features. Despite the woman's blatant vulgarity, Lilah supposed sourly that men must find her exceedingly appealing. Certainly her figure was. Her breasts were large as melons, the nipples boldly visible as they thrust against her loose white top. Her waist was large in comparison with Lilah's, but the voluptuousness of the breasts above and hips below made it look acceptably slender. Even as the woman stood still, smiling coyly up at Joss, her hips were moving, swaying the full black skirt she wore from side to side.

Today, obviously, Nell had gotten herself up to go hunting men. Her blouse had been pulled so far down over her shoulders that the top half of her breasts was bared. Her skirt was hiked short enough to allow much more than a glimpse of bare brown feet and slightly thick ankles. Her waist had been cinched tighter than usual with a sash of bright red silk. Her lips and cheeks had been roughed to nearly the same shade of red. Her eyes were fixed with infuriating avidity on the prey she had in her sights. And that prey was grinning at her with consummate charm and a complete absence of the outrage that Lilah, watching, felt.

Lilah approached, limping, steaming, to see Nell pouting prettily. Her rouged lips pursed as she boldly ran her eyes up and down Joss's tall form, lingering longest over certain unmentionable areas that were clearly delineated by his snug black breeches.

"You got an eye for me, handsome, I know you do. A lady can always tell. So what's stopping us from bein' friends? A fine gent like you has — needs." This provocative speech, uttered in a sultry voice marred only slightly by the speaker's Cockney accent, brought Lilah's teeth snapping together. If Joss did not send the creature about her business, now, she would . . . she would . . . What would she do? If she was not to betray her true sex, what *could* she do? Nothing, she acknowledged with bitter gall.

Her helpless fury increased as Joss reached out to put his hands on Nell's too-plump bare arms, running his palms up and down them while he smiled into her eyes. Lilah stopped in her tracks, watching, while a fierce, primitive rage simmered inside her.

He had no right to touch that creature, none at all! He was hers!

"You're a lovely woman, Nell, and I wouldn't be human if I didn't have an eye for you. But I fear that if I dealt with you as I'd sorely like to I'd have to take on the *Magdalene*'s entire crew. Which as a newcomer I'm somewhat loathe to do. It's no secret that every man on board is panting to take McAfee's place, and somebody'd likely slit my throat were I to steal the prize from under his nose."

Nell simpered at this, obviously pleased, and closed the small distance between her and her quarry, running her hands over the sapphire silk covering Joss's chest to link them behind his neck. Lilah thanked providence that he'd heeded her request to keep his shirt buttoned. If she had had to witness Nell touching his bare skin, she would have exploded for sure.

"I wouldn't have taken you for a coward, love. And it's you I want."

Joss grinned appreciatively down at the bold thing, his hands resting lightly on her waist while she hugged his neck and boldly rubbed herself against him. It was clear to Lilah that he was making no move to free himself. That is, not until he looked over the hussy's head to find her glaring at him. Their eyes met, and hers sent a message that he would ignore at his peril. Joss's eyes widened for an instant, he grimaced, and shifted his eyes back to the woman hooking herself to him. He shook his head at her, and pushed her gently away.

"You're a tempting wench, but I'm a careful man. I'll have to think on your offer for a while. Now take yourself off, woman, and let me get on about my business."

Nell pouted, but he sent her on her way with a grin that Lilah felt promised far too much and a familiar slap on her backside. This pleased the shameless hussy so much she giggled, and sent Joss a coy look and a blown kiss back over her bare shoulder as she flounced away. Clearly Nell did not take Joss's refusal as final.

Lilah let Joss have the full blast of her blazing blue eyes, quite forgetting her role as the addled Remy in her anger. It didn't help that, with the rising sun striking blue sparks in the black waves of his hair, now tied neatly back, and with his face now adorned by the same piratical mustache as the bold rogue who had first dazzled her, he was so handsome he took her breath away. Tall and broad-shouldered, bronzed and hard-muscled, he was a figure out of a woman's dream. It was no wonder that Nell found him appealing, but she couldn't have him. He was hers! The thought was fierce, the anger that came with it red-hot. He was hers, and he had no right to flirt with other women! And she meant to tell the two-timing creature so right quick!

Clearly sensing trouble, Joss grinned at her placatingly. When that didn't work he frowned, eyes narrowing, but Lilah was too angry to heed the warning in that significant look. She marched up to him, barely limping, the stone in her boot no match for her rage, and thumped him hard in the chest with her fist before he could see the blow coming and move out of the way.

"You — !" she began furiously, only to be forcibly silenced by his hand clapping over her mouth.

"Hush!" he hissed. His eyes moved beyond her. Lilah became aware of Silas and another pirate rolling a hogshead toward this sheltering spot beside the rail. Beyond them, the deck was swarming with activity as the crew went about their daily business. No one seemed particularly interested in the little tableau by the rail, but at any second someone could look up, notice her behaving in a most un-Remy-like way, and become interested. Knowledge of the danger she was putting them in affected her temper like a douse of cold water. It still steamed, but no longer blazed.

"You're right, Remy, it's too early for a lad like you to be rolling out of bed. At least when he's home with his mama. But you're not home with your mama now, so be a man, if you can." Joss obviously intended this speech to quell suspicion if anyone had noticed the little scene between them. Silas and the other pirate appeared to afford the pair of them only the most passing attention. Still, to say more could be dangerous.

Frustrated, Lilah managed one more killing glare at Joss before she dropped her eyes and resumed her role. Joss turned away without another word, going about his duties with his "nephew" meekly trailing behind.

The rest of that morning and most of the afternoon Lilah passed as she had the other days aboard the brigantine. Although the quarterdeck was for the most part off-limits to females (the only exception being if the captain was amorous), Nell and her black-haired, sloe-eyed sister were very much in evidence on the deck below. They lazed back on barrels and fanned their skirts provocatively so that the breeze could cool their legs and more. Lilah, sweating as she squatted in the infernal heat, stared down at the laughing pair with fierce dislike. Every once in a while she would sneak a hard look up at Joss, to see if he was ogling the charms the women so casually displayed. To his credit, she never caught him looking, but she knew that did not mean that he did not. Only that he did it when she would not see.

Absurd as it was, she had to admit it: She, Lilah Remy, well-brought-up young lady, sought after by the most eligible bachelors everywhere she went, acknowledged beauty, was so jealous of an ill-kempt pirate's wench that it was making her sick!

What would happen when Nell realized that she was really, truly rejected was anybody's guess. All Lilah knew was what would happen if Joss surrendered to temptation!

Remembering how, back at Boxwood, she had wished to fall in love, Lilah marveled at just how naive she had been. Being in love was not wonderful at all. Being in love was frustrating, maddening, painful.

"Sail ho!" The cry came from the lookout in the crow's nest high above.

The warning shattered the heat-induced lethargy of the afternoon. Every soul on the *Magdalene* dropped what he or she was doing to stare out over the vast blue expanse of ocean. A sense of excitement as tangible as a flame licked across the deck.

"Where away?" Logan called back.

"Astern to starboard!"

Footsteps echoed across the deck with a noise like a well-pounded kettledrum as the crew raced aft to see for themselves. Joss shielded his eyes with his hand as he strained to make out the sail against the glare of the afternoon sun. Logan lifted a spyglass. Lilah, keenly interested, had to content herself with staring through the rails of the quarterdeck while maintaining her mindless squat.

Excited babbling broke out along the astern rail as the men, with Nell and her sister in their midst, craned to see.

"What is she?" Lowering the spyglass, Logan cupped his hands around his mouth to bellow up to the lookout.

"A galleon, sir! Heavy laden, by the looks of her!"

Logan clapped the spyglass to his eye again. "Aye, she's riding low in the water." Then he lowered the spyglass, collapsed it, turned. He moved to the rail of the quarterdeck to stand looking down at his crew, his hands clenched so tightly around the smooth-polished mahogany that his knuckles were white.

"Have you stomach for a fight, lads? From the looks of her, she's holding wealth for all of us!"

"Aye!" shouted several voices at once.

"Good lads!" Logan took a deep breath. Then, "Stand by to come about!"

As that order was obeyed and the rudder went hard over, he shouted, "All hands take battle stations!"

The crew scrambled for their positions. Lilah watched with fascination as the grumbling, bumbling but — she'd thought — essentially harmless seamen changed before her eyes into an efficient, streamlined crew of cutthroats. For the first time since she had clapped eyes on them, they looked like her notion of bloodthirsty pirates. The implications made her go suddenly cold with fear.

Foxy, the apelike quartermaster, called off the names of the men, giving each a turn to go below and pick out small arms and other weapons. Speare, the helmsman, held the rudder steady, keeping the *Magdalene* headed straight for her prey. The lookout shinned down from the crow's nest, and joined the others in the push to go below for weapons. Chanting arose from many lips at once, low at first and then increasing in sureness and volume as the *Magdalene* plowed through the waves.

Yo, ho! Heave ho! 'tis a pirate's life for me!

A hold filled with gold and dead men gone cold,
Doubloons glittering bright beneath skulls black with mold!
Yo, ho! Heave ho! 'tis a pirate's life for me!

It took Lilah a while to get the sense of the words, and when she did she felt cold sweat break out along her spine. The pirates would kill for treasure, or be killed. Logan, his hazel eyes shining, paced the quarter-deck, muttering the pirate ditty under his breath. Watching him, Lilah no longer had any trouble seeing him as a merciless killer. The man was transformed by the chase, excited to the brink of insanity by the prospect of a battle. Beside him, packing away the sextant and the papers he used for calculations, Joss looked composed, but Lilah knew he must be as unsettled as she. In the heat of the battle, anything could happen. What was the likelihood that they would come through this unscathed and unexposed? Even if Captain Logan's crew won, many would die on both ships, possibly herself or Joss. And if they lost. . . . That possibility was nearly as bad. Pirates taken were customarily hanged by the neck.

As hard as she had ever prayed for anything, Lilah prayed the other ship would be fast enough to escape.

"We're short a gunner. Can you lay a cannon, San Pietro?"

"I have, in my time."

"Sugar-lips was a gunner. You can take his place by the aft cannon." Logan's eyes swept down to rest for a moment on Lilah. "You'd best stow your nephew below with the women. He'll be distracting you and getting in the way. And 'twill be safer for him."

Joss nodded once, curtly. Then, catching Lilah by the arm and indicating with a rough gesture that she was to follow him, he descended the ladder to the main deck.

The pirates swarmed all around them, turned younger, hardier, fiercer in the course of only minutes. Their eyes shone at the prospect of claiming a rich prize. An eager smile that looked more like a grimace parted more than one pair of lips. The chanting was quieter now, more a background hum as the men got ready to do battle. Lilah and Joss, pushing their way against the stream, were ignored.

"Will you really fight with them?" Lilah whispered, mindful of possible listening ears but unable to hold back the question as Joss flattened them both against the side of the forecastle to make way for a large cannon being rolled along the deck.

"I don't appear to have much choice. If they think we're against them, this lot will cut us down without a second thought. With pirates, it's either fight or die, and I don't intend to die if I can help it. Or let you die."

The cannon was trundled into position, lashed into place at the bow. Joss resumed pulling Lilah toward the hatchway. "Whatever happens, stay below. I'll come for you when it's over."

"No!"

"What?"

"You heard me. I said no!"

That this conversation was conducted in hissed whispers in no way detracted from its heat. Lilah's defiance stopped Joss in his tracks. Anger glittered in his eyes, darkening them to the deep green of a pine.

"I'm staying with you whether you like it or not. And if you argue with me, somebody's going to figure out that I'm not your addled nephew!"

"Maybe not my nephew, but definitely addled," Joss snapped, casting a wary glance around. "All right, have it your own way then. At least I'll be able to keep an eye on you. Alone, God knows what stupid stunt you'd pull."

This last was muttered under his breath

as he dragged her along the deck after him. Lilah, having won the victory she sought, was back in her role of Remy again, limping and looking vacant as she was hauled in Joss's wake.

"Handsome, wait!"

Nell hailed Joss as they passed the hatchway. Joss turned in response, and Nell threw herself against him. Joss automatically let go of Lilah's arm to catch the hussy, and before Lilah's widening eyes, Joss's head was pulled down and he was being thoroughly kissed.

"Take care, love," Nell said urgently, releasing him at last. Lilah, eyes forcibly lowered as she fought to hold to the persona of Remy, glared at the deck until Nell went back into the hatchway. Joss resumed his march toward the stern, and Lilah limped along behind, heart pounding with anger. When they reached the stern cannon, Silas was there, having just finished loading the big gun.

"She's all yours, mate," he said with a wink, and crawled away along the deck to check the next cannon. Lilah saw that the others on deck were crouching now, sheltering behind the raised bulwarks. She remembered what Joss had told her when they'd first come aboard: The bulwarks were designed to keep the enemy from seeing any activity on deck until the *Magdalene* was upon them. For all those aboard the other ship knew, the *Magdalene* was as innocent as they were themselves. The pirates meant to make their task easier by taking their prey by surprise.

For the moment, though, fury had driven fear from Lilah's mind. The only thing that interested her was Joss's reaction to Nell's kiss. As he hunkered down on one side of the cannon and she squatted on the other, she fixed him with a hot stare. He met her eyes, and scowled.

"What would you have had me do, push her away?" he demanded in a testy undertone, correctly interpreting that accusing look. Stevens and Burl came crawling along the deck just then to take their places aft of the stern cannon, so Lilah had to bite back her reply.

Silas brought cutlasses for Lilah and Joss from the ship's store. Joss had the pistol that had once belonged to McAfee, and he checked the powder to make sure it was dry. Lilah was apparently deemed too dim-witted to be trusted with a pistol, and she was given only a cutlass. Its cold handle seemed to burn her palm. The coming fight suddenly seemed all too horribly real.

The galleon, all things being equal, was

faster than the brigantine, but on this day all things were not equal The galleon was heavily loaded, while the brigantine, having been barren of prizes since the careen, was nearly empty. The wind blew dead astern for the brigantine, while the galleon, holding to a northeasterly course, was quartering. The galleon, having no reason to suspect anything amiss, was making no attempt to outrun her pursuer. Lilah, peeking occasionally over the bulwark like the others, felt her nerves tighten to a screaming pitch as she realized that it was just a matter of time until the *Magdalene* overtook her quarry.

"They think were just coming up to exchange news," Joss said. "From their quarterdeck, they should only be able to see Logan on the quarterdeck, Speare at the helm, and Manuel over there by the forecastle. They've obviously no notion yet that we're a threat."

"This'll be first blood for yer nephew, eh, San Pietro?" Silas asked. Without waiting for an answer, he lifted his head to peer cautiously over the bulwark. What he saw made him duck.

"Holy William, we're almost upon her," he cackled, and stroked the sharp end of his cutlass almost greedily. "Not more'n a quarter-hour, I'd wager."

Lilah's heart hammered as she exchanged glances with Joss, but surrounded as they were, there could be no further conversation between them.

"The *Beautiful Bettina* out of Kingston, Jamaica. What ship?" The hail came from the galleon, carrying faint but clear across the water.

Time seemed suspended as the galleon waited for her answer. On the quarterdeck Logan upped his hand in a slicing motion.

"Drop canvas or be blown out of the water!" came his roar, and in punctuation one of the *Magdalene*'s cannons boomed, sending up a white plume of water as the ball exploded off the *Beautiful Bettina*'s bow.

Thirty-nine

With all need for concealment past, the crew jumped to their feet, cheering and brandishing their weapons. Someone sent the *Magdalene*'s crudely drawn black flag skittering up the pole. As it unfurled, flapping wildly in the breeze, the crew cheered again, bloodlust in the cry.

There was another boom, and a white spume hurtled skyward just beyond the *Bettina*'s bowsprit as a second shot was fired across her prow.

Standing now with the rest, Lilah could see the tiny figures on the galleon's deck scramble for weapons. The *Magalene*'s strategy had been masterly, her surprise complete.

"Poor souls," she whispered, the horror of what was happening making her forget that she wasn't supposed to speak. Behind her, Silas cocked an ear and gave her a sharp look, but Lilah was too preoccupied to notice.

"Stern cannon!"

At the command, Joss motioned to Lilah

to raise the wood panel that hid the mouth of the gun until needed. Lilah did so, fingers stiff with fright, then stood by the sand bucket as Joss lit a match. Cupping his hand around it, he applied it to the wick. Powder sputtered as the wick caught, burned. Lilah winced, clapped hands to her ears.

The cannon exploded with a roar and an enormous backkick that would have sent it skittering across the deck if it had not been lashed into place. Smoke spewed, and through it the ball arched up. Lilah watched, fascinated, horrified as it spun on its arcing trajectory. She breathed a sigh of relief as it fell just short of its goal, kicking up another harmless geyser of water scant feet from the *Bettina*'s side.

"Come about!" Logan ordered.

The helmsman did as directed, and the *Magdalene* turned sideways in the water, slid right alongside her prey. The galleon was taller, but not more than six feet or so. Wood screamed as the ships scraped. Logan's crew cheered as they rushed the side. Fired from close range, another cannonball hit, bringing down the *Bettina*'s mizzen to a chorus of hoarse screams. Grapnel hooks, gleaming silver in the bright sunlight, were hurled upwards, hooked over the galleon's rail. From the deck of the *Magdalene* rose another earsplitting cry as the pirates prepared to swarm their prey en masse.

"Boarders away!"

Logan led the charge, and was eagerly followed. With the prospect of blood and loot to draw them, the pirates leaped up the nets that had been connected to the grapnel, easily scaling the distance to the galleon's rail. Half the crew seemed to go over at once; they were met with little resistance.

Then, from the *Bettina*'s deck, a cannon exploded. Shrapnel came flying over the rail to scour the *Magdalene*'s deck. Black smoke laced with flame appeared briefly above Lilah and Joss. This time the chorus of victory cries came from the *Bettina*'s deck. Bodies of men who had just been going over the *Bettina*'s rail when the cannon fired tumbled onto the *Magdalene*'s deck, thudding as they hit. More bodies got caught in the grapnel lashings, hanging grotesquely as blood poured from them. Those who had not yet made it over the rail fell back, dropping and scrambling for cover.

"Get down!" Joss yelled, coming around the cannon in a single bound to throw Lilah bodily to the deck.

"What's happening?" Lilah gasped as a second explosion from the galleon came whistling over.

"They were ready after all. That cannon was loaded with scrap metal. It probably took out half our crew!"

"Fire cannon!"

The command came from the *Bettina*. A round black cannonball hurtled over the *Magdalene*'s deck, taking the mizzen with it. The mast crashed down to the accompaniment of screams.

"Holy hell, Cap'n got it full in the face. Blew the top of his head clean off, by God! They were ready, suspecting a trap!" Blood ran down Speare's face. Lilah saw to her horror that his right ear was gone. "Why ain't you at that cannon, damn you? It's a bloody slaughter up there!"

"Too many of our own aboard. Cannon aren't picky who they kill," Joss told him.

"Boarders — again!"

The cry came from Foxy, who was trying to muster the crew now that Logan was dead. A few leaped up the nets at his words, only to be cut down by a hail of small arms fire as the defenders rushed the rail. More screams sliced through the smoke, more bodies thumped to the deck. One unfortunate lost his hold on the nets, then caught himself again with just his shoulders and head visible above the *Magdalene*'s bulwarks. He started to grin with relief, only to have the grin change to a look of surprise as the two ships, caught up on a wave, smacked together. Lilah watched bright blood pour from his mouth as he was crushed between the hulls. When the ships parted again, instants later, he hung on to the net for scant seconds, then dropped soundlessly from sight.

"Cut line! Cut line!"

The cry came from many throats at once. The pirates had had enough of the one-sided fight. In her entire life Lilah had never been so glad to hear anything as that order to retreat. Joss, after ordering Lilah to stay put, set to slashing at the grapnel holding the *Magdalene* to the *Bettina*. Pistol fire sounded from the *Bettina* as the unfortunates left behind battled to the death. Lilah remembered anew that there was no surrender for pirates; to surrender only traded death in battle for death by hanging.

More shrapnel raked the brigantine's deck as the men worked frantically to free her from her erstwhile prey. The sulphurous smell of gunpowder was everywhere Lilah could barely breathe, barely see through the pall of black smoke. She had passed the point of terror by now. She lay huddled beneath the sheltering bulwark, her arms providing what protection they could for her head.

Horror had rendered her emotions numb.

In a matter of moments, the *Magdalene* was safely away. Two pirates who had been left behind on the *Bettina* alive and apparently not badly wounded, leaped into the sea and began to swim frantically after the brigantine. Fire from defenders at the rail of the *Bettina* cut them down. They sank, screaming, as their blood rose to join the crimson puddles that had already spread over the surface of the sea.

A plume of smoke rose from where a cannonball had torn into the *Magdalene*'s deck. Men quickly extinguished it while more men worked to get the brig's sails up. Joss labored with the rest. Lilah felt renewed terror as she saw him shin up the jib to help with the torn rigging.

The wounded littered the deck. Their screams and moans were hideous to hear, but they were ignored as the survivors rushed to get the ship clear. Lilah was just taking hold of herself, telling herself that, pirates or not, she had to help men in need, when the cannonball came screeching overhead.

It hurtled down like a heaven-thrown thunderbolt, and when it hit it took the *Magdalene* with it.

The powder was stored aft, in barrels, and the ball found it.

The ship exploded, the sound a giant's enormous sneeze, its force lifting the *Magdalene* clear out of the water. When she fell back, shuddering and splintering, a great fan of jet-black smoke rose from her innards.

A second explosion sounded, the force of it knocking Lilah off her feet, slamming her headfirst into the bulwark.

When she recovered her senses, it was to find the *Magdalene*'s bow almost under water and a bright sheet of flame rushing toward her from the hatchway with the awful speed of a herd of stampeding horses. Lilah barely had time to do more than take a second horrified look before instinct sent her leaping over the rail, to fall down, down, deep into the bloodied sea.

Forty

Lilah clung to a barrel cover as the *Magdalene* went down. For what seemed like an eternity the brigantine appeared to balance on her prow, her stern high in the air, silhouetted against the soft blue sky. Her sails were bright crackling flags of crimson flame. Inky black feathers of smoke dirtied fluffy white clouds high above. Then, with hardly more than a whoosh, the ship slid downward, creating a giant whirlpool that sucked everything in the vicinity into its vortex before swallowing it whole. The ship and all that had been aboard her simply vanished from the surface of the ocean in the space of a few minutes. Swirling ripples rushed out from where the ship had disappeared, catching Lilah as she clung for dear life to the barrel lid. She was far enough from the center that she was not drawn down in the ship's wake. Others, not so fortunate, screamed as they were dragged under, never to be seen again.

Bodies and debris bobbed all around her. A man clung to what was left of a spar nearby. He was alive, but Lilah spared him scarcely a glance. Her eyes raked over the gently rolling waves, weighing every bit of flotsam, anything that might possibly be human that she could see. Her stomach churned; her throat was dry.

One thought occupied her mind to the exclusion of all else: What had happened to Joss?

He had been on the jib when the powder had blown. She had not seen him again. Had he been thrown clear? Or had he gone down with the ship? At the thought that he might be dead, that she might never see him again, Lilah wanted to scream, wanted to curse, wanted to cry. If he was dead, she could not bear it.

Two longboats crisscrossed the surface of the water, picking up survivors. They were from the *Bettina*, whose master was clearly too godly a man to see even pirates drown.

He would, instead, see them hang.

Joss could not be dead. She would know if he was, would feel it deep inside. He was alive, somewhere amidst the debris that was all that was left of the once-proud brigantine. She had to find him, now, before the *Bettina*'s crew did. They would think him a pirate like the rest. At the discretion of the captain, pirates, when taken, could be hanged summarily from a yardarm. No trial was required; it was the law of the sea. The gloomy truth was that those who had survived the *Magdalene*'s sinking might not see land again anyway. They might very well end their lives at the end of a rope at sea.

It occurred to Lilah that she herself might be mistaken for a pirate, but the possibility did not seriously worry her. She would explain the situation, and they would understand and restore her to her father. Joss was the problem. Convincing a captain to spare her was one thing; arguing for the life of a man, a gunner who to all appearances had been as much a part of the pirate crew as anyone, was another.

But none of that mattered at the moment. All that mattered was finding Joss. Alive.

Where was he?

Not wanting to cry out his name for fear of attracting the attention of the longboat and being picked up before she was ready, Lilah looked carefully around. Then, kicking, still clinging to the barrel lid, she half swam, half floated to an overturned lifeboat to which three men clung.

Yates was one, Silas another. Lilah did not know the third. The skin on Silas's face was blackened, burned raw in places. His hair was singed off. He looked dreadful, a creature from a nightmare. Still, he seemed to be suffering little pain, she thought as he stared at her for a moment without recognition or perhaps he was in shock.

"Remy? That you?"

"Yes, it's me, Silas."

Her voice, made hoarse by the smoke she had inhaled, was nonetheless far from Remy's inarticulate grunts. Now that the *Magdalene* was gone, there seemed no sense in keeping to her role. Besides, her worry about Joss was so acute that it drove everything else from her mind.

"By damn," Silas muttered, staring. "Yer a bloody wench. By damn!"

In addition to the change in her voice, Lilah realized that she had lost her kerchief and protective coat of dirt. Silas's recognition of her true sex was almost inevitable, but she no longer cared.

"Have you seen Joss? San Pietro?" she asked urgently, but Silas only stared at her, his eyes starting grotesquely from his scorched face.

A longboat came close, oars lapping through the water. Lilah saw that two survivors were huddled in the stern under guard by a man with a musket. A third survivor was sprawled in the floor of the boat, clearly unconscious. One of the *Bettina*'s crew crouched in the bow, leaning out over the water as he probed at a floating body with a boat hook. Two more manned the oars, but Lilah had eyes only for the man sprawled on the floor.

He was black-haired, broad-shouldered, tall and muscular, and wearing a sapphire silk shirt. He was Joss. She was sure of it.

Abandoning her barrel cover, she swam for the longboat, grabbed the side.

"Back off there!" The man with the musket swung the weapon around on her.

"I'm not a pirate," Lilah said impatiently, barely sparing him a glance "Help me aboard."

At the obvious femininity of her voice, all the men aboard who were capable of doing so turned to her.

"Lad or lass, it makes no matter. Pirates all," one of them said.

"I tell you I'm not —"

"Pull 'er aboard, Hank," said the one with the musket, who seemed to be in charge, to the one with the boat hook. Then, to Lilah: "If you try anything, we'll blast you to Hades. Lass or no."

Hands reached down to drag her over the side. Her attention was riveted on Joss. There was blood on the back of his shirt.

"What's wrong with him?" she demanded,

scrambling to kneel beside him.

The man who had helped her aboard shrugged.

"By Jehosephat, it's the idiot, Remy! She's his leman!" One of the pirates roused himself enough from his lethargy to stare at Lilah with a mixture of surprise and venom.

"Watch your language, you!" The man with the musket swung the weapon around so that it pointed at the speaker, who subsided.

Lilah ignored this interchange, instead focusing on discovering the extent of Joss's injuries. He was unconscious, soaking wet, scarlet bloodstains spreading like red ink on the wet silk covering his back. She traced the blood to its source, a deep gash in the back of his head, just above the skin of his neck. The hair there was sticky with blood and matted. She reached out a trembling hand to determine the extent of the injury. As she moved, the barrel of the musket caught her shoulder, pushing her back.

"You, sit over there with the others!"

"But —"

"You heard me. Sit! Or lass or no, I'll blow you straight to hell! Right here and now!"

Lilah looked up at that hard, unyielding face, and knew that he would do as he threatened. The man was young, probably not more than a few years older than herself, freckle-faced and gangly. But his expression was grim, his grip on the musket unwavering. Lilah realized that he considered her as much a member of the pirate crew as any of the captured men. She realized something else, too: He had been through a dreadful fight to the death, and as far as he was concerned, she was the enemy he'd narrowly defeated.

The longboat picked up Yates, Silas, and the third man who clung to the lifeboat, then reversed direction to make its way back to the *Bettina.* Lilah kept her eyes fixed on Joss. He moved once, flexing his back as if it hurt him, sending more blood spurting forth to trickle down his neck, stain his shirt. His head lifted, came down again so that the opposite cheek rested in the faint wash of the seawater that sloshed in the bottom of the boat. In his new position, she could see his face. Her every muscle ached to go to him, but she was sorely afraid that if she made the attempt she would be shot. So she stayed where she was, watching, aching.

Joss grimaced, his eyes flickering open, then closed. Lilah caught her breath, and made an involuntary move toward him. The muzzle of the musket caught her in the shoulder, thrusting her painfully back.

"Do that again and you're gone!"

"He's hurt, bleeding! He needs help!"

"Stay where you are! There'll be no mollycoddling of bloody pirates! What is he, your lover? That's too bad."

"He's not a pirate — I'm not a pirate! We were forced —"

"Sure you were."

Lilah glared at the man, who was looking at her with a combination of hatred and contempt, the small black hole at the end of the musket never wavering as he pointed it at her heart. Joss groaned, and she felt a spurt of anger.

"Look, you insufferable man, my name is Delilah Remy. My father owns Heart's Ease, one of the largest sugar plantations in Barbados. We were shipwrecked and —"

"Stow it," the man interrupted rudely. "I don't have the time to listen to fairy tales."

"Why, you . . . !" Forgetting where she was, Lilah started to her feet. The boat rocked precariously. The man roughly shoved her back down.

"Move again, and I'll throw you overboard, and leave you to drown!"

Looking at the grim set of his mouth, Lilah believed him, completely. Disgruntled, she crossed her arms over her chest and sat, alternating between glaring at the imbecile with the musket and casting worried looks at Joss as the longboat was rowed back to the *Bettina*.

Forty-one

On the deck of the *Bettina*, the pirates were herded into a tight little group under the main mast and kept under guard. Lilah was herded too, to her indignation. Joss, still unconscious, was hauled up from the longboat by means of a rope tied under his arms. He was dumped with as much care as if he'd been a sack of oatmeal near the others. Lilah, waiting until the guard was looking elsewhere, crawled furtively to his side. Shedding her soaked jerkin, she pressed it to the back of his head, trying to stanch the flow of blood. The cut was not large but it was deep, and still freely bled. The blow that caused it must have been severe. It was a miracle he had not drowned.

His was hardly the worst of the injuries. Like Silas, most of the survivors were terribly burned. Yates had had a foot blown off. Lilah and one other were the only ones to escape uninjured.

All in all, nine pirates including herself and Joss had been brought aboard the *Bettina*.

The rest were given up for dead, their corpses gone down with the ship or left for shark bait. A decent burial was not considered necessary for pirates, the carrion of the sea.

None of the women except Lilah had survived. Caught below decks when the ship exploded, they had probably been among the first to perish. She hoped the explosion itself had killed them quickly. She did not like to imagine them burned to death, or drowned.

Not even Nell. Her audacity in pursuing Joss was not deserving of such a terrible end.

The deck was a shambles, littered with pieces of scrap metal and sticky with blood. Her jib had gone down in the fight. It lay splintered across the deck, an ominous reminder of how much the galleon had lost in the battle. Her dead lay in a neat line before the forecastle, and they appeared to number more than a dozen.

Easy to spot as he moved with frenetic energy about the deck, the captain was a short, stocky man with a grim set to his mouth. At the moment he was standing before the forecastle, Bible in one hand, pistol in the other. A shot rang out. Lilah jumped, then realized the shot was a signal to all hands except the guards to gather together for the funeral service for their fallen shipmates.

By the time the prayers for the dead were over and the bodies were being tipped one at a time into the sea, Lilah was shivering with fear. There was no reason to expect mercy from those who had been so mercilessly savaged.

The captain marched over to stand in front of his prisoners. He eyed the bedraggled group with loathing.

"Pirates," he said. "Bah!"

Spitting on the deck to express his opinion of his captives, he turned to a lanky man who stood just behind him.

"No need to haul the scum to port. Hang 'em."

"Aye, Captain!"

From the man's alacrity, he was, like the captain, out for vengeance. The rest of the crew that Lilah could see were in grim concurrence. Those of the pirates who heard their sentence pronounced and were aware enough to understand their fate cried out and moaned, sobbing and begging for mercy. Silas lurched forward on his knees, scrabbling for the captain's leg as he started to walk away.

"Have mercy, sir, have mercy. . . ."

The captain booted him savagely in the

face. Silas screamed, clawed at his burned face, then collapsed on the deck, sobbing. Lilah felt sick with fear, and knew she had to act.

The captain was already moving away. Guard or no, Lilah shifted Joss's head out of her lap and leaped to her feet.

"Captain! Wait!" She would have run to him but the musket trained on her gave her pause. "Captain! I must speak with you."

To her relief the captain turned sharply at the sound of her voice, Lilah supposed because it belonged to a female.

"A lass." His eyes swept her, registered her sex. Then he shrugged. "No matter."

"But I'm not a pirate!" Lilah cried desperately, ignoring the killing looks cast her way by her companions in misfortune. "I am Delilah Remy, and I was shipwrecked —"

"Shut your mouth, you little slut!" One of the guards strode to stand between her and the captain, threatening to stave in her face with the butt end of his musket. Lilah looked past him, knowing she would not get another chance, her eyes and voice beseeching the captain to listen.

"Please, we were forced aboard the *Magdalene*, we were never part of the crew. We were as much victims of these pirates as you. . . ."

The musket butt lifted, was drawn back in preparation for a blow. Lilah cringed, raising her arm to shield her face.

"She tried to tell something of the same story when we fished her out, Pa. I was in no mood to listen."

Lilah realized then that the freckle-faced young sailor from the longboat was the captain's son.

From the corner of her eye, she saw a rope being thrown up to catch a yardarm. It snaked upwards, a thick brown arc against the sky, missed its mark and fell back. As she realized what this portended, Lilah shivered and redoubled her efforts.

"You must listen to me. Please, I beg you. . . ."

The captain turned back, crossed his arms over his chest. He and his son in an identical posture beside him considered her. Lilah knew that by no stretch of the imagination did she resemble the young lady she had once been, but she hoped that they would see something that would given them pause. She tried a tentative, tremulous smile. When that didn't work she stood mute, staring at the pair of them, chewing unconsciously, nervously, on her lower lip, her hands twisting together.

"Let her come here," the captain ordered

at last. The hovering guard stepped back. With a great feeling of relief Lilah went forward.

"Now tell your tale, and tell it quickly. And be warned, I mislike liars!"

Beneath the yardarm, the rope was thrown up again. This time it arched gracefully over the spar, was caught and pulled into position.

"My name is Delilah Remy. . . ." Lilah began, only to be interrupted by a sailor who ran over to inform the captain that the rope was up and the hangings could begin.

"Read a prayer over 'em, and get on with it."

The sailor was dismissed with a wave of the captain's hand. Lilah tried not to hear the despairing cries of her erstwhile crewmates as one of the sailors began a hasty chant of "Our father . . ."

Her one concern had to be for herself — and Joss.

Speaking as quickly as she could, she told him how she and Joss had come to be aboard the *Magdalene.* Her story was buoyed by the captain's son, who said: "The men I picked up did seem surprised to learn that she was a female, Pa."

"Hmm." The captain stared at her for a moment, nodded. "All right. Barbados is not far out of our way. Need to make some repairs anyway, so I suppose we can make port there as well as anywhere. If you're telling the truth, you'll be glad to get home. If you're not, well, I suppose you can hang just as well in Bridgetown as here."

He turned away, pleased with himself, and cast a sharp look at his son. "Give her a cabin, and some dry clothes, but make sure she's locked in."

"Aye, Pa."

"Captain!"

He turned back to look at her, from his expression clearly surprised to be importuned more about a matter already settled to his satisfaction.

"My companion — he is no more a pirate than I am."

"Which one is he?"

"The one lying amidships. Tall, with black hair. He's injured, unconscious."

"He was at the stern cannon! I saw him set a charge myself!"

The speaker was one of the sailors, a small coterie of whom had been listening with varying degrees of suspicion to Lilah's tale.

"That so?" The captain fixed Lilah with eyes that were suddenly ten degrees colder.

"He — he was forced. They would have killed us if he hadn't —"

"He was a gunner! I saw him, too, sir, hard to miss, he is, being so tall!"

The captain's eyes swung back to Lilah. At the look in them she nearly despaired.

"You can't hang him! I tell you he was forced —"

"Whatever the merits of your story, if he was laying cannon he's a bloody pirate. He hangs with the rest!"

With that pronouncement the captain started to turn away again.

"No! You can't!"

Lilah ran after him, caught his sleeve. He looked down at her impatiently.

"I warn you, lassie, I'm in no mood to listen to a young girl's heart-stirrings. I've lost nigh a third of my crew, one my own sister's lad. Plus I've got God knows how much damage to my ship. Do you know what it'll cost me to set her right again? I'll spare you, but not a man who fired a cannon on my ship. If he's your fancy-man, then I'm sorry."

"He's not!" The words came out in a rush as she sought frantically for those that would save Joss. The captain was concerned about money. . . . "He's not my — my anything! He — he's a slave, highly skilled, very valuable! He — he belongs to my father, and — he's worth more than five hundred American dollars! My — my father will want to be recompensed if he loses such a valuable property! If you hang him, you'll owe my father that money! But if you restore him to my father, and me too, I'll — I'll see that you are well paid for your trouble."

The captain stared at her, then at Joss. "Now, lass, spare me your tales. That's a white man and —"

"He's a slave, I tell you, and you've no right to hang him! He's what they call high-yeller, and my father owns him and he'll make you pay if you kill him! Five hundred dollars. . . ."

"Let's have a look at this slave!"

To a man the group around the captain walked over to stare down at Joss. Lilah went with them, her heart in her mouth. The pirates were being dragged, screaming, crying, away to hang.

Joss had regained consciousness, but barely. He blinked his eyes and lifted his head once before groaning and dropping back against the bloodied boards of the deck.

"Fetch a bucket of water!"

Someone did, and the bucket was emptied over Joss. As the cold deluge splashed him, slopped onto the deck, he lifted his head again, blinking. He moved an arm forward to serve as a pillow, resting his head on it.

His eyes stayed open and Lilah thought that he was groggy but aware. Then his eyes found her, and sharpened slightly.

"Can you hear me, boy?" the captain asked, bending at the waist to growl the question, his face scant inches from Joss's.

Joss nodded, the movement barely perceptible.

"You lay cannon against my ship?"

Lilah held her breath.

"Had no choice. Would have been killed, other— otherwise. Hope you'll — accept my apologies." He sounded as if he was struggling for breath.

The captain pursed his lips, squatted. "You know this — person?" He gestured toward Lilah. Joss's eyes lifted to her face, and he moved his head in what seemed to be assent.

"Aye."

"What is the person's name, and relationship to you?"

So he would test her identity, too, weigh her story against Joss's. Lilah noticed the captain was careful to use no pronouns that would give away her sex, and realized that Joss could not know they were aware of the truth behind what was left of her disguise He would try to protect her. . . .

"Remy." Joss's voice was hoarse, but he

stirred, trying to sit up. He winced and fell back, and it was all Lilah could do not to run to his side. "He's my . . ."

"They know I'm a lady, Joss," Lilah interjected. "You don't have to protect me anymore."

Joss looked at her. So did the captain. His look carrried a clear warning for her to be silent.

"Miss Remy claims that you're a blackamoor. She says you're worth five hundred dollars, and you're her slave. What do you have to say to that?"

Joss looked at Lilah again, his eyes suddenly growing hard.

"I never dispute a lady's word," he said finally, and his mouth twisted in what was almost a sneer.

"So you're a slave, belonging to Miss Remy here? Or her father? I want a plain answer, yes or no."

"Joss. . . ." The near-whisper was involuntary, drawn out of her by the sudden harshness of his features.

"You hush, missy!"

Lilah was silenced. She could only look miserably at Joss, knowing what he must be thinking. But what else could she have done?

"Yes or no? I don't have all day!"

Joss stared at her for a seemingly endless

moment, green eyes cold as ice. Then he said, "Whatever else she may be, the lady is not a liar. If she says it's so, then it's so."

That was enough for the captain.

"Hell, throw him in the brig, lock her in a cabin, and let's get back to business. The cargo won't keep forever, and I'm not of a mind to be owing five hundred dollars and be out a spoiled cargo as well. We'll sort the pair of them out when we get to Barbados. And I'm not forgetting the reward you promised, young woman."

Minutes later Lilah found herself being marched away under guard, with Joss being hoisted by two sailors and half carried behind her. As she approached the hatchway, she heard a hoarse scream from the front of the ship. The hangings had begun.

Her escort took her arm, his touch surprisingly polite, and turned her along a hallway while Joss's guards began to descend with him farther into the bowels of the ship. Lilah stopped.

"I would see him secured, if you please."

The three sailors looked at each other, shrugged, and permitted her to trail along as Joss was half carried down the narrow stairs.

The *Bettina*'s brig consisted of a single cell, dark and dank and comfortless. Lilah's heart sank as she saw where they meant to leave

Joss. But with luck it would only be for a few days, and in any case it was better than hanging. She only hoped that Joss would see it that way.

Lilah stood outside in the passageway as Joss was taken in and lowered to the bottom of the two tiers of bunks. The young sailor who was her escort was no longer holding her arm, apparently responding to her as a young lady now instead of pirate lass. With no one to prevent her, Lilah stepped inside the cell. The two guards had left Joss lying on his belly in deference to the wound in the back of his head. It was no longer bleeding, as far as she could tell in the sickly light of the single lantern that hung from a hook outside in the passageway. But his hair was matted with blood, and he still seemed weak and groggy.

"Joss . . ." she began, leaning over him, her voice low as the men waited for her by the cell door.

He lay with his head pillowed on his arm. In the darkness his eyes gleamed a hard, glittering green.

"You treacherous little bitch," he said. Lilah caught her breath.

"Joss. . . ."

"Miss, you'll have to come out of there now. Cap'n said you were to be locked in a cabin, and I have to get back on deck."

Lilah nodded in response to the sailor's summons, and turned away, her opportunity to explain gone.

As the door clanged shut behind her, was locked by one of the men who had carried Joss down, she spoke to her escort.

"Could you see that he has medical care? He . . . as I said, he's very valuable."

The sailor pursed his lips. "I'll ask Cap'n Rutledge. It's his decision."

And with that Lilah had to be content.

Forty-two

For three days Joss was left alone in the gloomy dampness of the *Bettina*'s brig except for a single visit by the ship's doctor, who looked at the back of his head, dusted the wound with a malodorous powder, and took himself off, never to be seen again. The decidedly spartan accommodations did not particularly bother Joss, but the solitude did. Not that he wanted to hobnob with the crew. He was happy to see them for the few brief minutes three times a day when they shoved a tray of food through the opening in the half-timbered, half-barred door.

The person he wanted to see, urgently, was Lilah.

He had much he wanted to say to her.

The more he dwelled on her actions — and with nothing to do but think, he dwelled on them at length — the more her betrayal infuriated him. After all they had shared, that she would tell the first sympathetic warm body she saw that he was a slave made him long to wring her slender neck. It made him want to shake her until her head was in danger of separating from her shoulders. It made him want to turn her over his knee and paddle her backside until his hand ached.

The faithless little bitch had claimed to love him, and he had believed her. Then as soon as she was back in reach of civilization, she had allowed the blind prejudices she had been raised with to reduce him to the status of a nonperson, not good enough to kiss the hem of her skirt, let alone her mouth. Let alone live with her, love her, marry her, father her children.

Bitch.

He had known it, somewhere in the back of his mind though he had hoped and prayed he was wrong, had known that in the end that tiny bit of blood would come between them. He had known that she would never admit, in the cold, hard light of day and society, to loving a slave. A Negro slave. Because that was what he was, as hard as it was to admit even to himself. That minute infusion of blood from an ancestor far, far back along his family tree mattered more than his education, his upbringing, his character.

That minute infusion of blood made him a black man, legally and socially.

Miss lily-white Lilah had bedded a man of

a different race. What did that make her? Or rather, what would that make her, if her fancy family and fine friends should discover it? At the very least, a social outcast. At the worst, a fallen woman, a strumpet, a whore.

Angry, bitter, Joss toyed with the idea of trumpeting their liaison to all and sundry just as soon as there was any all and sundry for him to tell. How the hoity-toity little bitch would cringe when the world knew her for the round-heeled hypocrite she was!

But he was a gentleman, damn it, and a gentleman did not boast of his conquests, no matter how badly the lady might have behaved toward him.

The little bitch had been hot as hell. She'd wanted him for a stud, damn it; that was the plain truth of it. And now that she was about to be restored to the bosom of her family she would marry that rawboned farmer, Keith or Karl or whatever his name was — if justice hadn't been served and he hadn't drowned. Even if he had, she'd marry someone just like him.

And she'd spend her nights lying in her husband's arms, suffering his touch while she pictured the steamy nights that the two of them had shared. He'd be her goddamn fantasy, and that thought made him madder than ever.

She'd wear another man's ring, bear his name and children, and all the while yearn for him. But the sanctimonious little hypocrite would never admit to it, except perhaps in her deepest soul. She would never come to him. Never.

He was a Negro slave. She was a white lady.

That was the truth of the matter as she and the world saw it, and he'd better get it through his head before he came within reach of the little bitch again. Strangling her would gain him nothing but a short dance at the end of a long rope.

He didn't want to kill her anyway. He wanted to spank her until she couldn't sit down, make love to her until she couldn't walk, and keep her properly under his thumb for the rest of his life.

He loved her, goddamn it all. Loved her so much that the thought of her with another man made him homicidal. Loved her so much that her betrayal made him sick to his stomach.

Well, first things first. He had had this slave business clear up to his eyebrows. No matter who his ancestors had or hadn't been, he was getting the hell back to England as soon as he could. And the little bitch could get on with her plans for a nice, tidy, boring life. He wished her joy of it!

That night, when the same wizened sailor who had brought his food for the last three days came again, Joss was on his feet, waiting by the door. In his best humble tone, Joss asked for a quill, ink and paper. Somewhat to his surprise, they were brought to him.

And with a grim half-smile he set himself down to write a long-delayed letter to his second-in-command at his shipping company in England.

Forty-three

The next morning the *Bettina* sailed into Bridgetown. Joss knew only that the ship had dropped anchor in a calm harbor. Their exact location was not revealed to him until two days later, when three sailors came to release him from the brig where he had spent nearly six days in isolation. To his silent fury, they clapped irons on his wrists before leading him topside. He was clearheaded now, able to walk without aid, but was a trifle weak from being confined without fresh air or exercise.

As he emerged into the sunlight for the first time in almost a week, Joss stopped in the hatchway, blinking furiously against the blinding glare. His escort nudged him in the back with a musket, urging him impatiently on.

As his eyesight gradually adjusted to the brilliance of the tropical afternoon, he became aware of four figures standing near the gangplank, watching his approach. Three were men, one of whom was, he thought, the *Bettina*'s captain.

The fourth, he realized as his escort brought him to a halt a few feet from the little group, was Lilah. She was fashionably dressed in a low-cut gown of palest pink muslin that bared her white shoulders and slender arms beneath tiny sleeves. A wide sash of deeper pink was tied beneath her breasts. A ribbon of the same shade was threaded through the tousled cap of palest gold curls that framed her small face. To his annoyance, the boyish style became her, emphasizing the fragile perfection of her features, the creaminess of her skin, the soft blue-gray of her huge eyes. The very loveliness of her infuriated him so much that it was all he could do to look at her without gnashing his teeth.

He restricted himself to a single icy glare.

She met this without so much as a flicker of her thick-fringed eyes. The soft half-smile that curved her lips never faltered as she said something to the short, stocky man on her right. Joss didn't know him, but it didn't require genius to deduce that he must be Lilah's father. He was perhaps sixty, burned a permanent lobster red from the sun, his hair a gingery version of Lilah's fairness, his figure portly but not yet totally run to fat.

The man on Lilah's other side he did

know. Joss cursed God, the devil or whoever was responsible because Lilah's erstwhile fiancé hadn't drowned after all.

Forty-four

"Joss. . . ." His name died as a mere breath in Lilah's throat, unheard by anyone. She couldn't go to him, couldn't acknowledge that he was any more to her than a slave to whom she felt grateful. Her father and especially Kevin were already angry and suspicious, ready to suspect the worst of Joss — and herself.

Because she'd spent almost two months alone with him.

If Bajan society knew only that and nothing else, she would be the subject of a raging scandal. If she'd been shipwrecked with a young, virile white man who was single and looked like Joss, her father would already be planning a shotgun wedding. But since Joss was of mixed race, he was almost a nonperson as far as society was concerned. The taboo against a respectable white lady taking a man like Joss as a lover was so strong that it almost precluded the possibility that such a thing could have happened. At least in her father's mind. Others in their social circle, some of whom had long been jealous of Lilah Remy's beauty and wealth, would likely welcome the spread of such gossip. Lilah could just picture them tittering behind their hands over her downfall. . . . The idea frightened her almost as much as did the prospect of her father's rage if he should discover what she had done.

She could not publicly admit that she loved a man of color, that she had given herself to him again and again. It was cowardly of her, she knew, but she just couldn't do it. Not to anyone, now or ever. Her good name meant too much to her. Her family meant too much to her. And Joss meant too much to her.

If she ever confessed, she would be signing Joss's death warrant. Lilah knew as well as she knew her own name that her father would see Joss dead before the sun rose on another day if he knew the truth of what had happened on that island.

The reality of the situation in which she could so easily find herself if either she or Joss were not discreet had been brought home to her with a vengeance by her father. When he had arrived on the *Bettina* that morning in response to Captain Rutledge's message sent to Heart's Ease when they docked the day before, her father had been overjoyed to see her, shedding sentimental tears and clasping her to his heart. Kevin too had kissed her, and she had let him, not knowing what else to do.

Then the pair of them had started asking questions about Joss. Had he offered her insult? Had he been overly familiar? Had he dared to touch her? How many nights had the two of them spent alone, and under what conditions?

It had been abundantly clear as the first battery of questions was fired at her that the only way she could keep Joss safe was to lie about every single thing that had happened between them. She had already aroused their suspicions by insisting that Joss's wounds be tended aboard the ship. Captain Rutledge reported that to her father as he pressed for payment for Joss's medical care to be added to the promised reward, along with a sum for both Lilah's and Joss's board on the ship.

Her father, primed by Kevin's terse account of her scandalous behavior over Joss in the Colonies, had been harsher than he ever had been with her. Only his long habit of adoration of his only daughter had enabled her to calm him down.

But if she were to show more care for Joss than simple gratitude dictated, she would endanger his life.

Lilah looked at him now, silently furious as he stood there squinting against the bright sunlight, and willed him to understand. Though she doubted that he would. Joss's nature was such that he wouldn't count the cost if he loved. But for herself — Lilah supposed, miserably, that she was a coward. But the consequences were too dear.

With a little pang Lilah saw that his clothes were tattered, the black breeches and sapphire silk shirt reduced to near rags. His feet were bare on the scrubbed boards of the deck. His hair had grown long, and without a thong to confine it, hung in deep blue-black waves to his shoulders. The lines of that rakish mustache were blurred by a near week's growth of beard. But even the unkept stubble could not disguise that his features were aristocratic, his mouth firm and well-shaped, his nose straight, his chin square. It could not disguise the slashing black eyebrows, or his eyes, which were the brilliant green of an exotic bird's plumage. It could not disguise the unbowed stance and steady gaze of a proud man.

Joking at the haughty tilt of his chin, the arrogant lift of his brows as he looked them over even as they stared at him, Lilah thought that no man could ever, possibly, have looked less like a slave.

Iron shackles circled his wrists, linked by perhaps a foot of chain. As they registered on her consciousness for the first time, Lilah caught her breath. Then she managed, just barely, to get hold of her emotions before she gave herself away. Quickly she cast a glance sideways, first at Kevin and then at her father; they were looking at Joss, their eyes hard.

Lilah prayed that Joss would not say anything that would give them both away.

"This is the slave?" Her father spoke at last, sounding disbelieving, addressing the remark to Kevin. Dear disapproving Kevin, who had made it to a populated island that dreadful night, had been home in Barbados for as long as she had been on that island with Joss. For as long as it had taken her world to be forever changed. Her heart to be forever changed, although Kevin did not know that. Could never know it.

"He's colored. I told you he could pass for white."

"I see what you mean."

Both men continued to study Joss as if he were a horse or some other livestock brought for their inspection. Lilah, able to stand that relentless green gaze no longer, looked up at her father.

"He saved my life, Papa."

"So you told me." He stared across at Joss a moment longer, frowning. "I don't like this. If word gets out that you were alone with him for weeks . . ." He shook his head. "He has my gratitude for not letting you drown, and for saving you from what could have been an even worse fate at the hands of those thrice-damned pirates, but the plain truth is that it would be best if he were sold. We could leave him here, have Tom Surdock put him up at auction —"

"No!" Lilah's response was instinctive. At the tightening in her father's face, she hurried to explain the urgent note in her voice. Her father and Kevin must not guess. . . . "If — if you sold him, he — he might say something to someone. Something about — about me being alone with him for all that time. He never touched me, of course, but if people were to find out that we were shipwrecked together . . . You know how people love to gossip."

Her eyes shifted for no more than a split second to Joss as she tried to gauge his reaction to her words. His expression remained impassive, though his eyes narrowed slightly, fixed on her face. Lilah prayed that he would keep quiet. She went cold as she remembered his slow-building temper that had on more than one occasion culminated in a fiery explosion. If he were to lose his temper now, were to give in to the fury she knew he must be holding inside, all would be lost for them both. But if he was furious, he was hiding it well beneath that carved-teak face. Her eyes touched his once, briefly, fluttered over his face as swiftly and tentatively as a butterfly's wings. Then she wrenched her gaze back to her father, who was shaking his head in refusal of her request.

Lilah spoke again, more desperately than before. "Papa, can't you see that it would be better to keep him on Heart's Ease, just until the talk dies down? You know that as soon as I get home, everyone will be just dying to hear the story of how I was shipwrecked. I can say there was another woman with me as well as a slave. But if he says something different . . . If they see him, see how — how white he looks, how — how . . . Well, I just think it's better if no one sees him, don't you? If we can keep him out of everyone's way at Heart's Ease, they'll find something new to talk about before long. Then — then you can sell him, if you want."

She cast another lightning glance at Joss, this one laden with guilt. If he read her silent apology, she saw no sign of softening in his face.

"I suppose you're right," her father grudgingly conceded after a long moment. Kevin said nothing, just looked at Joss with a narrow-eyed expression that Lilah didn't like. He who had been privy to much of the gossip about her previous acquaintance with Joss, and had witnessed Joss's shocking familiarity at the slave auction, had special reason to hate the fact that Joss had spent all those weeks with her alone. Kevin's dislike of Joss emanated from him as clearly as the faint smell of sweat. There would be trouble between those two sooner or later, if she did not find some way of heading it off.

But she could not worry about that now. She had to concentrate on convincing her father, Kevin, and the world, that Joss meant nothing at all to her except for the fact that he had saved her life. Gratitude was an acceptable emotion from mistress to slave, and for the delectation of the outside world that was all she felt for Joss. That wasn't much, not compared to what she really felt, but it would serve to explain any special effort she might make for him.

"You, boy. What's his name? Joss? You, Joss. Come here."

Her father spoke brusquely, the sudden change in his tone as he addressed the man he saw as nothing more than a slave startling. Lilah watched the two men cross looks sharp as swords, and held her breath. She willed Joss to keep his tongue and do as he was told. Her father had a temper every bit as volatile as Joss's. Though he was a kind master, Leonard Remy brooked no insolence from his slaves. And to him, Joss was a slave, a piece of property belonging to Heart's Ease, nothing more. The only problem was, Joss refused to recognize his lowly status, or realize the peril in which it placed him. In his own mind, he was still Jocelyn San Pietro, English sea captain and businessman, and a free man. The two men's differing perceptions of Joss's role were a recipe for disaster.

Lilah's one hope was to get Joss to the comparative safety of Heart's Ease without incident. There, in the natural order of things, Joss and her father would rarely set eyes on one another.

Once she had him safe on Heart's Ease, and the tension had eased somewhat, she would do what she could to get him free. If only Joss would trust her, and be patient until then! But knowing Joss as she did, she did not think he would be patient for long. The miracle was that he had been silent up to now.

Joss slowly walked forward, stopping a respectful few feet from her father, and Lilah breathed a silent sigh of relief. He was being cautious, waiting to see what would happen before he took any action. Thank the Lord!

"You saved my daughter's life. More than once." It was a statement, not a question. "Why?" The question was hard, shot at Joss like a bullet. Joss's eyes never wavered.

"I would not let harm come to any innocent person if I could prevent it."

The answer was perfect. Direct but revealing nothing of their secret. Lilah could feel some of the tension leaving her father's body. On her other side, Kevin stood as stiffly as ever. Suspicion was in his eyes, and he seemed to watch her as well as Joss as Joss spoke.

"You have my gratitude."

Joss merely inclined his head. Leonard shot a glance down at his daughter standing silent and pale beside him, then looked at Joss again.

"She says you've done naught to impugn her honor." It was both hard challenge and question.

"Papa!" Lilah was scandalized. She glared up at her father indignantly. How could he ask such a question with so many ears to hear?

"Hush, girl! 'Tis as well to have this out in the open, at once." He looked from Lilah to Joss, his eyes narrowed and weighing.

"Well, boy, answer! Have you done aught to be ashamed of with my girl?"

"Papa, you're embarrassing me!" Lilah's protest was fueled as much by alarm as embarrassment. Knowing Joss, she was terrified that his pride would not permit him to lie. And if he admitted to anything resembling the truth, he was a dead man and she was not much better off.

"I said hush!" His tone was as harsh as it ever got when speaking to his beloved only child. Lilah, silenced, could only look at Joss with silent pleading. He never even met her eyes. His attention was all on her father.

"You may rest assured that I have never, and would never, dishonor a lady, Mr. Remy."

Lilah caught the veiled barb in that, but she was too relieved at the diplomacy of the answer to quibble. So he was letting her know, oh so subtly, that he didn't classify her as a lady. Well, she'd make him pay for that — but later, much later, and in her own way.

"Very well, then." Her father's eyes shifted to her face briefly, and she felt about two inches tall as she read the relief in them. Clearly he believed that she was still as virginal as she had been when she had left Barbados. Well, guilt might be uncomfortable, but the truth would be far worse. Her father was appeased; far be it from her to disillusion him!

Leonard then addressed Captain Rutledge, who had held himself apart from the discussion.

"If you will, keep him aboard until I can make arrangements to have him transported to my plantation. I'll send some men by later today, or certainly no later than tomorrow morning, to collect him. I thank you again for your kindness to my daughter, and I know you will understand when I tell you that I'm anxious to be away home. My future son-in-law. . ." Here Leonard's voice swelled with pride, and he repeated the favored words with an affectionate glance at Kevin, "My future son-in-law and I are going to get this girl home and keep her there. No more jaunting about the world for her! I'll see her safe married, and no more of this worrying about her! Her stepmother is no doubt going out of her mind even as we speak, wondering what's taking me so long to bring her home again."

Leonard held out his hand to Captain Rutledge, who took it and pumped it with the first smile Lilah had ever seen on his face.

"Children are the very devil, aren't they? I've six boys, so you know I'm no stranger to worry meself!" He let go of Lilah's father's hand, and reached out to tweak her cheek in a teasingly avuncular fashion. "Go along of your father now, Miss Remy, and much happiness to you. I'm just thankful I didn't let my temper get the best of me when we hauled you out of the sea, and hang you and your man with the rest!"

"I'm thankful, too, Captain," Lilah said, able to think of no other reply. Then her father was tucking her hand in his arm, leading her away. As she was escorted down the gangplank, she was conscious every step of the way of a pair of emerald eyes boring holes in her back.

Forty-five

Home! Lilah had never been so glad to see any place in her life as she was to see Heart's Ease on that sun-drenched afternoon. As the carriage turned in to the long drive that led to the main house, Lilah felt the welcome shade from the twin rows of tall, leafy palms that lined the drive like an embrace. She looked toward the red-tiled roof of the house, which could just be glimpsed through the trees. Her excitement was such that she could hardly sit still. On either side of her, Leonard and Kevin smiled in indulgent amusement at her sudden attack of the fidgets. Aware of their grins, Lilah nevertheless craned forward eagerly to get her first look in nearly six months at the sprawling white stuccoed plantation house where she'd been born. She hoped never again to leave for much longer than overnight.

"Lilah!"

"Miss Lilah!"

At the sound of the carriage wheels, her stepmother, Jane, was first out on the verandah, and down the stairs. Behind her came Maisie, her skin shining like polished ebony in the heat as it always did, her whipcord thin body belying her reputation as the best plantation cook in Barbados. The rest of the house slaves piled out behind Maisie, tumbling down the stairs to greet the beloved daughter of the house.

"Lilah, welcome home!"

Lilah half fell out of the carriage into her stepmother's arms, hugging the gentle woman whom she had grown to love dearly over the years. Maisie stretched out her hand to pat Lilah's shoulder, then saw that her fingers were white with flour and drew back with a chuckle.

"Miss Lilah, we done thought you was dead!"

"Oh, Maisie, it's good to see you! It's good to see all of you!"

Once Jane released her, Lilah hugged Maisie, laughing as she disregarded the old woman's protests about floury hands. Looking over Maisie's shoulder at the smiling, weeping slaves, Lilah met a pair of eyes she had feared never to see again.

"Betsy! Oh, Betsy! I was afraid you had drowned!" Lilah fell into Betsy's arms and the two girls hugged each other soundly.

"You came a lot closer to drownin' than

I did, Miss Lilah! Our lifeboat was spotted by another ship in less than a day! The lifeboat you and Mr. Kevin was in was the only one that was lost — and when Mr. Kevin got home and said that your lifeboat had wrecked and you'd been swept away by the sea — well, I tell you, I never want to live through time like the one just passed! And to think of the adventures you've been havin', while we've been breakin' our hearts over you!"

"Terrifying adventures, Betsy," Lilah said, drawing away from her maid to smile at the rest of her slave family. "I am so glad to see you all I declare I could cry! But I won't — at least not until after I see Katy. How is she, Jane?"

"She's been grieving herself to a skeleton over you, of course. Her baby, lost at sea! You'd better go straight up."

"Yes, I will."

"I'll carry up water for your bath, Miss Lilah, and lay out some clean clothes. I know you'll be wantin' to get into your own things as soon as may be."

Lilah looked down at the cheap but pretty dress that her father had bought ready-made from a seamstress in Bridgetown when he discovered to his horror that she had only men's clothes. Compared to what she had been used to wearing ever since the *Swift Wind* went down this gown was magnificent. But as Lilah remembered her own wardrobe, from underwear to day dresses to the most elaborate ball gowns fashioned of the finest materials with the finest workmanship, she was suddenly eager to change. To be herself again.

"You do that, Betsy. And thank you all for the welcome home. I've missed every one of you more than I can say."

She swept up the steps and into the house with Jane and the slaves trailing behind her. Her father and Kevin would see to the horse and buggy, then most likely go about their business. The work on a sugar plantation the size of Heart's Ease was never ending, and required both men's full-time attention.

"Lilah, honey, is that you?"

Katy Allen occupied a small room at the top of the three-story house. Blind and bed-ridden, she scarcely ever went downstairs. She had come over from England with Lilah's mother, some sort of poor relation who was years older than the girl she was hired to chaperone, then stayed on until her charge's wedding and beyond. After Lilah's birth and her mother's death, Katy had taken on the role of the baby's nursemaid and, later her governess. She occupied a place in Lilah's heart second only to her father, and she wept as Lilah came to where she sat in the big rocking chair in the corner of the room and embraced her.

"It's me, Katy." Lilah felt her throat tighten as she hugged the frail old body, breathing in the sweet powdery scent that clung to the woman and had comforted her from earliest childhood.

"It is I, dear." Even at moments of extreme emotion, Katy could be counted on to remember her mandate as governess. This prosaic reminder made Lilah smile as she pulled back to look lovingly at the pale, lined face under its cap of snowy hair.

"It is I, then."

"I knew you hadn't drowned. No child who got into as much mischief as you did and survived would be taken like that."

"You shouldn't have worried." Lilah, undeceived by Katy's brave words, hugged her again. This time a tear, followed by a laugh and a sniff, coursed down the paper-white cheek.

"Don't you go away again, you hear?"

The old woman reached out and drew Lilah's head to her lap, where it had rested many times awash with childish tears, and stroked her hair.

"No, I won't, Katy. I won't," Lilah whispered. As the well-loved hand moved comfortingly over her shorn locks she vowed that she was home to stay.

Forty-six

Lilah heard through the grapevine that Joss arrived safely the next day. Though she was in a fever of impatience to see him, it was three days later before she judged it safe enough to steal away from the house after supper to pay him a surreptitious visit.

The long, lazy daylight hours, when her father and Kevin were both in the fields and Jane was occupied with the myriad tasks involved in running the house, would have been the best time for her to see Joss with no one the wiser. Unfortunately, he had been put to work digging cane holes with a gang of field hands the day after his arrival. His day began at half past five, when the plantation bell pealed its summons to the field hands to assemble in the main estate yard for instructions. He was issued a cup of hot ginger tea, and then driven out to the area in which he was assigned to work. His day lasted fourteen hours.

The slave compound offered no privacy, teeming as it was with activity as families prepared their evening meal or tended the small garden plots behind their huts. Lilah's visit to Joss's hut was sure to be seen and commented on unless it was very late, past the time when the slaves had gone to bed.

Finally, after three days, Lilah realized that the perfect opportunity would never arise. So she suffered Betsy to prepare her for the night, dismissed her, then struggled back into as many of her clothes as were necessary to make her minimally decent. Then she stole from the house.

The hour was just past ten. Her father and Kevin were playing chess in the library, thinking her safely in bed. Jane had retired for the night. As Lilah, shoes in hand, crept across the verandah she heard a voice call to Maisie and froze, her heart in her mouth. But the voice came from the separate kitchen at the back of the house, and Maisie's answer came from there, too. After a heart-pounding moment, Lilah judged it safe to go on.

As she made her way across the grounds toward the thatched-roof slave huts, Lilah was aware of every sound: the murmur of voices and rich laughter coming from the kitchen, where the slaves were still cleaning up after the evening meal and Maisie was setting the morning bread to rise; the soft lowing of the milk cows from the barn across the field; the occasional whinny of a horse from the stable. The night was warm, but a gentle breeze kept it from being unpleasant. The air carried with it a familiar mixture of smells — sweet sugarcane and molasses, manure, odors from the open cookfires that the slaves used to make their suppers, vegetation rotting in the heat, the heady scents of tropical flowers. The breeze whispered through the palm fronds, catching the flat paddles of the windmill where the cane was processed. The creaking sound as the paddles turned in the wind was so familiar that usually Lilah never even heard it. But tonight, with fear of discovery sharpening her senses, she did. Even the chirping of the crickets seemed extra loud, making her jump when one whirred close at hand.

The tiny huts were laid out in neat rows like streets. Lilah knew from Betsy that Joss had been given the hut of a slave named Nemiah who had recently died tragically, crushed to death by the huge stone that ground the cane at the mill. Lilah was too much of a Bajan not to feel uneasy about the hut — Obeahs made a powerful case for violently departed souls haunting their earthly habitats — but she knew Joss would ridicule any such notion.

His hut was at the end of the last row.

There were no fences erected around the slave compound, no guards posted. It would have been very easy for him to run — if there had been any place to run to. Barbados was a small island, just fourteen miles wide and twenty-one miles long. There was no way off except by ship, and escaped slaves were hunted down relentlessly. If he ran, Joss would never make it off the island. Harbor-masters would be alerted, and watch would be kept. Escape from Barbados was next to impossible. Lilah was sure that one of the slave overseers had acquainted Joss with the hopelessness of attempting such a thing. If not, he would probably already have tried it. Unless, of course, he was waiting to first talk to her.

The shutters had been closed over the windows, but light showed through the chinks in the mud-and-wattle walls. Joss was not asleep.

Lilah pushed at the door. It was closed, not latched, and swung inward easily. Moving quickly so as to lessen the chance that she would be seen and recognized, silhouetted against the warm light pouring from within the hut, she stepped inside, closing the door behind her, this time latching it. Then, her toes curling against the coolness of the dirt floor, Lilah turned to seek Joss.

He was lying on his back on a crudely constructed cot, clad only in his plantation-issued loose white trousers, one hand behind his head. An oil lantern smoked on an overturned barrel behind him, illuminating the hut's single room. The remains of a charred-looking meal sat on the rickety table against the wall behind the door. The cot, barrel, and a single hard wooden chair, were the only furniture. He had been reading a tattered copy of a book scrounged from somewhere. The slaves were forbidden to learn to read, but she supposed that Joss, having already known how when he learned of his enslavement, was a different case. As she stepped inside and closed the door he lowered the book. When she turned to face him he just looked at her, green eyes glinting in the uncertain light.

For a long moment they stared at one another without speaking. She drank in the length and breadth of him, the broad shoulders and hair-roughened chest, the handsome face. In that single comprehensive look she noted that his mustache had been shaved, and his hair was neatly shorn. He was clean, surprisingly so considering he had spent the day at hard labor, his hair still damp as though he had recently bathed.

"Hello, Joss." Lilah leaned back against

the door, her hands pressed flat against the rough panel, and smiled at him rather tentatively. What his reaction would be to her visit she could not guess.

By way of reply, his eyes narrowed and his mouth tightened. With an easy movement he swung his legs around, his movements careful, precise; he marked his place in the book with a feather and set it on the barrel beside the lantern. Only then did he look up at her. Those hard eyes told her all she needed to know: He was blazingly angry.

"Well, if it isn't little Miss Lilah, the belle of Barbados," he said at last, smiling in a tigerish way. "Tired of your lily-white fiancé so soon? Come to satisfy your craving for dark meat?"

His tone was savage, and he stood up as he snarled the last two words. Lilah's eyes widened as he advanced on her. She held up a hand, palm out, to ward him off. Her shoes dropped from her nerveless fingers to land with a soft thud on the dirt floor beside her bare foot.

"Joss, wait! I can explain. . . ."

"You can explain?" His voice was a mere rumble of sound, low and threatening, as he closed in on her. "You tell me you love me, bed me, then betray me the first chance you get and *YOU CAN EXPLAIN!*"

These last words were a muted roar, and as they exploded at her he reached out and jerked her toward him, his fingers bruising as they dug into her upper arm.

"Joss, sshh . . . Don't yell! . . . Stop it! What do you think you're doing?"

"Giving you a little of your own back, Miss Lilah!"

He jerked her across the tiny room, sat down hard on the cot, and yanked her over his lap with a speed and ferocity that left her helpless to do anything to save herself.

"No! Joss San Pietro, you let me up! Let me up this instant!"

As she squirmed to escape, he pinned her on his lap with one hard arm, and jerked up her skirt with his other hand.

"Stop it! Stop it this instant, or I . . . Oh! Ouch! Stop!"

His hand whacked her backside with a resounding slap. Lilah cried out. Quickly she muffled the sound with her hand pressed tight against her mouth as she realized a scream might well bring someone to investigate. At all costs she could not be found in Joss's hut, much less in such a compromising position! She kicked and squirmed and fought, but silently and to no avail. He smacked her bottom again, hard, and then again, the blows stinging madly. She tried her best to wriggle free, kicking and beating at his thighs with her fists, biting the inside of her cheek to keep from shrieking her rage at him. Her bottom burned with each blow, but he held her in an iron grip she could not break. Finally, as he showed no signs of either relenting or listening to her gasped pleas for a hearing, her temper blew. When his hand slammed down for what must have been the dozenth time, she bit him as hard as she could through the rough cotton trouser into the hard muscle of his thigh.

"Hell-born bitch!" With this oath he shoved her off his lap. Lilah landed on her hands and knees on the hard-packed floor.

"You low-down, dirty, rotten, smelly son of a bitch!" she hissed, leaping to her feet. So furious she could cheerfully have whacked him over the head with an axe, Lilah drew back her arm and slapped him across the face with such force that her palm stung.

He clapped a hand to his abused cheek, and jumped to his feet. Lilah had to scurry backwards to avoid being knocked over. As he towered over her, emanating rage like a stove gives off heat, her eyes blazed up into his and she gave not an inch. His eyes were as hot as hers, and his mouth twisted furiously. For a moment they glared at each other, murder at the forefront of both minds. Then, when he reached for her, meaning no doubt to shake her or commit some other act of mayhem against her person, Lilah suddenly remembered that this was the man she loved, the man who believed she had betrayed him. With a disgusted sound she stepped toward him, inside the arms that were seeking to hurt her. She lifted her hands to catch him by both ears.

"You dolt!" she said, her voice softening fractionally. Then, without loosening her grip on his ears, stretching up on tiptoe, she slanted her mouth across his.

Forty-seven

"Dolt, am I?" he muttered against her mouth, but his hands were not bruising her. Instead they settled almost reluctantly against her waist, not exactly holding her but not pushing her away, either.

"Yes, dolt," she repeated, her mouth lifting scant millimeters from his but her hands retaining their grip on his ears. "Stupid, blind man! If I hadn't claimed you as my slave to Captain Rutledge he'd have hanged you as a pirate!"

She kissed him again, lingeringly, using the lessons he had taught her against him. His mouth was warm and firm, tasting faintly of ginger. Resisting, he sought to pull his mouth away. Lilah tugged sharply on his ears. He yelped and his hands came up to free the prisoners.

"Did I not keep you safe and whole, have your wounds treated? How else could I have managed that, pray, without claiming you as . . . as property?"

Hands held fast in his now, she kissed him

again, running her tongue over the obdurate line where his lips remained firmly closed, nibbling his lower lip with her teeth.

"I'm the one who should be angry, not you! I've dared as much as my life is worth to come here tonight, and how do you greet me? What do you do? You beat me, that's what! For shame!"

"I did not beat you. . . ."

He was weakening under her ministrations, not surrendering but weakening. Lilah pressed her lips to the bristly underside of his chin, freed her hands to slide them around his waist, her palms relishing the contact with the satin-over-steel muscles at his waist.

"Then what would you call it?"

"Lovepats?"

"Hah! Lovepats! When I won't sit for a week!"

She ran her hands over the bare skin of his back, stroking the flat muscles on either side of his spine, rubbing her fingertips over his shoulder blades, pressing herself against him all the while.

"Whatever they were, they were well-deserved, and well you know it, witch! A small price, when you consider your words cost me my freedom!"

"Saved your life!"

"I thought we agreed that when we were rescued, you would say naught of my circumstances? I'd not be digging bloody holes for sugarcane every waking hour if you'd kept your tattling little tongue between your teeth!"

Despite his scolding words, much of the heat had left his voice. His arms had wrapped around her waist, his hands gently stroking the area they had so recently bruised.

Lilah pulled back to look up at him. "I truly had no choice. It was either tell them who I was and that you were my slave or watch them hang you. I would not have said what I did under circumstances that were any less dire, truly I wouldn't. It was no betrayal, Joss."

He looked down at her for a moment, his eyes moving over her face. One hand left its gentle massage of her posterior to ruffle her shorn hair, now shining clean and curled but definitely not the long seductive silk he had loved before. Still, as he had observed on the deck of the *Bettina*, it suited her.

"You know, I like you like this: a curly blonde boy with the face of an angel and the body of a woman. Tantalizing. I suppose Keith thinks so?"

The bite was back. Lilah's eyes widened.

Kevin was a subject she definitely did not want to discuss with Joss at the moment.

"I don't want to talk anymore. Aren't you ever going to kiss me, Joss?"

Her voice was plaintive, her eyes soft as they met his. He looked down at her for a moment, his eyes shining hotly as she pressed her legs against his.

"Please, Joss?" It was a seductive murmur, and he was a willing victim. One hand came up to cup the back of her head, tugging it backward, tilting her face up for his mouth. As his head came down he muttered something, but her blood was drumming so loudly in her veins that she didn't hear it.

His mouth touched hers, and her eyes fluttered shut. His lips were warm and soft as they found hers, his kiss gentle.

"I've missed you," she said against his mouth, her eyes opening. His eyes were dark with passion as they met hers.

"Now I don't want to talk," he growled, and took her mouth again.

This time the kiss was hard and deep. When he lifted his head a second time he led her to the cot. She sat on his lap, her arms twined around his neck, her head arched back against his shoulder as he pressed stinging kisses into the soft skin of her throat.

"What the hell are you wearing underneath this? Nothing?" His hand was moving over her breast, making the nipple spring visibly to life beneath the thin muslin.

"Just — a petticoat." Her voice was unsteady, and she shivered under the ministrations of that caressing hand.

"Is going around half naked another of your barbaric island customs?"

This growl surprised a tremulous little chuckle out of Lilah. "We wear as many clothes on Barbados as you do in England. But I had to dress myself. I didn't want Betsy to know. . . ." Her voice trailed off guiltily.

"About me," Joss concluded, his voice grim, his hand stilling in its fascinating journey over her body.

"Oh, Joss. . . ." she began miserably, sitting up in his lap.

"Hush," he said, pulling her back to kiss her again, fiercely, as if to stop her mouth and his thoughts. Then he was pushing her back on the cot, stretching out beside her, turning her toward him so that he could get to the buttons at the back of the gown, his mouth never leaving hers. She was scarcely aware when he peeled first the dress and then the single petticoat from her body. When she was naked, he shed his own trousers, nudged her over on her back. She arched and her legs parted instinctively as she waited with trembling anticipation for him to come into her.

But he did not.

Instead, he pulled her legs even farther apart and knelt between them. His hands slid, warm and strong, up over her slim calves, over the quivering softness of her thighs. He stroked her belly, her breasts, came back to her thighs again. Lilah caught her breath at the exquisite tightening that began inside her, in the place he so scrupulously forbore to touch. When his hands passed over her again, still without touching the place that needed touching most, she moved sinuously, inviting his hand to come where it would not. He concentrated instead on rubbing his thumbs over her nipples, kneading her breasts and belly before sliding his hands maddeningly down the insides of her thighs. When he began his teasing assault for the third time, she made a small protesting sound and her eyes opened.

The sight that met her eyes would have shocked her to the core six months ago. His face was hard and handsome, eyes like emeralds as they ran over the prize spread so delectably before him. He was kneeling between her wantonly parted thighs, seeming every inch the conquering, predatory male.

Following his gaze, looking down at herself, Lilah saw her own nakedness as if for the first time. She was all smooth white skin, unmistakably female. He was all hard muscle and unmistakably male.

Sprawled naked against the rough gray blanket, her own body was the most shocking thing she had ever seen. And he was seeing it, too, every detail mercilessly illuminated by the smoking lantern.

"Joss." It was a barely audible murmur, forced from her lungs by the years of ladylike modesty that had been drummed into her.

"Hmm?" He didn't stop what he was doing, didn't even pause in his sensuous massage, but his eyes met hers. They were green as emeralds, ragingly ablaze.

"The light," she managed faintly, barely able to breathe as he continued to inflict his particular brand of delicious torture on her.

He shook his head. "Oh, no. Not tonight, sweetheart. I want to see you — and I want you to see me. I don't want you to have any doubts at all about who is making love to you."

"But —"

"Shhh." He silenced her by stopping her lips with a hard, hungry kiss. For a moment he rested atop her, his weight a heart-stopping sensation in itself as he crushed her down into the thin prickly mattress that creaked on its rope supports. Lilah kissed him back, pressing against him, feeling delicious shudders of need race over her wherever their bodies touched.

When his mouth moved lower, found her breasts, took her nipples, she moaned and ran her fingers through his hair.

When he moved lower yet, pressing tiny stinging kisses along her abdomen, his tongue delving into her belly button, she moved invitingly beneath him. Her hands slid to his shoulders, tightened.

Then, when he moved lower yet, at last touching the woman-part of her with his mouth, not his hands, she cried out, her hands clutching at his hair, tugging frantically for him to stop. Her eyes flew open, and she looked at him wildly, driven half out of her mind by her own conflicting needs, wanting him to do what he was doing with every fiber of her being but knowing, knowing that it was shocking, wanton, wrong, and he must stop.

"Joss . . . no . . ." she gasped, trying to close her thighs against him. But he was there between her legs, holding them open, gently stroking her, giving her at last the kind of touching she had wanted — but determined to give her more, too.

"Shh, now. It's all right." He gentled her as he would have a frightened mare, his voice soothing, his touch distracting. Even as she geared herself up for one more protest he dipped his head again and kissed her, deep between her legs, shamefully, sinfully, and yet the heat and pressure of his mouth against her set her ablaze and she could no more have told him to stop than she could have gotten off that cot and walked away.

Her eyes shut and she was his to do with as he pleased.

By the time he poised himself over her, his shaft hard and throbbing and demanding entry, she was gasping, her body writhing, mindless with his loving.

"Tell me."

The words barely penetrated.

"Tell me."

He was insistent, holding himself just outside the place that cried out for him, making her give him an answer before he would give her what she craved.

"Tell me."

When she gave him his answer she gave it freely.

"I love you, love you, love you," she moaned against his mouth.

Then he took her to heaven and back again.

Forty-eight

Later, a long time later, Joss lifted his head from where it rested against Lilah's breasts. She stirred beneath him, her hands automatically clutching at him, but did not awaken. Joss rolled off her, stretched out beside her, settled her comfortably against him. Then he let her sleep for as long as he dared.

Finally he had to wake her. It would be dawn before long.

"Lilah." He stroked her hair. No response.

"Lilah." He tickled her eyelashes with his finger, tweaked a silken curl. Still no response.

"Lilah, my love, if you don't wake up this minute I'm going to push you out of this cot and onto the floor."

That threat, accompanied by a leisurely finger tracing the line of her parted lips then moving down over her arched throat to circle her beautiful breasts, at last produced a reaction. She murmured something, and rolled over. Only a quick grab saved her from ending up in the dirt.

He ran his eyes with a connoisseur's appreciation along her naked backside. In his many years of bedding many women, none had ever affected him like this one. None had ever made him fall in love.

What was it about her? She was beautiful, but so were most of the others. She was intelligent, which some had been but most had not. She was a lady, which narrowed the field considerably. Perhaps it was the aura of quality that clung to her whatever she was wearing, whatever she was doing, that had attracted him.

Perhaps it was her courage. Nothing cowed her for long, not gossip nor cholera nor near drowning, not being marooned on a deserted island nor discovering that island was not as deserted as they'd thought, not joining a pirate crew as an addled youth nor being caught in the middle of a sea battle. She'd risen ably to every challenge the last few months had flung at her, and he admired and respected her for that.

She made him burn hotter than a peat fire in bed.

She'd slapped his face, bitten his tongue and leg, yelled at him for things he couldn't help. She was a shrew and a witch most of the time, and occasionally, just occasionally, an angel. She'd turned him inside out since the first moment he'd set eyes on her, making him flame first with passion, then rage, then passion again. She'd even made him lose his temper to such an extent that he'd been provoked to physical violence, which shamed him now that he thought about it. Although it was his considered opinion that for Miss Delilah Remy a paddling had been far overdue.

She was an acclaimed beauty, her family's pampered darling, rich and used to being waited on hand and foot.

Even without the catastrophe of his bloodline, even if he'd still been the self he'd always known, an English seaman and businessman without the hideous nightmare of mixed blood and slavery, he'd not have been able to offer her a life to compare to what she had on Barbados.

His life in England was much different, simpler. He made enough with his shipping business to keep a wife in ample comfort, but not in such luxury as Lilah was accustomed to. He had only two servants, a house that was large but not fashionable, friends who were situated like himself. He was far removed from the social stratosphere. Even if he could have wed her without having the nightmare interfere, she would have been giving up something in the way of wealth and social status to become his wife.

He realized that, and didn't like it.

But with the addition of the nightmare, their situation became impossible. If she chose him, she would have to give up everything she'd ever held dear: home, family, friends, her whole life. It was a big step, and he wasn't sure she was ready to take it.

He was uncertain, and that was another thing he didn't like. Never in his life had he imagined that he would fall in love with a woman and worry about whether or not she would have him. His success with women had been too constant, too effortless. But with Lilah, he could take nothing for granted. Would she give up so much, for him?

She said she loved him. He thought she even meant it. But did she love him enough to go back to England with him? Because his life was not here, could never be here. He could not stay with her even with the best will in the world. She would have to come with him.

Or would that cursed soupçon of blood and all that it meant stand forever in their way?

He meant to put it to the test. At once, before he lost his nerve completely.

"Lilah!" Grim-faced now, he shook her shoulder.

"Mmmm?"

"Damn it, Lilah, wake up!"

This brought her awake, finally. She did not roll over, just turned her head to the side and blinked at him.

"Oh. Joss," she murmured, and smiled.

She looked so lovely, her eyes heavy-lidded with sleep, her mouth all soft and rosy, that he had to kiss her. That earned him a yawn, a smile, and another murmur.

"I wish I could stay. I love sleeping with you."

"Do you, now? I'm glad, because I'm hoping you'll be sleeping with me for the rest of your life."

It took a minute for this to penetrate. When it did, her eyes widened and she rolled over to stare at him. He had a complete and uninhibited view of her nakedness, but at the moment he was not interested.

"What does that mean?" The incomprehension in her eyes and voice made him smile despite the clenching in his stomach. To ease the tension his pride would not let her see, he shifted his gaze from her eyes to her mouth, which he traced softly with one finger.

"For a young lady who seems to have made a practice of collecting proposals, you're not very quick on the uptake. I'm asking you to marry me."

"M-marry you!"

There was a long silence, which he could interpret as appalled or not, as he chose. Her eyes were wide pools of pure blue, huge and shadowed.

"Mm-hm. Marry me." His voice was hard.

"Oh, my!"

He scowled. "That's hardly an enlightening reaction. Yes or no?"

Slowly, a smile curved her mouth. "Have you had much practice at this?"

"At what?" He was impatient.

"Asking ladies to marry you."

His scowl deepened. If she did not give him an answer soon, he would strangle her. He was more nervous than he had ever been in his life, and she, blast her, was smiling!

"As a matter of fact, you're the first one."

"I thought so." Unexpectedly she giggled, the sound delicious, a sweet girlish trilling. " 'Yes or no?' How romantic of you!"

"Well?" He was in no mood for her fooling.

She sighed, suddenly sobering. "Joss, it's not that simple. You know it's not."

"What's not simple about it? I'm leaving, shaking the dust of this thrice-damned island and its thrice-damned barbaric customs from my feet. You can come with me, or you can stay. If you come, I expect you'd prefer to come as my wife."

"Joss. . . ."

"Yes or no?"

"I wish you'd stop saying that! To begin with, you can't just leave Heart's Ease. I hate to remind you of it, but my father owns you. You're a slave. You can't just walk away. You have to have a pass to use the roads! They'll hunt you down, bring you back, punish you, maybe kill you."

"They'll have to find me first."

"They will. Believe me. Barbados is a small island, and it has a very efficient militia. In order to escape, you'd have to get off the island, and you can't do that. Within half a day of your disappearance, every captain of every ship in every port on Barbados would know about you. You'll be caught, sooner or later."

"So what do you propose? That I stay here in this bloody pigsty for the rest of my life scratching holes in the dirt? While you sleep with the Boss Man up at the big house and sneak down here every once in a while when you feel the need for a little excitement?"

"I didn't say that."

"No? You didn't say you'd marry me, either."

Lilah sighed and sat up. Despite his growing anger, his eyes were irresistibly drawn to her lithe, white-skinned body. Naked, she was the loveliest thing he had ever seen in his life, and she was driving him mad.

"I don't know if I can marry you. I love you. I'm so in love with you it's ridiculous. But marriage — Joss, how can I promise to marry you? You're a slave on my father's plantation! What do you want me to do, calmly walk up to him and say, Oh, by the way, Papa, I hope you don't mind but I'm not going to marry Kevin after all, I've changed my mind and I'm going to marry Joss, our slave? He'd die of an apoplexy — and if he didn't, he'd kill you. He really would."

"I'm leaving the first chance I get. You can come with me — or you can stay. It's your choice."

"Joss. . . ." It was almost a wail. "You cannot just leave! And I can't argue with you any longer, I have to go! It — what time is it?"

"Nearly four."

"Oh my goodness! I have to get back! Everyone will be waking up soon!"

She slid slender pale legs over the side of the cot and stood up, reaching for her petticoat. As she pulled it over her head she turned to face him.

"I want you to promise me — promise me!

— that you won't do anything stupid. You won't try to run until I've — I've had a chance to work on my father. I think I can get him to free you, if I dwell on how you saved my life, but it may take some time. Then you won't have to run — you can just leave."

He lay back on the bunk, crossing his arms behind his head, blatantly naked and not a whit bothered by it. His eyes were calculating on her face.

"Say I give you time to work on your father — how much time?"

"A few months. A year at the outside."

He shook his head. "Sorry, I'm not waiting that long. This farce has gone on long enough."

"Joss. . . ." Her voice was muffled as she pulled her dress over her head. "Fasten this, will you?"

She turned her back, and he stood up to fasten her dress. The action was so automatic, so much that of a husband or lover of long standing, that he could do it while still furious with her. When he was done, he turned her to face him, his hands on her shoulders.

"When I can, I'm leaving. Shall I come for you, or not?"

She stared up at him, her eyes troubled.

He noted absently that the material of her dress beneath his fingers was very fine, a delicate white muslin sprigged in a grayed-blue that almost precisely matched her eyes. With her crop of golden curls and her exquisite face, she was lovely enough to turn heads anywhere in the world. It occurred to Joss suddenly that, although this was his first marriage proposal, it was certainly not hers. Hell, half the bloody male population of this benighted island probably wanted to marry her, to say nothing of the pimply rich boys back in the Colonies! And he had thought she would say, Yes, thank you very much! to him? He must be mad. Joss scowled at her.

"Don't be angry. I can't decide something like this right here on the spot! I have to think about it, that's not unreasonable, so you can just get that mule-headed expression off your face! I love you, you know I do, it isn't that, but . . . but I need time to think."

"As I've told you before, you don't know the meaning of the word love," he bit out. "If I let you, you'd marry your bloody precious blockhead Kevin and have me on the side. Only that kind of arrangement doesn't suit me."

"That's not true!"

"Isn't it? Go on, get out of here! You have

to get back to the house before someone finds out you've been sneaking down here to diddle a slave."

"Go to hell!" Lilah rarely swore, but then she'd rarely been so furious. He was being so unfair it was absurd, the stupid ape, and if he would think about it rationally he would know it. But apparently a little rational thinking was too much to expect. He was so proud and so stubborn he couldn't see any farther than the end of his nose!

"Out. Now!"

When she still hesitated he picked her up bodily, carried her over to the door, opened it, and deposited her on her feet on the other side. She glared at him, opened her mouth to say something, then snapped it shut again without a word. Picking up her skirts, she ran, so furious that she wanted to get away from him as fast as she could. In her haste she completely forgot that she was barefoot.

Joss, cursing himself and her under his breath, grabbed his breeches, yanked them on, and started after her. She was already halfway across the field that led to the main house, her white dress easily visible in the gray light of near dawn. Joss stopped at the edge of the slave compound, crossed his arms over his chest and swore long and profanely until she disappeared from view.

He loved the little bitch. And despite what he said he knew he wasn't going anywhere without her.

He was leaving, all right, when the time was right. An accident of birth did not a slave make.

But when he left he was taking her with him. If he had to drag her by the hair of her head.

And Miss Delilah Remy could like it, or lump it. He didn't much care.

Forty-nine

Lilah crept up the servants' stairway at the back of the darkened house, feeling her way along the cool plaster wall, stepping nimbly over the loose step that she knew always creaked. In this, the hour before dawn, a hush lay over everything. A creak would sound abnormally loud. . . .

Her bedchamber was on the second floor overlooking the manicured lawn at the front of the house. Her father and Jane shared a suite at the opposite end of the hall. Lilah held her breath as she tiptoed past it, but nothing stirred. As she opened the door to her bedroom and stepped inside, she heaved a silent sigh of relief.

She was safe.

"Miss Lilah, is that you?"

Lilah whirled, her hand flying to her mouth as she tried to find Betsy through the darkness. The other girl had apparently been sleeping in one of the pair of chairs in front of the tall windows, waiting for her. She rose as Lilah's eyes found her, her slim body silhouetted briefly against the lighter gray of the window before she stepped toward her mistress.

"Shhh, Betsy!"

"Where have you been? I've been almost crazy with worry, wonderin' whether to wake the master, or Mr. Kevin. . . ."

"You didn't, did you?" Lilah's voice was sharp with fear.

"No, I didn't. I figured that you might not want them to know where you've been. Did I do right?"

"Yes, Betsy, just right. How . . . how did you know I was gone?"

"I came up to bring you a cup of chocolate. Maisie fixed it, 'cause she says you got too thin while you were on that island. But you weren't here, and I was scared, not knowing what to do. I thought maybe those pirates had come back and got you, or . . ." Her voice faltered.

Betsy had moved to stand before the dressing table, and before Lilah realized what she was about she used flint and steel to light a lamp. Then she turned to look at her mistress. Suddenly self-conscious in the soft yellow glow, Lilah lifted a hand to her bosom. Betsy took in that gesture, took in the disordered hair and swollen mouth, the less than complete toilette, and her eyes grew huge.

"You've been with that man, haven't you?" It was more a shocked gasp than a question. Lilah stared at her maid for a long moment, swallowing nervously without replying. Betsy was her dearest friend, but this secret was something that could not be shared. One whisper of gossip and she and Joss were ruined. . . .

"I don't know who you're talking about," Lilah said, turning her back and walking over to splash water on her face.

"Oh, yes, you do, Miss Lilah!" Betsy shook her head, her face taut with concern. "You been with that man, that one that's got the touch of the tarbrush. That — Joss. I remember how you were about him from the first night you met him. What you tole the master and Mr. Kevin about him not touching you whilst you were shipwrecked was a lie, wasn't it? You've done gone and let him bed you. Don't you try to lie to me, Miss Lilah. I know you like I know myself!"

"Oh, Betsy, I know it's bad but I can't help it. I'm in love with him!" Lilah had to confess; Betsy did know her, all too well. She could never hide this from her.

Betsy sucked in her breath. They stared at each other, one with horror, the other with anguish. Then Betsy reached out to take Lilah by the shoulders, gave her a little shake. There was no more mistress and maid, only two old and loving friends.

"Miss Lilah, you can't do this. You know you can't. You can't go sneakin' down to the quarters, beddin' with a man like that! You're a lady! If the master were to find out, or Mr. Kevin . . ." Betsy broke off, and shuddered visibly.

"I know! But I love him! He — he wants me to run away with him. To marry him." Lilah's voice broke as tears sprang to her eyes. Betsy took one horrified look at her mistress's white face, then folded the girl in her arms, rocking her gently against her.

"You are in a mess of trouble, aren't you, honey? But you already know what you've got to do. You can't see him anymore, you just can't. As to marryin' him — Miss Lilah, you might just as well think of marrying my Ben. It's the same thing."

Lilah lifted her head, pulled back a little from Betsy, a vivid picture of Ben, the plantation cobbler, appearing in her mind's eye. He was good-natured, handsome, a skilled worker — and ebony black.

She shook her head. "No!"

"It's the truth, Miss Lilah. You just don't want to admit it. You been like that ever since you was a little girl, not wanting to see anything that didn't suit you."

Lilah's chin came up. "Tell me something, Betsy — if Ben were white, would you still love him? Would you still want to be his woman?"

Betsy's eyes widened as she thought this over. Then she shook her head in consternation. "I see what you mean. Oh, honey, I don't know the answer. I only know that you're asking for a heap of misery and heartbreak if you don't stop this."

At the stubborn look on Lilah's face, she folded her mistress close again, hugged her.

"Damn all men," she muttered fiercely. Lilah, head resting tiredly on Betsy's shoulder, was inclined to agree.

Fifty

It was late afternoon of the following day. Lilah was sitting on the back verandah steps talking to Jane as her stepmother rocked nearby and did the delicate stitchery that adorned all her husband's handkerchiefs. Lilah, who had never been any good at stitchery, sat with her hands clasped around her knees, feeling deliciously lazy in the somnolent heat. She would have been perfectly content with the world if it had not been for two things: her worry over what to do about Joss, and Jane's topic of conversation. Her stepmother was intent on making plans for Lilah's wedding.

"There's no point in putting it off, is there, dear? Now that you've finally made up your mind to wed Kevin, I mean."

Lilah cast her eyes out over the estate, touching on verdant grasses and bright pink bushes and, just visible over the tops of the fringed palms, the paddles of the windmill as they turned slowly with the breeze. If she hoped for any distraction that would let her turn the subject, however, she hoped in vain. Heart's Ease was as peaceful as it always was at that time of day, before the men and the slaves came in from the fields, before the preparations started for supper.

"I just got home, Jane. So much has happened that I really haven't given much thought to . . . to getting married."

"Well, it's time you did then!" Jane said with a comfortable little laugh, looking up from her work to eye her stepdaughter. "Kevin loves you very much, you know. He was beside himself those weeks when you were lost."

"Was he? I worried about him, too."

"I think six weeks would give us enough time," Jane decided.

"Six weeks!" Lilah was appalled. Jane looked at her, frowned.

"Are you getting bridal nerves already? My heaven, you will be in a state the night before! But don't worry, dear, every woman feels like that before her wedding. After all, it's a big step. Marriage is for life."

"Oh, Jane — six weeks," Lilah said faintly, feeling as if a trap were closing in around her. "I . . . I don't know if I'll be ready. . . ."

"Two months, then," Jane said, as if the subject were closed. "That's really better, anyway. It'll give us time to have your dress made up — it'll be the most beautiful dress any bride ever had, you'll see. We'll plan a lovely feast and invite everyone we know from all over the island. Your father's told me to spare no expense, and I won't. After all, how often does one's only daughter get married?"

She stood up, workbasket in hand. "I must go in now, dear, I have things to see to in the house. Why don't you go for a walk? I'd appreciate it if you'd fetch back a jug of syrup from the mill to pour over Maisie's tildy-cake. Besides, I think Kevin might be over there. I know you haven't seen much of him since you got home, but please don't take it for lack of ardor on his part. You know how busy he and your father are in grinding season."

Jane left, and Lilah sat where she was a moment longer, her mind as active as her body was still as she tried to sort through the awful dilemma that confronted her. After all that had passed between herself and Joss, could she marry Kevin? It was the sensible thing to do — but the idea of permitting him the intimacies that Joss claimed appalled her.

Lilah jumped up, shaking out her skirt, and began to walk purposefully toward the mill. As Jane had pointed out, she hadn't spent much time with Kevin in the week she'd been home. He'd been caught up in the work involved in grinding season, the plantation's busiest time, while she . . . if truth were told, she'd been avoiding him.

If more truth were told, since she'd fallen in love with Joss, she could barely tolerate Kevin's kisses, relatively chaste though she'd learned they were. And whenever they were alone, he seemed to always want to kiss her.

How was she going to stand being married to him?

This was the question she had to resolve, and soon. Soon enough to call off all the wedding plans that Jane was so happily hatching. Soon enough to put a stop to everything before it was too late.

Her life was suddenly so complicated. Why couldn't she have fallen in love with Kevin instead of Joss? Kevin was kind, hard-working, fond of her, on excellent terms with her father. He was the perfect husband for her. What was wrong with her to prefer Joss with all his drawbacks to Kevin with all his assets?

Maybe, just maybe, she hadn't tried hard enough to fall in love with Kevin. Maybe if she gave herself a chance . . .

Which was why she was walking toward the sugar mill. She meant to give herself every chance.

Fifty-one

The sugar mill was a scene of intense activity. A half dozen slaves were piling heaps of newly cut cane in front of the mill for crushing, while toward the rear more slaves were shoveling out the golden mounds of "bagasses," or what was left of the cane after it had been chopped into pieces and crushed several times to extract the juices. From inside the mill came the sound of running water, which was added to the juice along with "milk of lime," designed to filter out any impurities. To one side of the mill were enormous flat troughs, where the water was allowed to evaporate in the sun from the juice mixture, leaving the thick, brown syrup that Jane wanted for the cake. Lilah was so familiar with the sugar operation that she scarcely paid any attention to the sounds or sights involved in the process. Instead she scanned the area for Kevin.

He was mounted on a bay mare, leaning on his saddle, a wide-brimmed hat on his head as he supervised a slave leading the mule that, because of lack of wind, was operating the stone crusher.

"Kevin!" Lilah waved, hailing him. Even as she did, even as his eyes swung toward her, she realized that she had made a huge mistake. The sweat-drenched slave leading the mule in circles was Joss. He looked up to meet her eyes as Kevin smiled, waved, and urged his mount toward her.

Lilah stared back at Joss, feeling absurdly guilty, before tearing her eyes away to smile at Kevin, who was swinging down from his horse.

"Good afternoon," he said, smiling broadly, slipping the reins over his arm and tilting his hat back as he bent over to give her a resounding kiss. Lilah, knowing herself to be in full view of Joss, stepped back nervously. Kevin frowned.

"Is something wrong?"

"I . . . I . . . Jane sent me for a jug of syrup."

"Maisie's made tildy-cake, hmm? I can't wait. I love her tildy-cake."

"I know." She smiled up at him, feeling more at ease as she recalled the chunky boy who, upon first coming to Heart's Ease, had eaten so much tildy-cake one night at supper that she'd come upon him later, being sick out behind the orchard.

Kevin tied his horse to a nearby fig tree, took her arm, and strolled with her toward the troughs. Their route brought them within feet of Joss. Lilah cast him a sideways glance. She saw that though his face was impassive as he dragged the mule around, every muscle in his body was taut with tension. He didn't look at the pair of them ambling so cozily arm in arm, but she knew he was aware of them with every fiber of his being.

As she had been, when he had been with Nell.

"Jane has been after me to set a date for our wedding," Lilah said suddenly. They had stopped by the side of the mill, and Kevin sent one of the slaves to fetch a jug.

"Has she?" Kevin slanted a look down at her, shrugged. "Any time you say. The sooner the better, if you ask me."

Lilah hesitated. This was hardly the place for such a conversation, but unexpectedly, she wanted everything settled. If he gave the right answer, it would make what she very much feared she was going to do easier.

"Kevin, why do you want to marry me?" She asked the question earnestly, turning so that she faced him, one hand resting on his forearm that was bared by his rolled-up sleeves.

"Why do you think? Because I love you, of course, silly goose. You know I've been in love with you for years." It was not the answer she wanted, but she rather suspected he was telling her what he thought she wanted to hear. He looked down at her with a gathering frown.

Lilah gazed into the hazel eyes and weather-beaten face that she knew so well. Over his broad shoulder she could see Joss, naked to the waist, grimy and sweating in his loose white trousers, jerking savagely at the harness of the recalcitrant mule. Any sane woman choosing a mate between the gentleman planter and the half-naked slave would have no choice to make. So did that make her insane?

Whether it did or not, Lilah knew, suddenly and with no doubts at all about the correctness of her decision, that she couldn't marry Kevin. She didn't love him, and she didn't think he loved her either. Not like a husband should love his wife. Not like Joss loved her.

She would have to tell Kevin of her decision, soon. But not now. Not with Joss a witness to what she very much feared would be an unpleasant confrontation. Kevin was unlikely to take his congé lightly since it also meant losing Heart's Ease.

"You know I love you, don't you?" Kevin murmured, his hands stroking over her bare forearms, then tightening to hold her in place as he bent his head toward her. Before Lilah could answer he was kissing her, lingeringly this time, in full view of the slaves; in full view of Joss.

As Lilah walked back across the yard with her hand tucked in Kevin's elbow and her mouth throbbing from his kiss, she was all too aware of a pair of eyes turned vivid emerald with anger watching her from a suddenly savage face.

Fifty-two

This time, when Lilah snuck out of the house, it was near to midnight. It had taken that long for her to be sure everyone was asleep. She dared not tell even Betsy that she was going to see Joss. If Betsy knew of her mistress's activities and kept silent, she would be another target for Leonard Remy's wrath. And Leonard Remy's wrath would be terrible if he discovered his daughter's perfidy. Which sooner or later Lilah very much feared he had to do.

She ran across the night-dark yard, holding her skirts clear of the dew-wet grass. When she got to the slave compound, she slowed to a walk. The huts were all dark; the slaves long since asleep.

Even Joss's hut was dark.

As before, the door was unlatched. Lilah let herself in, closed the door, and stood for a moment leaning against it. She heard not a sound, not a rustle of bedding, not a breath.

"Joss?" Even as she said it she knew she

was alone. He was not there. Once her eyes grew accustomed to the dark, she looked around. As she had thought, his cot was empty. The hut was empty.

Lilah was suddenly, sorely afraid that he had done as he had threatened and left without her.

Where else could he be, so late at night, when all sensible people were in their beds?

When she had come to see him before, he had just come back from bathing.

It was a slim possibility. Lilah left the hut, the door with its leather hinges swinging silently shut behind her. Walking carefully so as not to make any noise, she headed for the far edge of the slave compound where the cane fields began. This close to the house, the cane had yet to be cut, and it rustled continuously as the balmy wind ruffled through it. It had been years since she had been this way, and it took her a few moments to find what she was looking for. Then, a terrible fear driving her, she picked up her skirts and ran down the path to the pool where the slaves bathed. The path was narrow, and tall stalks of cane brushed her bare arms and skirt, caught at her hair. Night creatures hissed and slithered as they got out of her way. She never spared them a thought. She had to find Joss before it was too late. . . .

Bursting into the clearing, panting, Lilah scanned the silent black surface of the water where she and Betsy had spent so much time as young girls.

"Joss?" Her voice was soft, despairing. "Joss?"

No answer. She walked to the edge of the pool, careful not to lose her balance on the slippery vines that grew around its perimeter. Think, she willed herself, think: What route would he take? If she could figure it out, it was possible that she could overtake him before he got too far away. . . .

He was floating on his back in the water, watching her. Lilah saw him just as she was starting to turn back.

"Jocelyn San Pietro! Why didn't you answer me?" Relief washed over her like a tidal wave, perversely igniting her temper. Hands on hips, she stood glaring down at him. He was almost at her feet, turned parallel to the shore as he floated in the shallow pool. Only his water-sleeked black head rose above the surface of the water. The rest of his body was a pale blur.

"Maybe I didn't want to talk to you." His voice was hard, insolent. "Maybe I've had a bellyful of you and this whole bloody situation."

Lilah sighed. "You're angry because Kevin

kissed me. If you'll come out of there, I can explain."

"I don't want your explanations. I've had a bellyful of them, too."

"Joss, you're being unreasonable."

"And I'm bloody tired of you telling me I'm unreasonable!" His voice was suddenly explosive. His eyes in the darkness were shards of green glass.

Her voice turned soft, coaxing. "I'm not going to marry Kevin."

"What?"

"You heard me. I'm not going to marry Kevin."

"Oh? Do you always kiss men you're not going to marry? Come to think of it, I guess you do."

"Don't you want to know who I'm going to marry instead?" She ignored his blatant attempts to start a fight. What she had to tell him was too important, too wonderful to be put off by his ill humor.

"Not particularly."

Blast the man, did he have to be difficult at a time like this?

"I'm going to marry you, you bad-tempered beast!" She glared at him. He scowled right back at her.

"Am I supposed to say I'm honored?" The deliberate sarcasm made her fists clench. At all costs, she was not going to fight with the infuriating creature when she was accepting his proposal of marriage! Taking a deep breath, she forced her voice to stay even.

"Would you please come out of there so that we can talk?"

"No, I will not."

"Then I'll come in!"

"Suit yourself."

Gritting her teeth at his studied indifference, Lilah quickly undressed. Joss watched her in silence. Then, as she untied the tapes to her petticoat, he got to his feet. Water streamed off him, rained into the pool that now came no higher than his hips.

"You are the most maddening, aggravating, mule-headed man that it's ever been my displeasure to meet!" she snapped.

"And yet you're going to marry me?" He was mocking her but still angry, his voice scarcely above a growl as he stalked naked from the pool and walked right past her to pick up his trousers.

"At the moment I'm not so sure!" she spit back, furious. Then, drawing a long-suffering sigh, she relented, walking toward him. "Yes, I am!"

He eyed her, his trousers forgotten. Something in his expression gave her pause. Lilah stopped walking, stood for a moment looking at him. Never in a million years had she pictured this kind of reaction from him! She'd expected him to shout for joy when she told him she'd decided to toss her cap over the windmill at last and become his wife!

"Have you told lover-boy the wedding's off?"

"If you are referring to Kevin, he's not my lover, and you know it!"

"Have you told him?"

She looked at him, shook her head. "Not yet."

"I thought not." He shook out his trousers, put a foot into one leg of them, oblivious to the fact that he was still soaking wet.

"What difference does it make when I tell Kevin? Don't you even care that I've said I'll marry you?" The words were almost a wail.

His face tightened, and he put his other foot into his trousers and pulled them up. "Oh, I care. I just don't believe you."

"You don't believe me!" *She* didn't believe *him*. "You don't believe me!"

"That's what I said."

"You have got to be the stubbornest, stupidest . . ." She broke off, advancing on him with murder in her eyes. "I love you, you blithering idiot, and I am going to marry you!

Do you understand me?"

She reached him, thumped him in the center of his chest for emphasis.

"Ow!"

"And another thing, while we're on the subject of how utterly unsatisfactory you are! For all the times you've made me say the words, you have never, not once, told me that you love me!"

"Never?" His voice was suddenly meek.

"Never!"

"Not once?"

"No!"

"And you'd like me to?"

"Yes!" It was a hiss.

"I do."

"You do what?"

"You know."

She literally ground her teeth. "Jocelyn San Pietro, if you do not tell me, now, this minute, that you love me in so many words, I am going to go straight home and marry Kevin! Do you hear me?"

He smiled then, a slow-dawning smile that was as charming as any she'd ever seen. He gripped her hands, pulling her a step closer so that she was standing right up against him with only their clasped hands between them.

"Would you really marry what's his

name?" The anger had totally left his voice; he sounded almost as if he was teasing her.

"Yes!" Then, an instant later: "No."

There was a pause. Then she said, "I'm waiting."

He looked down at her, his grin going all lopsided. "I have trouble saying the words."

"Oh?" The single syllable was definitely not encouraging.

"I've never said them before."

"Never?" That caught her attention, softened her. She looked up at him, up at the big handsome man whose wife she'd promised to become, and felt her heart catch. "Is that the truth?"

"Suspicious little thing, aren't you?" The grin still lurked around the corners of his mouth, but his voice turned serious. "It's the truth, I swear."

For a long moment she just looked at him. "I'm still waiting," she prompted when it seemed as though he'd stand there, silent, all night.

His lips quirked. He opened his mouth, closed it again.

"All right," she said, suddenly obliging. "I'll help you."

She freed her hands from his, stood on tiptoe, slid her arms around his neck. He was still wet, but as she pressed against him, she didn't even notice.

"I . . ." she said, drawing his head down so that she could brush his lips with hers.

"Love . . ." She deepened the kiss, stroking his lips with her tongue tantalizingly, forging within to probe at the hard smooth line of his teeth.

"You." She pulled her lips away. When he followed them with his own, his hands tightening around her waist, she shook her head at him.

"Say it!"

"Help me some more," he said, his voice husky despite the amusement that laced it.

Lilah looked at him, at the night-black hair that was wet beneath her fingers, at the hard, handsome mouth, at the green eyes that darkened and glittered as they moved over her face, and felt her breath catch.

"All right," she whispered, and lifted her mouth to his again.

Fifty-three

When she kissed him this time, employing on him all the devastating little tricks he had taught her to such good effect, his hands slid down over the backs of her thighs, bare beneath the hem of her chemise. He ran them up again, over the buttocks, to caress the silky bare skin of her waist, his hand forging under the one garment she had left to her. But when his hands tightened on her and he would have bent her backwards, taking control of the kiss, she pushed against his shoulders and pulled her mouth free.

"Oh, no. Not until I get what I want. Say it, Joss. A big strong man like you can't be afraid of three teensy little words."

Though his eyes had heated, his mouth quirked in a teasing grin. "Going to torture me, are you? Go ahead. I think I like the idea."

"Mmmm." She pressed tiny kisses along the bristly line of his jaw, down over his throat, along his shoulders. His skin was warm, wet, and just faintly salty, and she loved the taste of it. Her lips could feel the blood pulsing beneath his skin.

In her sudden fascination with the taste and texture of his flesh, she quite forgot that her object was to coax a confession of love from him. She bent her head, followed the line of his breastbone down, her lips brushing over crisp curls of hair, over hard muscles and flat planes. In her lingering exploration of his chest she encountered a male nipple peeking out at her from its bed of black hair. Intrigued, she touched it with her tongue, flicked it. To her pleased amazement, it hardened just like her own did. He drew in a sharp breath as she took it between her lips, nibbling. His hands clenched on her waist. Her lips traveled across his chest to his other nipple, performed the same exercise on it.

"Lilah . . ." Her name was more groan than anything else. She glanced up at him, saw that there were flames in his green eyes. She realized with some surprise that his whole body had gone rigid with tension. The idea that she could have such an effect on her worldly tutor in lovemaking made her smile like a cat with a bowl of cream.

"Ready to surrender yet?" she purred, straightening to nuzzle his neck while her tinge's stroked the nipples she had just thoroughly kissed. Pressing her body against him, feeling the heat and strength of him, sent a thrill of excitement through her. His chest was hard against her nearly naked breasts, and she could feel her nipples tighten in response. Against her bare thighs she could feel the tantalizing abrasion of his coarse cotton trousers. Farther up, pressing against her belly, was the steely strength of his manhood, swollen and ready.

At her half-teasing question he managed a laugh, though the sound was thoroughly shaken.

"Never."

"Be warned, I take no prisoners," she murmured and she proceeded to show him what she meant.

Her hand slid down the front of his chest, stroking his heated flesh, and her lips followed, planting little stinging kisses along a line to his belly. As she kissed him above the low-riding line of his trousers, he sucked in his breath, his hands coming up to weave through her hair and press her face closer yet. She found his navel, explored it with her tongue. He pulled her head back, his eyes hot, and she suddenly realized that she could pleasure him as he had pleasured her.

The thought was shocking, exciting, wanton.

She knelt, barely conscious of the damp ground, and tugged at his trousers. They slid down over his hips, past his thighs, to crumple about his feet.

He was naked, vulnerable . . . and hers.

Acting on instinct, her hands cupped the hard roundness of his buttocks, and her mouth kissed gently that part of him that had made her a woman.

"Sweet Christ!" The words were a gasp, uttered as though he were dying. She looked up at him inquiringly, to find that he was staring down at her with eyes that smoldered, burned.

Then he was pushing her onto her back on the soft carpet of moss, yanking the chemise up out of his way and parting her thighs with his knee in a single violent motion.

She clasped her arms around his back and lifted her hips to meet him as he thrust wildly inside her.

At last, when he had brought her trembling to the brink and then pushed her over, she got what she wanted. As his body convulsed inside her he groaned the words in her ear: "I love you, I love you, I love you."

Over and over, like a litany.

Fifty-four

Later, much later, he helped her dress, grinning lazily as she teased him about the words she still could not get him to say outside of the throes of passion. Then he pulled on his own trousers — again! — and wrapped a hard bare arm around her waist as they made their way back along the path that led to the slave compound. She leaned against him as they walked, enjoying a rush of pure happiness unlike anything she had ever known.

She was sure of it now: Falling in love with Joss was far and away the most wonderful thing that had ever happened to her. Whatever the difficulties, whatever it cost her, she wanted to spend her life with him, loving him. As his wife, and the mother of his children. At the thought of children a dreamy smile curved her lips. She'd like a little boy who looked just like Joss. Or a little girl for that matter. Or both. A whole tribe! On that giddy thought, she giggled.

"Now what's funny?"

She kissed the bare shoulder against which she leaned. "I was thinking of children. A whole tribe of them."

"Our children?"

She nodded.

"I take it from that that you meant what you said."

"What?"

"About marrying me."

She stopped walking to look up at him, suddenly serious. "Yes. I meant it."

He turned to face her, his hands coming up to slide along her shoulders as he looked down into her eyes. The big orange globe of the moon, already paling and hanging low in the sky with the approach of day, was just visible over his left shoulder. All around them, the world was still shadowy and dark, alive only with small nocturnal creatures and the soft rustle of the cane.

"To marry me, you'll have to give up all this: your home, and your family, and even some of the luxuries you're used to."

The words sounded as though he was saying them almost against his will. Lilah gazed up at him, at the suddenly austere face that she loved more than anything in the world, and felt her heart turn over. He loved her enough to point out the drawbacks of her choice. . . .

"Are you trying to tell me you can't support a wife?"

"I can support you, but not, I'm afraid, entirely in the style to which you're accustomed. I earn a good living, but I'm comfortable, not wealthy."

"Mmmm. And to think I was hoping to marry for money. Oh, well." Her attempt to lighten the moment was sweet, but she knew how serious he was now by his next words.

"In all likelihood you'll never see your family again. Under the circumstances, I won't be coming back to this — to Barbados. And if you marry me, your father is very likely to write you off as dead." He seemed determined that she understand precisely what she was doing, now that she had made up her mind to do it.

"I know all that." Her voice was soft. A faint shadow darkened her eyes. He saw it and his mouth tightened.

"If you marry the Boss Man, you'll inherit all this, be able to pass it along to your children. You'll have the life you've always known, the life you've always said you wanted."

"I know that, too."

That he loved her enough to put her needs and wants before his own put every last, lingering doubt to rest. A plantation, even one as beloved as Heart's Ease, was just that. One thing she had learned over the past few months was that it was people that really mattered. The tragic thing was that in this situation she could not avoid hurting those she loved — her father, Jane, Katy, Kevin and the rest. But she would do it for Joss, whom she loved with a wonderful shining glory she had never in her life expected to feel.

Whatever choice she made, she would, she knew, hurt herself.

But she could live without her family, without Heart's Ease. She couldn't live without Joss. Not and be happy.

She chose Joss, now and forever. When she tried to convey that to him he listened to her very gravely, then tilted up her chin so that he could study her face by the soft glow of the moon.

"Are you sure?"

"Yes."

He smiled then, a rare smile that softened his whole face. "You won't regret it. I'll take good care of you, I swear."

She reached up and kissed him.

When they resumed their walk back toward his hut, they started making plans.

"But it would be so much simpler if you

would just wait until I can talk my father into freeing you," she argued as she had for the dozenth time as they skirted the edge of the slave compound. Joss's hut was on the far side. As they approached it their pace slowed. Unconsciously, each sought to prolong the moment of parting.

"I'm not waiting for any longer than I have to. What I want you to do is make an excuse to go into Bridgetown, and book passage to England for a man and his wife — make up names. The night before the ship's to sail, we'll take horses and ride to Bridgetown. With luck, we should make it just in time to catch the ship before she sets sail with the dawn tide."

"If they catch us . . ."

"If we wait for you to talk your father into freeing me — which I think is extremely unlikely, by the way — or for my people in England to finally find me — and I guarantee they're looking, but probably not on the right trail — we could wait years. I'm not inclined to pass my days at hard labor and my nights waiting for you to sneak into my bed. Besides, the longer we wait, the more dangerous it gets. If we're found out before we can get away, all hell will break lose."

He was right, of course, though the

thought of fleeing from Heart's Ease like thieves in the night, never to return, brought butterflies to her stomach. But what choice did she have?

"I'll tell Jane I need to shop for my trousseau. She won't make the least objection if I want to go to Bridgetown for that."

Joss made a face. "I take it you're not planning to tell the Boss Man that the wedding's off."

"I think it would be better if I didn't. It might make him wonder about the reason, and it might not take him long to think of you."

"I suppose he'll figure it out when you run off with me." Lilah looked up at Joss, and was relieved to see that he was grinning. "Lord, I'd love to see his face when he gets the news!"

"Kevin's really very nice," she protested halfheartedly as they reached his hut.

"We'll have to agree to disagree on that. Come in for a minute. You left something behind on your last visit that you need to retrieve."

"What?"

"Your shoes."

Joss was opening the door as he spoke. He stood back for Lilah to precede him. She did, and stopped dead two paces inside the door. There, on Joss's cot, just barely visible in the gloom, sat Kevin.

The pair of slippers she'd left behind dangled from his hand.

Fifty-five

For a long moment Lilah and Kevin stared at each other, equally appalled. Joss walked in behind her, said something, saw Kevin, and froze. Kevin didn't even glance at him. His attention was riveted on Lilah. Slowly he placed her shoes beside him on the cot, reached over, struck flint on steel, and lighted the lantern. By its yellow light he looked across at her again. Stunned speechless, Lilah had not moved. Behind her, Joss recovered enough presence of mind to close the door so that their confrontation, whatever came of it, would be private. He leaned against the door, palms flattened back against the wood, eyes watchful.

"Kevin. . . ." Lilah said at last, her throat so dry that his name emerged as little more than a croak. The expression on his face was indescribable.

"You . . . little . . . slut," he said, and stood up. Lilah saw that he was fully dressed down to his boots. The only thing missing was his cravat; the throat of his shirt was open. In the tiny room he looked massive. Behind her Lilah felt Joss straighten, tense.

"No," she said, gesturing to Joss to stay where he was. Every protective instinct that she possessed warned her that Joss would be the primary target of Kevin's fury. Joss moved anyway, taking a step forward so that he stood just slightly behind her. However much she protested, the feel of his solid strength at her back was comforting. Disaster had struck, and her mind raced in crazy circles as she tried to think of a way out for them.

Kevin fumbled at the waistband of his tobacco-brown breeches. When he withdrew his hand seconds later, Lilah was horrified to see that he was holding a pistol.

"No!" she said again, holding up a hand to ward him off. "Kevin, please! I . . . I know how it must look to you, but —"

Joss quickly gripped Lilah's shoulders and tried to shift her to one side, out from between his body and the pistol. Heart pounding, Lilah refused to budge.

Kevin laughed, the sound harsh, bitter. "You should move, Lilah. This is for him."

Naked hate was in his voice on the last word.

"Kevin." Her blood thudded in her ears as she sought for a way to placate him. "Kevin, you . . . you're wrong in what you're thinking. I . . . we —"

"Don't insult his intelligence, sweetheart." Joss's voice was cool and insolent as he seemingly addressed her but looked at Kevin. She winced at the blatant provocation in Joss's words and voice. "Since he's discovered our secret, you might as well admit that you've been sleeping with me for months."

The noise Kevin made sounded like something that might have come from an enraged bull. Dark color rushed to his face, turning the blunt features an ugly shade of puce. His mouth twisted into a snarl. His hazel eyes burned as they fixed on Lilah's face.

"You . . . you . . . how could you?" Kevin sputtered, his chest heaving as he drew in a great draught of air. Then he continued in a strangled voice: "How could you let him put his hands on you? Any other man would be bad enough, but him — for God's sake, he's not even white!"

"You don't have to be lily-white to bed a lady and make her like it, Boss Man."

The deliberately jeering note in Joss's voice terrified Lilah. Why was he saying such things, goading Kevin so? She did not believe that he would be deliberately reckless so he must have some sort of plan.

"Did you hear him, Lilah? Did you hear

what he thinks of you? He's gloating, gloating because you let him touch you! He's probably bragged about it to all the other bucks — God, it makes me sick! You'd be better off dead than defiled by the likes of him!" Kevin was babbling now, his voice rising in pitch, his eyes moving from her face finally to rest on Joss's above her.

"I'm going to blow a great bloody hole right through the middle of your pretty face, boy," Kevin said to Joss, as if he relished the thought. Then his eyes shifted to Lilah again, and he made a sideways gesture with the pistol. "Get out of the way. It's always possible that I might miss."

"Move aside, Lilah," Joss said in her ear, too low for Kevin to hear.

"No!" Lilah was frantic. She knew Kevin well enough to know that he truly meant to shoot Joss in cold blood where he stood. Pressing back against Joss, she shielded him as best she could with her body, clutching the fabric of his trousers in both hands so that he could not shift her aside. "Kevin, don't do this! Don't kill him! Please, I —"

"You have approximately one second to move."

Kevin lifted the gun. Joss's hands tightened until they were almost painful on her shoulders.

Without warning the pistol boomed. Joss flung Lilah aside with such violence that she crashed into the opposite wall before falling, dazed, to the floor. Scrambling to her knees, her stomach churning with horror, she looked up in time to see Joss knock Kevin to the ground with a flying leap. Apparently he had gone for Kevin in a low, fast dive just as the pistol went off, just after he had shoved her out of the way. Kevin went down with a grunt and a curse, throwing punches with vicious intent. Joss slugged him in the stomach, in the back, the blows landing with sickening thuds. Then the two were rolling around in the dirt, scrabbling for supremacy as they fought like savage dogs.

The battle seemed fairly equal, with both men meting out and absorbing a tremendous amount of punishment. Lilah gasped as Kevin locked his fingers around Joss's throat. She looked around for a weapon to come to Joss's aid.

The pistol had fallen beside the cot. Fired once, it was now useless.

Wildly she sought some other weapon — the lantern! She would blow it out, and smash it over Kevin's head.

As she started for it, edging around the room close to the wall so as to stay well away from the men, Joss brought his feet up under him, heaved, and sent Kevin sprawling over his head. Then he straddled Kevin, held him with one hand digging viciously into his throat, and punched him in the face with ferocious power. Kevin grunted, quivered. His hands clawed impotently at Joss's thighs. Joss reached for the useless pistol, closed his hand around the barrel, and brought the mother-of-pearl handle crashing down on the side of Kevin's head.

As he repeated the blow, the door crashed back on its hinges.

Fifty-six

"What be goin' on in here?" The man who filled the doorway was enormous, black, clad in the same loose white trousers that Joss wore. Lilah stifled a scream at his sudden appearance, watched as Joss turned to glare at the intruder. More disaster! Then, miraculously, her mind started to function again.

The situation was not quite beyond saving.

"Henry — it is Henry, isn't it? I need your help. Mr. Kevin's had a . . . . a fit of some kind, and J-Joss here had to subdue him. I need you to stand guard over him, not let him up until I can get back here with help."

Henry, whose identity she remembered because he was the biggest of the field hands, taller even than Joss and huge with muscle, frowned. But the habit of obedience was ingrained in him, and he obviously knew her for the master's daughter.

"Yes, Miss Lilah," he said, and stepped into the room, looking uncertainly down at Kevin's unconscious form. Joss, after shooting a quick, surprised glance at Lilah, lowered the pistol and stood up, stepping away from the body. Joss was barefoot, dressed only in the trousers that now sported a long rip down one leg. His chest and arms were covered with red marks from the punches. His hair was wildly disordered, and blood trickled from one corner of his mouth. He wiped it away with the back of his hand, and looked at her again. Despite all that had happened, his green eyes were bright. Like most men, Lilah suspected with an inward spurt of disgust, he probably secretly liked nothing better than a good fight.

"You come with me," she said, nodding to Joss, every inch the mistress. "Henry, I'm counting on you to keep Mr. Kevin here until I get back with help. Do you understand?"

"Yes'm, Miss Lilah. I understand." The big man squatted down by Kevin's prostrate body, scowling direly at the seriousness of his charge. Lilah, motioning to Joss to follow her, stepped quickly outside. Her eyes widened as she saw the crowd that had gathered in the narrow track between the rows of huts. Apparently a goodly number of the field hands had been awakened by the shot and had come to investigate.

Lilah looked at the mass of faces, recognized several through the graying light, chose one. "Mose, you go in there and help Henry. You're both to keep Mr. Kevin in that hut and quiet until I get back. You hear?"

"Yes'm, Miss Lilah." Mose detached himself from the group that Lilah saw numbered perhaps twenty, and went into the hut, sidling past Joss, who was just coming out.

"The rest of you, go on back home. You've no business hanging about," she said sharply to those who remained. As they began to disperse, she motioned to Joss, who fell in with deceptive meekness behind her. Once the two of them were safely out of sight, she looked wildly over her shoulder at him. To her amazement, he was grinning.

"As I believe I've said before, you're a female in a million! That was a stroke of pure genius." Admiration shone from his eyes as they moved over her. "How long do you think we have before the Boss Man gets away from them?"

"I don't know — Papa will miss him at half past five, when he doesn't ring the bell."

"Then we've got a little more than an hour. I have to get away. You don't have to come with me. It'll be dangerous, there'll be pursuit. I can send for you when I'm safe in England."

Lilah stopped walking abruptly. Joss stopped too, his expression suddenly serious.

Beyond him, perhaps half a field away, she could see the white stucco walls and red roof of Heart's Ease, dark and still in the hour before dawn. The house and all those in it were everything she had once held dear. The moment had come when she had to decide, finally, irrevocably, whether or not to give up her home and family and every bit of the security she'd always known for this man. If he left without her, she greatly feared that she would never see him again. Even if he got away, got back to England, she would be trapped. Her father would never let her go to him.

Chances were, he would not get away. As he'd pointed out, there'd be pursuit. But perhaps if she were with him, she could keep him from being killed out of hand.

In any case, her choice had already been made. Whatever came of it, good or ill, she was throwing in her lot with Joss.

"I'm coming with you, and we don't have time to argue," she said with finality, and caught his hand. "Come on, we have to get away before Kevin starts raising a ruckus. The stables are this way."

Fifty-seven

Before noon they were within sight of the red roofs and sun-washed pastel buildings of Bridgetown. Lilah and Joss reined in on top of a grassy hill overlooking the serene wash of the ocean to the west and the bustling town sprawling out from the sapphire curve of Bridgetown Bay just ahead. From their vantage point they could also see a considerable way back down the road over which they had traveled. The heat was intense, the sun bright; the horses, her own sorrel mare Candida and a big bay gelding called Tuk, were tired out.

Dismounting to rest the animals, which had been pushed hard by their headlong flight, Joss and Lilah sprawled wearily in the long grass as the horses lowered their heads to drink from the stream that cut across the hillside. So far there had been no sign of pursuit. It seemed as if their decision to flee directly to Bridgetown, where they would sell the horses to buy passage on whatever ship might be sailing with the next tide, had been the right one. As Lilah had pointed out, nothing would be gained by trying to hide themselves on Barbados until her father forgot about them. Her father would never forget about them. Their only hope was to find a ship that was leaving Barbados for any destination whatsoever before word could be gotten to the harbormaster that they were being sought. Later, when they were safely out of the reach of her father and the militia, they could worry about getting to England.

Sitting with her back against the huge twisted trunk of a baobab tree, Lilah idly stroked Joss's hair — he was stretched out, his head resting on her lap — and considered their situation. She was exhausted, dirty, hungry, and frightened. The night before she'd had no sleep, and her lemon-yellow muslin dress, never intended to withstand the rigors of riding, was hideously crumpled and stained. In addition, she was only half dressed, not having bothered with stays, stockings, or more than one petticoat when she had donned her clothes to go in search of Joss the night before. Still, she was better off than Joss. He was barefoot, unshaven, clad only in the ripped trousers, with bruises turning livid all over his torso. It occurred to her that they might have a problem she had not previously considered: What respectable ship's captain would agree to take aboard such disreputable-looking passengers, without papers or baggage of any kind?

She said as much to Joss.

"We'll pay them enough so that they won't ask too many questions. The horses should bring a good price. Enough to get us aboard a ship, at least, with a tidy bit left over. And I thought to buy us both what clothes we need before we approach the ship. Then we'll have baggage and we'll be dressed appropriately. That should make things easier."

He sat up, smiled at her, his eyes crinkling at the corners. With his unshaven jaw and bare chest he looked the complete brigand. Despite her worry Lilah smiled back. Cost what it might, she still had no doubts, none, about her decision. If only they could get safely away!

"Come on, we've rested long enough," Joss said, his thoughts apparently running parallel to hers. He stood up, wincing at the soreness of his bruises, and held a hand down to her. Lilah allowed him to pull her up, then ran a questing hand along his ribcage.

"Are you sure nothing's broken?" she asked worriedly. He had taken quite a beating from Kevin — and he had been the victor. She shuddered to think what Kevin must feel like now. Or what he was doing. What her father was doing.

"Positive. Don't worry, I've survived far worse than a few bruises."

"I know." She smiled at him again, really smiled this time. He looked down at her for an instant, his eyes turning grave. Then he bent his head and kissed her.

As they mounted their horses, Lilah chanced to look back down the road. What she saw brought fear shooting through her: a dozen or so uniformed riders cresting the next rise over, coming fast.

"Joss. . . ." Mouth drying, she could not say more, but wordlessly pointed back down the road.

He looked, and his face tightened.

"They're militia! Do you think it's us they're after?" Her voice was high-pitched with dread.

"From the way they're riding I'd say it's likely. I sure don't propose to stay here and find out for certain. Come on!"

They urged their tired horses into a gallop, heading for town. The land thereabouts was entirely under cultivation, and there was no place to hide even if they'd wanted to.

The pounding of the horses' hooves against the hardpacked dirt road echoed the fear-quickened drumming of Lilah's heart. Bending low over Candida's neck, urging her to greater speed despite the distance she'd already traveled that day, Lilah knew deep in her heart that they were not going to get away. Joss raced beside her, his face grim, his bare back gleaming bronze in the bright sunlight. He rode the horse as if he'd been born to it.

From behind them a musket spat. The ball whizzed past her ear. Instinctively Lilah ducked. Every thought but one vanished: Her worst nightmare was about to come true. They would be caught and returned to Heart's Ease, where Joss would face her father's vengeance. And Lilah knew all too well that to Leonard Remy, nothing could be more hideous than the fact that she and Joss had been lovers. Her father would see Joss dead.

Another musket barked behind them. The ball whistled past, closer to Joss this time. He ducked, looking back over his shoulder to where the militia were closing fast. His jaw tightened, and his mouth clamped into a hard, straight line.

"Pull up!" he ordered, his face grim.

Lilah turned her head, looking at him in open-mouthed astonishment. She could not have heard him properly. . . .

"I said pull up!" It was a roar this time, and there was no mistaking the words.

Another musket ball sang through the air, a hair to Joss's right. Joss leaned dangerously far out of the saddle to grab at Candida's reins. He caught them, and despite Lilah's wild cry of protest, pulled both Candida and Tuk to a rearing stop.

"No!" Lilah cried out, fighting him for control of her horse.

"They're shooting at me, but they're not particular. They could very well hit you," he said grimly, releasing her reins as he wheeled Tuk to face the onrushing horsemen. Lilah was free to run, but without him beside her there was no purpose in it. Besides, she realized, as Joss must have, that being taken was inevitable. Their tired horses could not outrun the fresher horses behind them.

Like Joss, she wheeled her horse to face their doom, waiting at his side in proud despair.

In the instant before the horsemen were upon them, Lilah looked at Joss.

"I love you," she said, knowing that she might never again have a chance to tell him. Tears rose to her eyes, spilled down her cheeks. He saw the tears, and his eyes darkened. Leaning over in the saddle, he kissed her once, quick and hard. In full view of the onrushing militia.

"I love you, too," he said. His eyes met hers, and her heart turned over at the expression she saw in them.

Then the militia thundered up, surrounding them. Lilah's reins were jerked from her hands, while Joss was wrestled from his horse to the ground. Lying on his stomach in the dirt, shackles were fastened around his wrists and he was put in irons.

"Don't hurt him!" Lilah cried out, unable to stop herself although she knew that to plead for him was a waste of her breath. "He hasn't done anything!"

"He's a bloody horse thief, to begin with, and he damned near beat my overseer to death! Before I'm much older I mean to see him hang!" boomed a steely voice. Shocked, Lilah looked around to see her father riding toward her. He'd apparently been at the rear of the group, and she'd missed spotting him in the sea of uniforms. Not accustomed to hard riding, he had nevertheless managed to keep up with men thirty years his junior in pursuit of his errant daughter. That alone told Lilah just how furious he must be. Feeling the door of the cage slam shut against her, she looked hopelessly, helplessly, at Joss. He was being yanked roughly to his feet. Half a dozen members of the militia surrounded him, pistols at the ready. More militiamen, still mounted, held muskets. They were well and truly caught. There was no escape.

Leonard Remy took Candida's reins from the uniformed man who held them, and greeted his daughter with no more than a single icy glance. Lilah swallowed. She had seen her father in many moods, including thunderous rages, but she had never seen him like this. He looked as though his face had turned to stone, and his heart with it.

"I thank you, Captain Tandy, for your good work. I'll be taking my daughter home now, and I trust you know what to do with that scoundrel there."

"He'll be taken to St. Anne's Fort, sir, and imprisoned there to await trial for the crime of horse stealing, and any other charges you might care to bring. You can contact Colonel Harrison, head of the garrison, or —"

"I know him," Leonard interrupted testily. "You'll be hearing from me, I assure you."

Without further ado, her father nodded curtly at the officer. He held Lilah's reins in a grip so tight that his knuckles were white with it. Shock at what was happening dried her eyes. In Barbados, horse thieves were hung. But as terrible as that fate was, it was better than being dragged back to Heart's

Ease as a runaway slave, to be summarily executed by her father. His apparent intent not to take personal vengeance on Joss puzzled her, but she did not dwell on it, not then. There was so little time left, time only to make one last desperate appeal to the father who had never denied her anything in her life.

"Papa, please! Won't you try to understand? I love him. . . ."

Before Lilah could guess what he was about, Leonard Remy twisted in the saddle, his meaty hand swinging around to make sharp contact with the side of her face. The blow sounded as loud as a shot, even over the stamping of the horses, rattling of the tack, and the voices of the men. Lilah gasped, her hand flying to her injured cheek, her heart stinging even more than her face. He had never struck her before, ever.

"Shut your mouth, daughter!"

Lilah stared at her father in dumb shock. Some of the militiamen gaped, some pointedly looked away. Joss's eyes fastened on the pair of them, flamed emerald with rage, but, chained, he was helpless to come to her defense. Horses and men stood between them, too many to permit the exchange of so much as a final word.

"Do not shame yourself, or me, further.

Or I swear I'll take you home gagged and tied." Leonard Remy's voice was a growl almost as cold as his eyes.

"Papa, please. . . ." It was a piteous plea.

"No more!" he thundered, face reddening with choler, eyes bulging as he glared at her.

Then he yanked at Candida's reins so that Lilah, unwarned of the mare's sudden start, was almost unhorsed. She had to grab at the saddle horn for balance. Urging his horse to a brisk canter, he set off for home, dragging his heartsick daughter behind him.

Fifty-eight

To Lilah's complete disbelief, when they arrived home her father ordered her locked in her room. He had hardly spoken to her on the road except to tell her in icy tones that she had disgraced him and herself by her wanton behavior. To her tearful pleas for Joss, he responded with a rage that was frightening.

Lilah gathered that he had told the militia nothing of the fact that Joss was a slave, or anything about Joss's bloodline. He had simply summoned them on the pretext that his daughter was eloping with an adventurer who had also attacked his overseer and stolen his best horse. Those charges alone were enough to get Joss hanged. But hanging, in Leonard's loudly expressed view, was too good for the villain who had ruined his daughter. He had done what he could to preserve what was left of Lilah's name by omitting the fact that her companion in shame was a runaway slave. By doing so he had forfeited his chance to take personal vengeance on one he regarded as kissing kin to the devil incarnate. Although the scandal that was inevitable when news of Lilah's aborted elopement leaked out would be extensive, they could still hope that, eventually, it would die down. If anyone outside the immediate family ever discovered that the rogue Lilah had run off with was a man of color and a runaway slave, the resulting infamy was something none of them would ever live down.

The evening after her return home in disgrace, Lilah was summoned to the library. Lilah had never been "summoned" anywhere before, and she followed Jane, who had been sent to unlock her door and fetch her, downstairs with more than a little trepidation. But she kept her chin up and was outwardly composed, allowing none of the humiliation or fear she felt to show. She meant to fight for Joss, and herself.

The library was paneled in teak and lined with shelves of leather-bound books. Though it was dark outside, the oil lanterns cast a golden glow over everything. The room was furnished with an Aubusson carpet in soft rose, a massive mahogany desk and a leather chair, and several other armchairs with small tables beside them. It was Leonard's sanctum, and Lilah had spent many a pleasant evening in there when she was younger, playing chess with her father.

The wooden jalousies that covered the windows in lieu of curtains were cranked outward, allowing a soft breeze to cool the room. Despite the breeze the room was warm, but Lilah felt cold as she looked over at her father, who was seated behind the desk. His expression as he looked up at her upon her entrance was one of distaste. Lilah immediately felt soiled, unclean, and was furious with herself for feeling so. She refused to be ashamed of her love.

Jane followed Lilah into the room. Leonard immediately motioned to Zack, one of the houseboys who'd been stationed by the door, that he could go.

Kevin was also present, seated in a chair near the desk. A white bandage was wrapped around his head where Joss had hit him with the pistol. One side of his mouth was swollen and discolored, and he sported a painful-looking black eye.

Thrown into prison, treated as scum, Joss's wounds wouldn't have received the care that Kevin's had. Lilah's heart ached at the thought. Immediately she banished it from her mind. If she was to have any hope of persuading her father of the merits of her plan, she had to keep a cool head, and not let her emotions interfere.

"Hello, Kevin," she said evenly, crossing the room toward her father. Kevin's eyes flickered, but he didn't reply.

Neither of the men rose as was their wont as she entered, nor said a word of greeting, nor was she asked to have a seat. She stopped before the desk, waited, head high though her knees had begun to tremble at the icy quality of the silence. Both men continued to stare at her as if they'd never seen her before, as if she had suddenly grown two heads.

The silence stretched out, grew fraught with tension. At last Jane broke it, saying in a timid voice: "Leonard, don't you think Lilah might be allowed to sit?"

Her husband flashed her a narrow-eyed look, and then his eyes immediately returned to his daughter.

"Sit, then," he barked. Lilah looked at him, searching for a hint that he was not as closed to her as he seemed. The grim, blunt-featured face seemed to belong to a stranger rather than the father who'd always adored her. Feeling a dull pain take root in the area near her heart, Lilah sat in a small upright chair. Three pairs of eyes fixed her, pilloried her. She felt like a prisoner in the dock. Her heart knocked against her ribcage as she looked from one familiar face to another, and found a softening for her only on Jane's. She had known her father would be furious if he had ever discovered her love for Joss, but never in her wildest dreams had she imagined that his rage would be so all-consuming. It was almost as if he hated her.

Leonard drummed his fingers on the desk top, looked over at Kevin then back at Lilah, his face hardening until it could have been carved from granite. His eyes were distant, cold. Lilah had to bite the inside of her cheek to keep tears from filling her eyes. She knew that by acting on her feelings for Joss she had cut herself off from her father's love forever.

At last Leonard spoke. "I need not go over how sickened I am by the abomination you have committed, or how shocked and grieved I am that you, my daughter, would debauch herself with a slave. No words I can say can convey the depths of my revulsion for what you have done. You're not the daughter I thought I knew."

"Papa. . . ." A lump lodged in her throat, turning the word into a croak. Her eyes beseeched him. He silenced her with a gesture, appearing not the least bit moved by her obvious distress.

"At the present I am solely concerned with

salvaging what we can from this debacle. Word of your transgression is doubtless already spreading across the island like wildfire; you may rest assured that you will no longer be received by any but our closest friends. And they will only allow you in their homes for my sake, and only because they don't know the true extent of your depravity. Of course they will think that your ruin was with a white man. No one could ever imagine the true depths to which you have sunk."

Lilah did not try to interrupt this time. Tears were too perilously close to the surface to permit her to speak.

"Tempted as I may be, your stepmother has persuaded me not to totally cast you off. If you are ever to have the slightest chance of taking your place in society again, you must wed at once. Kevin here says he is still willing to have you. I salute the nobility of spirit and kindness for me which prompt him to such a sacrifice. Though it ill becomes one who loves him like a son to do so, I have taken him up on his offer because there is no other way for you, my blood daughter as much as it shames me to claim you, to avoid absolute ruin. You should feel grateful that Kevin is willing to offer you the protection of his name. I, in his place, would not be so generous.

"Father Sykes will be coming at noon tomorrow to perform the ceremony. Under the circumstances, it will be done as discreetly as possible, with only family in attendance. Kevin tells me he is prepared to treat you with kindness despite what you have done. I hope you are properly grateful to him."

Lilah breathed deeply once, twice, meeting her father's eyes with pain in her own.

"I'm sorry to have caused you such grief, Papa," she whispered. "Please believe I never meant to."

Then she turned her eyes to Kevin. Kevin, whom she had known from childhood, nursed through the cholera, loved, though not in the right way. Kevin, who still wanted to marry her. Why? For Heart's Ease? She thought that was part of it. But perhaps he wanted to marry her because in his own way he did love her.

He was watching her, his hazel eyes shadowed. Her conscience smote her. If he had truly loved her, he must be hurting now. She hated to hurt him more, but wed him she could not.

She wet her lips, and spoke in a low, steady tone. "I'm sorry you were hurt, Kevin. I never meant for things to happen like this. I truly thought I could learn to love you, that we could wed and be happy. I see now I was wrong."

Her eyes shifted to her father. "Papa, please hear me out! I know I've shocked you, disappointed you, disgraced you. I'm sorry for that, because I love you. But I love Joss too."

Her father made an outraged sound, slamming his fist on the desk and starting up out of his seat in a burst of fury. Lilah stood too, facing him bravely, trying to get the words out before sorrow at what she was doing to her family closed her throat.

"I'll never wed Kevin, never, and you can't compel me to do so. I realize that if I stay here at Heart's Ease, unwed, I'll be ruined, and you, all of you, will be shamed. So I'm asking you to let me go. Let me go and let Joss go and we'll go away to England and start a new life. You need never see or hear from me again, if that's your wish, and you can leave Heart's Ease to Kevin, who surely deserves it."

"Enough!" Leonard came around the corner of the desk, bellowing like a wounded moose. Lilah stood her ground as he closed on her, knowing she had to be strong if she was to have any chance of seeing Joss again.

"You will do as you're told and be damned grateful! You'll wed Kevin tomorrow, and if you so much as mention that damned blackamoor's name in my presence again I'll whip you as I should have when you were a little girl!" Leonard growled, leaning threateningly close to Lilah's face.

"I'll not marry Kevin, tomorrow or any other day, Papa. And there's nothing you can do to make me." Her voice was very steady despite a slight trembling of her lower lip.

Father and daughter stood nose to nose, one glaring and the other looking on the verge of tears, but adamant for all that. Leonard's bulk was overwhelming next to Lilah's slenderness, his weather-roughened features coarse compared to the delicacy of hers. Yet there was a sameness in both of them that spoke of wills that would never bend, and it was obvious an impasse had been reached. He ordered, and she would not obey. Checkmate.

Kevin got up, wincing as if the movement pained him. "Leonard, if you would permit me. . . ." he said, looking at the incensed older man as he caught Lilah's arm and pulled her gently aside.

Badly shaken by the unprecedented battle of wills with her father, Lilah allowed Kevin to lead her off to a corner of the room, where he took both her hands in his and stood looking down at her. It was a moment before he spoke. "You had better marry me, you know. Your life will be miserable if you don't."

"You don't want to marry me, Kevin," she said quietly, looking up into the face that Joss had battered so badly. She had never meant to hurt any of these people, and here she was hurting them all. For Joss. And herself. Because she would never be happy without him. "I don't love you, you see, not in the right way. Not in the way a woman should love her husband. I'm fond of you, but that's not enough. I've learned that. I'll make you unhappy, and you don't deserve to be unhappy. You're a very special man, and you deserve someone who'll love you more than anything in the world."

"I suppose you think you love that buck of yours?" A sneer twisted his mouth, wiping the kindness from his eyes. Lilah sighed.

"His name is Joss, and he's a man just like you are. Who his mother was doesn't make a tad of difference. Yes, I love him. I love him more than I ever thought I could love anyone, and I'm not ashamed to admit it. Now, after hearing that, do you really want to marry me?"

Kevin frowned as he weighed her words. "Together we'd make a good team, Lilah.

We've known each other for years, we both love the plantation, and if you married me people would soon forget all about this aberration of yours. Your father would forget. I'll run the sugar operation and you'll run the house and we'll have children. In twenty years we'll hardly remember that this happened."

"I'll remember," Lilah said softly. "I'll always remember."

"I'll help you forget. Please marry me, Lilah. I love you." There was pleading in his eyes, and in his voice.

She looked up at him steadily. "No, Kevin."

"Enough of this!" The interjection came from Leonard, who crossed the room to take Lilah roughly by the arm and pull her around to face him. "You will marry Kevin tomorrow, and there's an end to it! If you refuse, I'll sell that maid of yours, what's her name, Betsy, that you're so fond of! I'll pack her right off to auction before you can so much as spit!"

Lilah's eyes widened on her father's face. If she didn't obey him he would do as he threatened, she knew. And she also knew that there was only one way to stop this talk of marrying Kevin once and for all. She would have to reveal a secret so new that she had only become aware of it a few days before.

Her spine stiffened and all hint of tears suddenly fled. She had to be strong, and she would be. If she gave in, she had too much to lose.

"Kevin doesn't want to wed me, Papa. Or at least, he won't when he knows the truth." She paused, took a deep breath. With all eyes on her, the words were difficult to say. Unconsciously her fists clenched at her sides, pressing into her thighs as she forced the words out. "You see, I'm with child. I'm carrying Joss's child."

Fifty-nine

The next morning, to Lilah's horrified surprise, iron bars were installed outside her bedroom windows, making it impossible for her to open them more than a few inches. Apparently Leonard feared that she would try again to flee from Heart's Ease. Merely locking her in her room would not be sufficient insurance that she would stay there. Lilah was perfectly capable of climbing out her second-floor window.

In truth, Lilah had been planning just such an escape. It had become abundantly clear that there was no chance of persuading her father to drop the charges against Joss to set him free and let him return to England. Not even in return for her promise to marry Kevin would he do that. Leonard hated Joss with a virulent hatred that would not be appeased until Joss had paid with his life for what he had done to Leonard Remy's only daughter.

A frightened, subdued Betsy was permitted to see to her mistress's needs during the day, but to Lilah's combined fury and humiliation Jane or Leonard escorted Betsy to Lilah's door, unlocked it, locked the two girls in together, then let Betsy out again when her tasks were done. At night Betsy was locked in her own tiny third-floor room, so that she could not steal downstairs and help her mistress to escape. As it sank in that her father had her well and truly trapped, Lilah had never felt so helpless, or so frightened, in her life.

She was a prisoner in her own home, cut off from everyone, everything. In Bridgetown, the man she loved was imprisoned, facing trial for his life, for the crime of loving her. He did not even know that she was carrying his child. . . . When she thought that he might be hanged, might die without knowing, she feared she would go mad. For the sake of the tiny bud of life she carried within her she forced such thoughts from her mind. She must just have faith that things would work out for the best, no matter how impossible it seemed.

As days passed, turned into a week and more, it became obvious that her father was not going to relent. Lilah became convinced that her father meant to keep her locked up until she bore her child, and then would take the child away from her by force. His rage at her condition had been terrible; Lilah grew more and more certain that he was capable of such a heinous act. To him, a grandchild of mixed race would be an abomination.

Try as she might, she could conceive of no way to help herself, no way to help Joss.

Ten days after her imprisonment, she was lying on her bed, hot and dispirited and trying to nap. The early weeks of pregnancy were beginning to take their toll. She was constantly tired, and occasionally nauseous. She knew she should be trying to conceive of some plan of escape, but she had no energy to even think. The truth was that, unless she could persuade her father to relent or Jane to defy him, escape was impossible.

The sound of hoofbeats on the drive leading to the house broke through her lethargy. Visitors had been few since her return from the Colonies, and even fewer since her disgrace. Curiosity prompted her to get up from her bed and cross to the window overlooking the front drive. Pulling aside the drape to blink at the brilliant afternoon sunlight, Lilah saw that their caller was a man, a stranger. He was young, she observed without much interest as he swung down from his horse, perhaps in his mid-thirties, well-dressed with a lean, muscular build. His hair was a bright butter-yellow, nearly as blonde as her own. Her father had occasional business callers, and Lilah assumed that, since the man wasn't known to her, he must fall into that category. She watched him until he disappeared beneath the overhanging roof of the verandah, then let the curtain fall again, returning to throw herself on the bed.

That night Betsy came to help her undress as she always did, with Jane as her silent, tight-mouthed escort. Lilah suspected that her father had forbidden her stepmother to speak to her, and Jane, ever the obedient wife, would not dream of defying her husband. Betsy said nothing until Jane locked the door behind her, leaving the two girls alone together. Then she hurried over to Lilah, who was sitting in the chair before the window, feeling more lively than she had all day. The small doses of Betsy's company that she was permitted were the bright spots of her days.

"Miss Lilah, I done got somethin' to tell you, about that Joss," Betsy whispered, glancing around nervously as if the very walls had ears. Betsy was not permitted to stay with her long, so she had learned to work as she talked, and was now undoing her mistress's buttons.

"What?" Such paranoia was contagious,

and Lilah found herself whispering too. Which, when she thought about it, might be more cautious than foolish. Never in her wildest dreams would she have imagined that her own father could treat her so inhumanely, despite the magnitude of her offense. If he was capable of locking her in her room for weeks, allowing the man she loved to hang, and possibly even stealing her baby, he might be capable of dreadful retaliation were he to discover that Betsy was bringing her news of the man he had grown to hate above all others.

"That man that was here today — he was looking for him. At least, for a Captain Jocelyn San Pietro — that's him, ain't it?"

Lilah nodded.

Betsy went on. "This man works for your Joss in England. He says he got a letter from him saying that he'd been sold as a slave and bought by your pa. That man — David Scanlon, his name was — he come to buy your Joss's freedom!"

"What did Papa say?" It was hardly more than a breath, as hope welled up inside her. Lilah turned to look at Betsy, her gown half unbuttoned, all thoughts of preparing for bed forgotten. Although she knew it was foolish, she could not help the sudden leap of her heart.

"He said he never heard of Jocelyn San Pietro, and ordered the man off Heart's Ease."

"Oh, no. Did the man just leave? Didn't he . . . he try to get Papa to tell him anything?"

"Your papa isn't the easiest man in the world to talk to when he's angry, and he is surefire angry about this! I ain't never seen him this way before, and that's the truth! But the man did tell him that if he got word of your Joss, he could find him aboard the *Lady Jasmine*, in Bridgetown Harbor. He said he'd be stayin' there until he got word of your Joss."

Lilah frowned into space while Betsy stepped around behind her to finish unbuttoning her dress. Her mind raced. How to let this David Scanlon know of Joss's fate?

Betsy lifted the dress over Lilah's head, and turned her attention to the knots on her stays. Lilah suddenly had the answer.

"Betsy, do you think you could get a letter out of here for me?"

Betsy's hands stilled at Lilah's waist. "I could try, Miss Lilah. I surely could do that."

"There's no time tonight, Jane will be back any minute, but tomorrow I'll write a letter to this Mr. Scanlon and let him know where Joss is and what's happened. Maybe he can do something to save him."

"Maybe." Betsy didn't sound too hopeful, but Lilah was. This friend of Joss's might just be his salvation. But first she had to write the letter — fortunately her own writing materials were in her desk, because she doubted that she'd be allowed any were she to ask — and Betsy had to smuggle it out of the house. That was the difficult part.

"How would you get it out of the house, Betsy? I'd hate for you to be caught."

"Lord, I'd hate to be caught." Betsy's voice was prayerful as both girls thought of Leonard Remy's wrath. "But I can just slip it in my bosom until I see my Ben — he comes to the kitchen sometimes in the afternoon now — and give it to him. He'd do most anything for me."

"Thank heavens for Ben!"

"I says that a lot."

Both girls giggled, the first time Lilah had laughed since her aborted elopement with Joss. It felt good to smile again, and the brief spurt of lightheartedness didn't quite fade as Betsy eased her stays off, then untied the tapes of her petticoats and helped her step from them. Lastly she rolled down Lilah's stockings and pulled her chemise over her head, quickly replacing the garment with an immaculate white night rail.

"What would I do without you, Betsy? You're the only friend I have left." Lilah smiled with real affection at her maid as Betsy buttoned up the night rail.

"I'm not the only one that grieves for you, Miss Lilah," Betsy said seriously, following her mistress over to the big four-poster and pulling the covers down for her. Lilah climbed up on the high mattress. "Mama and Maisie think it's a real shame, how your pa's treatin' you. And Miss Allen is real upset, too. She wanted to come down to comfort you, but the master said no. I think she would have come anyway, you know she never pays him much mind, but there's no one who dares to help her downstairs, and she can't manage by herself."

"Dear Katy," Lilah said, her eyes misting. A lump rose in her throat as she thought of all those whom she loved: Joss, Katy, Jane, even her father despite everything, all as estranged from her as if she had died. What a dreadful coil she had gotten herself into by loving Joss! And yet, if she could do it all again, what exactly would she not do?

The key sounded in the lock, signalling the end of their time together. Betsy stepped nervously away from the bed. As expected, it was Jane, come to let Betsy out and lock Lilah in. For the first time since Lilah's announcement of her pregnancy, Jane stepped inside the room. She was carrying a silver tea tray.

"Betsy, you go on up to your room now, and wait there for me. I'll be up presently to lock your door."

"Yes, ma'am." Betsy bobbed a little curtsy to Jane, and with an uncertain glance at Lilah left the two alone. Jane set the tea tray on the table beside the bed, then, just as Lilah's eyes wandered to the unlocked door with a seed of hope, returned to turn the key in the lock.

"I finally persuaded your father to let me talk to you," Jane said as she stored the key securely in the pocket of her voluminous skirt. "Oh, Lilah, this has been so hard for all of us! How could you have . . . but never mind, I didn't come here to scold you. I just can't understand how you could . . . could ruin yourself with a man like that! I suggested to your father that perhaps your mind was injured in the shipwreck. It's the only explanation I can come up with that makes sense. You were always such a perfect lady before. . . ."

The hesitancy of Jane's words robbed them of some of their sting. She was more sorrowful than accusing as she came toward the bed, her unfashionably full skirts rustling. Lilah sat up, moving a pillow behind her back, and leaned against the intricately carved headboard as her stepmother pulled a chair up beside the bed and sat down.

"My mind's not injured, Jane! I love him, and that's the simple truth. I wish you could just meet him as an equal, talk to him, just once, you and Papa. He's . . . he's wonderful. He's educated, and a gentleman, and handsome and charming and —"

"Let's not talk about him," Jane said, not quite managing to repress a shudder as she reached for the silver teapot. Pouring the tea, her hand trembled slightly, and Lilah realized with compassion that Jane had been badly shaken by the destruction of her family. Her love for Joss had had ramifications she had never even considered. . . .

"Here, dear, drink this and we'll talk," Jane said, passing the cup to Lilah. The brew was strong, and very bitter. Lilah made a slight grimace at its taste. Jane must be more upset than she seemed if she could not brew palatable tea. But Lilah was so glad of the slight softening her stepmother's visit indicated that she managed to drink the foul-tasting liquid without a word of complaint.

"Dear, I must first preface what I have to say by telling you that, despite everything, I still consider you as a daughter. I want what's best for you, best for all of us, as does your father. He is so angry because he loved you so much, was so proud of you, and then you . . . do this. You know how proud he is! This is nearly killing him!"

"I'm truly sorry that I've hurt either of you," Lilah said, lowering her cup as a lump rose in her throat. "I never meant to! I never meant any of this to happen, but . . . I . . . I can't honestly say I'm sorry it did. I love Joss —"

"Please don't mention that man's name! To hear it on your lips makes me feel quite ill!" Jane said with a visible shudder.

Lilah sat up a little straighter, her chin coming up. "You and Papa are just going to have to accept it: I'm with child by Joss, a slave. I'm also in love with him. I'd marry him if I could. Please, Jane, if you love me, help me! Help me persuade Papa to free him, to let us both leave Barbados and go somewhere where his blood won't matter so!"

Jane swallowed, looked away, then back. "You know your father will never agree to that. Drink your tea, dear, don't let it get cold."

Absently Lilah took another sip. "I know Papa is planning to try to take my baby away from me. I won't let him."

Jane looked away again. "You haven't considered, Lilah. The . . . the child you carry will be of mixed race. It will be an outcast. You will be an outcast. No loving parent could wish such a hideous fate on a beloved daughter."

Lilah drained the last of the tea from the cup and handed it back to Jane, who set it on the tray beside her own untouched cup.

"My child won't be an outcast if only you'll persuade Papa to let Joss and me go! We can go back to England together, marry —"

"That won't alter the man's blood, Lilah. You have to look at this realistically. However attractive you may find him, he is not for you. It's better if you let go of the idea that you can ever make a life with him."

"But Jane —" Lilah's argument was interrupted by a sudden, terrible cramping deep inside her. She broke off in mid-speech, her eyes widening, her hands clasping her belly. The pain was sharp, twisting — awful! She had never felt anything like it. . . .

Her face must have mirrored her distress, because Jane got to her feet, her own face whitening. "What is it, dear?"

"My stomach. . . ." Lilah could say no more, because another pain caught her, making her writhe in agony.

"Oh, dear, oh, dear, I didn't know it would hurt you so," Jane murmured, ashen. As the pain subsided slightly to be replaced by another even more vicious, these words percolated through Lilah's pain-clouded consciousness. Her eyes opened, and she stared with horror at her stepmother, who was hovering over her anxiously as she twisted in the bed.

"Jane, Jane — what have you done?" It was a hoarse cry.

"Darling, we talked . . . we thought it was best . . . you can't have this child, Lilah! It would be a bastard, a . . . a mulatto!" Another pain knifed through Lilah's belly. She lay on her side, panting, her knees drawn up as she stared at her stepmother.

"It was in the tea!" Lilah gasped, understanding suddenly. Jane had gone to an Obeah and gotten the root that the natives used when they wanted to end a pregnancy. It had been ground and mixed into the tea. . . .

"When this is over, when you're better, you can marry Kevin and we can forget this whole dreadful ordeal ever happened," Jane was saying rapidly as sweat broke out on her upper lip. Her eyes were large and dark with an echo of Lilah's pain, her hands gentle as they fluttered over her stepdaughter's brow.

"Get away from me," Lilah said through teeth gritted against the pain, utterly rejecting Jane's touch. "You're killing my baby!"

"I'm sorry, darling, so sorry it has to hurt like this, but it's for the best, one day you'll understand and be grateful. . . ." Jane was babbling, her face white as she watched her stepdaughter thrash with agony. Lilah closed her eyes, shutting out her stepmother's face, her whole being concentrating on not expelling the tiny life inside her.

As she sank into a vortex of pain, her mind repeated the same words over and over: "Please God, please don't take my baby!"

Sixty

It was near midnight of the following day. Lilah lay in bed, wan and exhausted, unable to sleep although the rest of the household was long since in their beds. Occasional cramps still twisted her insides, but with nothing like the agony that had wrung her on the previous night. The worst was past, and she had not lost her baby.

Jane and her father were no doubt bitterly disappointed; Lilah knew she would never forgive them for what they had attempted to do. Her last tie to parents and home was broken by their act.

She realized now just what her father and Jane and Kevin were capable of, and she was frightened. Not for a moment did she believe that they would stop trying. To them, this child was an atrocity, something not fit to be born. They meant to end her pregnancy if they could. She could not eat or drink anything brought to her without fearing that they would make another attempt on her baby's life before it even once saw the light of day.

The horror of it was, they had her as securely as a rat in a trap. Weakened now, and locked in her room, there was no escape from the evil her family had planned for her in the name of love. What was she to do?

As Lilah lay there, frantically trying to come up with some means of saving her child, she heard the gentle clink of a key being inserted into the metal of her door's lock. Sitting up in bed, eyes wide as she strove to see through the darkness, she heard the sound of the key turning, the click of the lock disengaging.

Terror rose in her throat, set her heart to thudding. Was this another attempt on her baby's life? Or having failed to end her pregnancy, would they perhaps even go so far as to try to kill her, to save themselves from shame?

Someone, she could not determine who in the darkness, slipped through the door, shut it again. Lilah sat tense, immobile, straining to see. It was like a horrible nightmare, only she was all too certain that she was awake.

"Who is it?" Her voice was squeaky with fright. It took all her courage just to ask the question. Her hand crept toward the candlestick on the bedside table. If they intended her harm, she would fight. . . .

"Shhh, Miss Lilah!"

"Betsy!"

"Shhh!" Betsy crossed to the bed, moving swiftly, silently, and bent down to hug her mistress. Lilah clung to her fiercely.

"What are you doing here? How on earth did you get out of your room? Did Jane let you go?"

"No. Miss Allen came and let me out. She sent me down to let you out. She heard you screaming and crying last night, and she made Miss Jane tell her what they'd done. She said that what you done was wrong, but what they was tryin' to do to a poor helpless little baby was even worse. So this evenin' she got hold of Miss Jane's keys, stole 'em right out of her pocket when Miss Jane went up to say good night, and then when Miss Jane was gone, she felt her way along the hall to my room and let me out. Then she tole me to come down here and let you out."

"But Katy — Katy can barely walk! And she's blind!"

"I know, but she managed it for your sake, honey. She loves you. She couldn't get down the stairs to your room, so she sent me. Now get out of that bed and I'll help you dress and you get! Then I'll lock your door, and scoot back to my own room. Miss Allen's gonna lock me back in, and drop Miss Jane's keys somewhere like they just fell out of her pocket. In the morning, when you're gone out of a locked room, they won't know how you done it."

"Oh, Betsy, thank you!"

Lilah scrambled out of bed, the small needling cramps that were the residue of the doctored tea forgotten in her sudden excitement. She was free! Quickly, her mind performing mental acrobatics, she made plans. She would ride to Bridgetown, go to that Scanlon man who had inquired for Joss, and tell him of Joss's plight and her own. He was her only hope.

"Help me dress! I need my riding habit. . . ."

In minutes Lilah was completely clad except for her boots.

"Where will you go, Miss Lilah?" Now that the moment of parting had come, Betsy sounded suddenly fearful. Lilah shook her head.

"It's better if you don't know. Oh, Betsy, I'll miss you!"

The two girls hugged, stepped back. Lilah looked at her maid uncertainly through the darkness.

"Betsy, if you want to come with me, I'll — I'll set you free. . . ."

Betsy shook her head. "No, Miss Lilah,

but I thanks you. There's Ben. . . ."

Lilah smiled. "I wish you much happiness, Betsy, always."

"And I you, Miss Lilah."

Lilah felt tears mist her eyes. But there was no time for that now. If she was to make good her escape, she had to get away as quickly as possible.

"Tell Katy thank you. Tell her I love her," Lilah said, and then she slipped out the door, along the corridor, down the stairs, leaving Betsy behind.

Some quarter of an hour later, on the third floor of the house, an old woman, sitting by an open window in the dark, heard the distant sound of hoofbeats and felt tears come to her eyes.

"God go with you, my dear," she whispered into the night.

Sixty-one

Lilah rode as she had never ridden before in her life. Speed was of the essence, she knew, because her absence would be discovered before the day was very old. Jane usually escorted Betsy in with her breakfast around nine. By that time she had to have found the ship — what was its name? the *Lady* something, *Jasmine*, that was it — and the man named Scanlon. She had to tell him her story, and where to find Joss, and hope that he could help them.

It was perhaps an hour before dawn when she crested the hill where she and Joss had rested their horses some two weeks before. This time she didn't even pause, didn't even look at the beautiful panorama of sleeping town and undulating ocean glittering beneath the stars. She rode at a full gallop to the very edge of town, and then only slowed her pace because she feared attracting too much attention. Even at this hour, the wharves were awake. Small fishing boats were putting out to sea, cargo was being loaded on ships set to sail with the tide. Lanterns lit the worn wooden docks, gleamed off the skin of men laboring to roll barrels up long gangplanks. Bits and pieces of sea chanties, sung as the men labored, spiced the cool salt wind that blew in off the sea.

Candida trotted along the edge of the wharf while Lilah strained to read the names of the tall ships that bobbed gently at anchor alongside. During the wild ride the pain in her abdomen had returned. Resolutely she ignored it.

The *Lady Jasmine* did not appear to be among those tied to the wharf. Ah, there she was at last! She was the second to last ship, anchored just beyond the spot where two Bajans argued spiritedly over the price to be paid for a barrel of "kill-devil," as the local rum was called.

Sighing with relief, Lilah slid from the saddle, and tied Candida to a post with the fervent hope that she would not be stolen by any of the disreputable-looking persons who took advantage of the dark hours to roam the quay. Then she hurried across the wharf, skirting the increasingly acrimonious quarrel, to the *Lady Jasmine*'s gangplank. It was blocked by two barrels rolled across it for just that purpose. A guard had been posted, but sat on the gangplank, leaning against the barrels, sound asleep. Much good he did. . . .

Ignoring a sudden sharp cramp in her belly, she edged around the guard and the barrels, hurrying up the gangplank. Another pain struck her at the top, causing her to clench her teeth.

"Who goes there?" The brusque hail came just as the pain subsided. The *Lady Jasmine* was totally in shadow and Lilah had to strain to see who was addressing her. She gulped down nervousness and stepped onto the deck.

"I . . . I've urgent business with a Mr. Scanlon. It concerns Joss San Pietro."

"Indeed?" There was a scraping sound. A light flared, was touched to the wick of a lantern, caught and spread. The lantern was lifted so that the light shone on her face. The man holding it remained veiled in darkness. "And who are you?"

"Does it matter?" Lilah was both anxious and frightened. "I have to see Mr. Scanlon. It's quite urgent, I assure you."

"I'm Scanlon," said the figure, and as he lifted the lantern higher Lilah saw the glow of butter-yellow hair. "How can I help you?"

"Joss — Joss is in gaol, at St. Anne's Fort. My — my father had him arrested for horse thieving. He's in love with me, you see, and . . . Ah! Oh!"

"What's wrong?" Mr. Scanlon said sharply as Lilah doubled over, clutching her stomach. "Are you ill?"

"I think I'm losing my baby," Lilah gasped, and felt a warm rush between her legs even as she crumpled senseless to the deck.

Sixty-two

Joss lay on his back on the husk-filled mattress that was all that came between himself and the dirt floor. Around him men of every shade betwixt white and black snored and rattled, though the noises they made were not what kept him from joining them in sleep. His mind was busy with schemes for escape. Impossible schemes, he knew. He was in a gaol inside a fortress with walls twenty feet thick. Chains linked his wrists and ankles. He had no weapon. Two guards played cards outside the locked cell door. Two more guards were on duty farther down the hall. He had no money for bribes, and no friends save Lilah on this thrice-damned island. So figure a way out of this hole, San Pietro, if you can, he jeered at himself.

All male prisoners, regardless of race or offense, were kept in this one large cell. The reason for that was simple: The rest of the gaol, apparently having been damaged in a severe hurricane some years before, was still under repair. Most crimes on Barbados seemed to be linked to what his fellow prisoners called "kill-devil"; out of seventeen prisoners he was the only one who, if he ever came to trial, might conceivably hang. The rest, except for a pair of inept thieves who had tried to relieve a lady of her reticule and been beaten half senseless by the very object they'd tried to steal as the lady proved to be a warrior of considerable valor, were an ever-changing lot.

He had to escape, or he would hang. He existed in daily expectation of being hauled up before whatever passed for justice in this tiny slice of hell, and finding himself facing Leonard Remy. That Lilah's father would exact every bitter drop of revenge from the man who had ruined his daughter Joss had no doubt. He was only surprised that it was taking the man so long to get around to it.

Whenever he thought of Leonard Remy, he worried. The man had slapped his daughter, and Joss broke into a cold sweat when he considered what he might be doing to her even as he, Joss, lay waiting for his day in court. Would he harm her? His own daughter? The mere thought made Joss feel murderous. But there was nothing he could do to aid her. Not unless he could figure out a way to escape.

Footsteps approaching along the hardpacked dirt of the corridor brought Joss out of his half-savage revery. The guard had just been changed, and it was hours early for the repulsive dish of raw mashed fish that generally served as breakfast. Perhaps another drunk to be locked up?

The guards looked up from their card game, squinting as they peered at the newcomers. The stone wall on either side of the barred door prevented Joss from seeing the objects of those narrow-eyed looks.

"Oh, Hindlay, it's you," one of them grumbled, relaxing. "What the bloody hell do you want now?"

"I want you to open that cell damned quick," came a growl, and four uniformed members of the militia were herded into view, held at gunpoint by half a dozen rough-garbed sailors.

Joss blinked, grinned suddenly, and got to his feet. Another inmate woke up, saw what was happening, and ya-hooed.

"It's a bleedin' jailbreak," he whooped, and ran for the door that the scowling guard had just opened. Awakened by his cry, those who weren't too drunk followed. Joss, the only one wearing shackles due to the seriousness of his crime, made his way toward the door a little more laboriously. He stopped before the seething guard, holding out his arms wordlessly. The guard, gritting his teeth, unlocked the shackles on wrists and ankles.

"I thank you, sir," Joss said, and smiled as the guards were roughly bound, tied, and pushed into the cell that he was vacating. His yellow-haired rescuer turned the key in the lock, then nonchalantly pocketed it.

"Good evening, Jocelyn." David Scanlon inclined his head with exquisite courtesy. The sailors with him saluted Joss with varying degrees of punctiliousness.

"Good to see ya, Cap'n."

" 'lo, Cap'n."

"Good to see you, too, Stoddard, Hayes, Greeley, Watson, Teaff. Davey here got you up to no good as usual?"

The men grinned. "Aye, sir."

"Speaking of no good, my friend . . ." Davey was herding them all with quick efficiency from the now guardless gaol as he spoke. "That appears to be exactly what you've been up to since we last met."

"My late lamented career as a horse thief, you mean? Not quite what it was made out to be, believe me." Joss clapped his friend on the shoulder. "Thanks for coming so quickly, Davey."

"You're entirely welcome, of course." Davey was looking around with his usual caution before he nodded to the others. Then, with Joss beside him and the rest following, he strolled cooly toward the open gates of the fort. "Actually, I wasn't referring to that. I was referring to your quite unprecedented action in dishonoring one who was obviously, before she met you, an innocent young lady."

Joss stopped walking, stared at his friend, stiffened. "Lilah — you've seen her?"

Davey inclined his head. "More than seen her, my friend. She appeared on the *Lady Jasmine* about two hours ago, obviously in some distress. She told me where to find you."

Joss ignored all but the relevant part of that. "What do you mean obviously in some distress? What's wrong with her? Where is she now?"

"Still on the *Lady Jasmine*, in the captain's cabin, to be exact. I'm sorry to tell you that she seems to be in the process of losing your baby."

Sixty-three

Standing braced on the deck of the *Lady Jasmine*, Joss watched with something less than his usual appreciation as her sails filled with wind and she quartered toward the mouth of Bridgetown Harbor. Not even the rainbow of pinks and purples that were all that was left of the fading dawn had the power to lift his spirits. There was a hollowness deep inside him that he feared would never go away.

At that moment Lilah was in his cabin. Macy, the ship's doctor, was with her. In the brief glimpse he'd had of her before Macy barred him from the room, she'd been writhing and moaning in pain. He'd been white himself when Davey had dragged him away.

Now he wrestled with hideous fear. Would she die? If she did, he would want to die himself.

"You can go in now, Captain."

Macy had emerged from the cabin at last. Joss took one look at the blood that stained his shirtsleeves and felt his stomach lurch along with his heart.

"Is she . . . is she —"

But he couldn't wait for the answer. Even as Macy tried to tell him, Joss was turning away, striding purposefully to the captain's cabin.

Inside, the room was shadowy. The promised brightness that was dawn had so far barely penetrated.

Lilah lay on his bunk, a small mound under a pile of covers. He thought she was asleep. Her eyes were closed, her lashes black fans resting against cheeks that were as white as death.

He felt his heart turn over. She looked so young, so very small, so defenseless lying there. Only the cropped head of golden curls seemed to belong to the dauntless girl he loved.

"Lilah?" It was a husky whisper as he approached the bunk. Her eyes slowly opened. For a moment she seemed to have trouble focusing. Then she saw him.

"Joss," she breathed, and smiled faintly. Then her lips quivered and her face crumpled. "Oh, Joss, I lost our baby!"

Tears coursed from her eyes to roll down her cheeks like rain. Shaken to the core, Joss dropped on his knees beside the bunk, took her gently into his arms.

"Don't cry, sweetheart," he whispered tenderly, stroking her hair as she wept. "It tears the heart out of me when you do. Please don't cry, Lilah."

"I've been so frightened," she murmured. "I've missed you so. Hold me, Joss."

Joss slid into the bunk beside her, careful not to jar her in any way. She clung to him, never even noticing that he was dirty and half naked and probably smelled. She burrowed her head into the hollow between his shoulder and neck and told him everything, weeping until she had no more tears left. Then she drifted off to sleep.

Still Joss lay there, holding her slight weight against him, filled with a fierce tenderness the likes of which he had never felt before.

He stroked her cheek, her hair, kissed the silky top of her head.

"I've got you safe, sweetheart," he whispered. "I've got you safe now, Lilah my love."

Epilogue

One year later almost to the day, Katherine Alexandra San Pietro lay in her mother's arms, nursing contentedly as she was rocked sleepily back and forth. Katy, as she was called, was not quite six weeks old and had not yet developed any concept of day and night. Consequently, she was unaware that it was three A.M., or that she was in grave danger of being dropped on her head as her mother nodded and all but fell asleep in the rocking chair.

"Here, sweetheart, let me take her. You go back to bed."

Joss's voice roused Lilah enough to prevent Katy from taking a tumble. She blinked, smiled sleepily up at her husband, and allowed him to take the baby. Then she stumbled back to bed.

It was broad daylight when Lilah woke again. She opened her eyes to the sun pouring through the bedroom window of the big, comfortable house in Bristol, and realized with a rush of horror that Katy had not wakened her with the chickens as was her wont.

Had something happened to the baby?

On that horrible thought Lilah was ready to leap out of bed. Then she heard a contented gurgle and looked around.

Joss lay beside her, sprawled flat on his back, which was surprising. Her husband usually slept on his stomach, and hogged two-thirds of the bed, too.

The gurgle came again. It could be his stomach, but she didn't think so.

Pulling aside the blanket, Lilah had to smile. There, stretched out on her papa's hairy, muscled chest, lay Katy, wide awake and cooing contently as she bobbed her head up and down.

"Oh, you precious thing." Lilah smiled, leaning down to scoop up the baby.

"Dare I hope you are referring to me?" Joss was awake after all, Lilah discovered as he opened his eyes and grinned.

"Certainly," Lilah said obligingly, leaving Katy where she was for a moment longer to plant a kiss on his mustachioed mouth.

His hand slid behind her head, pulled her mouth down for a heartier sample. Lilah felt the familiar heating of her blood, her hand came up to rest on his chest. . . .

And Katy promptly howled.

Joss released her, Lilah sat up, and this time succeeded in picking up the baby.

"Spoilsport," Joss grumbled to his daughter, hitching himself up against the pillows.

"But we love you," countered Lilah, smiling at him.

"And I," said Joss, eyeing his two golden-haired, blue-eyed ladies as they cuddled and cooed on his bed, "love both of you."

The employees of Thorndike Press hope you have enjoyed this Large Print book. All our Large Print titles are designed for easy reading, and all our books are made to last. Other Thorndike Press Large Print books are available at your library, through selected bookstores, or directly from us.

For information about titles, please call:

(800) 223-2336

To share your comments, please write:

Publisher
Thorndike Press
P.O. Box 159
Thorndike, Maine 04986